EXTREME MEASURES

Also by Vince Flynn

EXTREME MEASURES

A THRILLER

VINCE FLYNN

ATRIA BOOKS

New York London Toronto Sydney

ATRIA BOOKS

A Division of Simon & Schuster, Inc.
1230 Avenue of the Americas
New York, NY 10020

First Atria Books hardcover edition October 2008

ATRIA BOOKS and colophon are trademarks of Simon & Schuster, Inc.

For information about special discounts for bulk purchases,
please contact Simon & Schuster Special Sales
at 1-800-456-6798 or business@simonandschuster.com.

Designed by Rhea Braunstein

Manufactured in the United States of America

10   9   8   7   6   5   4   3   2   1

ISBN-13: 978-0-7432-7042-7
ISBN-10:   0-7432-7042-8

To Robert Richer and
the men and women of the
National Clandestine Service and
National Counterterrorism Center

ACKNOWLEDGMENTS

To Emily Bestler, my editor, and Sloan Harris, my agent, for your wise council and friendship. To David Brown, for your ideas and humor. To Judith Curr and Louise Burke, for your vision and commitment; I couldn't be happier that I'm staying put for four more books. To Ian Chapman, Kate Lyall-Grant, and the rest of the Simon & Schuster UK family, thank you for the great strides you've made in the last few years. To Laura Stern, Kristyn Keene, Niki Castle, and Allie Green, thank you for putting up with me. To Jamie Kimmers, we're going to miss you. To Ron Bernstein at ICM for sticking with me and selling the movie rights to the Mitch Rapp franchise.

To Paul Evancoe, a fellow author, friend, and a great patriot, for his spot-on advice. To Dr. Jodi Bakkegard, for once again keeping me in line. To Dorothy Wallner, for being so good to my family. And to my wonderful wife, Lysa, who has kept things together during a very hectic year. You're the best.

We sleep soundly in our beds because rough men stand ready in the night to visit violence on those who would do us harm.

—WINSTON CHURCHILL

EXTREME MEASURES

CHAPTER 1

BAGRAM AIR BASE, AFGHANISTAN

MIKE Nash glanced anxiously at his watch and then eyed the twin flat-screen monitors. Both prisoners were sleeping soundly. If all went according to plan, their slumber wouldn't last much longer. The prisoners had been picked up seven days earlier on a routine patrol. At the time, the young GI's had no idea whom they had stumbled upon. That revelation came later, and by accident. The brass at the Bagram Air Base in Afghanistan quickly separated the two men from the other 396 enemy combatants and alerted Washington.

Nash was one of the first people called. The secure phone began ringing at 2:23 in the morning the previous Sunday. The watch officer at the National Counterterrorism Center gave him the news. Nash thanked him, hung up, and contemplated whether or not he should get out of bed and head in to the office. Catching a couple of high-value targets was exciting, but Nash knew from experience that people would be tripping over each other trying to take credit. Having just returned from London, he needed the sleep a hell of a lot more than he needed recognition.

Less than a minute later the phone started up again. This time it was his boss's boss, Irene Kennedy, the director of the CIA. Nash listened without comment for a good twenty seconds and then replied, "I'm on it." With that, he kissed his wife, got out of bed, threw on some comfortable travel clothes, checked on each of his four kids, grabbed his go-bag, which was always packed, left a brief note by the coffeepot, and was out the door. Given his job, it was all too likely that his family would not be surprised by Nash's absence when they awoke.

Twenty minutes later he arrived at the private airstrip and climbed aboard a fully prepped Gulfstream V. As soon as they were airborne, Nash's thoughts turned to the two prisoners. He didn't need to look at their files. He'd already memorized them. He had been building them for years, each time a new piece of intelligence came in. That was one of Mike Nash's gifts. It didn't matter if it was baseball stats or the details on the who's who of terrorists around the world. If he read it, he could recall it. Nash began to construct his line of questioning. With as much instinct as logic, he laid his traps and anticipated their lies. It would likely take weeks to completely break them, but they would talk. They always did.

Somewhere over the eastern Atlantic he received his first secure message that there was a problem. As the plane raced along at 47,000 feet the drama unfolded via a painful exchange of updates from Langley. Three senators, who had been at the base on a fact-finding mission, had caught wind of the two new detainees and requested to see them. The base commander, through either sheer stupidity or a calculated desire to please those who could advance his career, relented and let the senators sit down with the high-ranking prisoners.

If Nash had been forced to compile a list of the three politicians he most despised, two of these "Fact-Finders" would have been on it, and the third would have made honorable mention. As chairmen of the Senate Committee on the Judiciary, the Senate Committee on Armed Services, and the Senate Select Committee on Intelligence, they were a powerful group. They also happened to despise the CIA. After their one-hour meeting with the prisoners, the three senators told the base commander in very stark terms that his ass was on the line. The chairman of the Judiciary Committee went one step further and told him if the Geneva Conventions weren't followed to the letter she would haul him before her committee and make him answer for his crimes in front of the American people.

The fact that one of the prisoners had earned his stripes with the Taliban by blowing up coalition-built schools with little Afghani children in them seemed to be of little consequence to the chairman of the Judiciary Committee. Neither did she care that the prisoners and their organization were not signatories of the Geneva Conventions. Apparently, she had other priorities. Affording tolerance, respect, and compassion to the bigoted, sadistic, and cold-hearted sounded very noble in principle, but in reality it was a great way to lose a war.

One of the most difficult aspects of Nash's job was dealing with the opportunistic politicians he answered to. These same senators had clamored for action in the months after the attacks on New York and Washington. Behind closed doors they expressed concern that the CIA wasn't being aggressive enough with their interrogation techniques. They pushed for the use of extreme measures, and gave Langley assurances they would be protected. Now, Nash was reminded of the fable about the scorpion who promises the frog he will not sting him if the frog gives him a ride across the river. They were now halfway across the river, and just like in the fable, instincts had taken over, the stinger was out, and they were all on the verge of drowning.

Nash looked at the two prisoners sleeping peacefully in their warm, clean beds. On the left screen was Abu Haggani, a senior Taliban commander in charge of suicide operations in Afghanistan. It was estimated that his attacks had claimed the lives of more than three thousand civilians and another forty-three coalition soldiers. The man was notorious for intentionally targeting women and children in an effort to intimidate his fellow Afghanis from cooperating with coalition forces. The second man was Mohammad al-Haq, the Taliban's liaison with al-Qaeda and one of Mullah Omar's most trusted aides. While Nash unashamedly relished the thought of inflicting severe pain on Haggani, it was al-Haq who interested him most. The man was an integral link between al-Qaeda and the Taliban. The secrets he held would be invaluable.

Nash had been allowed a maximum of four hours with each man per day for the first three days. Everything was strictly supervised and recorded. No stress positions, no sleep deprivation, no loud music or yelling, no hitting or slapping, no manipulation of diet, and no manipulation of temperature in their cells. Even the mere threat of physical violence had to be approved by lawyers back in Washington.

On Wednesday, Nash's session was ended early when he told al-Haq that he had spoken to General Abdul Rashid Dostum. The former Northern Alliance commander and leader of the Uzbek community was widely known for his hatred of the Taliban. Nash told al-Haq that he had arranged to have him transferred to Dostum's custody in the morning. Al-Haq nearly shit a brick over the prospect of being handed over to a man who was every bit as vicious as he and his colleagues. The fear in al-Haq's eyes was obvious. Nash watched him closely as the prisoner searched for a way to forestall the nightmare. Nash had put dozens of men in this situation before. They always looked down at first and then nervously to the left and then the right as they scrambled to come up with something that would save their asses. The truth didn't matter so much at first. Nash just wanted them talking. He could sort out the lies later.

Unfortunately, just as al-Haq was about to start talking, an air force officer burst into the room and stopped the questioning. Nash was put on the phone with the Justice Department lawyers back in D.C. and warned that he had crossed the line. The incident set off a firestorm between the CIA, the White House, the Justice Department, and Senator Barbara Lonsdale, the chairwoman of the Judiciary Committee. While the lawyers argued, Nash began to look for a way to get around the wall rather than over it. That was when he put a call in to Mitch Rapp.

Nash glanced at his wristwatch. It was a few minutes before midnight. Rapp and the cavalry were due to arrive any minute. The two sleeping thugs were in for a rude awakening. They'd been given three square meals a day, beds nicer than the cot Nash was sleeping on, prayer rugs, a fresh copy of the Koran, and hot showers. Their defiance had grown with each passing day as they realized they would not be subjected to torture. That false sense of security was about to vanish in a very real and possibly violent way.

CHAPTER 2

TRIPLE FRONTIER, SOUTH AMERICA

THE man walked slowly around the room, his hands clasped firmly behind his back. He observed the seven men seated at the rough-hewn plank table with growing concern. It had been six months since they'd left Pakistan, and still they weren't ready. They were close, but that was not good enough. The slightest misstep could bring disaster, as it had brought to others who had gone before them.

Karim Nour-al-Din thought back on their journey and all of the painstaking work he had put into forming his elite unit. They had traveled to Peshawar as a group, handed in their weapons, cut their hair, shaved their beards, and had photos taken for their new passports. A week later each man took possession of an expertly forged set of documents, two credit cards, and plane tickets. Some traveled through Africa, others the Orient and the Pacific Rim. Not one of them, however, traveled through Europe, Australia, or the United States. They were off-limits. Two weeks later they converged on one of the world's most wicked and depraved cities.

Karim had never been to Ciudad del Este, and it would not have been his first choice, but as soon as Ayman al-Zawahiri had suggested it, Karim knew that was where he was going. The number two man in al-Qaeda was rarely open to suggestions and never open to debate. Those who had been bold or foolish enough to argue with him were all gone. So when Zawahiri suggested the remote South American city, Karim simply nodded and reasoned he would make it work. He arrived in the city first, and after spending one day roaming its filthy streets, he decided he would have to risk Zawahiri's wrath and move his men.

Ciudad del Este was run by drug dealers, flesh merchants, gunrunners, and mobsters. Counterfeiting of currency as well as products was rampant. There were more gambling houses than houses of worship. Tax cheats, rapists, pedophiles, and murderers all ran to Ciudad del Este to evade the long arm of the law. Perfectly located in the Triple Frontier where Paraguay, Brazil, and Argentina came together, the city was a free-for-all. The competing authorities, the dense jungle, and the murky water of the Parana River combined to create a toxic stew of all things illicit.

Zawahiri had even gone so far as to tell him that he would like Ciudad del Este. He said the city would remind him of Peshawar, the Pakistani city that was the main supply center in their struggle to expel the infidels from their lands. But the only things the two cities had in common were drugs, guns, and poor people. Other than that, they couldn't have been more different. Peshawar was a city on a war footing. It was a city with many opinions and clans, but a unified purpose. It was a city on a religious mission.

Ciudad del Este was a godless place. Chinese, Mexicans, Colombians, Syrians, Lebanese, Palestinians, Eurotrash, Russian thugs, and every other sort of reprobate roamed its streets, each person caring only about himself. There was no larger purpose, no restraint whatsoever. The very lawlessness of the place was bound to attract the attention of the Americans.

Karim reasoned the CIA would have little trouble penetrating the various factions. He imagined their intelligence assets crawling all over the city of nearly two hundred thousand. With their endless sums of cash and their technological advantage it would be easy for them to discover what was going on. He and his men would be photographed within the week, and within the month they would begin to disappear. Just like the other teams that had been dispatched. If the Americans, British, and French weren't afraid to grab his fellow warriors off the streets of major European cities, what would stop them from doing it in this lawless place?

Karim spent two days searching for a solution and then stumbled across something that he thought might work. He met a Lebanese arms dealer who had been implicated in the assassination of Prime Minister Rafiq Hariri. After two years of living on the run, his name had finally been cleared, no doubt because large amounts of cash were given to the right people. Now, he was returning to his native Lebanon. The man had a remote parcel of land he was looking to unload. With a hushed tone and conspiratorial glance, he explained to Karim that if was the perfect place to get away from the city.

The man was right. The 250-acre site had been cut out of the rain forest and was accessible only by helicopter or on foot. The closest road was almost ten miles away, but the trek through the rain forest made it feel more like a hundred miles. The site's buildings consisted of nothing more than concrete slabs, corrugated metal roofs, and screens running along the perimeter. There was a diesel generator to run the lights. Considering his lack of options, Karim thought the place was perfect. He bought it all for $50,000 and had the money wired to the man's account. His men, who had arrived by then, were transported to the camp and the training began in earnest.

That had been nearly six months ago, and they had come a long way in a relatively short time. Karim looked down with satisfaction as the first man finished assembling his bomb. It was Farid, of course. He was always first. Three more men completed the task in quick order. Karim checked his watch. Not so long ago it took them almost an hour to assemble the bombs. The goal was ten minutes or less. They were at nine and counting. Two more men finished with seconds to spare, leaving Zachariah as the only one to fail.

The lone Egyptian in the group set down his tools and looked up with a sheepish smile, "My uncle would be very disappointed."

A couple of the men chuckled. Karim did not. He found none of this amusing. They were scheduled to depart in a few days, and thanks to this idiot sitting before him, they were not ready. Karim had driven them without rest for nearly six months in an effort to hone them into elite warriors. He had succeeded with at least four of them. Two more were adequate, but he would have to keep a close eye on them. One was a total failure, and he was holding them back.

Karim turned away from the group and looked through the rusty screen at the steady rain. He felt isolated. Everything was foreign about this place. It was too lush, too humid, and there were far too many bugs. The desert was a much better place to commune with Allah, and the high altitude of Afghanistan was a much, much better place to discuss tactics with the other leaders. He missed the counsel and advice of his equals. He was alone in the jungle, faced with an extremely difficult decision. He had to decide what to do about Zachariah, and he had to do it quickly.

CHAPTER 3

BAGRAM AIR BASE, AFGHANISTAN

NASH heard them coming, as did the airman sitting at the duty desk. The young man from Arkansas checked the flat-screen monitor. A look of concern spread across his face. Nash knew he was looking at the video feed from the security camera mounted at the main door. Bagram Air Base was a busy place even at 12:21 in the morning, but most of the action was taking place over on the flight line. The Taliban liked to move at night, so the air force and army pilots were out hunting. Forwarding operating bases were being resupplied with bundle drops, Special Forces teams were loading up for insertions, and the wounded were coming in and going out. The base occupied some 840 acres and averaged more than four thousand personnel at any given time. It was a city unto itself, but even so, the building they were in was off the beaten path.

The main internment facility sat near the middle of the base, nearly a half mile away. The Hilton, as they liked to call it, was fully automated, with surveillance devices built into each of the eight cells and two interrogation rooms. All cell doors, as well as the main steel door that led to the cells, had to be remotely opened from the control shack. There were only two ways in and out, and both required the proper ID card and pass code. Nash had given Rapp both in advance.

Nash casually strolled over to the desk and asked, "What's up, Seth?"

The nineteen-year-old looked anxious. "It looks like we've got some unexpected guests."

"Who is it?" Nash asked, knowing damn well who it was.

"I don't know."

There was a metallic clicking noise as the locking mechanism on the main door was released. Footsteps could be heard, and then six men wearing olive-drab-and-tan Airman Battle Uniforms, or ABU's, entered the room. Mitch Rapp led the group. He had a black eagle on each side of his collar, which meant he outranked the airman by a mile. As he approached the desk, the airman jumped to his feet and snapped off a salute. Rapp returned it and said, "As you were. Are you Airman First Class Seth Jackson?"

"Yes, sir."

"I'm Colonel Carville. Air Force Office of Special Investigations." Rapp's right hand shot out to the side. He snapped his fingers and the man behind him placed an envelope in his palm. Rapp retrieved the letter from the envelope and held it up so the young airman could read it. "This is from the secretary of the air force," Rapp said in a commanding, clipped voice, "authorizing me to take temporary command of this interrogation facility. Do you have any questions, Jackson?"

The young airman nervously shook his head from side to side. "No, sir."

"Good." Rapp turned to Nash and eyeballed him from head to toe. Nash was wearing an olive-drab flight suit with no name or rank. "Who are you?"

Nash grinned. "I'm afraid that's on a need-to-know basis, Colonel."

"OGA," Rapp said in disgust. The acronym stood for Other Government Agency, which was a euphemism for the CIA. "You goddamn spooks. You're more trouble than you're worth." Rapp turned back to Jackson. "You're on duty until oh seven hundred?"

"That's correct, sir."

"Follow me. You too," he said to Nash. Rapp led them back through the doorway. There were offices on the left and the right. Rapp opened the door on the left and said to one of the men in his entourage, "Chief, remove the phone and keyboard from this office and make sure this spook doesn't leave until I say so."

Rapp walked across the hall and opened the other door. Looking at the young airman, Rapp said, "Jackson, in here. I'm going to assume I can trust you to not make any phone calls . . . no e-mails . . . no communication at all. Is that understood?"

"Yes, sir."

"Good. Grab some shut-eye on the couch, and don't leave this room unless I say so. Is that clear?"

"Yes, sir."

Rapp shut the door, walked back across the hall, and opened the other office door. Nash was standing on the other side with a big grin on his face. The two men shook hands and then walked back down the hallway past the control room and into a small cafeteria. Four of the five men who had entered with Rapp were waiting. Nash walked up to the oldest man in the group and extended his hand.

"General Dostum, thank you for making the trip."

At five feet eight the general was four inches shorter than both Nash and Rapp. His most striking feature was the contrast between his black beard and close-cropped gray hair. The former Northern Alliance general slapped Nash's hand away and gave him a big hug. He laughed and in heavily accented English said, "I would do anything for you, Mike."

Nash had been the first American to meet with General Dostum after the assassination of Northern Alliance commander Ahmad Shah Massoud. He paved the way for the arrival of warriors from the U.S. Army's 5th Special Forces Group and an eventual offensive that dislodged the Taliban from the north. Dostum may have been a ruthless warlord, and one of Afghanistan's largest exporters of opium, but he was also very loyal to those who had helped him wrest his land from the Taliban and al-Qaeda.

Nash regarded Dostum and said, "Even if it means getting you in trouble with the U.S. military?"

"Your military has more important things to be concerning itself with. It would be wise for them to turn all prisoners over to me."

"Wouldn't that be nice?"

Rapp looked at his watch and said, "General, we're a little short on time. To be safe, we should be finished and out of here by oh six hundred. That leaves us about five and a half hours." Rapp turned his attention to Nash. "You want to cover anything before we get started?"

Nash had put a lot of thought into the best way to utilize their time. He had decided that he and Dostum would handle al-Haq, while Rapp would be in charge of interrogating Haggani. They'd already gone over their strategy, but with Rapp involved, Nash felt one thing bore repeating. "Remember, no marks."

"How do you expect me to get him to talk?" Rapp complained.

"Be creative."

"I can't just shoot him in the knees?"

General Dostum nodded enthusiastically at the idea. The two of them made Nash very nervous. "Guys, we can't leave any marks."

Rapp smiled. "Don't worry, I brought along something special." Rapp looked across the room and said, "Marcus, did you bring the rats?"

CHAPTER 4

TRIPLE FRONTIER, SOUTH AMERICA

KARIM had fought against the Americans in Afghanistan and seen firsthand the effects of their training. His fellow jihadists liked to claim that the Americans' impressive kill ratio was due solely to the fact that they controlled the skies, but Karim knew otherwise. He had come up against their hunter-killer teams: autonomous deep-penetration units that wreaked havoc behind enemy lines. Karim had been in the region only a month when they received a report from the locals that a single American helicopter had dropped off seven men on a nearby peak.

Shortly after midnight Karim's commander ordered a full assault on the position. Nearly two hundred men participated in the attack. Two platoons of roughly thirty men apiece started up the mountain, while the rest of the men were held in reserve. The first group attacked from the east and the second from the west. The lead elements of both groups made it to within ten meters of the peak, and then everything went wrong. From their elevated and fortified position the Americans sprung their trap. A total of five men made it back down the mountain without injury. The wounded were left to cry for help in the cold mountain air.

The undisciplined commander immediately ordered a second attack and called for the mortar teams to open fire. They quickly learned the Americans had a sniper with them. All six men manning the three mortar tubes were killed within seconds of firing their first round. Another wave of sixty men headed up the mountain, this time firing as they went. Two hours later, a handful of men limped off the mountain, swearing a company of Rangers was dug in on the peak. The commander would hear none of it. He turned to Karim and ordered him to take his newly formed unit of thirty-eight Saudi freedom fighters and attack the position.

Karim looked back on that night as a defining moment in his life. He understood the situation both tactically and psychologically. The commander was Taliban and had been in charge of the area prior to the American towers' coming down. If word got out that he couldn't dislodge seven Americans from his own backyard, he would be humiliated. The man would rather waste two hundred good men than face the public embarrassment.

Standing in the mountains that night, Karim was overcome with an incredible sense of calm. He did not bother to argue with the commander. He knew if he refused the order he would be branded a coward and sent back to Saudi Arabia to live the rest of his life in humiliation. If he led his men up the hill it was likely he would be killed along with many of his men. With his options limited, he decided on the most simple, straightforward solution there was. Karim pulled out his pistol, shot the commander in the head, and took charge. He sent runners for more men and artillery and had the wounded evacuated. In the half-light of dawn, just as the lone artillery piece was being moved into position, Karim heard the steady thumping of a helicopter fighting to stay aloft in the thin mountain air. As the noise grew he grabbed a pair of high-powered binoculars and focused on the peak. He watched in awe as seven men climbed into the belly of the American beast and disappeared over the other side of the ridge.

After that lopsided engagement, Karim had thrown himself into studying the American Special Forces. What he quickly learned was that it was not simply better weapons and tactics that made them so effective, it was selection and training. Of the seven men now seated at the table, he had commanded five of them in Afghanistan, and had handpicked them for the operation. The other two were foisted on him by Zawahiri. The arrogant man had insisted they were two of his best. When Karim found out that Zachariah was Zawahiri's nephew, things became more clear. The talentless hack had been sent along to keep an eye on things and report back to his uncle.

The Egyptian was dragging the rest of the team down. He finished last in every exercise and because of him the success of the mission was now in jeopardy. Karim thought of the Americans and their training. The selection process for their elite units was grueling. Some of them, like the SEALs, had an eighty percent rate of attrition. Karim tried to remember the word they used. It had something to do with water. After a moment it came to him. They called it washing out. Karim liked the phrase—it had a religious undertone to it. Like washing away the impure or unworthy.

He looked down at Zachariah. Sending him back to his uncle was very risky, for two reasons: the first, Zawahiri was liable to cut off their funding and recall the entire team; the second, the halfwit was likely to get picked up by a customs official somewhere along the way and expose the entire operation. Karim had another moment of clarity. The Egyptian's smug face and half-finished bomb made the decision all that much easier. The mission was more important than any one man. Karim drew his 9mm pistol from his thigh holster, pointed it at Zachariah's head, and shot him.

CHAPTER 5

BAGRAM AIR BASE, AFGHANISTAN

NASH approached the cell bay door and listened for a buzzing noise that would tell him the lock had been released. Rapp was right on his heels, breathing down his neck like a bull ready to enter the ring. Between the two of them they had interrogated well over a hundred terrorists, informants, and enemy combatants. On nine previous occasions they had combined their talents and pried open the minds of men such as Abu Haggani and Mohammad al-Haq. Sucked them dry over a period of months. Individually, Rapp and Nash were very effective. Combined, they were like a hurricane; relentless, swirling, pounding, and then the final surge. There was no doubt they could break them, the only question was, Could they do it in such a short period of time?

There was a clicking noise and then a steady buzz. Nash shoved open the door and they moved into the cell bay. There were four cells on the left and four on the right, with a wide walkway down the middle. Each cell was a self-contained cube, elevated one foot off the ground, with a gap of a foot between each pair of cells. In addition to the cells being wired for video and sound, the doors were made out of one-way Plexiglas.

Nash and Rapp marched the length of the cell bay and stopped at the last door on the right. Nash reached out and hit the light switch. If it had been up to him the lights would have stayed on 24/7, but the air force was running the show.

Rapp looked in on the prisoner, the wrinkles on his brow showing his disapproval. "They didn't shave his head or beard?"

"No."

Rapp's frown deepened and he mumbled a few curses to himself.

"The Detainee Treatment Act says it's degrading," said Nash with feigned earnestness.

"Degrading," Rapp said gruffly. "The guy lives in a cave nine months out of the year. His specialty is convincing the parents of Down syndrome kids to let him use their children as suicide bombers. The word *degrading* isn't in his vocabulary."

Nash would make no effort to defend the rights of an animal such as Haggani, but tonight would be unlike any of their previous efforts. He needed to keep Rapp from going too far, from leaving marks that would be seen by the military interrogators in the morning. "We both know he's a piece of shit, and any other time I couldn't care less what you do to him, but you're going to have to pull your punches tonight."

The only assurance Rapp was willing to give him was a slight nod. "Let's get started. We're wasting time."

Nash grabbed a small digital two-way radio from his pocket, clicked the transmit button, and said, "Marcus, open number eight for me, please."

As soon as the door buzzed, Rapp yanked it open and stepped into the small cell. In a booming voice he yelled, "Good morning, sunshine." Rapp snatched the covers off Haggani and screamed, "Time to get up, you piece of shit!"

Abu Haggani was wearing an orange prisoner jumpsuit. He rolled over with the look of a feral dog on his face and let loose a gob of spit that hit Rapp in the chin.

Rapp blinked once before letting loose a slew of curse words.

"I forgot to tell you, he's a spitter," Nash cautioned.

"Goddammit," Rapp yelled as he drew his sleeve across his face, his temper flaring.

Haggani kicked his legs and began thrashing at Rapp. Rapp jumped back quickly and almost tripped over Nash. He caught his balance and then caught Haggani's right ankle as it came within inches of striking him in the nuts. Rapp grabbed the foot with both hands and took a big step back, yanking the terrorist from his bed. Haggani hit the floor with a thud, and before he could recover, Rapp twisted the foot ninety degrees to the left. The move caused Haggani to straighten out and expose his groin. Rapp turned 180 degrees and brought the heel of his jump boot crashing down. There was a whoosh of air as the wind was driven from Haggani's lungs. The man groaned loudly and reached to protect his crotch.

Swearing loudly in Dari, Rapp dragged a far more cooperative Haggani from the cell and started down the hall. Nash rushed ahead and opened the next door. As Rapp reached the threshold, Haggani came to life again. He pulled himself forward and grabbed onto Rapp's right leg. He opened his mouth wide and went for Rapp's thigh. Rapp saw it coming, and just as Haggani's teeth were about to connect, Rapp unleashed an elbow strike that caught the Afghani above the right eye. The blow hit with such force that Haggani's head snapped back and then his whole upper body collapsed to the floor. His eyes rolled back into his head and his entire body went limp. A thin line of crimson about an inch long appeared where the terrorist's right eyebrow ended. That's all it was for a second or two, and then the blood began cascading from the cut.

"For Christ sake, Mitch," said a wide-eyed Nash.

"What'd you want me to do? Let him bite me?"

"No, but you didn't have to cut him." Nash bent over for a closer look. "I think he's gonna need stitches."

"There's nothing we can do about it now." Rapp grabbed Haggani by the feet again and pulled him through the door, down the hall, and into the interrogation room on the left. Two men were inside, waiting. "Put him in the chair and tie him down," Rapp ordered. "I don't want him moving, and if he spits on you, you have my permission to slap the shit out of him."

Rapp walked back out in the hallway and into the cell bay. Nash was waiting in front of the first cell on the left. There, sitting on the edge of the bed with prayer beads in hand, was Mohammad al-Haq. The forty-nine-year-old senior Taliban member looked more like he was seventy. His hair and beard were almost completely gray. His posture and gnarled hands spoke to the harsh life he had lived while fighting for almost thirty straight years—first as a revolutionary in the seventies, fighting against his own government, then for the Soviets in the early eighties when it looked like they would win, and then for the mujahideen when the tide turned against the Soviets. After the conflict with the Soviets, al-Haq worked with the various factions of the Northern Alliance, including General Dostum, before he yet again switched sides and jumped over to join up with the Taliban as they rolled to victory. Al-Haq was the ultimate opportunist. His past indicated he would be very easy to turn.

Nash opened the cell door and said, "Mohammad, I'm afraid the time has come."

The bearded man looked up at him with nervous eyes. There would be no spitting or kicking. "For?" he asked in English.

"To reacquaint you with your old friend General Dostum."

The man looked heavily at his prayer beads, and then, at the urging of Nash, got to his feet. The three of them left the cell bay and entered the other interrogation room. Nash placed al-Haq in a chair with his back to the door. Rapp walked around the other side of the table, leaned over and placed both hands on the surface, and stared into the prisoner's eyes. In Dari he asked, "Mohammad, do you know who I am?"

The prisoner hesitated and then looked up. His eyes searched Rapp's face for a moment and then he nodded.

"Do you think you have been treated well during your stay with the United States Air Force?" Nash asked.

"Yes."

"Well, the party is over, Mohammad," Rapp said as he moved around the table. "I brought your old buddy General Dostum down here from Mazar-i-Sharif. He is eagerly anticipating your reunion."

He glanced warily at Rapp and with as much conviction as he could muster, said, "I do not believe the general is here. If he was, he would be standing in front of me right now."

Nash and Rapp shared a look that al-Haq construed as nervous. The terrorist wiped his sweaty palms on his jumpsuit and added, "I have become a student of your country. I see how important it is for your leaders to feel that they are enlightened and compassionate. They would never allow me to be turned over to an animal like General Dostum. The senators I met with earlier in the week assured me that I would be treated humanely."

Rapp laughed. Nash shook his head. Al-Haq allowed himself a smile at what he thought was a small victory.

"Your thinking," Nash said, "is not far from the truth, but you left out one important thing. We're CIA. We don't play by the rules. Our job, our only job as ordered by the president, is to hunt down and kill you and your merry band of backward, bigoted nut jobs. Now, you may have found some comfort in the assurances of those politically correct senators who visited you earlier in the week, but let me tell you something, they have the shortest memories of any animal on the planet. We have assured the president that in our opinion an attack on the continental United States is imminent. He has talked to each of those senators, two of whom are up for reelection, and asked them how they are going to explain their behavior to their constituents if the U.S. is hit by a terrorist attack."

Nash was making all of it up. There had been no discussion with the president, and therefore the president had not gone to the senators in question. They were way off the reservation, but the prisoner did not need to know that.

"Those senators bailed on your ass like that." Rapp snapped his fingers. "So it's down to two choices for you. You either talk to General Dostum or you talk to us. With us, it's only going to be as painful as you make it. With General Dostum it will be painful. You will sleep in your own shit for as long as he keeps you alive. He will allow his men to do unspeakable things to you. You will experience pain that you didn't think possible. You will beg him to kill you, and after he has had his fun, he most certainly will."

Rapp took a step back, folded his arms, and shrugged. "With us, as long as you cooperate, you will most certainly live. In twenty years or so you will probably be set free. You can even look forward to playing with your grandchildren someday."

"The choice is simple," said Nash, almost pleading with the man to make things easy.

The Afghani's face was pinched in thought, like a card player trying to decide if he should fold or put everything in the pot. After a long moment he looked up and said, "I do not believe you. If General Dostum was here, he would be standing in front of me."

"Well that can be arranged," said Nash as he moved across the room. He opened the door and left the small interrogation room.

Rapp smiled at him. "You're an idiot. The general wants you so bad he's offered me money. Fifty thousand cash if I look the other way and let him take you back to Mazar-i-Sharif. And you know how much this man likes his cash."

Nash returned with the general a few seconds later. Dostum approached al-Haq from behind and placed both hands on the man's shoulders. There was an obvious physical contrast between the two men. Dostum was carrying an extra twenty pounds at least, whereas al-Haq was emaciated from years of living on the run in the mountains.

"Mohammad, I have looked forward to this for years." Dostum

spoke in Uzbeki, which Rapp and Nash did not understand as well as Dari. "I have many things planned for you. There are many of your old friends who can't wait to see you."

Nash watched al-Haq close his eyes. He tried to stand but Dostum's powerful hands kept him in place. Nash cleared his throat. "I think we should allow you two a few minutes alone."

"That is a wonderful idea," Dostum said, switching to English. "Please send in my bodyguards."

As Rapp and Nash started for the door, a terrified al-Haq began pleading with them to stay.

CHAPTER 6

CAPTAIN Trevor Leland stopped outside the door, reached for the knob, and froze with indecision. When you worked for a man like General Garrison, this was one of those moments that could make or break your career. The base commander liked his sleep and had left specific orders not to be disturbed. Leland thought of how Garrison would react to the intrusion and lost his nerve. He withdrew his hand and began walking away. After a few steps, though, he slowed his pace and started to reconsider. He'd been an aide to Brigadier General Scott Garrison for nine months, and found it extremely difficult to satisfy the man. It was by far the most tasking assignment he'd had in his six years in the air force. Garrison, like Leland, was an Air Force Academy graduate. That was about where their common ground ended, however. They disagreed drastically on how to lead and be led.

Leland thought of his own career. The general wasn't likely to do him any favors, even if he performed to expectations. There was something the general didn't like about him. Leland thought he knew what it was, but he didn't want to admit it. He was a charmer. He'd figured out pretty much every CO he'd served under and been able to win them over. Not this time, though. Garrison was a tough nut, and Leland was having a really hard time trying to figure out how to turn things around. He had even tried to win over the other officers on Garrison's staff, but so far he had received little sympathy.

For at least the tenth time in as many minutes, Leland went over his options. If he woke him up, and it turned out to be nothing, Garrison would make his glum job downright miserable. If he didn't wake him, though, and the rumors proved to be true . . . Leland shuddered at the mere thought of what would happen. He remembered the senators who had been at the base earlier in the week. Leland had gone out of his way to smooth things over and make sure the politicians had everything they needed. Garrison wasn't about to do it. He hated the politicians and dignitaries who came rolling through his base for a photo op so they could tell their constituents or friends that they had been over there, that they'd been to the war zone and survived.

So it was up to Leland to kiss their asses. He knew how the game was played. Powerful senators regularly lobbied on behalf of the officers they liked. Leland had promised them that the prisoners would be treated humanely and by the book. One of the senators had told him they'd better be or she would haul his ass before the Armed Services Committee and eat him for lunch.

Leland thought about the senator's words as he laid out his options yet again. If he woke him up, and it was for nothing, Garrison would go nuts. He was scheduled to go on leave in ten days and planned to meet a couple of academy buddies in Istanbul. He'd been looking forward to it for months. If this turned out to be nothing, Garrison wouldn't hesitate to punish him by canceling his leave. If he let him sleep, on the other hand, and the rumors turned out to be true, the man would do a lot more than cancel his leave. He would probably have him transferred to one of the tiny firebases up in the mountains where he could expect to be shelled once or twice a day. Leland took a deep breath and made his decision. A firebase was a far worse punishment than missing Istanbul.

Leland moved quickly now. He didn't want to lose his nerve. He tapped lightly on the door, even though he knew it would do no good. The general was a sound sleeper. Gently opening the door, Leland walked over to the bed and cleared his throat.

"Excuse me, sir." The general kept snoring, so Leland reached out and repeated himself. The general didn't stir. Leland grimaced and lightly touched the general's shoulder.

General Garrison flinched and made a loud snorting noise as he snatched a breath. He rolled over and said, "What . . . who is it?"

"It's me, Captain Leland, sir."

"Leland, what in the hell do you want?" Garrison growled through a dry throat. "I thought I told you not to disturb me."

"You did, sir, but there's something . . . something that I thought I should bring to your attention." He took a step back.

"Something," General Garrison said in an irritated voice as he sat up. "This had better be good, Captain, or you're going to be out calling in close air support for the rest of your tour."

Leland took a dry gulp, his worst fears confirmed. It seemed he would never be able to satisfy the man. "A plane arrived shortly after midnight, sir."

"Planes arrive all the time," Garrison snarled. "This is an air base, Captain. That's what happens . . . planes land and planes take off."

Leland was suddenly regretting his decision, but there was no turning back. "I think it might involve the prisoners, sir. The two high-value ones."

The news had a sobering affect on the general. "What do you mean, the two prisoners?"

"The plane was an Air Force G III. Six men deplaned, all wearing BDU's. They had two Humvees waiting for them."

"Who are they?"

Leland grew increasingly nervous. The next piece of information had been passed along as a rumor. "I have not been able to verify this, sir, but I was told by someone on the flight line that the men are from the Office of Special Investigations."

Garrison threw back his blanket and swung his feet onto the floor. After mumbling a few curses he looked up at his aide and said, "Office of Special Investigations?"

"Yes, sir."

"How long have you known?"

"About forty minutes, sir."

The general stood. "Air Force Office of Special Investigations arrives on my base, unannounced, in the middle of the night, and it takes you forty minutes to notify me."

Leland stood ramrod straight and looked over the top of the general's head. "Sir, you left specific orders not to be disturbed."

"I left specific orders not to be bothered with all of the trivial bullshit that you think is important. When the Office of Special Investigations shows up in the middle of the night, it's about as bad as it gets for a CO. It ranks just an ass hair under a plane crashing or attack on the base."

"I'm sorry, sir."

"Where are they now?"

"I'm not sure, sir, but I think they might be at the Hilton."

Garrison was in the midst of pulling on his flight suit. He stopped with both feet in and fixed a stare on the young captain. "The Hilton?"

"Yes, sir."

The anger spread across the general's face. "How in the hell did you ever graduate from the United States Air Force Academy?"

CHAPTER 7

NASH and Rapp had made it clear to General Dostum that, as much as they would like to hand al-Haq over to him, it was not going to happen. The general was reluctant at first, but when Rapp offered to deposit a sizable amount of cash in his bank in Geneva, the general agreed to the plan with enthusiasm. Their little charade had been rehearsed in advance, and was so far proceeding according to plan. Nash reasoned that once al-Haq agreed to talk, Dostum would be the perfect person to initiate the interrogation. The two men had fought alongside each other for eleven years. Al-Haq had committed his unforgivable sin during a pitched battle against the Taliban for the city of Mazar-i-Sharif. When it became obvious that the Taliban was going to carry the day, al-Haq crossed over with his men and switched his allegiance. Dostum was forced to retreat and eventually flee the country. Al-Haq would think long and hard before he lied to his former friend.

Nash and Rapp monitored the first few minutes of the session from a one-way viewing window. When it was obvious that Dostum wasn't going to choke al-Haq to death, Nash relaxed a bit. His plan was to move onto the other prisoner while Dostum got things rolling. He turned and looked at Marcus Dumond, who was sitting behind the watch desk. Rapp had brought him from Langley. The thirty-one-year-old was the Clandestine Service's resident genius when it came to security systems and computers.

"You getting all this?" Nash asked.

"Yep," Dumond answered.

"And you have control of the cameras? Base security isn't catching any of this?"

Rapp had made Dumond shave his Afro for the trip, and he couldn't stop rubbing his newly polished head. He looked at Nash the same way he looked at anyone who dared question his ability to work magic.

"Base security is looking at a one-hour loop from every camera in this facility. I am recording the interrogations, both audio and video, onto this flash drive." Dumond held up a small silver box no bigger than a checkbook.

"Good." Nash turned back to Rapp and said, "Are you ready for a little fire and brimstone?"

"In a minute. Where do they keep the towels?"

"Storage closet over here." Nash led Rapp down another hall and opened the door to a janitor's closet where fresh orange coveralls, bedding, and towels for the prisoners were kept. Rapp grabbed a towel and wet it in the mop sink.

Already concerned over the cut above Haggani's eye, Nash asked, "What do you have in mind?"

Rapp wrung out the towel and said, "You've seen his type before. The only thing you can do is beat on him until he heels."

"Mitch, we have to be careful."

"Don't worry, no matter how pissed off I look, it's all part of the act."

"Right. And that's supposed to make me feel better?"

"No," Rapp said with a smile. "You just do your fire-and-brimstone thing, and I'll play the sadistic bastard who looks like he wants to tear his head off and piss down his throat."

"That's a real stretch for you. You sure you don't want to switch roles this time?"

"I'm sure." Rapp laughed. "I don't have your ministerial zeal."

"Fine. Just remember . . . no more marks."

"I'll do my best," Rapp said, as if he was already admitting he couldn't.

Rapp's attitude gave Nash pause. "You're looking for a fight, aren't you?"

"Maybe."

"Then maybe we shouldn't go in there. Al-Haq is already talking. Let's get as much out of him as we can tonight, have Irene bring it to the president, and if all goes well, he'll be transferred to our custody, and we can spend the next thirty days debriefing him."

"No," Rapp said with conviction. "I want a shot at Haggani. I've wanted to get my hands on him for a long time. I want to hear from his own mouth how he thinks it's noble to kill little kids, and then I want him to feel some real pain. I want him to understand what he's put these people through. I want to break him down bit by bit, and then I want to suck his brain dry. And then I'm going to personally hunt down every person in his little pipeline of suicide bombers and put a bullet in their head."

Nash had known Rapp long enough to know he meant every word of what he'd just said. "Mitch, it might take weeks just to get him to talk."

"It might, but he also might break within an hour." He jerked his head toward the interrogation room. "Let's get started."

Nash reached out and grabbed Rapp's arm. "Mitch, I've been here all week. These senators put the fear of God into these air force guys. Let's not give them any reason to call Washington."

"I'm not going to back down from this fight, Mike. I've had it with these damn politicians who don't have the stomach to take on these bastards. It's only a matter of time before we get hit again and then you watch these pricks run for cover. Every single one of them who's been handcuffing us is going to blame us for failing to stop these guys."

"You're probably right, but there's a smart way to do this and then there's the . . ."

Rapp held up a hand and cut him off. "You don't have to go in there with me. You've got a family to worry about. I don't. I'm free and clear. I've got nothing to slow me down. Nothing they can hold over my head."

Nash was tempted to take him up on the offer, but they had been through too much together. He owed Rapp too much. "Just try not to leave any more marks."

"I'll do my best." Rapp walked back down the hall and paused to look in on General Dostum and al-Haq. He took it as a good sign that the two men were talking. Rapp moved down the hall and opened the door to the other interrogation room. As he entered, he said, "Abu, I hear you've been playing dumb all week." Rapp reached Haggani's side and added, "We both know you understand English."

Rapp expected it this time. Was waiting as the same feral look spread across Haggani's face. With his arms and legs bound to the chair, the prisoner tilted his head back, cleared his throat and then lunged forward unleashing a gob of spit. Rapp held up the towel and blocked it.

"Bad move, Abu," Rapp said as he draped the towel over Haggani's head and reached into the right cargo pocket of his pants. He fished out a black stun gun and gripped it firmly in his right hand. Haggani was violently trying to shake the towel from his head, but was having little success. As soon as he stopped moving, Rapp placed the two charge electrodes against the wet towel in the general area of the terrorist's mouth. He pulled the trigger and pressed firmly, holding it down for three long seconds. The high-voltage, low-amperage electrical charge crackled as it spread through the wet towel. Haggani's body went rigid for a second and then convulsed several times.

Rapp withdrew the gun, grabbed the towel, and took a step back. A disoriented Haggani fought to keep his head up.

"Abu, have you ever heard of Ivan Pavlov?" Rapp searched the man's still-dazed eyes. "Based on your limited educational experience, I doubt it. He's a Russian, or I should say, was. He's been dead for a long time, but that's not important. The man was a genius . . . the father of classical conditioning. Most people know him because of the study he did with dogs. He'd ring a bell, wait a few minutes, and then feed the dogs. After a while the dogs would salivate in anticipation of being fed when they heard the bell ring . . . pretty basic stuff. It's called conditioned response and it works with humans as well as dogs. Take your little nasty habit of spitting on people, for example. The guards should have broken you of the habit right away, but they didn't, so I'm going to have to do it. Not a big deal, though. It shouldn't take us more than ten minutes to cure you of the tendency."

Haggani's eyes blinked several times. He shook his head and then opened his mouth and flexed his jaw.

Nash watched, unfazed, from the other side of the table. He'd seen Rapp go through this with prisoners on four other occasions. The towel was used to both block the spit and spread out the charge so they wouldn't leave any marks on Haggani. Nash had used stun guns himself on many occasions. Especially on the prisoners who were fond of throwing their feces and urine at the guards. Every human rights organization had released statements condemning the use of stun guns on prisoners as torture. Nash wondered how they would feel if they had someone throwing shit on them every day when they walked into work.

Rapp got the towel ready. He stepped a little closer and asked, "Are you done spitting?"

Haggani tilted his head back again and pursed his lips.

Rapp tossed the towel back over Haggani's head and hit him with another three-second shot from the stun gun. The results were the same. Haggani's recovery, though, took a good half minute longer.

Nash and Rapp exchanged a brief look. Between the two of them they'd had only one prisoner go beyond three hits in a sitting. Almost all required shocks a day or two later, to help cement the conditioning.

A minute passed and Rapp pulled the towel off Haggani's head. He didn't speak this time. He stood within striking distance locked in a stare with Haggani waiting for him to decide which path he would take.

Nash stared at the cut and swollen bump above Haggani's eye. The blood had run down his face onto his neck and was now soaking the collar of the orange jumpsuit. It showed no signs of slowing. Nash knew that sooner rather than later he would have to get a first aid kit and clean up the prisoner. There was no way of hiding the injury, though. That was going to create some major problems in the morning.

There was a knock on the door. Nash walked over and opened it. General Dostum was standing in the hallway, smiling. "He wants to talk to you."

Nash did not want to talk in front of Haggani, so he said to Rapp, "I'll be back in a minute." He stepped into the hallway, and as soon as the door was closed he asked, "What's up?"

Dostum rolled his eyes. "The man is a snake. He thinks only of himself. I knew he would want to strike a deal."

"Did he give you anything?"

"He says he has information that would be very helpful and timely to the U.S."

"You believe him?"

"He was in a position to know important things, but he is a liar. It is up to you to sort it all out." Dostum grinned.

Nash thought of his strategy. He knew from experience that you never walked into an interrogation room without a plan. He had an idea where al-Haq would want to take this. He patted Dostum on the shoulder and said, "Thank you. I will go in alone. Please watch, though, and don't be afraid to interrupt if you think he is lying."

CHAPTER 8

WASHINGTON, D.C.

W HERE in the hell is Mitch Rapp?"
The question was tossed out like a hand grenade lobbed at an enemy position. It rolled down the long, shiny mahogany conference table, striking fear in all. Eyes were averted, a few throats were cleared, and one man was actually smart enough to get up and head for the door. One by one, though, all eyes turned to the woman sitting at the opposite end of the table. As director of the CIA, she was responsible for Rapp.

Irene Kennedy looked down the length of the ridiculously long table at her questioner. He was a lawyer, of course. They were all lawyers these days; the FBI agents on her left, the Department of Justice people on her right—even the handful of people from State more than likely had law degrees. Kennedy had intentionally left her lawyers back at Langley for this early-morning meeting. Tactically speaking, this was a reconnaissance operation, and for that she'd brought along two men with plenty of experience. She eyed the antagonist at the far end of the table. Over the last two weeks she'd heard a steady stream of complaints about the man. Watching him operate for the first time, she wondered how two parents could have so thoroughly failed to equip their child with the most basic manners.

Wade Kline was the newly appointed chief privacy and civil liberties officer at the Department of Justice. He was a fairly attractive man, at least until he opened his mouth, at which point he became decidedly less so. His new position at Justice was created to appease the ACLU crowd on Capitol Hill, who felt that America had become a police state. Before taking the post, Kline had spent a decade as a prosecutor working for the New York State Attorney General's Office.

"Well?" Kline asked with obvious impatience.

Kennedy's face remained unimpressed. She had learned the espionage business at the arm of Thomas Stansfield, a Cold War legend. Like her mentor, she was widely known to be an unflappable player; respected by most, despised by a few and feared by more than she realized. All of that went with the job, of course. She was the director of the Central Intelligence Agency, and it was easy for people to imagine a hidden, sinister side to an otherwise classy and pleasant woman.

Kennedy eyed Kline and told herself to stay calm. At thirty-nine he was too young to be throwing his weight around, and old enough to know better. Kennedy had seen plenty of men and women like Kline come and go over the years. Five months ago the New Yorker would have had no chance at getting under her skin, but a lot had changed since then. There was no doubt about the source of her discontent. It could all be traced to a single traumatic event that had sent her careening down a road of doubt and pain, an event she tried every day to forget.

"This is not a difficult question," Kline pressed. His suit coat was off, his tie loose, and his white shirtsleeves rolled up.

Kennedy's brow furrowed as if she was studying a strange insect. "Mr. Rapp," she said in an even tone, "is unavailable."

"Unavailable." Kline contemplated the word. "That's pretty vague."

"Not really."

"I beg to differ." Kline paused, scribbled a note to himself, looked directly at Kennedy, and asked, "Where is he?"

It was obvious to Kennedy that Kline had spent a fair amount of time strutting in front of juries. Surely he didn't think she would simply announce the location of her top counterterrorism operative to the Justice Department's newest politically appointed watchdog. Feeling a tinge of anger over the man's arrogance, Kennedy said, "Where and what Mr. Rapp is doing is none of your business."

"I couldn't disagree more, Ms. Kennedy."

Despite the warnings by her legal counsel, Kennedy was shocked by the man's arrogance. She took off her reading glasses. "It's Director Kennedy, Mr. Kline, or Dr. Kennedy, if you would prefer."

A cocky, self-satisfied grin spread across Kline's face. "Doctor, director," he said in a more pleasant tone, "either one works for me."

Kennedy did not flinch. She made no effort to respond in any way. Her thoughts headed down an unconventional path, exploring the man's potential weaknesses, wondering how he would react to pain.

"Back to Rapp, if we could." Kline tapped his pen on his yellow legal pad as if to refocus the conversation. "I've been asking to see the man for more than a month, and frankly, I've about run out of patience."

"Mr. Rapp is very busy."

"Aren't we all, Madam Director."

"Some more than others," she said, a touch of impatience creeping into her voice.

Kline did not miss the change in tone. He nodded to Kennedy as if to say *game on* and then asked, "Where is he?"

"I know you're relatively new to Washington, but surely you are aware that much of what my agency handles is classified."

"So you won't even tell me if he's in the country?"

"Not unless I'm authorized by the president, or you can prove to me that you have somehow miraculously received a security clearance that is far above your pay grade." The last part was a not-so-subtle reminder to Kline that in the power structure of the federal government, he was more than a few rungs beneath her.

Kline clicked his pen shut, stuffed it in his shirt pocket, and closed his leather briefing folder. "I can play hardball as good as anyone, Madam Director." He stood and snatched his suit coat from the back of the chair. "This is my last warning. If Mitch Rapp isn't standing in my office a week from today, I can promise you, I will make your life miserable."

Kennedy felt her anger rushing to the surface. Part of her wanted to unleash it, wanted to teach this egocentric man a lesson, but there was another part of her that held back. Intuition warned her that no matter how satisfying it might feel, it would be a mistake. She watched him march to the door and then stop.

"One other thing," Kline said as he flipped open his briefing folder and scanned his notes. "You have a man named Mike Nash who works for you."

Kennedy returned his stare, wondering if he'd simply made a statement or was asking a question.

"I want him in my office Monday morning. If he isn't there, I'll send the FBI for him." Kline closed his folder and was gone.

One by one the other people seated at the table turned to look at Kennedy. She ignored them, her gaze fixed on the open doorway. The man had just openly threatened the director of the most powerful spy organization in the world, which either meant he was insane or he had something on her. The fact that he had brought up Rapp was not all that surprising. People had been coming after him for years, but Nash was another story. Kennedy had taken great care to keep him under the radar. He was increasingly handling some of the agency's most delicate operations.

One of the two men she'd brought along leaned over and whispered in her ear, "I just got a text from the office. We need to get you out of here."

Kennedy shot him a concerned look.

Rob Ridley, the deputy director of the Clandestine Service, saw the alarm on her face and said, "It's not that." Ridley knew she was thinking an evacuation had been ordered. Since 9/11 it was not uncommon for high-ranking government officials to be taken out of the city at the first whisper of trouble. In recent years it had slowed down, but that was now balanced against fresh intel that pointed to something big. "That thing . . . it just started."

"What thing?"

Ridley's eyes darted around the room. "The thing over in Afghanistan."

"Oh, that thing."

"Yeah, that thing. I don't think you want to have a conversation about it in this building."

Kennedy looked around the Department of Justice conference room while she thought of Rapp and Nash. She checked her watch. The time would be about right. She knew what they were up to. She'd signed off on it herself. She motioned for Ridley to lead the way and politely ignored several of the other attendees who wanted to have a word with her.

As they reached the elevators her thoughts returned to a feeling that had been nagging her. Someone at Langley was leaking highly classified information. Accusations were appearing in the press that were far too close to the truth. The Intelligence Committees were becoming increasingly antagonistic, and now she had to deal with this hungry deputy attorney general who was trying to make a name for himself. A sense of foreboding crept over her, like a looming storm on a humid summer day.

CHAPTER 9

BAGRAM AIR BASE, AFGHANISTAN

RAPP sat on the edge of the metal table, looked down at the bound terrorist, and asked, "Is it seventy-two or seventy-seven?"

Abu Haggani lifted his head cautiously and stared at Rapp, confusion in his eyes.

"Virgins," Rapp said. "Seventy-two or seventy-seven. How many do you guys get when you go to paradise?"

Haggani muttered something under his breath and looked away.

"I'm not giving you crap," Rapp persisted. "I've read the Koran several times and that's one of those facts I can never keep straight. Not that it matters much. I mean what's the difference . . . seventy-two versus seventy-seven? It seems a little like overkill, don't you think?" Rapp paused to see if Haggani would respond. He didn't, so Rapp pressed on. "Have you ever read the Koran, Abu?"

Haggani fixed Rapp with a hard stare and in Dari said, "I know what you are trying to do."

"What's that?"

"You are trying to provoke me. We know about your methods. We have undergone training to defeat your tricks."

Rapp knew it was true. Most of their once secret interrogation programs had been blown wide open. Many of their methods had been dissected by politicians and the press alike. Terrorists had been released and had run back to Afghanistan and other parts, where they were thoroughly debriefed by the very organizations they denied belonging to. The whole mess drove Rapp insane, but there was only so much he could control.

Rapp clenched his left fist and then flexed his fingers. "Abu, I am not trying to provoke you . . . at least not yet. I'm not one of the talkers. I don't have the patience they do . . . like my friend who was in here earlier. He's next door talking to Mohammad, and we both know how that is going to play out. Mohammad is going to sell you and the rest of your friends down the river. You will eventually, as well, but it will take more time, and of course it will be significantly more uncomfortable."

"You will never break me," Haggani said with pride.

Rapp let out a long sigh. He'd seen this kind of bravado before. Once things got physical, it wouldn't last long. "Abu, torturing guys and breaking them down is not something I look forward to, although your case is a little different. I think you're such a despicable fuck that I might actually enjoy our little session."

"You do not scare me."

"Well, I should." Rapp laughed. "I scare myself sometimes. You see . . . I'm not like the guys you've been talking to this week. I have a real conviction about this little war we're fighting and I'm pretty intolerant of people who don't have the stomach to do what it takes to win this thing. Add to that the fact that I pretty much don't give a shit what people in Washington think of me and it makes me your biggest nightmare."

Haggani shook his head and snorted. "Empty threats."

Rapp reached out and put a hand on a galvanized metal box sitting on the other side of the table. Something inside stirred. The box shook and there was a scraping noise. "I've only used what's in this box one other time, and let's just say the guy I used it on was a hell of a lot tougher than you. He lasted less than thirty seconds." Rapp was lying. He'd never used this particular method, but there was no sense in telling Haggani.

The terrorist looked anxiously at the box and, with a false bravado, said, "I have rights. You are not allowed to treat me like this."

Rapp saw an opening. Maybe Haggani wasn't as tough as they thought. Rapp thought of Nash, the way he would draw prisoners into a debate. How he would press them with logic, use the words of the Koran to undermine their weak arguments. Nash's strategy was straightforward: get them talking. It didn't matter what they talked about, it just mattered that you established a pattern. Gave yourself a chance to watch the subject, study his habits, and learn as much about him as possible. The tough questions would come later. Rapp had none of Nash's patience, however. But still there was a part of him that was intrigued by Haggani's request for proper treatment. He thought of one of Nash's favorite questions, looked at the terrorist and asked, "Abu, do you think I should show you compassion? That I should respect your rights as a human?"

"Yes," he answered with absolute sincerity.

"And how would you treat me if I had been captured on the battlefield and brought to one of your caves?"

Haggani ignored the question. "Your senators who I met with promised me that I would be treated with dignity. They gave me their word."

"They are politicians. They say what makes them feel good and then they move on."

Haggani shook his head in firm disagreement. "We have access to the Internet. To satellites. We have followed the debate in your country over the treatment of prisoners. Those senators meant what they said to me."

"You go ahead and believe that, Abu, but I have no intention of treating you with dignity. You think of yourself as a holy warrior, but you are nothing more than a butcher. A mass murderer."

"You know nothing of my ways."

"Is that so? Let's talk about the schools."

"What schools?"

"The ones you blew up. The ones filled with little children." Rapp expected one of several reactions from Haggani, but not the one he got.

Haggani smiled proudly. "We know how to sacrifice. We are not afraid to martyr ourselves for Allah."

The anger came quickly. It started to rise up and Rapp stuffed it back down. Said, "You haven't martyred yourself, tough guy, and I doubt you gave those kids a choice in the matter."

He held his chin high and said, "I am not afraid."

"You're not afraid to send little kids to their death. That makes you a coward and a butcher, and if you had read the Koran you would know that."

"What do you know of the Koran?" Haggani roared back.

Rapp grinned. "Apparently more than you . . . since I've actually read it."

"I have it memorized."

"Bullshit. You know as well as I do that you were taught the suras by some twisted Wahhabi cleric who told you only what he wanted you to know. Kill all the Jews. Kill the infidels. Cover your wives and daughters. Beat them if they disrespect you. The West is evil. We are just and good, blah . . . blah . . . fucking blah. I am so sick of the hate you pieces of shit teach each other and your children."

"You know nothing."

"I know Allah," Rapp screamed, "is going to send your ass to hell for killing His children!"

"You have no right being in my country. You are infidels and Allah will punish you and your nation for this war."

"You ever think maybe it's the other way around?" Rapp brought his face within inches of Haggani's. "That God is punishing your nation for how you have twisted and misused the words of the prophet? America hasn't been at war. We've suffered the one attack. Your nation has been at war for almost forty years. Over a million people have died. Allah is mad as hell with you sick fucks. He's been punishing you and he's going to keep punishing you."

Haggani unleashed a gob of spit, hitting Rapp square in the face.

Rapp didn't bother to wipe away the spit. He didn't bother to grab the stun gun. His head reared back and then snapped forward; the hardest part of his forehead striking Haggani on the soft bridge of the nose. It was like a hammer hitting a banana. Haggani's nose flattened and blood began oozing from his nostrils.

Rapp stood and circled the prisoner. He looked at the blood and the misshapen nose. He knew Nash would flip, but he didn't care. He was sick of all the bullshit. "You're not getting any virgins," Rapp barked at Haggani. He thought of Nash's words; how he used their religion to dismantle their twisted ways. "Djinn," Rapp uttered, the one word that seemed to drive the ones like Haggani nuts. "You are a Djinn, and you don't even know it. You know the Koran forbids suicide and yet you have convinced dozens and dozens of Allah's children to throw their lives away. You have killed thousands of Allah's followers. The seventh sura, Abu, do you remember?" Rapp switched to Arabic and began reciting the verse from the Koran, "Many, moreover, of the Djinn and men we have created for hell. Hearts have they with which they understand not, and eyes with which they see not, and ears have they with which they hearken not. They are like brutes: Yea, they go more astray: these are the heedless."

Rapp switched back to Dari. "That is you, Abu. You believed those twisted Wahhabi clerics, and now you will have to answer to Allah. Before the sun rises I am going to kill you." Rapp paused, grabbed Haggani by the chin, and forced him to look him in the eye. "That's right, I am going to kill you, and unless you repent you're getting on an express elevator to hell."

CHAPTER 10

NASH entered the interrogation room and set a pack of Marlboro cigarettes and a lighter on the table. The cigarettes had started out as a device; something for him to do during the long pauses that inevitably punctuated the interrogation sessions. Many of the prisoners eventually partook, and it helped build a sense of fellowship that Nash was more than happy to exploit. Unfortunately, it was now much more than a device. After six years, he was using them on a daily basis, sneaking one or two, here and there. His wife had caught on and wasn't happy—both for his health and for the message it might send their teenage daughter should she find out. He tried his best to limit his smoking to these overseas jaunts, but it was becoming increasingly difficult to separate his job from his personal life. The stress, he had to admit, was getting to him.

Nash picked up the pack and offered a cigarette to al-Haq. The Afghani took one eagerly. Nash held the flame a foot in front of the terrorist. Al-Haq hesitated and then leaned forward. Little things mattered in these sessions. Getting a man to take a cigarette was good but getting him to lean across the table and meet you halfway was even better. Nash lit his own cigarette, sat back, crossed his legs, and exhaled a big cloud of smoke.

"I would like to make a deal," al-Haq said in a businesslike tone.

Nash hid his surprise—studied him for a few seconds. Thought to himself, *This one is different. In all the time I've been doing this, not one of them has started the conversation, much less announced that they were ready to deal.* "Let's hear it."

"I have information . . . very valuable information that I think your government would be willing to pay for."

"Pay for?" Nash said in a voice that lacked any emotion even though he was fighting to suppress his excitement.

"Yes."

"What makes you think they would be willing to pay for it?"

"I think considering the political climate in your country it would be much easier to make a business deal with me."

They study us more than we think, Nash thought. Al-Haq was right about the leaders in Washington, but Nash wasn't willing to admit it. At least not yet. Instead he said, "Why would I give you cash when I can have General Dostum squeeze the information out of you?"

Al-Haq took a pull off his cigarette and answered, "For many reasons, but most importantly, the information I have for you is very time-sensitive. If I am forced to endure the humiliation and pain that will no doubt be employed by the general, I am likely to be less than forthright. Eventually, you will get most of what you want, but it might be too late."

"And why should I believe you?" Nash watched as al-Haq considered the question. He got the sense that the man was contemplating how much he should divulge.

"You picked up a cell in Mauretania seven weeks ago."

Nash's face gave away nothing. They had in fact intercepted an al-Qaeda cell in Mauretania with the help of the French. It had been kept very quiet. Not a single mention of it had been reported in the press. Most of the men had been thoroughly debriefed, but there were a few holdouts, including the cell's leader. Nash looked al-Haq calmly in the eye and said, "Go on."

"There was a second cell."

Nash nodded.

"Intercepted in Hong Kong. We think by the British."

Nash was intimately familiar with the incident. It was in fact the British who had picked up the group. He'd spent the week before last in London being briefed by his counterpart at MI6. The cell was composed mostly of Pakistanis who spoke very good English. "I am familiar with the situation."

"Well, there is a third group."

"I'm listening," Nash said calmly, even though he wasn't calm. His worst fears were being confirmed.

"I need assurances."

"We can work that out."

Al-Haq exhaled a cloud of smoke and laughed. "I am going to need more than the word of a professional spy."

"What would satisfy you?"

"I have a lawyer in Bern. I will need a letter from your president guaranteeing me the following . . ."

Before he could list his demands, Nash cut him off. "That's not going to happen. There is no way the president is going to get anywhere near something that even remotely makes him look like he is negotiating with a terrorist."

"The letter will only be used if you fail to follow through on your part of the bargain."

"It's a nonstarter, Mohammad."

Al-Haq ignored him. "There is a two-million-dollar reward for my arrest. I want that money for turning myself in, and I want a new identity. If we can agree on that, and a few more things, I will cooperate fully with you. I will tell you everything I know, but you must report . . ." His voice faded.

"Report what?"

"That I am dead."

Nash understood immediately. He wanted to protect his family. Nash stuffed his cigarette in his mouth to hide his deep satisfaction. He was staring at what amounted to their first high-level defection. *This could be huge,* he thought to himself. Nash leaned forward and pointed his cigarette at al-Haq. "Mohammad, I think I can make this work, but the agreement will have to be between the director of the CIA and you. If I get any politicians involved, they'll screw it up."

Al-Haq thought about it for a long moment and in a voice filled with doubt and anxiety said, "I need assurances."

"I will get you assurances. I know I can get you the money, but this is the type of thing that has to be handled in the dark. There is no other way."

Al-Haq didn't like what he was hearing. He had no faith in this man or the organization he represented. He shook his head, his face showing his discomfort.

"Mohammad, if you want to go public, there's a way I can sell this," Nash said in a reasonable tone. "The president would love nothing more than to announce that you've defected. Have you stand up in front of the cameras and repudiate al-Qaeda and the Taliban, but if you do that your family is going to be slaughtered."

The words hit al-Haq like a knife in the side. After a moment he said, "I do not want that."

"Then the only option is to do this in the dark. In fact we might even want to announce that you've been killed."

"That would be very convenient for you."

"I think it is a mutually beneficial solution."

"But can I trust you?"

"You'd better."

"Why?"

"Because if you don't, I'm going to be forced to turn you over to General Dostum. I might not get the information out of you as quickly as I'd like, but ultimately, you'll give me what I want."

Al-Haq fidgeted in his chair. His eyes darted from one wall to the next and then back to Nash. "There is not much time."

"What do you mean?"

"The third cell . . ." Al-Haq's voice trailed off.

"What about the third cell?" Nash asked while trying to stay calm.

"No." Al-Haq stabbed his cigarette in the ashtray and put it out. "I need assurances."

Nash scrambled to think of something. "If I got the director of the CIA on the phone would it help?"

Al-Haq nodded. "What about the money?"

"We could wire the money to your attorney first thing in the morning." Nash watched him closely, could tell he was on the fence. Nash put out his own cigarette. "You're going to have to trust me, though. I'll get the director on the phone, but you are going to have to give me more than just the fact that there is a third cell."

"I know the man who is leading the cell. I know several others in the group. I know where they have been training, and what American city they will attack, and when they will strike." Al-Haq folded his arms and looked across the table with confidence.

"What city?"

"I will tell you when I have my deal."

"All right," Nash said as he stood. "Give me a few minutes to get the director on the phone." Nash could feel his heart racing. This could be big, but it would have to be handled with great care. There were too many factions in Washington. Too many people who would be more than happy to screw it up.

CHAPTER 11

THREE Humvees rolled up to the Hilton and came to a slow stop. General Garrison stared past the thick bulletproof glass of his vehicle at the two Humvees that were already there. He muttered something to himself and then cautiously got out of his vehicle and began to circle the two Humvees. This was only the fifth time Garrison had visited the facility in the nine months he'd been running the base. He was of the mind-set that, as far as his air force was concerned, nothing good could come from this place. The capture of the two high-value targets and the subsequent visit by the three senators had proven that.

Garrison had not spent four years at one of the world's premier military colleges to be a jailer. He was lauded by his peers as a logistical genius and had proven that he had a knack for moving pieces on the chessboard. That was why he was here, to keep the planes and supplies moving, to push the flight crews and the ground crews, to run an air base. Not to run a jail. Foreign fighters, terrorists, interrogations . . . in Garrison's mind that was the stuff the army should be handling, or better yet, the CIA. Put them up in the mountains somewhere. Out of sight. Out of mind.

None of that mattered now, of course; the senators had changed the entire dynamic, had made both their public statements and private threats. Garrison had let the little kiss-ass Leland show them around. Everything was going smoothly on his base, just the way he liked it, and then this confluence of events conspired to make his job infinitely more complicated than it needed to be. There wasn't a CO in the armed forces who liked the idea of one, let alone three, opportunistic politicians poking around their command. Ultimately, they never cared about all the things that worked. They cared only about what didn't work, and that meant they were looking for a scandal. Now, through no choice of his own, his career rested on the proper treatment of two men who did not evoke much sympathy from the young men and women who would be guarding them.

Garrison studied the two Humvees that according to rumor had been driven here by members of the Air Force Office of Special Investigations. There weren't many things in the air force that could make Garrison nervous, but OSI guys were one of them. Any way he tried to slice it, nothing good could come from the OSI's showing up at his base unannounced and in the middle of the night. To make matters worse, they had come straight to this building that housed a problem waiting to happen.

Leland placed his hand on the hood of one of the vehicles and announced, "It's still warm."

Garrison looked at the door.

"I think they've been here going on an hour, sir."

Part of Garrison thought if he simply went back to bed they would be gone in the morning, and he could play dumb about the entire thing. Maybe even make a few calls to the Pentagon and ask why the OSI guys were poking around his base. As much as he'd like to do that, though, it was too risky. He had to think about those senators. The woman, Barbara Lonsdale, was a real ballbuster. The thought occurred to him that she might be the reason why the OSI was here.

Garrison turned slowly to Leland, "You think your friend Senator Lonsdale sent these guys over here to keep an eye on us?"

Leland looked back in the direction of the flight line and then replied, "I don't think so, sir. As chairwoman of the Judiciary Committee it is more likely that she would have sent the FBI."

"Yeah . . . but she also sits on Armed Services." Garrison studied the big warehouse off to his right. The only damn thing in the building was the two prisoners. *Maybe,* he thought, *they're here to transfer them to a different facility.* The OSI was after all part of air force security.

In a hopeful voice, Leland said, "Maybe they're getting ready to transfer the prisoners."

"If that is the case," Garrison replied, "I sure would like to think they'd notify the base commander." The thought pissed Garrison off. He took command very seriously. This was his base, and ultimately, he was responsible for everything that happened within the fence. Garrison pointed to the door of the building and said, "Let's go. There's only one way to deal with this."

Garrison, Leland, and eight air force security officers entered the outer building through a three-foot-wide steel door. Once inside they walked across the warehouse to a separate, smaller building that was the Hilton. Leland used his security card and code to get past the next door, and the group filed into the small lobby. With no one in sight, Garrison continued down the hallway past two offices and entered a larger room that contained the duty desk, some tables, and two people that Garrison didn't notice because he couldn't take his eyes off the two flat-screen TVs directly across from him. The prisoners were not asleep in their cells.

Garrison saw Mohammad al-Haq sitting alone in the one room. He looked relaxed and in roughly the same condition as when he'd last seen him. But in the other room a man in an air force uniform was questioning Abu Haggani, who looked horrible. Garrison stepped closer to the monitors and felt his chest tighten. He saw the blood on the prisoner's face and his worst fears were realized. Someone under his command had beaten the prisoner. Some eighteen-year-old, no doubt. Some kid who'd made it in because the air force had lowered its recruiting standards. None of that mattered, of course. Special Investigations was on-site and sooner or later they would put the CO in their sights.

Garrison was in a bit of shock. All of his sacrifice, his years of hard work, was about to go right down the drain. His thoughts turned to that idiot woman who had been in charge of Abu Ghraib. She had failed her command in the most miserable way. Garrison felt the unfairness. He had never asked for any of this. He had made it clear to his superiors that the CIA should be running the facility, not the military. *The air force should not be in the business of guarding these animals,* he thought. His job was to keep this lifeline open and running smoothly, to supply the troops and evacuate the wounded.

He remembered the senators and his mood sank again. That ball-busting senator would drag his ass before her committee and humiliate him in front of an ungrateful nation. All of his hard work, all of his sacrifice would be destroyed because of some juvenile airman who couldn't practice a little restraint.

Up on the screen, the air force investigator who was talking to the bloodied Haggani suddenly reached out and grabbed him by the throat. Garrison was trying to comprehend just what in the hell was going on when Leland stepped forward.

"Sir," Leland said as he concentrated on the screen, "there's something familiar about that man . . . I think I've seen him before . . . back during my first tour."

Garrison was less concerned with who the man was and more concerned with why he was choking a restrained prisoner. Nothing he was seeing made any sense.

Leland watched the screen intently, waited for the man in the air force BDUs to give him more than a profile. Suddenly the man turned and pointed at the camera. Leland finally got the look he'd been waiting for. His eyes narrowed at first and then opened wide. He could barely contain his excitement. "Sir, that man is not OSI!"

Garrison looked at his aide like he was speaking Latin.

"Sir, he's CIA. I know he is. A few years back when I was on my first tour here they were talking about him. He's some interrogation specialist."

"CIA," Garrison repeated in a skeptical voice. He turned to the screen. Looked at the blood, thought of the choking and the man's actions, and it all suddenly made sense. "You're sure?"

"Absolutely, sir."

Garrison thought of the implications. CIA operatives dressed in air force uniforms, beating prisoners. What were they going to do, simply leave him with the mess in the morning? Have him try to explain why these guys had had the shit kicked out of them? Garrison was getting madder by the second. He personally had no ax to grind with the CIA, but this was ridiculous.

"Sir," Leland said, "would you like me to arrest him?"

Garrison thought of the drama that could come of this if it was ever made public. Again, nothing good could come of it. Reluctantly, he nodded, and gave Leland the order to put the man in custody.

CHAPTER 12

RAPP didn't spend a lot of time questioning the civility of what he was doing. Civility was for people living in cities with law and order. This was asymmetrical warfare, where one side, due to political pressure, was playing by the old set of rules, while the other side played by no rules at all. It was a down-and-dirty street fight, with knives and guns and hands and teeth and anything else that could be brought to bear. Washington didn't want to recognize that obvious fact, so Rapp made his peace with it. He didn't like it, couldn't really even understand how they thought, but he was done fighting them. What they didn't know wouldn't hurt them, so he, and a select few like Nash, ventured out and risked it all to try to stop the enemy from another spectacular strike like 9/11.

There'd been a few politicians who'd pulled him aside and thanked him for his actions. Told him to keep it up and make sure we don't get hit again. "Do whatever it takes," they would say, and then they'd go on TV and decry Guantánamo, the rendition program, and detainee treatment in general. Sure, there were a few wise old men in Washington who understood what they were up against. Men who realized someone had to be willing to climb down into the gutter with this scum and slug it out. One-hundred-million-dollar fighter planes and billion-dollar aircraft carriers were great for the heavy lifting. Five-million-dollar tanks came in very handy in a fight, but against an enemy that refused to put on a uniform and refused to meet you on the field of battle, they went only so far. Eventually someone had to reach out and wrap their hands around the throat of the enemy and pick apart their network.

At the moment, Rapp was trying to do just that. With his left hand he tightened his grip around Haggani's larynx and forced his head back. He looked down into the man's deep brown eyes and searched for some hint of his mental state. He'd done this more times than he could count, and had found he could usually get a pretty good sense of how things would go. Most showed outright fear, a few looked back with the crazed eyes of someone who had serious mental issues, there were even a couple whose eyes reminded him of Charles Manson's—that wide-open "I see right through you into the essence of your soul" look of a zealot high on his beliefs. Those guys were the worst. They screamed and thrashed like some toddler throwing a completely irrational temper tantrum. They were so bad you wanted to beat them just to shut them up.

The eyes gave him a clue, but you never knew with these guys. Some of them folded at the first hint of violence—tried to talk their way out of it. Which was fine with Rapp. The more they talked the easier it was to catch them in their lies. Like a python squeezing the air out of its prey, he would strip away the deceptions until the subject's only chance at life, a lung full of air, was the truth.

Rapp stared intently at Haggani's eyes, searching for a clue. It took only a few seconds for him to categorize what he saw, and it wasn't good. Rapp wanted to swear out loud, but knew he couldn't let Haggani see his frustration. He recognized the look in Haggani's eyes. It was an expression of absolute conviction. There wasn't a drop of fear in either orb. It would take weeks to break him. Rapp's grip eased for a second, and he thought of calling everything off, cleaning Haggani up, and throwing him back in his cell. They could focus on al-Haq, and then possibly later on arrange to have Haggani transferred to a more discreet location where an entire team could work on him.

But maybe, Rapp thought, *just maybe I can bait him into making a few mistakes.* Rapp increased the pressure, his fingers digging into the taut tendons of Haggani's neck. "I know about your plan." Rapp searched his eyes for a flicker of recognition. "We've intercepted both cells. They've told us everything. You've failed yet again." Rapp saw something, an acknowledgment that his words had stirred something in Haggani's limited brain. Rapp eased his grip just enough so the man could reply.

"You know nothing," Haggani said in a hoarse voice. "You will never stop us. For every warrior you strike down another will take his place."

Rapp casually released his grip. The important thing was to keep him talking. "You guys blew your load on nine-eleven. You got lucky. You caught us with our guard down, but what have you done since?"

"Madrid and London, and there will be many more."

"Madrid and London," Rapp scoffed. "You might have got the Spaniards to blink, but all you did was piss off the Brits."

"The entire West is afraid of us."

"The West thinks you're a bunch of cowards. You intentionally kill innocent people because you're too big of a pussy to take on our troops. You're a coward, Abu."

"You know nothing."

"What do you say I take those handcuffs off, and you and I find out just how tough you are?"

Haggani considered the offer and looked across the room at the thick man who had bound him to his chair. He looked back at Rapp and said, "He will join in on your behalf."

"I don't need any help. Not against some baby-killing little pussy like you."

"I don't believe you."

Rapp laughed and circled around the table. "Just like I said, you're a coward. You blow up schools where you know little kids can't fight back. You attack office buildings where innocent men and women are simply trying to make a living."

"There are no innocents in the West."

"If that's true, why haven't you hit us again? All you had was nine-eleven. You haven't done jack shit since then."

"We have killed over fifty thousand of your soldiers."

All Rapp could do was laugh at the outrageous number. He had come across this before. Al-Qaeda and the Taliban loved to exaggerate their successes. "You haven't even killed five thousand, and you know it. You guys are getting your asses kicked. One by one we keep picking you off. Your leadership is in shambles, you're living in caves, and your recruiting is way down. People are tired of sending their boys off to die at your incompetent hands."

"You know nothing."

"Educate me, then. Tell me about all your successes."

"You will see soon enough."

Rapp saw what he was looking for. He moved quickly to Haggani's side and leaned in close. "We know all about the third cell. Your little butt-buddy Mohammad is across the hall right now giving us all the details."

Rapp saw the anger flash in Haggani's eyes. Saw the registration of betrayal as he realized a weaker man was putting everything in jeopardy. Rapp also knew what was going to happen next, having baited others in the same way. The lips pursed, the cheeks sucked in slightly, and then just as Haggani was poised to let loose a gob of spit, Rapp's right hand shot forward. The flattened hand and curled knuckles struck the larynx like a battering ram. Haggani gasped, his open mouth filled with spit, his eyes bulging from his head as his body absorbed the shock. He was frozen for a moment and then fell forward, gasping for air.

"The teams have been dispatched," Rapp whispered in his ear. "Within twenty-four hours they will be in our possession, and you will have failed yet again. Did you really think the plan would work? Did you really think we would allow you to just walk into our country and . . . ? "

Rapp was in mid-sentence when the door opened. He turned to see four sizable men with black Air Force Security Forces patches on their shoulders filing into the interrogation room. Rapp looked to the man with the most stripes on his collar and snapped, "What in the hell are you doing?"

"Excuse me, sir," the man said, "would you please step out into the hallway? The general would like to speak to you."

Rapp eyeballed the man from head to toe and then looked the others over. "I'll be with you in a minute, Sergeant."

In a less-than-commanding voice the man persisted. "The general would like to see you now, sir."

Rapp glanced down at the prisoner and then back up at the senior master sergeant. "You tell the general to cool his fucking heels, or I'll get Secretary of Defense England on the phone and make sure the general spends the rest of his career in a missile silo in the middle of Bum Fuck, North Dakota." Rapp watched him look toward the door and then back at him. He was on the fence. "Sergeant, I suggest you get your ass out of here right now, or I'll make sure you accompany the general on his new assignment."

The sergeant had been in a lot of tricky spots during his thirteen years with the air force, but this one took the cake. An up-and-coming one-star was out in the other room. The guy had been running the base for less than two months, and had made it really clear that he believed in the old axiom that shit rolled downhill. Now he was staring at the very man that general had told him to arrest—a colonel wearing an Air Force Office of Special Investigations unit patch, who was threatening to call the secretary of defense himself. And if that wasn't bad enough, the guy looked like he might literally rip his head off if he didn't exit the room and do so on the double. Not liking the lay of the land, the sergeant decided to pull a tactical retreat to the hallway.

CHAPTER 13

THIS was a moment to be savored, Nash thought to himself. Like most jobs, his was filled with frustration, boredom, and all kinds of tedious bullshit, and recently, more political correctness than was healthy for an organization tasked with penetrating perhaps the most politically incorrect group of men on the planet. But occasionally there were flashes of excitement, of brilliance, when it all came together to mesh in an unqualified success. Moments when all your hard work and personal sacrifice paid off. Where you rolled the dice and broke the house, and felt like you were actually pushing the boulder back up the hill.

Nash had experienced a lot of highs in his life. A Pennsylvania state football championship his junior year in high school, a wrestling title his senior year, falling in love with his wife, the births of his children, becoming an officer in the Marine Corps, successfully leading his men in battle, and countless other things. None of it compared, though, to the high-stakes game he now played. The stakes had never been so big, the challenge never so great. The big picture was pretty straightforward; keep America and her allies safe from the likes of Haggani and al-Haq. How they went about doing that was where it got complicated. There were those like Rapp who made no bones that the best way to accomplish their goal was to kill every last one of them. Keep killing until they were all gone, or they no longer had the will to fight.

Nash sympathized with Rapp. He knew someone had to have that attitude. Someone had to be willing to go toe-to-toe with these guys and beat them at their own game. Make them flinch, keep them up at night wondering when a bomb was going to fall on their heads or a team of commandos was going to sneak up on them and cut every last man's throat. It had all been done, and it had kept the enemy off balance. It had not been localized to Afghanistan, Pakistan, and Iraq, though. European, Middle Eastern, and Asian financiers had been targeted. Most had taken the warning, but a few who had chosen not to listen had fallen victim to tragic, accidental deaths. The same went for the arms merchants, the pimps of war. They knew the risky game they played by supplying the Taliban and al-Qaeda, but the allure was too much. Many had been killed and many more would forfeit their lives before it was over.

Nash would never admit it to his wife or friends, but there was no bigger rush, no bigger thrill, than when they took down one of the high-value targets. He'd helped arrest a few and killed just one, but it was the highest high he'd ever been on. It felt like all of his life's victories rolled into one. Everything had been set to take the target down in the Pakistani border town of Chaman. He and Rapp had worked through unofficial channels, bribing Pakistani Intelligence officials left and right until they had located the man. They were operating with a small team of only six men, all of them trained shooters. The target got spooked as Rapp and two others came through the front door of the building. Nash was in back, alone, when the guy came flying out the door, a big, ugly AK-47 in his hands, ready to blow away anyone who tried to stop him. Nash stood in the shadows of a doorway, and as the man ran by he extended his silenced gun and sent a single hollow-point 9mm round into the back of his head. The man took a few more steps, his body running on autopilot, and then collapsed, skidding to a stop on his own face.

This time it was different in several ways. The most obvious was that Langley knew what they were doing. In Chaman they were operating on their own without a net. This was a victory they could share with the Hill. It was something the politicians could celebrate. They had captured a few people as important as al-Haq, but none of them had ever willingly cooperated. He had to work to squeeze every drop out of them, and even then the information they provided had to be treated with suspicion. Al-Haq was coming over without a fight. Sure, there had been a few threats, but no one had laid a hand on him.

Nash's boss, Rob Ridley, was thrilled. He had given Nash the green light to proceed, while he got Kennedy to sign off on it and provide some type of legal assurance to al-Haq. Nash told Ridley of his idea to get al-Haq to go public. Get him to tell the world how al-Qaeda and the Taliban had strayed from the path. Ridley loved it. "If they could find a way to get his family out," Nash told him, "I think he would do it in a heartbeat."

"One success at a time," had been Ridley's comment before he congratulated Nash and told him he'd get back to him within the hour. Nash hung up the phone and checked his watch. He'd been gone less than five minutes. He didn't want to rush this, didn't want to seem too eager. He paced back and forth in the small office, calming himself and thinking of how he would play his hand when he went back into the room. He still had all the cards, and while he had General Dostum around, he should use him for leverage. Nash decided he'd push al-Haq a bit harder. He thought the earliest they'd have the assurance from Kennedy would be an hour. Probably two.

Nash thought of ways to push him. *Tell him the big hitters in D.C. didn't believe him*, he thought to himself. *Tell him the other two cells had been debriefed and hadn't said a word about a third cell.* That was a lie, of course. They had, and there was other disturbing stuff floating around out there, murmurs on the World Wide Web that something big was coming. Nash believed al-Haq, but for now he would make him think the deal was in jeopardy.

Nash checked his watch again and took a couple of deep breaths to try and ease off the natural high he was on. He yanked open the office door, set his jaw in a more grim position, and started down the hallway. As he stepped into the big observation room, he found himself staring at the backs of a group of men who were not supposed to be there. Up on one of the screens Rapp was yelling at a couple of MPs.

Nash turned nervously to his right and found Marcus Dumond, the young CIA hacker, looking like he was about to crawl under the desk.

Just then he heard General Garrison, the base commander, growl, "Did he just say Secretary of Defense England?"

"He did, sir," the younger officer next to him replied.

"You'd better be right about this, Leland. If that man isn't CIA and you get me in hot water with the secretary of defense, you are going to be shoveling shit for the rest of your tour."

Nash felt his stomach turn, and thought to himself, *These guys could screw this thing up real quick. How in the hell are we going to talk our way out of this?* The very next thing he thought of was damage control. Dumond had been recording the sessions. The last thing they needed to do was hand over proof of their crimes.

Everyone else in the room was so intent on the TV showing the interrogation room that Nash saw an opportunity. He looked down at Dumond, pointed at his small external drive, and then jerked his head toward the hallway behind him. Dumond nodded, grabbed the drive, and quietly stood. As he passed by Nash, the general must have noticed the movement, because he began to turn around. Nash stepped forward quickly to block the general's view and distract him.

In a booming voice Nash announced, "What in the hell is going on here?"

CHAPTER 14

O NCE the MPs were gone and the door was closed, Rapp turned and looked at his prisoner. What he saw pissed him off to the point of wanting to drive his fist through Haggani's face—shove the cartilage behind his nose up into his brain and kill the bastard right on the spot. He felt the camera on his back, though, and knew he was already in enough trouble. Choking the man . . . he might be able to talk his way out of. Killing him . . . not a chance. He thought of Nash and Dumond. *What was going on out there?* Had Dumond been quick enough to erase his interrogation of Haggani and smart enough to save Nash's with al-Haq, and just what in the hell was the base commander doing up and about? The guy was supposed to be an anal-retentive freak about his sleep.

"What is wrong?" Haggani asked in a mocking tone. "Are you in trouble?"

Rapp glanced at him for only a second. Just long enough to register the smug look on his face. He clenched his fists and told himself not to do it. He walked to the far side of the room, where one of his men, Joe Maslick, was leaning against the wall. Maslick was an inch taller than Rapp and tipped the scales at 220 pounds. He was too big for most undercover operations, but perfect for something like this, where intimidation and presence were more important. Rapp knew how sensitive the room's recording devices were, and since he had no idea if Dumond had turned them off, he decided to be extra careful. He pointed back at the prisoner and then cupped both hands over Maslick's left ear.

In a voice barely louder than a whisper, Rapp said, "I'm going out first. If I can talk our way out of this, great, but if I can't, and you see me get up in that general's face, I want you to get our people out of here. Grab Dostum, get back to the plane, and get the hell off this base. Mike and I will deal with the fallout."

Maslick cupped his hands over Rapp's ear and whispered, "We can overpower these guys."

Rapp knew this was the approach Maslick would take. The man did not know the meaning of the word *retreat*. Slugging their way out would be a short-term solution that would only make things worse. "No way," he whispered, "that'll just buy us a little time and then the shit will really come down. Trust me—you get everyone out of here, and I'll take care of it."

"I'm not leaving you behind to take the fall."

"You are," Rapp said firmly, "and don't worry about it. I've got plenty of favors I can call in. Just get everyone out of here. End of discussion."

Rapp and Maslick walked across the room. As they passed Haggani, the terrorist began laughing.

"Leaving so soon."

"Don't worry, I'll be back."

"No, you won't."

Rapp stopped and looked down at the prisoner. There was a definite change in the way Haggani met his stare. Gone was the rage and bravado, the stubborn defiance. It was replaced by something very different; something that embarrassed Rapp on a level he didn't think possible. It was contempt; scorn for an opponent deemed unworthy.

"This is why you will never beat us," Haggani said in a voice that was simple and matter-of-fact; one warrior to another. "You are not tough enough. Your country is too divided . . . too concerned with the rights of your enemies."

"Don't confuse me with those people back in Washington. I'm not done with you. Not by a long shot."

Rapp led Maslick out of the interrogation room and down the short hall to the observation room. As he reached for the doorknob he reminded himself that these air force guys respected men who took charge. Unlike the civilian world, where leadership was a fluid concept, in the military there was very little gray. Rank ruled the day and there was only one man on the other side of the door who could beat the two black eagles on Rapp's collar. He thought of General Garrison, the base commander. He'd skimmed the man's personnel file on the flight over, and now he was cursing himself for not paying closer attention. He had a few vague recollections of him. He was an Air Force Academy grad and on the young side for a brigadier general, which meant he was either really good at his job, really lucky, or a really good kiss-ass. Whatever the answer, Rapp supposed it didn't matter, since his only chance was to meet this thing head-on. He'd bluff them long enough to get the others out of there and then come clean, or at least partially clean.

Rapp readied himself and then pulled open the door. He stepped into the other room and was surprised to find everyone with their backs to him. Rapp moved forward a few steps and motioned for Maslick to continue to the right, where General Dostum was standing. Everyone's attention seemed to be focused on the hallway that led to the offices and the main exit. Three men were talking. One was Nash, who was the only person facing him. Rapp couldn't see the faces of the other two men, but they appeared to be rather upset by the way they were shouting and pointing.

"So you're denying that man is CIA?" the taller of the two asked in a stern voice.

"Listen," Nash said, "I think you two need to calm down."

Rapp did a quick scan of the room. He found everybody on his team except Dumond. He looked again and still couldn't find him. Unsure of whether this was a good sign or a bad sign, Rapp turned his attention back to the conversation.

"Calm down?" the older man asked more forcefully. "This is my damn base, Mr. Nash. If that man is CIA and he is impersonating an officer, I'm going to throw both of you in lockup."

That had to be General Garrison. Rapp straightened up, cleared his throat to get everyone's attention, and yelled, "What in God's name are all you people doing here? This facility is in lockdown."

One by one, heads turned and feet shuffled as everyone did a 180 to meet the new voice of authority. General Garrison eyed Rapp warily and asked, "And you are?"

"Who I am is not what's important. What is important is that this facility is off-limits until oh seven hundred." Rapp motioned from one side of the room to the other. "None of you are authorized to be here right now."

"By whose authority?" asked the man standing next to the general.

Rapp took note of the two bars on the collar and said, "The secretary of defense, Captain."

"Why weren't we informed?"

"I don't think the secretary of defense feels the need to go around explaining himself to captains," Rapp growled. He directed his attention to the general and said, "Sir, I suggest for your own good that you vacate this facility and let me do my job. Trust me . . . this is not something you want to get in the middle of. Whoever got you out of bed didn't do you any favors."

General Garrison turned and gave Captain Leland a hard stare.

"Sir," Leland said, "this man is CIA. I will stake my entire reputation on it."

Rapp saw movement to his right, but didn't want to look. He hoped it was Maslick leading Dostum and the others toward the door. "Your reputation is not what's at stake here, Captain. It's the general's career." Rapp turned his glare back to Garrison. "There are some very important people in Washington who are waiting for me to finish what I was sent here to do."

"Does that include impersonating an officer in the United States Air Force?" Garrison asked.

Rapp didn't know what to say, so he said nothing.

"How about beating a bound prisoner to a bloody pulp?" Leland asked.

"That's it," Rapp growled. "Everybody out of here." He turned away from the two officers. "I need to have a word in private with the general and his aide." Rapp began shooing people down the hallway toward the exit. Everybody moved except Nash.

"Slow down there," the captain said, "I don't think you're in any position to be giving orders around here."

Rapp turned on him before he could say anything else, like telling the MPs to stay put. "General, I suggest you tell Dudley Do-Right here to shut his piehole. What I have to tell you is highly classified. The president, the secretary of defense, and only a few others have been briefed. I can't very well tell a roomful of enlisted servicemen." Not bothering to wait for a response, Rapp told the others to get moving and then said to Nash, "You too." Rapp mouthed the words *Get on the plane.*

Nash shook his head. "No."

"Don't argue with me." Rapp grabbed Nash by the arm and started walking him down the hallway. In a low voice, he added, "Get back to D.C. I can handle the political heat . . . you can't. Tell them you verified the third cell and get Mohammad transferred to our custody."

"Mitch, this is serious shit."

"I've been in far worse. I'll talk my way out of it."

Nash looked back down the hall at the two officers and said, "Don't count on it. That Leland is a real pick."

"I'm not exactly easy to get along with," Rapp said with a grin. "Just get everyone on that plane and get the hell out of here."

CHAPTER 15

THE two officers watched the mystery colonel lead the CIA man down the short hallway, where they stopped and exchanged a few words. Without taking his eyes off them, Captain Leland said, "Sir, I don't like this. I don't trust these spooks."

"It can't hurt to hear him out." Garrison had finally shaken the sleep from his head. The drastic swings of fate had helped push the dull fog away and he was now operating on a level that was more appropriate for command. *The fog of war was not localized to combat,* he thought. Only moments ago, his entire career had flashed before his eyes, corkscrewing downward in a tailspin that would surely result in a spectacularly tragic fireball. Now he was confronted with something entirely different. He watched the two men speak. He had never liked the idea of these spooks lurking around his base. They were insolent bastards who seemed to be always looking for a way to cause trouble, but they were more important to this fight perhaps than any other in modern history. The one wearing the rank of colonel turned and was coming back to them.

"Sir, I think you should lock him up."

Garrison put his hand out in a silencing gesture. "I want to hear what he has to say first." The idea that the man might really be doing the bidding of the president was worth exploring.

"Don't expect the truth."

"It won't hurt to listen to him, Captain."

"General," Rapp announced as he stopped a few feet in front of them, "I apologize for all of this, but this is a difficult situation."

"There's no excuse for what we saw you doing to that prisoner."

"Captain, when I want your opinion, I'll ask for it."

"This is a United States Air Force base. You have no authority to tell anyone on this base to do a thing. I suggest . . ."

"I suggest you shut your fucking mouth," Rapp snapped, "I'm a GS-Sixteen, Captain, so that makes me the equivalent of a flag officer. I'm a special advisor on terrorism to the director of the CIA, the director of National Intelligence, and the National Security Council. I'm on a first-name basis with the secretary of defense, and the president has me on speed dial, so unless you're a hell of a lot more important than your entirely unimpressive appearance or those two bars would lead me to believe, I suggest you butt the fuck out and let me talk to the general."

Leland's complexion flushed with embarrassment. Rapp, feeling like he had finally got his point across, looked at the base commander and said, "I want to start off by apologizing for all of this. My methods aren't pretty . . . Alerting you about what I was up to was not something you would've welcomed."

"You were just going to sneak in and sneak out?"

"Yes."

"And I would be left in the dark."

"Your judgment would be left intact."

"And the marks on the prisoner? How would I explain that?"

"That was not intended. He tried to bite me." Rapp looked up at the monitor, as did the two officers. Haggani was still tied to his chair.

His blood-streaked face looked horrible. Rapp grimaced and offered, "It's not as bad as it looks."

"It looks bad, Mr. . . . ?" The general left the question unfinished.

Rapp wavered and then thought, *What the hell, I'm in deep enough already.* "Rapp . . . Mitch Rapp."

"You work for the CIA?" Garrison asked.

"That's right."

"You're a spy," Leland said.

"Counterterrorism specialist."

"What exactly does that entail?" the general asked.

"It involves dealing with people like that." Rapp pointed at the screen.

"Dealing," the general repeated the word, "that's pretty vague."

"We walk in different circles, General. I don't expect someone who puts on a uniform like yours to ever fully condone what I do. You guys have to have your rules . . . your discipline. You need that to remain an effective fighting force. Me . . . I'm the guy who sneaks out under the wire late at night and crawls up next to these guys and cuts their throats."

"Is that what you tell yourself so you can sleep at night?" Leland folded his arms across his chest, a look of contempt on his face.

Rapp cocked his head and studied the captain. He couldn't care less what this wet-behind-the-ears officer thought of him, but with the intent of buying more time for Nash and the others, he supposed he should engage him. "I sleep like a baby, Captain. How about you?"

"It's because of people like you that we're losing this war."

With a raised eyebrow Rapp said, "I wasn't aware that we're losing it."

"This is about hearts and minds, and you know it. Not torturing prisoners so we can get false confessions out of them."

"False confessions . . . that's what you think this is about? That man sitting in that room right there; do you even know who he is?"

"It doesn't matter who he is or what he's done. As an officer of the

United States Air Force, I am sworn to uphold the Geneva Conventions."

"You're also sworn to protect and defend the United States of America. So which comes first, the Geneva Conventions or your fellow citizens?"

"They coexist equally."

"I'm sure they do in your little perfect world, Captain, but out there in the real world, on the other side of the wire, things aren't so academic."

"That's where you're wrong, Mr. Rapp."

"Really . . . I love being told how things are by some prick in a clean uniform who thinks he has all the answers. Tell me how it is, Captain. Tell me how many terrorists you've killed. Tell me how many times you've been shot."

Leland shifted his weight from one foot to the other, his chin stuck stubbornly out. "General, I think we're wasting our time. May I please put him under arrest and have him thrown in lockup?" Leland's hand slid down to the top of his thigh holster.

"Captain," Rapp said in a casual voice, "I'll break your wrist before you ever get that thing out of the holster."

"Relax, Captain," Garrison said. "I want to hear him out first. So," he said, looking at Rapp, "this classified information you were talking about?"

It really was classified information, and Rapp now had to decide how far to go with these two. Telling the captain to leave would have technically been the right thing to do, but Rapp didn't want to free him up to check on the others. He would have to give them a heavily sanitized version of what was going on.

"About a month ago an al-Qaeda cell was intercepted on its way to the United States. A second cell was intercepted a few weeks later. We were very alarmed to find during interrogations that these cells were highly trained in commando tactics. They had researched their targets thoroughly. They'd preshipped their weapons, and I'm not just talking guns. . . . I'm talking high-end explosives, fuses, remote detonators . . .

the works. They could've done some serious damage. At any rate, during the interrogations . . ."

"You mean torture," Leland said.

Rapp looked at the senior of the two officers and said, "General, with all due respect, if he says another word I'm going to knock him out. And trust me when I say, I'll never be punished for belting some smart-ass, low-level officer who was interfering with me trying to stop a terrorist attack on the United States. And make no mistake about it . . . either of you. This operation . . . my little midnight visit to your base . . . is about acting on solid intel that a third cell is still out there." Rapp paused to let the revelation sink in. "That's right, there's another group. We estimate eight to ten men, all highly trained."

"What do you want with these two," General Garrison asked, "when you already have the other men in your custody?"

"The men we have are only foot soldiers. None of them were involved in the recruiting or planning of the attacks."

Garrison nodded and then pointed at the twin monitors. "And these two?"

"Both of them are high up. In fact right before you came walking in, al-Haq was talking about making a deal."

Garrison looked at the ground for a moment and then asked, "So what do you expect me to do?"

"Go back to bed. Act like this never happened. I'll be gone in the morning, and hopefully I'll have enough information to run down this third cell and intercept them before they deploy." Even as Rapp said it he knew it wouldn't happen. Still, he had to go through the motions.

The base commander looked over at Leland and then said, "Give us a minute to discuss."

"Sure. It's your command, General." Rapp stayed firmly planted between them and the hallway that led to the exit.

General Garrison led Captain Leland to the far corner and asked in a hushed voice, "Your thoughts?"

"I don't like it. I don't like him, and I don't trust him. I think he's a liar."

"I didn't ask if I should date him, Captain. A little more nuanced opinion is what I'm looking for."

"Sorry, sir." Leland paused, set aside his personal feelings of dislike, and said, "In these situations, what gets command in trouble is never the crime. You have done nothing wrong, sir. What gets command in trouble is the cover-up. Usually the old boy network . . . academy grads looking out for each other." Leland exchanged a brief look with Garrison. Like they shared an unspoken bond. The general gave him no such look in return. "It starts out innocently enough, because no one thinks they are going to get caught. They usually do, though, and when that happens it's never pretty. Instead of one career being ruined it ends up being two, three, four . . . sometimes dozens."

"Your point being . . . if I go back to bed and act like nothing happened, eventually someone will find out I knew he was here."

"That he impersonated an officer, tortured a prisoner, and God only knows what else."

"So you think we should lock him up?"

"Yes!" Leland said with conviction. "You have done nothing wrong, sir. Your only concern should be to follow regulations."

"But what about this third cell?"

Leland didn't like that the general wasn't recognizing how dangerous this could be to not only his own career but Leland's as well. "What about Senator Lonsdale? How do you think she will react when she gets wind of this? And trust me, sir; it is not if, it's when, and when she does, she is going to want your balls on a platter. She said as much before she left. Your career will be over, sir."

Garrison looked back across the room at the man from the CIA. He was right. It would have been better if he'd never gotten out of bed. He glanced at the two monitors, watched the two fanatics sitting in their chairs. This whole thing was a mess. "And how," he asked Leland, "do we live with ourselves if what he says is true . . . if we get hit with another attack?"

"He has no proof of that, sir. That's what these spooks do. They run around chasing shadows. Crying wolf."

"That doesn't mean he's not right."

Leland sighed in exasperation. "That is not our job to decide."

"So you think I should lock him up."

"Yes, sir. It's the only responsible thing for you to do."

"And then what?"

"It will get kicked up the chain of command, and they will deal with it."

Garrison thought long and hard about it. He couldn't shake the feeling that he was making a mistake, but he saw no other way. "Fine," he said with no enthusiasm, "place him under arrest and notify Centcom."

"Yes, sir." Leland was beaming with satisfaction as he snapped off a salute.

"And, Captain, I want this kept quiet. No gossip. For now it stays between the two of us and our security detail in the other room. The Pentagon and the president might have an entirely different take on this than you do."

"I doubt it, sir." Leland turned to go arrest Rapp.

"One other thing, Captain."

Leland stopped and looked back at his CO.

"Don't look so damn pleased with yourself. Before this is all over, I have a bad feeling we're both going to wish you had never gotten me out of bed."

CHAPTER 16

WASHINGTON, D.C.

THERE hadn't been many dates and no real relationships to speak of. The ones with any sense simply stayed away and the ones who pursued her made her nervous for the simple fact that they should have had more sense. Then there was the very real fear that she would be set up by a foreign intelligence service. It had been done before, using a woman's heart, or in a man's case something else, to put them in a compromising situation. So there were background checks, surveillance by Langley's counterespionage gang and probably the FBI as well. She questioned none of it. To do so would have been reckless.

Irene Kennedy had resigned herself to the simple fact that she would probably never find true love and almost certainly never re-marry. The first go-around had gone badly, as they pretty much always do when referred to in the past tense. She rarely looked back on it with any deep regret. It had started out well enough. He was interesting, handsome, and very intelligent. Her mistake had been underestimat-ing his relationship with his mother. The woman treated her son as if he were still eight years old. He was a mama's boy who thought only of himself. Looking at it after the fact, Kennedy could see she enabled his behavior. She was a pleaser. She loved him and wanted to make him happy. It was three years into their marriage when she gave birth to their son Thomas that things took a turn for the worse. When confronted with the hard truth that her husband wouldn't change a diaper, handle a feeding, or get up with Thomas in the middle of the night, it was hard to deny the simple fact that the man was a selfish prick.

It would have been another story if he'd been the breadwinner and she'd been a stay-at-home mom, but it was the opposite. He was a college professor who acted as if he was God's gift to the intellectual elite of the world. Kennedy soon grew tired of the inequities of the partnership. The tipping point came one Saturday afternoon when she found herself mowing the lawn with young Thomas sleeping in a baby backpack, while the professor was off working on his dissertation. It took nearly two years for the divorce to be finalized, but it was then that she knew it was over, when she knew she no longer loved the man.

Still, she never regretted the marriage, for the simple fact that it had given her a son whom she adored. Kennedy had made it a priority to make sure her son did not turn out like his father. The only real challenge came every summer when Thomas would spend a month at his father's family summer retreat on Nantucket. It was really the only time he spent with his father since he was now teaching in France. There were lots of tennis and golf and sailing. He never changed, though. He was a good kid who got good grades and stayed out of trouble. Her mother helped a lot, and then there was Rapp.

Kennedy reached for her glass of wine and looked through the open French doors of the semi-private room. Her date was late. As she took a sip of the pinot noir, she thought of the influence Rapp held over her son. *He was a complex man . . . no, that's not right,* she thought to herself. *He's probably the least complex man I know.* Rapp's line of work was complicated, rare and very dangerous, but to Kennedy he was perhaps the most transparent man she had ever known. There were plenty of people at Langley who were tacticians; those who dreamt up grand, complex plans that would weaken or destroy the enemy, plans that would harvest intelligence and give them an advantage over their enemies. Invariably, Rapp would pick these plans apart. As someone who had spent almost his entire career in the field, he was painfully aware that there was a direct relationship between the complexity of a plan and its chances for failure.

Rapp preferred the simple, direct approach, which usually involved firing a bullet into the back of someone's head. That was the stark truth, and Kennedy spent a fair amount of time trying not to think about it. Her mother, though, had expressed her concerns. When Rapp's wife was killed several years ago, Kennedy's mother had come to her and stated in unequivocal terms that she thought it extremely reckless that her daughter allowed her grandson to spend so much time in the company of a CIA assassin. Kennedy hated the word. Hated the idea that someone who had sacrificed so much could be dismissed and tarnished by a simple word. Put Rapp in a uniform and give him a rank, and he would be a hero. They'd have pinned so many medals on his chest, he'd tip over. He wasn't part of the military, though, so certain people looked down on him, even her own mother.

Kennedy couldn't blame her. Her mother did not understand how anyone could do what he did for a living. Kennedy smiled as she thought of how her mother would react if she knew the whole story— if she were given access to Rapp's file. Even worse, how she would react if she read her own daughter's file. At least with men like Rapp and Nash the anthropological evidence was in plain sight. One look at them and it was obvious that they were hunters. Her own daughter, on the other hand, had not a hint of predacity in her entire appearance or demeanor. She was the epitome of high-powered Washington class. Her clothes were always stylish but never over-the-top. She showed just enough skin to retain her femininity and never so much as to be thought a slut. Her smooth, shoulder-length hair was the perfect accent to her narrow face and button nose.

Never was there a hint that beneath the disarming, pleasant smile lurked a woman whose patience was gone. A woman who now, on an almost weekly basis, gave men like Rapp and Nash the approval to break laws, to lie to congressmen and senators, to kidnap and torture, and, yes, to kill. It was never cavalier or done for the perverse pleasure of doing it simply because she could. The decisions were made with great care and consideration, but nonetheless they were made, and Kennedy had to live with them, had to live with the lies. She knew Rapp could handle it, but she was increasingly worried about Nash. Where Rapp kept to himself, especially since the murder of his wife, Nash was forced to confront the lie. Married, with four kids, he crossed over on a daily basis, back and forth from suburbia to the black-ops world of counterterrorism—soccer and lacrosse games followed by late-night interrogations and the occasional liquidation.

They'd come up with plenty of words to help them cope with their less-than-noble deeds; *detainee*, as opposed to *prisoner*, opened up the door for *extreme interrogations*, which, of course, had a much nicer ring than *torture*. A suspect underwent *rendition*, as opposed to simply being *kidnapped*. All of the political speak drove Rapp nuts. He blamed it all on the lawyers, and he was probably right. The truth was they were in a dirty business that was populated by some less-than-reputable people. Rapp liked to remind everyone, "We're not cops. We're not soldiers. We're spies, and spies do nasty shit to nasty people."

Nowhere in their charter was there anything about fighting fair. The enemy certainly didn't, and their people treated them like heroes. In America you were forced to sit through meetings like the one she'd just finished at the Justice Department. Meetings with people who didn't know the first thing about the silent war that was being waged. Your reward for your sacrifice was to be hounded by some politically appointed prick like this Wade Kline. At a bare minimum your reputation got trashed in the press, or worse, you ended up indicted and drowning under a mountain of legal bills. Kennedy's anxiety rose as she thought of Rapp and Nash and what they were up to. One slip-up and the vultures would pounce.

Her date appeared at the top of the staircase with an apologetic smile on his face. Kennedy wasn't the slightest bit irritated that he was twenty minutes late. She pushed back her chair to stand, but her date rushed over and gestured for her not to bother.

"Sorry I'm late," he said as he bent over to kiss Kennedy.

She offered her cheek and said, "Don't worry, any chance I get to have a moment alone is one I'll gladly take."

The man laughed genuinely and took his seat directly across from Kennedy. He unbuttoned his suit coat and retrieved a pair of reading glasses from his inside pocket. William Barstow ran an investment firm in town and had been divorced for a little more than a year. Kennedy had never met the ex or the two kids and was in no rush. She'd sat next to Barstow at a fund-raiser for the Kennedy Center, and he'd made her laugh. It might sound like a small thing to most people, but there wasn't a lot to laugh about in her life. As the event wrapped up, Barstow asked her out, Kennedy said why not, and now they were five dates into what was so far a pretty easy relationship.

They were at the Ruth's Chris Steak House on Connecticut Avenue. The service was excellent, as was the food, but more important, it was one of a handful of restaurants in town that had a good working relationship with Langley. Not far from embassy row, the place was often used for meetings and was rumored to be wired to the hilt. Kennedy liked it because it had a room on the second floor that had two glass walls which at least gave the illusion that you were part of the busy restaurant. It was far less stifling than some of the other private rooms in town, the ones where you felt like you were seated in a closet. Her security team was familiar with the place and could sweep it and employ their countermeasures with relative ease.

Kennedy looked across the table at her date. He was the John Wayne type, that was for sure. A big barrel chest, with warm brown eyes and a disarming grin, which belayed a very serious man who, she had no doubt, could lose his temper at work. She worked with plenty of men just like him, although their suits weren't as nice. His drink arrived a moment later, and he held it up to toast Kennedy.

As the two glasses clanged, Barstow said, "To an evening without interruptions." With a conspiratorial wink he added, "I left my phone in the car."

Guilt washed over Kennedy's face. Based on what was going on in Afghanistan, she knew there was almost no chance of getting through the evening without a disruption.

Barstow noticed the look on her face. "Did I say something wrong?"

"No . . . it's just that . . . there's a good chance I will have to take at least one call."

"That's all right, your job is a little more important than mine."

Kennedy heard no malice or jealousy in his voice. It was a gesture of honest humility. "Thank you. I'll try to keep it short."

Barstow ordered a fabulous bottle of Bordeaux and they made small talk over salads. He got the wedge and she got the baby arugula. Kennedy enjoyed asking him about the financial markets. He had a master's degree in economics from the University of Chicago and he usually had a fresh take on the world. Like most economists he also used hard facts to back up his theories. He would have been really good in her line of work.

Three waiters filed into the room with the main course and sides. A petite filet was set down in front of Kennedy as well as steaming side orders of asparagus and mushrooms. A giant slab of meat was placed in front of Barstow as if it were a bar of gold. Kennedy knew it was the porterhouse, and if Barstow acted the way he did last time, he would eat only half of it and take the other half home for his dog. At least, that was the story.

Kennedy savored the aroma of what would be her first steak in four weeks. It was all she allowed herself. The wineglasses were refreshed and then the waiters filed out. Kennedy and Barstow looked at each other in anticipation. Barstow looked to be torn between making another toast and digging into his slab of red meat, which would feed a small family for a week. Kennedy grabbed her steak knife and fork and was poised to go to work, when she sensed something amiss. There was a flurry of movement on the other side of the glass doors. It was

men in dark suits, not waiters in white jackets. Kennedy badly wanted
to ignore them but knew she wouldn't. Carefully she turned her head
and instantly knew the meal was over.

Looking back at her through the glass was Rob Ridley. The deputy
Clandestine chief was a perennial smart-ass. He loved to tease and
joke, but there was none of that on his face tonight. He was as grim as
Kennedy had ever seen him. Kennedy slowly set her fork and knife
down and dabbed the corners of her mouth with her napkin.

After a heavy sigh she said, "Bill, you'll have to excuse me. It appears that interruption I was anticipating has arrived."

Barstow tried to look sympathetic, but in truth was already inhal-
ing his first cut and looked like he might pass out. Kennedy went to the
door and drew it back. Ridley stepped forward, his eyes as concerned
as Kennedy had seen them in some time.

"What's wrong?"

"We've got big problems."

"How big?" she asked.

"Really big."

"Mitch?"

"Yep."

Kennedy sighed. It sounded like he was finally going to get the
fight he was looking for. She had resigned herself to the fact that it
would happen sooner or later. The conflict was unavoidable, and
Rapp's attitude that they fight it on their terms was probably right, but
it still didn't feel right.

"I'll brief you on the rest of it in the car," Ridley said.

Kennedy turned to say good-bye to her date, saw his expression of
understanding, and felt very guilty that he would have to eat alone. She
considered the time difference, looked at her own meal, and made
her decision. Turning back to Ridley she said, "I'll be down in thirty
minutes."

CHAPTER 17

TRIPLE FRONTIER, SOUTH AMERICA

MORALE was not good. It was something he had failed to account for and Karim rarely failed to account for the important things. That was his strength. He was a scholar first and a warrior second. To be fair to himself, though, he had considered it briefly. In the final few seconds before he killed Zachariah he thought of how the execution would affect the other men. As he drew his sidearm, pulled the trigger, and watched the hollow-tipped round spray the back of Zachariah's head against the screen, he felt certain that his action would galvanize the men, unify them, force them to put their differences aside and focus their talents on this important mission. He saw now that he had misjudged them.

It was their faith, he decided, a lack of true devotion. Tribal rivalries had also played a role, to be sure, and Karim chastised himself for not seeing that beforehand. Islam was notorious for its infighting; the petty rivalries that had kept them apart for so many years. The four Saudis under his command were fine. They would fight with efficiency and courage to the last man. Even the lone Afghani seemed to be taking it well, but then again the Afghani had served under him for more than a year and had fought bravely in countless incursions with the enemy. Because they had been to battle together they had that trust. The Afghani would be fine. They were the toughest, most selfless fighters Karim had ever known.

The Moroccans, however, were a problem. He now saw that, if anything, the team was more deeply divided than before. He briefly considered executing one of them, but found it impractical. He was not above using fear to motivate, but in this instance he was dealing with a finite supply of men. Karim had studied the brutal tactics of men such as Lenin and Stalin. There was something to be learned from them. Their sheer audacity and thirst for power was unmatched. Most impressive, though, was their ability to seize power and then hold on to it by the most heinous means necessary.

Karim thought of Lenin and Stalin often. Asked himself if he had it in him; the greatness of those two men, the ability to lead a revolution, to take power from others, to kill every enemy, real and imagined, until your power was unquestioned, secure, and you were ready to implement real change. He knew he could be cruel. Knew he had the conviction to see things through, to indiscriminately kill as many as it took. It was Allah's work he was doing, after all, and Allah would sort out the believers from the nonbelievers when they were dead.

Karim's job was to turn back the tide. Stop the heathens and the infidels and their steady march, their assault on Islam. Their liberation of women, their thirst for pornography, their acceptance of an abomination like homosexuality—all were the work of the devil. Their music, their movies, their entire culture was an assault on the family. Their entire culture was a cancer on the world, a slow and steady attack on Islam. Whatever the cost, no matter how many innocents were caught in the cross fire, they had to be stopped.

This particular operation was not the end for Karim. It was a grand stepping-stone for something far greater. Allah had come to him during his unending hours of prayer, had told him of his plans. How he wanted him to take back the cradle of Islam from the traitors, from the corrupt lovers of money and wealth. But before he could accept that responsibility, he had to prove himself. Not to Allah, but to those whom he would need for the next fight.

Karim would not martyr himself like the others. For obvious reasons, he had failed to share this with his men. Allah had grand designs for him. He was to one day lead a revolution that would change the world. Karim was destined to unseat the Saudi Royal family and purge his country of their corrupting influence. The entire family, ten thousand plus relatives, would have to be killed. Karim knew a few would escape, knew the world would be shocked, but the numbers were insignificant compared to Lenin and Stalin. Millions had died at their hands, and for what, a godless system that rewarded only the uppermost echelon of bureaucrats. Muslims would understand, and in the end that is all that would matter. But first he had to deal with America, and to do that successfully, he needed to raise the morale of the two Moroccans and get his team acting as one.

Karim pushed open the rickety screen door and stepped onto the soft grass. Six months in this suffocating place. Much had been accomplished, but not enough. The mid-morning sun was finally high enough in the sky to drive the disease-carrying insects into the shadows. He knew the men would be thankful for that, but now they had to contend with the suffocating wet heat. Even his fellow countrymen found the wicked combination of heat and humidity a formidable opponent. Water was the key, just like in the desert. *The men must drink plenty of water,* Karim thought to himself. He'd made sure they took their malaria medicine as well. He hadn't poured his talent and energy into this operation only to see it fail because of some tiny little bug.

There was shouting from the men. Karim looked across the clearing to see what it was about. Six of them were assembled on the far end of the clearing approximately 150 meters away. They were all wearing jungle cargo pants and faded green T-shirts. Like Karim, each man wore a thigh holster with a 9mm Glock and two extra clips of ammunition. Karim made them do it because he wanted them to get used to always carrying a weapon. He also did it because he secretly hoped a drug cartel would stumble upon the camp and pick a fight. It would be a great way to test the men.

Karim knew they were standing at the point where the obstacle course both began and ended. Even from this distance he could tell the encouragement was only half-hearted. His eyes swept the course, looking for the seventh man. He was still trying to get used to that. A few days earlier it had been eight. One of the Moroccans rounded the far corner of the obstacle course. He couldn't tell if it was Ahmed or Fazul, they were so similar. The man dropped to his belly and began crawling under a layer of barbed wire that was perched a mere eighteen inches above the ground. After he'd crawled thirty feet he popped up and headed straight for a twenty-foot wall. He hit the wall in stride, grabbed the rope, and started up. Halfway up he slipped, gathered himself, tried again, slipped once more, and then gave up, dropping to the ground. Out of breath, he bent over, his hands on his knees, gasping for air. Karim's gaze intensified. He had not come this far to watch someone quit at something they should have mastered months ago.

After a few more deep breaths, the man shook his head in frustration and jogged around the wall, to the next obstacle. The other six men began laughing and taunting him. Even though it was almost impossible to tell the two Moroccans apart from this distance, Karim knew it was Ahmed. He had led Fazul, the other Moroccan, into battle and knew Fazul was tougher than any wall. Karim's anger was set afire. That any man under his command would give in so easily was infuriating, but the fact that the others found it humorous was intolerable.

His worn black jungle boots were moving, carrying him along one of the many paths that cut through the tall grass like spokes on a wheel. His stride was short and quick, his anger building with each pace. One of the men noticed him coming and alerted the others. The laughing and jeering came to a nervous halt. The men spread out and while not coming to attention, they prepared themselves for the approaching fury. Karim stopped eight paces from the group just as Ahmed crossed the finish line. The gangly Moroccan stumbled and then fell to the ground, tumbling twice and coming to a stop at Karim's feet.

There was a better than fifty-fifty chance he would have kicked him in the ribs if it weren't for the fact that a nervous laugh managed to escape the mouth of one of the men. It was Farid, the most talented of the group, and as he struggled to suppress his ill-timed expression, the others joined in. It had a cascading effect, and soon they were all giggling like little schoolgirls.

Karim stepped over Ahmed, drew his 9mm Glock, and pressed the tip of the muzzle to Farid's forehead. Karim's action and the image of one of their fellow jihadists dying at the hands of their commander only a few days earlier sucked any and all humor out of the situation. The men straightened, throwing their shoulders back and staring straight ahead. Even Farid managed to stand tall with the weight of the cool steel pressing against his forehead.

"Amir," Farid barked as quickly as he could, "I apologize for my bad judgment,"

"Do you find this humorous?"

"No, Amir, I do not." Farid chose to call him *Amir*, which was the Arabic word for commander.

"Then why are you laughing?"

Farid hesitated, not sure how he should answer. Finally he said, "I was wrong to have done so. I will not let it happen again."

"No, you will not," Karim said in an icy tone, "or I will put a bullet in your thick skull."

Farid blinked once, the sweat on his brow stinging his eyes. "Yes, sir!"

Karim lowered the gun, turned on the others, and barked, "Do the rest of you find humor in this?" They replied as one that they did not. The anger had not dissipated an ounce for Karim. It continued to build as he walked behind each man, fighting the urge to crack them across the back of the skull with his heavy gun.

Command was a lonely position, especially in the jungle thousands of miles and a world away from the war. Their failure was his failure, and he did not like failing. How could he get them to snap out of it, to understand what was at stake? How could he get them to understand just how serious the Americans were? As much as he despised them, Karim had no illusions about their formidability.

The men had all joined the fight willingly, and over the years Karim had met far too many who had talked bravely of war. Cafés and mosques all across Saudi Arabia were filled with them. Only a handful was brave enough, stupid enough, or devout enough to actually pick up a weapon and do something about it. The idea with his group was that they would be both brave and devout. Zachariah had been devout, and smart, but he was lazy. Never bothered to take what they were doing seriously enough. That was the element he had to contend with; young men with nothing better to do. Many of them had been sent by wealthy fathers who wanted to bask in the honor of giving to the cause. More than a few of these fathers also quietly paid to have their boys kept off the front lines. The vast majority showed up with no military training, and worse, a casual, false perception of battle. Even the most well-trained and well-equipped soldiers could soil themselves in battle. Take the novice, though, full of rhetoric and propaganda and see how he performs the first time the Americans drop one of their bruising, ear-shattering 2,000-pound-laser guided bombs. Karim had witnessed entire battalions of men refusing to move for fear that American warplanes were lurking in the dark skies above.

These men were not cowards. He had seen all but two of them fight in battle and all were worthy. Even Ahmed, for all his inability to simply get over the wall, had his strengths. A self-taught sniper, he was by far the best shot with both a pistol and a rifle. Karim had big plans for him. A well-trained sniper on the prowl in a peacetime urban area would be an invaluable weapon. A thought occurred to Karim as he continued to circle his men. Maybe he was pushing them too hard. Maybe it was destroying their confidence. It was against his nature to pull back. Everything he had accomplished in life had been done by pressing forward. By trying harder.

Maybe that was not the answer with this group. In less than a week they would begin their insertion into the heart of the enemy, where they would have few allies. The tension would be tenfold. Karim thought of the other two groups. He'd received word that they'd been intercepted, but there had been nothing in the press. That meant they were more than likely floating aboard some nondescript ship in the middle of the ocean, being tortured. How had they been caught? Did they trip themselves up? Was there a traitor somewhere in their organization? All of these questions and more had kept Karim awake at night for weeks.

Something came to him at that moment as he looked over his tense men. It was guidance from Allah. He knew that almost immediately. Increasingly he could feel the hand of Allah in everything he did. Guiding him, prodding him, gently nudging him on this journey to the belly of the beast. His future was suddenly less certain; his destiny to one day lead a revolt in the holiest of lands. Maybe it would all end in America. Karim couldn't help feeling slightly disappointed, but it lasted only a second. He knew Allah was testing him. Making sure he was humble. Getting him to stay focused on the task at hand. *So be it*, Karim thought. *If America is to be my final battle, I will make it a glorious fiery ending.*

Karim turned his attention to Ahmed, who was still breathing heavily. He had yet to address a very important issue; with Zachariah gone the structure needed to be realigned. Karim had designed the team to function much like the Navy SEALs and their swim buddy system. Each man had been assigned a partner to train with. The eight men could be split into two fighting forces of four, or four smaller teams of two. Karim had put much thought into it. This would give him the strength to make the initial assaults and the flexibility to deploy smaller units that would be harder to detect once the powers that be figured out what was going on.

"Ahmed," Karim said as he extended his hand, "I would be honored if you would accept me as your partner."

The Moroccan was shocked. "Amir, the honor would be mine."

Karim smiled. "You are a fine soldier and I have great faith in you." He glanced at the other men and took pride in their approving smiles. To lighten the mood further he said, "I will have to make sure we don't have to climb any walls."

CHAPTER 18

KARIM looked out across the clearing, not sure what to expect, but he thought he would feel something. Some momentous change, a gnawing anticipation for what lay ahead, a sense of pride in what they had accomplished. Something, anything, but all he felt was emptiness. He looked from one side of the clearing to the other. Surveyed the obstacle course they had all run a thousand times, the pistol range, where he had turned each of them into expert marksmen with their Glock 19s. And not just into static marksmen; he'd turned them into gunfighters. They'd learned to shoot with both their left and right hands, extended two-hand grips, close-in single-hand grips, on the move, on the ground, standing and sitting. They'd covered every conceivable situation, and they were all drastically better. But were they good enough?

Karim felt it. The tightness in his chest. The shallow breaths. It was another panic attack. He had told no one. So far he'd been able to convince the men they were just migraines, but he knew better. He'd had headaches before, and these were not headaches. They were far more terrifying. Normally he was visited by the pangs of doubt right before he fell asleep. When he was alone with his thoughts. When he was desperately trying to empty his consciousness of all his worries so he could simply sleep. It was hopeless, though. The more he tried the worse it got, and now it was happening to him in the middle of the day.

The illness, or whatever it was, always came the same way. It started as doubt; doubt in his own ability and that of his men. They had done so much, had come so far, but was it far enough? Where was the sense of accomplishment, or finality, or at least the satisfaction that they were leaving this awful place? The place that had almost doomed them from the start. Karim thought back to those first few weeks when the men had all taken ill, their bodies assaulted by the horrid stew of moisture and insects. It was the one thing he had failed to take into consideration. He knew his men would have to adapt to the new climate, but assumed their youth and health could handle it. They had, after all, survived fighting against the Americans in the cold, rough mountains of Afghanistan. Karim had hated the cold, but never again would he curse it. The cold, dry mountain air killed all of the things you couldn't see; the tiny microbes and bacteria that would assault the body. Those unseen enemies flourished in the moist jungle air.

Surprisingly it was the U.S. Army that had rescued them, or more precisely one of their handy field manuals on tropical survival. Karim had gotten the men the proper medicine and clothing and had instituted a strict policy on hygiene. It took almost a full month before everyone was cured of their rashes and diarrhea. From that moment on they had made great progress. They were stronger, fitter, more knowledgeable, and more confident, but was it enough? What was he failing to account for?

"Amir."

Karim turned to find Farid standing a few feet behind him, a look of concern on his face. "Yes."

"Are you all right?"

"Yes. Why do you ask?"

"You do not look well. Excuse me for saying so."

"I feel fine." Karim lied.

"The men are ready."

"Water?"

"Full rations, as you ordered."

"Do they know we are leaving?"

Farid could not hide his own surprise.

"I didn't think so." Karim looked back toward the huts and their rusty tin roofs. The men were standing next to their packs, preparing for what they thought would be just another long march through the jungle. "Bring them over. Tell them to leave their packs."

Farid barked out a quick order and the six men hustled over. They lined up from left to right, the distance from one man to the other a full arm's length. They'd done it so many times over the last six months, they could simply eyeball the distance.

Karim surveyed his elite squad. Seven of them from left to right. The tallest was a hair over six feet, and the shortest a bit under five eight. They were all in peak physical condition. What little extra weight they may have carried on their agile frames was now gone. They were an impressive group with their broad shoulders, bulging muscles, and narrow waists. Their entire bearing had been changed. They stood straight, with shoulders back and chests out, their eyes front and center, waiting for an order. The posture alone had taken nearly a month. He'd had to transform them, slowly strip all the bad habits they'd learned fighting for al-Qaeda and the Taliban. They had been encouraged to look down on the Americans and their formality of command. The way the Americans marched around like robots. Karim saw it for what it really was; an efficiency that stripped away an individual's identity. It was one of the many things that made them such daunting opponents, and it was the foundation of their effectiveness. When an order was given they could move with amazing speed and efficiency.

Karim looked over the men and realized for the first time just how proud he was of them. He gave the order for the men to relax and then with a thin smile on his lips he said, "My warriors, Allah has told me you are ready. There is nothing more we can do here."

"We are leaving?" It was Ahmed, one of the Moroccans.

"Yes. We will leave within the hour."

One by one the men looked to each other. Some smiled. Others looked nervous. Karim saw this, stepped on his own anger, and told himself it was natural. As horrible as this place had been, it had served its purpose. It had become home to them. "I know some of you are anxious. Some of you are nervous, and one or two of you are probably afraid. All of these feelings are natural. When God asked the prophet Jonah to go to Nineveh and decry the wickedness, he was afraid. So afraid, he ran in the opposite direction, where he ended up in the belly of the beast. Even one of the great prophets was afraid. It is normal to have such feelings. Even to doubt in our cause . . . our mission. We have each other, though. We have become family. We will keep each other strong, and we will not run. We will go willingly, and with great courage, into the belly of the beast, and we will inflict such harm and pain that the beast will no longer have the stomach to meddle in our affairs."

A few of the men shouted and pumped their fists in the air. The more solemn ones simply nodded.

"To stay longer is to give the enemy more time to prepare." Karim began to walk the length of the formation with his hands clasped behind his back. Now came the hard part. "I have not told you this until now because I did not want to distract you during your training." He stopped at one end and looked back down the line. "The other two units have not been heard from in almost a month. It is feared that they have been intercepted."

There were murmurs of shock and disappointment. "But there has been nothing in the news," said Farid.

"That is true." The men had access to two laptops with Internet links, and Karim encouraged them to read several U.S. newspapers every day. "I would hold out some hope if it had been reported in the papers. That would mean the CIA would have acknowledged their capture, and in turn they would have to document their treatment.

The fact that there has been no word means they will drain them of everything they know."

"Do the other units know of our plans?"

Karim looked at Fazul Alghamdi, whom he had fought alongside in Afghanistan. "Only in vague terms."

"They know which city we will attack," Farid said in an agitated tone.

"Yes, they do, but it is a big city. As we have discussed, there are many targets."

Fazul looked forlorn. "They were good men."

"Yes, they were. They were brave men, but they put too much faith in their belief that Allah wanted them to succeed." Karim had spent a great deal of time as of late trying to sort this out. With the thoughtfulness of an imam he said, "Allah wants us to succeed, but he wants to challenge us. He wants to test us. He wants to see how committed we are to defeating our enemy."

"We are all committed, Amir," said Farid, speaking for all of them.

"Good. This is why I have preached preparation and vigilance. I have admonished many of you for what I feel is a lack of respect for our enemy. You are weak if you fall prey to this. You are immature and you are afraid . . . like a schoolboy who is jealous of a pupil who gets a better mark on an exam. The truth is that the Americans are extremely good, and if we are not careful, we will end up like the others . . . captured and I'm sure tortured."

"We will not disappoint you, Amir," said Farid.

"Good." Karim would always worry about the men. He had poured everything he had into getting them ready for this mission, and he knew he would never be completely satisfied. That was his nature. Those concerns, though, had taken a backseat to something that was weighing very heavily on him. He knew the Americans were good, but he was not naive enough to think the other two units had been intercepted by sheer luck. More and more, Karim was convinced the leadership of al-Qaeda had been compromised.

"I have one other concern," Karim announced in an extremely dire voice. "I am afraid that Zachariah may have been passing information along to his uncle."

The two Moroccans, who were closest to the Egyptian, shared a nervous look.

Karim picked up on it and asked, "Am I right?"

Both men nodded.

Karim told himself that he could be angry about it later. His suspicions confirmed, he felt very vulnerable standing in the clearing. He got that feeling he'd had many times in Afghanistan. The one where he could almost sense one of the American drones circling high above. A faint buzz that foretold death from the sky. He was suddenly very glad that he had killed Zachariah and even more glad that he had made other preparations.

"Does anyone have any questions before we leave?"

"Where are we going?"

"The airstrip." Karim looked to the north. "If we make good time we should be there by nightfall."

"And then on to Mexico City?" Fazul asked.

"No."

"But what of the plan?"

"We can no longer trust our own people. Somewhere along the line the Americans have penetrated our leadership. We are on our own."

"But how will we get into America?"

"I have made other arrangements."

"What are they?"

"I will tell you when the time is right." The men accepted this without further question. Karim looked at Farid and said, "Set the buildings on fire. I don't want any clues left behind in case the Americans learn of this place."

"Yes, Amir."

Karim scanned the blue sky above them in search of a sign that they were being watched. The mere act of doing so made all the men nervous. "I think we should leave this place as quickly as possible."

No one argued. The men moved from one building to the next, using the oil from the lanterns to start the fires. The two laptops, extra radios, maps, and satellite phones were all thrown into the raging fire. Fourteen notebooks filled with research on individuals, buildings, entities, and organizations were all torched. Karim had made them memorize their battle plan. From this point forward nothing was to be put on paper. All communication with the al-Qaeda leadership was to cease.

With the fires raging behind them, the men moved along a narrow foot trail. Karim stood at the edge of the jungle as each man disappeared under the dense canopy. He was happy to finally leave this place, and more than a little content to be cutting all ties with his commanders. There was nothing else they could do for him. He and his men were on their own. They would face Goliath, and they would strike a mighty blow for all of Islam.

CHAPTER 19

WASHINGTON, D.C.

IKE Nash lay on his side, the wind knocked from his lungs, his arms pinned beneath his body. His eyes fluttered, then opened only to find a sea of dust and debris. With great effort he rolled onto his back. A jolt of stabbing pain shot through his body. After a moment it passed and was replaced by a strange, comforting warmth that spread beneath him. It was oddly silent, the air filled with a pungent odor. Slowly, steadily, the pain in his ears began to build. A figure emerged from the dust, holding a rifle. A slack-jawed Nash stared up at the man, trying to make sense of it all. Where in the hell was he? None of this made sense.

It was the weapon that brought him halfway back to reality. It was an M4 Carbine. Nash didn't know why he knew what it was, but he had an almost instinctive familiarity with the weapon. The man standing above him swung his rifle around, dropped into a half crouch, and began firing. Shell casings tumbled from the ejection port, peppering Nash's head. The hot brass on his cheek was like a slap to the face. His perception of reality went from narrow to panoramic in a split second, and then back again. The last few tumblers fell into place and Nash realized there had been an explosion. That warm feeling spreading beneath him was his own damn blood.

Nash tried to move. Knew he had to move. Once the shooting started, you had to move. Movement meant survival. The opposite meant death, or worse, capture. He rolled onto his side and felt a warm, sticky goo begin to pour out of his ear. The man standing over him dropped to a knee and began running a hand over Nash's back while his eyes and weapon swept the area. The man jerked his weapon to the left and unleashed another volley while Nash rolled flat onto his back again.

Nash watched the man hit the magazine release on his weapon. Saw the empty metal box fall free. Watched the man slam a new magazine home without looking. He fired another volley, glanced down at Nash, and screamed a question. Nash couldn't hear a thing the man was saying, but he finally realized who it was—Mitch Rapp.

Somewhere in the distance there was a rhythmic banging noise; oddly familiar, but distinctly out of place. Rapp grabbed him by his shoulder harness and began dragging him out of the line of fire. Nash's back was suddenly on fire with pain as he was pulled over the debris from the explosion. As the first wave of pain passed, he came to the horrifying realization that he couldn't feel his legs. The strange banging noise grew louder.

Nash's eyes snapped open, and he was instantly transported thousands of miles from the Federally Administered Tribal Areas of Pakistan to his home in suburban Washington, D.C. His right arm slid under the sheets and found the warm skin of his wife. His eyes focused on the familiar pink-and-white crystal chandelier she had insisted on hanging above their bed. He sighed, closed his eyes, and wiggled his toes. The banging noise started up again. It was coming from down the hallway and was neither unfamiliar nor unwelcome.

Nash rolled onto his side, threw back the covers, and swung his legs onto the floor. He was wearing a pair of gray flannel pajama pants and nothing else. He put his elbows on his knees and ran his hands through his short brown hair. At thirty-eight he was still in peak physical shape, but the chiseled exterior hid inner flaws. A stabbing pain shot from one temple to the other, so much so that it hurt to open his eyes. It reminded him of his days in the Marine Corps when he used to drink way too much. If only he were so lucky. He'd been to three separate specialists and none of them could tell him why he was waylaid with a splitting headache every morning when he got out of bed. Apparently, massive explosions could do more than just give you a concussion.

All complaining aside, he was grateful he could walk. It had taken four surgeries to pluck all the shrapnel from his back. The last one was the most delicate, since it involved removing a piece of razor-sharp metal from between his L3 and L4 vertebrae. After that surgery his progress had been amazing.

Other than the physical scars of the molten hot shrapnel that had peppered his back, there were few signs that Mike Nash had changed, but those close to him could tell he was holding on a little too tight. His wife had warned him. Thomas Dudley, the psychiatrist he worked with, had been pulling him aside every chance he got—trying to get him to talk about what he'd been through. Told him he needed to find a way to blow off some steam.

An unfortunate choice of words, considering the debacle that had taken place the previous evening. The last thing Nash wanted to do was revisit that subject. He was an expert at mental triage. He had learned it well on the wrestling mats and football fields of his youth. The Marines had further perfected the survival skill, and the CIA had given him the equivalent of a master's degree. *Repress and move on,* that was their motto. Maybe there would be time to deal with all of it later. Maybe it would simply fix itself. He sure as hell hoped so, because life had become decidedly less enjoyable.

His thoughts turned to Rapp. Nash told himself he had no right to complain about a thing. The man had jumped on a grenade for all of them. The shit storm of all shit storms was about to come raining down on them and Rapp had walked right into it. Told the rest of them to get away. Nash glanced over his shoulder at his wife, thought of the great years they'd had together, and wondered how she and the kids would handle it if he got indicted. Rapp was convinced he could take the heat and keep the attention off everyone else, but Nash had his doubts. Congressional investigations were bad enough, but his one had the earmarks of something much bigger. It smelled like one for the Office of Special Counsel and that meant it could last for years, their net getting bigger and bigger, and catching all kinds of crap none of them could have predicted.

The banging noise down the hall grew in its ferocity. His wife stirred. Nash stood and walked stiffly across the room and down the hallway. Two other bedroom doors were firmly closed, but the last one on the left was ajar. The mystery noise was emanating from the smallest room on the second floor. Nash stopped just outside and peeked through the crack. Inside he caught a glimpse of one-year-old Charlie as he ran from one end of the crib to the other and then back again like he was a professional wrestler bouncing off the ropes and working up a head of steam for a clothesline or an atomic leg drop.

After a few more laps he stopped and grabbed on to the side rail. His tiny fingers clutched the white wood, his cheeks puffed with air and he gave it everything he had. Back and forth, back and forth. Bang . . . bang. Bang . . . bang.

Mike Nash got a huge kick out of this little kid's determination. He pushed the door open another foot and waited to be seen.

Charlie caught the movement and looked over the top rail with his big brown eyes. A huge smile spread across the baby's face. He sprang up on his toes, threw out his arms, and squealed, "Dada. Dada."

Mike Nash brimmed with unbridled love. He hadn't seen the little fella in a week. He crossed the small nursery, grabbed Charlie under his outstretched arms, lifted him up, and brought him in tight. Nash kissed him on his shiny, red cheek and then went to work on his neck. Charlie giggled and then squealed with laughter.

"Good morning, Chuck," Nash said in a whisper. "Did you miss me?"

Charlie took his two pudgy hands, slapped his father's face with surprising force, and then tried to grab as much skin as possible. Nash broke free by shaking his head and then started snapping his teeth at Charlie's fingers. Charlie pulled his hands back and squealed in delight.

Nash placed him on the changing table, unzipped the boy's pajamas, and with the efficiency of a Marine gunnery sergeant field stripping an M-16, went to work. A fresh diaper was unfurled and put in place. The tabs on the puffy diaper were simultaneously pulled back, but before it was yanked free, Nash grabbed a washcloth to place over Charlie's groin in case he decided to hose down the nursery. He'd learned that lesson the hard way with Charlie's oldest brother. Nash tossed the used one in the diaper pail, gave the boy the once-over with a wet wipe, and then secured the new diaper.

The two headed downstairs, with Charlie clutching his father's neck. Nash stopped at the front door and looked out the small window. He tried to remember if he'd heard anything last night about the weather. This traveling from one continent to another could really confuse you. He'd gotten home late and all of the kids were asleep. Unfortunately, they'd grown so comfortable with his coming and going that none of them bothered to wait up. Nash punched in the security code and turned off the alarm. He cracked the front door and peeked outside. The air was humid for a change. It looked as if spring had finally arrived.

CHAPTER 20

BAGRAM AIR BASE, AFGHANISTAN

RAPP lay on his bunk and stared up at the ceiling. They'd taken away his uniform and given him an orange jumpsuit just like the ones worn by the other prisoners. He took it all in stride. He'd been in far worse situations. It would do him no good to start ranting and raving and demanding that he be treated with more dignity. The truth was that he found it humorous that they had chosen to put him in the very same facility that housed Haggani and al-Haq. Rapp figured this was the only place they had where they could keep him isolated until Washington weighed in on the unique situation. The main prison was filled with hundreds of combatants and terrorists. Putting Rapp in with that group was almost unimaginable, but that dimwitted captain had actually suggested they do just that. Fortunately, General Garrison seemed to have a decent amount of common sense and intervened.

This thing was going to get kicked up to the highest levels in Washington, and his allies on the Hill would be indignant that they had treated Rapp no better than a common terrorist. His stint at the prison was at two days and running. He knew because he still had his watch. They'd ordered him to hand it over, but he declined. After a brief discussion the four guards who were processing him decided it wasn't worth the fight. They'd already seen what he'd done to one of the prisoners as well as Captain Leland, and since they liked neither the spitting terrorist nor Captain Leland they decided to cut him some slack. He'd been brought six meals and expected his seventh any minute. The food was nothing great, but it wasn't bad. It sure the hell was better than anything these guys were eating up in the mountains.

So far the only real surprise was that no one had shown up to bail him out. He figured it must have been the time change and the fact that it had happened over the weekend. Whatever the case, Rapp knew they would be coming soon. He'd be dragged back to Washington, and then the real show would start. The solitude had given him plenty of time to figure it out. To think about each person, what they would say and how he would meet it all head-on. It was time. They had been running from this fight for far too long. The amount of time, energy, and money they spent trying to hide what they were doing from their own government was ridiculous.

Rapp heard the metallic click of the lock on the door being released and sat up, thinking his next meal had arrived. When the door opened he saw the familiar face of Rob Ridley. The deputy director of the National Clandestine Service looked at Rapp with a combination of amusement and concern.

"You've really done it this time, my friend."

"Could you have taken any longer?" Rapp asked in return.

Ridley held up his camera phone and said, "Don't move. I need to record this moment for my personal archives."

Rapp made an obscene gesture and said, "I'm glad you can find some humor in it."

Ridley dragged a chair into the small cell and closed the door. "It's not every day I get to see my idol in prison orange."

All Rapp could do was smile at Ridley and shake his head. It was good to see him, but he wasn't about to tell him that. "Seriously, where in the hell have you been?"

Ridley sat and let out a long sigh. "This is a complicated situation, Mitch."

Rapp took the fact that his friend closed the door as a bad sign. "So some prick wants to keep me in here and show me a lesson?"

"Kind of. Here, I brought something for you." Ridley handed Rapp a paper bag.

Rapp took it and looked inside. He pulled out a worn leather baseball glove, a baseball, and a copy of *Mein Kampf*. "What the hell is this?"

Ridley was known as one of the biggest pranksters in the agency, which had endeared him to many. He flashed Rapp his signature boyish grin and said, "I just thought I'd help put you in the mood. You know, *The Great Escape* with Steve McQueen. You, stuck here in the cooler . . . playing catch against the wall . . . reading Adolf Hitler's autobiography. I just thought I'd help get you in the right frame of mind, since you might be here for a while."

"You're a dandy." Rapp laughed while he put on the glove and began pounding the ball into the old mitt. "Great movie, by the way."

"One of the best." Ridley held up his phone for Rapp to see and then gave him a wink.

Good, Rapp thought. He carried the same phone. It would emit a ten-foot umbrella of white noise and render the cell's listening devices useless. The cells were wired to record everything. It would stand to reason that since he was a U.S. citizen anything he said would not be admissible in court, but that was a pretty low threshold, considering what they were about to discuss.

"Seriously," Rapp said, "what took so long?"

"There've been some complications."

"Such as?"

"Such as you hitting a United States Air Force officer and almost breaking his wrist."

"You can't be serious," Rapp groaned.

"Did you have to hit him?"

"I didn't hit him."

"Really," Ridley said in a tone of disbelief. "How did he get the shiner?"

"He fell."

"Come on."

"Seriously . . . he tried to pull his gun on me."

"And?"

Rapp stopped pounding the ball into the mitt. Stopped moving entirely. "You can't be serious."

"I'm very serious. Some of this we have a shot at fixing, but you striking this guy has caused quite a stir."

"I didn't strike him. He went to draw his gun." Rapp shrugged. "I felt it was excessive force."

"You expect me to believe that?"

"It wasn't the only reason, but I sure as hell don't like guns being pointed at me. Especially by some snot-nosed little prick like that."

"Fair enough. That's basically what I told them, but this captain is making a big stink out of it. Any other reasons why you may have done it? Just between you and me."

"Of course . . . he was getting ready to call the MPs in and send them to arrest the others. I needed to buy a little more time for the others to get away, and I didn't hit him. He was bringing his gun around on me, I grabbed it, twisted it free, and in the process, he fell and hit his head on a chair."

"I had a chance to talk to the base commander in private."

"General Garrison."

"Yeah . . . he pretty much corroborates what you just said, but this captain is . . ." Ridley stopped and rolled his eyes.

"A little puss, is what he is. I should have broken his fucking jaw."

Ridley moaned. "That type of attitude is not going to help." Ridley leaned forward and placed his hands on his knees. "I think if you make a heartfelt apology to the captain we could probably get him to drop this whole thing."

"Hell no."

"Don't be unreasonable."

"I'm willing to face the music. I told you that before I came over here. It's time to force this issue."

"That's fine, and Irene agrees, but this stuff about you hitting an officer isn't going to play well with the very people we need to support you."

"Yeah . . . well, have you met him yet?"

"Yes."

"And?"

"I can see where he might bug some people."

Rapp frowned. "The guy is a prick with a capital P."

"And he has a huge shiner and is wearing a sling, and if he ends up in front of one of the committees wearing his service dress uniform, he is going to garner a boatload of sympathy from the exact people we are counting on for support."

Rapp drove the ball into the mitt a few more times and then asked, "So what do you want me to do?"

"You know what I want you to do."

"Crap."

"It's not that hard. Just shake his hand and say you're sorry. We've explained to him that you have a very colorful history and even intimated that the president owes you a few favors. That he would more than likely look favorably on someone who was willing to help him out in such a delicate situation."

"Who's the we?"

"Stephen Roemer, special assistant to the secretary of defense."

Rapp thought about his options for a moment and then swore. "If this kid cops an attitude . . ."

"I'll make sure he doesn't. The important thing is that we get you out of here so we can get moving on the other stuff. There's still going to be an investigation and hearings and God only knows what else. Now, if you don't want to apologize . . . you can sit in this cell for the next month or so while a bunch of lawyers decide your fate."

"Hell no."

"Then do it."

"Fine."

"Make it sincere, Mitch. We need you back in D.C."

"I said fine," Rapp growled.

Ridley reached into the bag next to the chair and pulled out a khaki flight suit. "As much as I'd love to see you have to walk around in your prison garb, I think it might send the wrong message."

"I thought you said I might have to stay in here for a while?"

"That was before you agreed to play nice. Now, hurry up and put those on. You have to apologize, and then we have a plane to catch."

"Fuck," Nash blurted out as he reached for his copy of the *Washington Post*. Right about the time he found the front-page headline, he heard his son parrot him. Nash paused, waited a moment, and looked at Charlie, hoping he'd misheard him.

Charlie took a pull off his bottle, sighed, looked at his father as if he was bored and said, "Fuck."

Nash grabbed Charlie by the hand and said, "No, little buddy. That's a bad word."

Despite Nash's efforts, Charlie said the word again.

Any other morning Nash would probably be laughing, but he heard his wife stirring upstairs. If she came down and heard her little angel swearing like a Marine she would flip. He put on his most stern face, pointed at Charlie, and said, "Bad word."

Charlie frowned, pointed right back at his father, and said, "No." A moment passed and then he repeated the four-letter word, but this time with more vigor.

Nash heard his wife coming down the stairs and began to panic. Grabbing the spoon off the table, he quickly scooped it into the baby jar and shoved the food into Charlie's mouth just as he was beginning to utter his new favorite word again.

Maggie Nash entered the kitchen wearing a loose white robe, her raven black hair cascading past her shoulders. She headed straight for Charlie and kissed him on the forehead. Charlie started squirming with excitement and tried to speak, but Nash was right there with another load of puréed squash and peas.

Maggie grabbed a bottle of lotion off the counter, poured some into her hands, and began to rub it over the scars on her husband's back. She tilted her head to the side and threw back her hair. "About last night," she said cautiously, "I don't want you to overthink the whole thing." She worked the lotion into his muscular shoulders and added, "It's not uncommon."

Nash frowned and mumbled, "I'd rather not talk about it."

"It's all the stress of your job, honey. It's normal for men to . . ."

"Please," Nash cut her off. "Not in front of the baby."

She took a step back. Placed her right hand on her hip. "The baby can barely say Mommy and Daddy. I don't think he's about to blurt out 'erectile dysfunction.'"

Nash winced at the mention of the medical condition. This was just like his wife. She'd want to talk about this over and over until they'd looked at it from every possible angle, and then she'd want him to talk to a shrink. But he was fine. He'd been with Maggie for fifteen years and not once had he failed to rise to the occasion. He tensed and said, "We are not going to talk about this."

"Don't you dare," she snapped.

"Don't what?" he barked back.

"Act like your father." She gave his shoulder a shove. "I'm not going to watch you die of a heart attack before you reach fifty because you're too macho to talk about your problems!"

"You need to relax."

"I'm not the one who has a hard time relaxing." She turned and started for the other side of the kitchen. "You proved that last night." As she yanked open the cupboard in search of a mug, she began her sermon on Nash's father.

He'd heard it many times. Maggie had loved him. Thought he was a great man, but it sure did suck that his grandkids never got to know him. Nash was debating whether to sit there and take it or fight back, when Maggie yanked the coffeepot out of its cradle a little too force-fully, catching the filter basket, and swinging it into the open position. Since the machine was not done brewing, the basket was brimming with hot, muddy coffee. The sludge sloshed over the edge onto the white marble counter, the floor, and Maggie's white robe.

Maggie jumped back, held out her arms, and said, "Fuck!"

Nash glanced sideways at Charlie and saw the recognition in his son's eyes as he stared in wonderment at his mother. Silently, Nash urged him on. He watched the baby-food-covered lips open and a split second later the dreaded word flew out of Charlie's mouth with more gusto than he could have ever hoped to coax from him.

With a look of sheer horror on her face, Maggie turned and looked at her little angel. Charlie smiled and belted out the word one more time for good measure.

Nash stood, handed his wife the jar of baby food, and said, "Nice work, honey."

CHAPTER 22

TRIPLE FRONTIER

K ARIM held the binoculars to his eyes and scanned the airstrip from one end to the other. It had been a good, hard march the day before. The men had practiced excellent discipline. As the crow flies, the narrow valley was only three miles from their camp. As with most things in the jungle, though, the most direct route was also the most dangerous. They'd learned the hard way that it was foolish to fight the jungle, so they took the footpath that followed a dry stream west and around the steepest, most treacherous part of the ridge that separated their valley from the next.

Karim had known about the airstrip from the start. The Lebanese man he had bought the land from had warned him to stay away from the neighbors. The strip was used by a drug cartel as a collection and distribution point for their cocaine trafficking. That knowledge alone had got Karim thinking.

For the first month Karim stayed away from the place, but as his men became more proficient in their maneuvering and concealment, he decided to have a closer look at the airstrip. He had a security concern. He didn't like not knowing what was going on such a short distance from his camp. He also saw an opportunity. A chance to shake up what was becoming a monotonous routine for the men. It was a training tool, an actual facility, manned by real people who carried guns.

They kept their distance for some time. The top of the ridge offered them a clear view of the dirt runway and the ramshackle buildings down at the one end. Karim used the Navy SEAL philosophy of two-man teams to collect his information. He'd send the pairs out early in the morning and tell them they would be relieved at noon the following day. He ran them like this for sixteen days, each two-man team pulling four shifts. It was a great training exercise, and the men reacted well to the challenge. Anything to break the daily monotony of the obstacle course was a good thing.

The men took meticulous notes as ordered and soon Karim had a detailed idea of how the place worked. At first it seemed there was no structure to the set-up, but out of the chaos a pattern emerged. None of the men appeared to be older than thirty and most of them looked to be teenagers. Rarely did anyone rise before ten in the morning, and when they eventually did venture outside they were lethargic, cranky, and most likely extremely hungover. Every night the men would stay up late gambling, drinking, and watching porn movies. Twice, prostitutes had been flown in. It was not unusual to see a man stumble from the bunkhouse well after sunrise and vomit.

The guns were always present, though, and they carried a myriad of weapons, from AK-47s, to MP-5s, to all different kinds of pistols, and as far as he could tell, less than twenty percent of them used the same ammunition, another sign that it was a sloppy operation. They would hold their own impromptu shooting practice, firing at the previous evening's beer and liquor bottles. Never had he seen them get through a session without one of the weapons jamming. Invariably, the others found this to be hilarious. Karim used it as an opportunity to show his men how not to act.

One evening Karim had executed a mock attack. He split the team into two groups and then led them to within a few feet of the barracks where the men were drinking and gambling. The exercise was a great confidence builder, but for Karim there was no feeling of accomplishment that they had crept to within a few feet of a bunch of drunk and coked-up men. These idiots were not a worthy test for them and he took great care to point out to the men that the Americans would be far more vigilant.

As he peered through his binoculars Karim thought of that first day, when he crested the ridge and looked down at the ramshackle operation. Within seconds he asked himself, *How would I assault this place? How would I deploy my men? What were the odds of total success? What were the chances of failure? What would he do if he lost one or more of his men?*

This was how the military mind worked, he thought to himself. *It is a gift. We look at a target in the same way a sculptor looks at a block of stone or a carpenter a hunk of wood.* Except his job was much harder. His subject was not static. It would fight back if given the chance. That was why he had to surprise them. Karim had seen in Afghanistan what could happen when the bullets started flying. Tactics, maneuvering, concealment, and marksmanship would carry the day, but there was always the chance that a stray bullet could bounce around until it hit a piece of flesh. He could not afford to lose a single man. Not until he arrived in America and the real battle began.

Farid slithered up next to him and looked down at the empty strip of dirt and grass. "Your orders, Amir?"

"We'll move out in thirty minutes. Send two men to sweep the trail in front of us and have them radio back."

"May I ask what you have planned?"

Karim continued looking through the binoculars. "A plane will arrive at approximately nine. We're going to secure the airfield before it lands."

"So the plane is ours?"

"Yes."

"You have had this planned for months."

Karim lowered the binoculars, allowed himself a grin and said, "Why would I do something like that?"

"Because you don't trust Zawahiri?"

"That is part of it."

Farid stared down at the landing strip for a long time.

"You have something on your mind?" Karim asked.

Without looking, he asked, "Do you trust us?"

"Of course."

"Then why do you keep so much from us?"

"Security. Too many people know too many details. The first two teams have failed. We are the only hope."

Farid watched the wind sweep down and bend the tops of the trees. "You have trained us like the American Special Forces, but you do not command like one of them."

The honest words were a slap to the face. "How do you mean?"

"At your urging, we have all done much reading these last few months. I think you've read too much about the great American generals."

Karim was annoyed by what he was hearing, but he said, "Go on."

"I have read some of the same books. They all talk of the need to keep yourself aloof so your judgment isn't affected. I suppose in the regular army it makes sense, but everything I have read about their Special Forces says otherwise. The enlisted men participate in the planning of the mission."

"Your point?"

"I think you need to stop keeping secrets from us. You need to trust us. In a few days you will have no choice."

Karim didn't like hearing the words, but a part of him knew they were accurate. "Fair enough. When we reach our next destination I will tell the men of my plan."

Farid smiled, "Thank you, Amir."

"Just remember, this is not a democracy."

"You do not have to worry about that. The men have too much respect for you, and more than a little fear." Farid slithered backward on his belly and then disappeared into the brush.

CHAPTER 23

LANGLEY, VIRGINIA

THE assistant told Nash they were expecting him. He glanced at the two bodyguards standing post outside the CIA director's office and opened the heavy soundproof door. Irene Kennedy was seated behind her desk with the handset of her secure phone held to her right ear. She glanced up and gave him a *where in the hell have you been* look, before spinning her chair away and looking out the window. Nash silently cursed his wife. Standing in the middle of the big office, he wished he could have dragged her in here so she could feel what it was like to piss off the person who ran the Central Intelligence Agency.

Two men were sitting on the couch opposite Kennedy's desk. The gray-haired gentleman on the left mouthed a swear word and put one hand to his ear like he was holding a phone. It was Chuck O'Brien, the director of the National Clandestine Service and a thirty-two-year veteran of the CIA. He had been trying to get ahold of Mike since 6:00 a.m. and it was now almost 9:00.

Nash had two separate CIA-issued phones that he was expected to carry on his person at all times. As soon as he heard the female TV anchor talking about the *Washington Post* article, he knew what had happened. When he returned from Afghanistan, Maggie had met him at the door wearing a thin robe and a lustful expression. She handed him a glass of wine, informed him that the kids were in bed, and suggested he go upstairs and take a shower. He stopped in the den first and plugged in both phones. After he had gone upstairs to shower, Maggie had turned off both phones. She wasn't crazy about his working for the CIA, and she had a serious problem with the fact that the higher-ups at Langley demanded her husband be plugged in twenty-four hours a day every day of the year. She was right, they were right, and as usual he was stuck in the middle trying to keep everyone happy.

Nash glanced at an empty chair but chose to remain standing. Some might have thought it an old habit from the Marine Corps, but they would be wrong. Nash didn't like the seventh floor. Didn't really like headquarters at all. The discomfort had nothing to do with Kennedy. At least not personally. They got along fine. He respected her, even feared her a bit, which was healthy in his line of work. The discomfort, he reasoned, was due to the fact that he didn't belong. The seventh floor was an arena in which he was not suited to compete.

The top floor of the headquarters building was filled with bureaucrats. Nash would be shocked if one in ten had any real field experience. That did not make them bad people, but it spoke to their narrow perspective. Most were good husbands and wives, fathers and mothers. They were active in their kids' lives and their communities. They were people who had sacrificed and were willing to sacrifice more. They were patriots, but they had been browbeaten by the media and henpecked by the politicians. They were like children who were punished for the wild ways of an older brother. Mike and his fellow operators in the Clandestine Service were the wild sibling in the relationship. In many ways the bureaucrats' distrust of men like Nash and Rapp was inevitable.

"No, Mr. President," Kennedy said as she spun her chair back around. "I can assure you no such operation has been sanctioned by the CIA." She listened for a second and then replied, "They like to get upset, sir. It gives them a reason to go on TV and let their constituents know they're still alive." She listened for another moment and then said, "Yes, sir. I'll be there at four."

Nash stood in the middle of the spacious office and did his best to look bored and unfazed by the revelation that the president was already involved.

Kennedy placed the white handset back in its cradle and looked up at Nash. "The president is very anxious."

Nash didn't know how to respond so he simply nodded.

Kennedy held up her copy of the *Washington Post* and said, "This is not good."

"I would agree."

"Please tell me it is a complete fabrication."

"It is a complete fabrication."

The man sitting next to Nash's boss scoffed in disbelief.

Nash turned and looked with contempt at Glen Adams, the CIA's inspector general. The man had been hounding him for fourteen months and counting. Mike could think of nothing more satisfying than putting him in a headlock and pounding the snot out of him.

Kennedy glanced at Adams and then back at Nash. "Our esteemed inspector general doesn't agree with you."

"I've been warning you for months," Adams said in an I-told-you-so voice. "He's a loose cannon. My money has him running the whole damn operation."

Nash felt his headache returning. He closed his eyes for a second and then looked at Adams. The *Washington Post* article flashed across his mind and he wondered if Adams might be one of the unnamed sources that the reporter quoted. Nash took a step closer to the couch and in response to Adams's accusation said, "Prove it."

"That's not my job, but I have no doubt, based on this article, that the Justice Department and the FBI are already in the process of doing just that."

"Yeah, I wonder if anyone in this building gave them a head start."

"Don't make this about me," Adams said in a sad voice.

"Fuck you."

"Mike," Kennedy said forcefully.

"This is bullshit," Nash said directly to Kennedy. "I want to know how many terrorists this waste of sperm has captured. How many people in his office have been killed in the line of duty since nine-eleven?"

"This isn't about me, Mr. Nash." Adams shook his head and casually flicked a piece of lint from his pants leg.

"No, it sure the hell isn't, because I can't think of a single thing that you've done to protect the American people from another attack."

"We all have our role to play," said Adams.

"Some more important than others."

Adams sighed as if he was bored. "I'm not going to allow you to bait me into a fight when I have nothing to do with this."

"The hell you don't." Turning back to Kennedy, Nash asked, "I wanna know if I'm under investigation by the Gestapo here."

Before Kennedy could answer, Adams said, "That's none of your business."

"What about my rights?"

"You surrendered them the day you walked through the front door."

"What about you? Who investigates you?"

Adams laughed. "That's funny, Mr. Nash. Who investigates me?" He shook his head. "I don't need to be investigated. I play by the rules."

"Spoken like a true sociopath."

"Let's just calm down," Kennedy cautioned.

Nash's headache got worse. He looked at the woman he'd always respected and suddenly lost his patience. "Fuck this."

"Excuse me?" Kennedy was shocked.

"This is all a bunch of bullshit. You're telling me to calm down. I saw the front page of the *Post*. It's all a bunch of lies, but it doesn't matter. The politicians are going to want to burn someone at the stake and this little smug prick here is trying to offer me up."

"There is no need to talk to me like that."

"You're scum, all right. You're a traitor to your own country." Looking back at Kennedy he said, "How much do you want to bet he's one of the anonymous sources mentioned in the *Post* story?"

Adams stood abruptly. "I don't need to take this. My work here is above reproach, and I for one have done nothing to embarrass this agency." Adams started for the door, and as he passed Nash, he said, "I doubt you can make the same claim."

Nash's right hand shot out and grabbed Adam's fleshy bicep. He spun him back around and said, "Don't ever compare what you do around here with what I do. When you have a bad day, a file gets lost. When I have a bad day, one of my boys gets killed."

Adams tried to pull his arm away. "Get your hands off me!"

Nash ignored him. "You're not on the field. You're not on the team. Hell, you're not even in the arena. You're at home with a bottle of beer and a bag of chips watching the game on TV, criticizing our every move, when the truth is, your fat, lazy ass wouldn't last five minutes out there."

"Mr. Nash!" Kennedy yelled as she stood. "That is enough."

"It sure is." Nash let go of Adams and started for the door. He grabbed the handle and looked across the office at Kennedy. "The next time you need someone to go to Afghanistan and get shot at, you can send this prick." Nash yanked open the door and was gone before Kennedy or his boss could say another word.

CHAPTER 24

BAGRAM AIR BASE, AFGHANISTAN

THEY were waiting for him in General Garrison's office; the special assistant to the secretary of defense sitting on the left side of the general's desk and Captain Leland the other. With only one chair remaining, Garrison stood and told everyone to take a seat at the eight-person conference table. The general ambled over to the table. He looked ready to be rid of this entire problem, even though he knew it wasn't going to simply disappear. For now, though, he was glad to have the opportunity to get this man off his base, so he could get back to the business of supplying the men and women with what they needed to wage war.

As reported, Leland was wearing a blue sling. It clashed with his camouflage BDUs and looked a bit ridiculous. Rapp watched the captain slowly and painfully rise to his feet. He was instantly reminded of some huckster plaintiff with a neck brace trying to convince a jury that he was in agony. It took great restraint for Rapp not grab him by the neck and kick him in the ass. Leland shuffled over to the table and carefully lowered himself into the chair to the right of the general.

Rapp didn't want to sit, but he knew he had to. He chose the seat directly across from General Garrison so he wouldn't have to look straight at Leland.

"Well," Ridley started off, "We don't have to drag this out with a lot of unnecessary talk. We've taken enough time as it is. Mitch has agreed that he will offer his sincere apologies, and then we'll get out of your way." Ridley looked at Rapp. "Mitch."

Rapp looked down at his folded hands and then traced a finger along fake grains of the pressed-wood tabletop. Without looking up he said, "I'm sorry about all of this."

Ridley looked nervously around the table hoping that would be enough, but already knowing it wasn't. After a long silence he cleared his throat.

Rapp looked up at General Garrison and said, "I'm sorry it had to happen."

"Excuse me?" Leland said in disbelief.

"I'm sorry it had to happen. I wish you hadn't got involved in this."

"That's your apology?"

"Yes," Ridley interceded. "He feels very bad about this. He knows you were simply trying to do your job."

"He doesn't feel bad about what he did to me. The man is a monster . . . he's a sociopath. He's incapable of remorse."

"What the fuck do you know?" Rapp asked.

Leland sat back and said, "I told you." He looked at Garrison and added, "This should be referred to the Department of Justice."

Rapp, looking at Garrison, said, "Is he always this big of a prick?"

The general looked up with bloodshot eyes and in a tired voice said, "I wish both of you would give it a rest."

"I have done nothing wrong, sir," Leland protested.

Ridley, sensing that things were spinning out of control, waved a hand to get everyone's attention and said, "Obviously, nerves are still a little raw. I would like to assure you, Captain Leland, that Mr. Rapp will be dealt with harshly. Director Kennedy has assured me that he will be punished for striking you, and . . ."

Before Ridley could continue, Leland turned to his CO and the assistant secretary of defense and said, "I don't trust any of them. I want to press charges."

"You're a prick." Rapp came out of his chair lightning-fast. "And you have an overinflated sense of how important you are in this whole thing. There's thousands of officers who can do exactly what you do, Captain, and thousands more who can do it a hell of a lot better than you. Look at you." Rapp waved an open hand at Leland. "I twisted your wrist and you fell, and now you're sitting here looking like a wife who's been battered by her husband. Aren't you even remotely embarrassed? You're a damn officer in the United States Air Force. Can you at least pretend to be a warrior?"

"I want to press charges, and I want him thrown back in lockup."

"Shut up, Captain," Rapp snapped. "Me taking that gun away from you was the luckiest thing that ever happened to your dead-end career. If you'd shut your mouth for a minute and listen, you'd realize just how lucky you are. You're going to get promoted to major immediately, and then you'll be on the fast track for colonel. Any post you want, you name it."

"I am not looking to prosper from this."

"He's right, Captain." It was the first words spoken by the assistant secretary of defense. "Secretary England wants you to know he considers your cooperation in this matter a personal favor, as does the president. He knows that Mr. Rapp here can be little rough, but wants you to understand that every American, including you, owes him a debt of gratitude."

Leland felt the room spinning. He was hit with a sudden fever. He couldn't believe what he was hearing. It went against everything he'd been taught at the Air Force Academy. Why couldn't his superiors see that this was wrong?

"You say the word, Captain. You want Colorado, California, Hawaii . . . Europe? You name it."

An exasperated Leland said, "I want justice."

"I told you he was a prick."

Leland looked up to see Rapp talking to the other man from the CIA.

"We're out of here." Rapp looked at Garrison and Roemer. "I'm sorry for all of this. I really am. I never wanted to put the military in the middle of this, but we're running low on options."

"You're just going to let him walk out of here?" a shocked Leland asked.

For the first time, Rapp felt sorry for the young officer. The guy was way out of his league and he hadn't a clue. "Captain, you have to let go of this," Rapp said in an almost pleading voice. "This entire thing is way above your pay grade. I told you not to draw your weapon. I told you I would cooperate, but you wouldn't listen to me. Maybe if you knew where I've been and what I've done for the last eighteen years you could understand why I did what I did. That's about all I can tell you. I'm sorry I had to get physical."

"But you're not sorry that you hit me?"

"I didn't hit you. I disarmed you, and you fell on your face."

"You assaulted me," Leland half screamed.

Rapp was out of patience. "You know what, Captain, good luck with your career. I'm out of here."

"No, you are not," Leland shouted. "General, do something."

The general sighed and put his hands over his face. "Captain, give it a rest."

"But, sir, I must protest . . ."

Ridley opened the door.

"That's an order, Captain. I want you to wait forty-eight hours, weigh all your options, and then file your official report. Until then, I don't want to hear another word about this issue. Have I made myself clear?"

Ridley didn't wait around for the answer. He pushed Rapp out into the hallway and closed the door behind them. Moving quickly down the hallway, he looked straight ahead and said, "Boy, that went well."

"I told you he was a pain in the ass."

"And you're just a treat to deal with." Ridley glanced at his watch. "Let's hurry. We have a plane to catch."

CHAPTER 25

LANGLEY, VIRGINIA

THE elevator doors opened, and Mike Nash was relieved to see it was empty. He stepped in, hit the button for the ground floor, and leaned against the far wall. The bright overhead lights made his headache worse. He covered his eyes with his right hand and began muttering to himself, knowing damn well his morning stood a good chance of getting worse.

The doors were within inches of closing when a large, callused hand shot through and gripped the rubber seal. The doors opened, and in stepped Chuck O'Brien. At six foot three O'Brien was a couple inches taller than Nash. He was a Dartmouth grad who had come to the CIA by way of Naval Intelligence. More than twenty years Nash's senior, he was still a physically imposing figure.

Fortunately, the elevator was almost as large as the type you would find in a hospital. Nash watched as O'Brien went to the far corner. He knew his boss would be less than enthusiastic that he had lost his cool in front of the director.

As soon as the doors were closed, O'Brien said, "What in the hell is wrong with you?"

"What in the hell is wrong with me?" Nash asked as he pointed to himself and sprang off the wall. "I've slept maybe ten hours in the last five nights, I've got that prick Adams all over me, the *Post* puts this shit on the front page, Mitch is sitting in a cell over in Afghanistan and I go to bed every night and wake up every morning with a headache that feels like someone is shoving a screwdriver through my eye socket, and you want to know what's wrong with me."

O'Brien glanced up at the camera in the corner as a reminder to Nash to watch what he said and then with a clenched jaw said, "You need to calm down."

"And you need to watch my back," Nash snapped back. "That's the deal. I do my job, and you keep idiots like Adams away from me."

"I can't control Adams, and you know that."

"Then don't call me in here and waste my time. I've got more important shit I should be dealing with right now."

"What just happened up there was not my fault. If you had your phone turned on we could have dealt with this in a more timely manner." O'Brien jerked his head in the direction of the camera.

"I know it's up there," Nash snapped. "He's probably watching us right now." Nash turned around and flipped off the camera. "Are you listening, Adams, you prick? There's a third cell out there, buddy, but am I looking for them? Nooooo! I'm here making sure all the forms have been filled out in triplicate and I haven't trampled on some terrorist's rights."

O'Brien pulled Nash's hand down just as the doors opened. He dragged Nash out of the elevator and into the lobby. "Do you have any idea how a guy like Adams operates? He builds his case slowly, over a long period of time, and episodes like this all go into his file." O'Brien pulled him in close and whispered, "And while I understand and agree with all of your frustrations, you are giving the man everything he wants. He'll take this stuff up to those hacks on the Hill and the Justice Department and he'll make you look like a raving lunatic."

"Well, maybe I am," Nash said with a wide-eyed, crazy look.

"Don't say that."

Nash yanked his arm free. O'Brien followed him through security and across the lobby to the main door. When they were outside Nash said, "I'm not kidding."

"About what?"

"Sometimes I feel like I'm going nuts."

"You are not."

Right before they reached the visitors' parking lot, Nash spun around and said, "Then answer me one question. Which side is Adams on?"

"He's on our side."

"Bullshit. Maybe the FBI should investigate his ass. Maybe he's on al-Qaeda's payroll. You ever think of that?"

"I'm done talking about him," O'Brien said, obviously exasperated. "We've got more important things to worry about." The gray-haired O'Brien pointed at Nash's car and said, "Let's take a ride."

Both men climbed into the front seat of Nash's blue Chrysler minivan. Nash started the vehicle and cranked the stereo. The station was tuned to *Elliot in the Morning* on DC101. The host finished abusing a guest and then cut to "Rockstar" by Nickelback.

As the car backed up, O'Brien said, "Please tell me you pulled the plug on this thing."

"It's in the works." There was one loose end, but Nash saw no reason to get O'Brien worked up about something neither of them could control.

"Damage?"

"Damage?" Nash thought about it for a second. "We're fucked. We were on the verge of a couple of breakthroughs. Now we're flying blind just when everything is pointing to something big." He put the van in drive and said, "This couldn't have happened at a worse time."

They turned left out of the parking lot and began winding through the campus. Neither spoke for several moments. They were both, however, thinking the same thing. O'Brien finally asked, "Who leaked?"

"It wasn't me or anyone who works for me."

"You can't be sure of that."

"I'm as sure as I need to be. If I had to put my money on it, I'd say it was someone in your office or some other clown on the seventh floor."

O'Brien laughed. "You're a dandy."

"How so?"

"I think you are going out of your way to piss me off." He reached over and turned the loud music down a bit.

"Well, I'm not really feeling a lot of love and support from your office today."

"Well . . . unless you have some evidence, don't go around blaming my people for this thing falling apart. You'll get a reputation as one of those needy field guys who never gets enough support."

Nash sighed in frustration. "Don't turn this back on me. I've got a tight group, and I'm telling you, not a one of them would narc us out."

"And I'm telling you to take another look at them, from top to bottom, and you need to do it immediately. If the full scope of this thing gets leaked the agency is going to disappear up its own ass."

As they wound around the back side of the massive employee lot, Nash said, "This operation has saved lives."

"It doesn't matter. The FBI will tear our balls off. We've stepped all over their turf."

"The FBI didn't have the balls to put these mosques under surveillance, so we did."

"It wasn't the bureau's fault. It was the Department of Justice who told them no."

"They didn't tell them no. They told them the Judiciary Committee would freak out."

"So back to my point . . . they didn't have the balls to do this, even though it makes complete sense, so we have to step in and do it for them and now it's our asses on the line."

"There are plenty of good people over there who are going to do everything they can to protect us."

"What about Mitch?"

"Ridley is over there right now trying to sort things out."

"And?"

"Listen, this is going to piss you off even more, but Irene says she wants you as far away from this Mitch deal as possible."

"Why?"

"For a couple of reasons, but most importantly, you have to roll this other thing up and you have to do it today. You don't have time to be sticking your nose in this other deal."

Nash took his eyes off the road. "Sticking my nose in it . . . I'm up to my neck in it. Al-Haq wants to strike a deal with us. I had him convinced to come over. You guys need to send me back over there so I can push this thing over the goal line."

"No, and I'm not going to argue with you about this. Irene is adamant. She wants you as far away from this other thing as possible. It will be handled."

"By who?"

"None of your business. Now put it out of your head. She wants you to go see Stan this morning."

O'Brien was referring to Stan Hurley, a retired spook. Nash thought about the crass old operative and his unconventional ways. "Do I have to?"

"Mike, put yourself back at Officer Candidate School. I'm your DI. Look over here at me and imagine I'm wearing that ugly green Smokey the Bear hat and I'm about to bite your head off if you say another word. You're not working for Microsoft. This isn't a debate club. There's shit going on here that she isn't telling me about and she sure as hell isn't going to tell you, so I'm handing down an order and I expect you to carry it out. Do you understand me?"

Nash stared straight ahead. "Yes, sir." He wasn't so sure, based on his current mental condition, that he could handle the notorious Hurley. "Where is he?"

"Bethesda Naval Hospital. I saw him yesterday."

"Is he all right?" Nash was surprised.

"He's fine. He had his hip replaced when you were over in Afghanistan." O'Brien checked his watch. "He's expecting you. Drop me back at the main door. Oh, and one other thing. The Intelligence Committee wants someone up there at two. I'm sending you."

"Come on . . ."

O'Brien looked at him sideways. "Are you done pissing and moaning, Major?"

Nash knew the use of his Marine Corps rank was intended to remind him that a chain of command was still in place. "Yes."

"Good. And no arguing when you get in front of the committee. Keep your temper in check. Don't give them a reason to hate you any more than they already do."

CHAPTER 26

TRIPLE FRONTIER

THE men moved into their final positions thirty minutes before the assault was to begin. So far the morning had gone according to plan. The noises of the jungle masked their movement. Exotic birds sang and chirped, rodents scurried and scratched and a whole host of things living in the trees made the most bizarre noises of all. After more than six months, Karim was finally used to it. Maybe he would miss this place after all. As if on cue, a mosquito landed on his exposed wrist and began drawing blood. *No,* Karim decided, *I will not miss this place.*

After breakfast, which consisted of energy bars and some salty peanuts, he'd given them one more chance to pray. No one complained about the food. They'd grown used to it. They'd packed four days of light rations, just in case something went wrong. Water was the main thing, though. They had plenty of that and purification tablets if they ran out. After breakfast they did a weapons check, and then Karim spent a moment with each man, asking him to recite his duties for the raid. All seven knew what was expected of them.

The planning session the night before had been brief. They were, after all, using the same plan they had already practiced several months earlier. It was a variation on a simple L-shaped ambush. Technically, it was a raid, since they were attacking a fixed position, but the men kept referring to it as an ambush, and Karim saw no sense in correcting them. It was fairly straightforward, with the assault force of four men providing direct fire, and the support force of three providing indirect fire. The only real deviation he made was to position Ahmed three hundred meters down the runway and slightly up the rise, so he could provide cover with his long rifle should anything unexpected occur. He didn't like the idea of retreating, at least not here, for it meant failure, and if they couldn't execute this simple plan, maybe they deserved to die here in this inhospitable place.

As Karim looked through his Trijicon Reflex Sight he wondered yet again if this would really be a test or simply a slaughter. If it went according to plan it would be the latter, and Karim saw no reason why it wouldn't. He was far more nervous about the other part of his plan— the one involving their transportation. It was by far the biggest risk he was taking. There would be dozens of assets waiting for him to make his journey to Mexico City, and he was about to not only disappoint them, but not even tell them what he was up to. Karim had decided the organization had been penetrated and he had neither the time nor the assets to figure out where. The choice was actually simple. Just disconnect himself from the entire organization. The al-Qaeda leadership would have to learn of his exploits in the paper.

With his camouflage-striped M-4 carbine leveled, he looked through the sight at the bunkhouse, a mere thirty meters away. He had one man on his right and two more to his left. They were spaced five meters apart; each man lying on his belly at the edge of the jungle. They'd all applied black and green face paint for the assault. With their camouflage uniforms and floppy hats they were all but impossible to see, even in broad daylight.

The bunkhouse was almost identical to the one they had lived in for months. It was elevated a meter or so off the ground and covered with screens along the sides. The big difference was that these men had sheets along the perimeter of the sleeping area so they could block out the sun. Karim never allowed his men the luxury. They awoke when the sun rose and slept when it went down. Just as Karim had figured, it was almost nine and still no one had emerged to do any work.

He'd figured this thing would go down one of two ways. The first was that they would riddle the bunkhouse with bullets while the men slept. He was hoping it wouldn't come to that. He'd spent the better part of a year teaching these men to carefully pick their targets. To have them simply hose down a building blindly was beneath them. He'd considered planting a bomb under the structure, but he had to balance that against his desire to keep things quiet. Not that he expected anyone to stumble upon them or come to the aid of the drug runners. He didn't, but he wanted this first engagement to be as perfect as possible. He wanted it to last no more than twenty seconds, and he wanted it to be totally silent.

That was the interesting thing about guns. For those who had never experienced combat, the loud report of a rifle did funny things to the body. Time would stop, fear would grip the brain, and the body would be stuck in a moment of limbo that was usually followed by panic. To those who were used to the noise, though, the reaction to gunfire was instantaneous. Find the source and return fire, and good soldiers could do it within seconds. Karim wasn't going to give them that chance. He was going to draw them out. The plane would fly over once at nine, buzzing the strip. He was confident that would wake the men from their slumber and draw them outside. With or without guns, it did not matter. Their attention would be directed skyward. They would never notice the four men concealed to their right or the other three behind them.

At ten minutes before the hour, Karim heard someone stirring within the bunkhouse. A moment later a man appeared. He stumbled down the wood steps and relieved himself right there next to the building. When he was done he walked over to the well and stuck his head under the faucet. After he'd doused most of his face and upper body with cold water, he stumbled over to the open-air warehouse where they stored their drugs. He disappeared between two pallets of neatly wrapped cocaine and then reappeared a moment later, wiping the white powder from his nose. He moved around the other side of the building and Karim lost sight of him. A short while later, he heard a churning noise. It was very mechanical. Suddenly, there was a loud rumble and a plume of dark smoke belched into the air. Then came the unmistakable rumble of a diesel engine revving. It was the tractor.

Karim's thoughts lurched backward to the previous evening. It had been Ahmed—no, that was not right, it was Fazul who had mentioned it. They were talking about how lazy these men were and that it was a rarity to see anyone emerge from the bunkhouse before noon. Fazul said that on one occasion he had seen a man grading the runway with the tractor well before noon. The conversation quickly moved in a different direction. Karim was now struck with the horrible visual of the plane turning away because the tractor was blocking the runway.

The gears ground together and a howling clutch shattered the calm morning air. All of this racket would undoubtedly wake the others. Karim thought of them stumbling out of the bunkhouse one at a time, spreading themselves around the compound. He couldn't allow it. He needed to keep them together. If they spread out, things would get very complicated.

The tractor lurched into view. Karim moved his rifle to the right and put the red dot of his sight on the man's head. He was approximately eighty meters away. Karim had the shot. He knew no one else would take it unless he ordered them to do so. He had been specific about that, "No one shoots until I give the word."

The soft pad of Karim's right index finger moved onto the curve of the trigger. He began to increase the pressure and then thought of a better solution. Each man was wearing a headset that was plugged into a digital radio. Before heading out this morning they had all placed them in transmit mode and checked to make sure they were working. "Ahmed," Karim whispered into his thin mouthpiece.

"I see him."

"Do you have a shot?"

"Yes."

"When he gets to the runway, before he makes his turn, shoot him in the head."

"Yes, sir."

Karim had no illusion that the man would keep his foot on the gas after he was hit. He wouldn't. The silenced Heckler & Koch PSG-1 would fire the 7.62x51mm NATO cartridge and would likely separate the man from the tractor in a very violent way. Karim was hoping the momentum of the tractor would carry the vehicle clear to the other side of the runway. If not, they would have to move it themselves.

As Karim was watching the tractor through his sight, he was startled by the loud noise of a screen door slamming shut. Not wanting to move the rifle, he slowly lifted his head from behind the sight and scanned to the left. There, standing at the base of the steps, was a second man wearing nothing more than a pair of dirty white underwear. He was facing Karim, underpants pulled down, eyes closed, holding his pecker in his hand, relieving himself. His eyes suddenly opened, and for a moment he seemed to stare right at Karim's position. Then his head snapped around and craned skyward.

It took Karim a second to realize that the man must be looking at an incoming plane. Surrounded by the thick undergrowth, Karim had yet to hear the plane, but he knew it had to be what the man was looking at. The man began barking orders in Spanish and darted back into the bunkhouse before Karim could make a decision. A moment later the man reappeared, this time in a pair of jeans, a rifle in one hand and a T-shirt in the other.

The man took a dozen long strides toward the warehouse and then stopped. Karim could hear the plane now. Based on how loud it sounded he guessed it was nearing the far end of the runway. Karim didn't like the fact that the man was moving away from the bunkhouse, but the situation was still manageable. Then unexpectedly the man raised his rifle and aimed it down the length of the runway. At that same moment the screen door slammed again. Karim didn't bother to see who or how many men just left the bunkhouse. The thought of the man firing on the plane forced his hand.

Karim maneuvered the red dot onto the man's head and kept both eyes open. He didn't wait for the man to fire his weapon. He knew it would cause the others to grab their own rifles and come running out, possibly more alert and ready to fire. This thing had played itself out as far as he was willing to let it go. It was time to abandon the perfect plan and get to the killing.

Karim was a good shot, one of those guys who didn't have to put a lot of thought into it. The technology helped, of course. More and more it was like a video game. Put the red dot on the person and squeeze the trigger. Never pull it, always squeeze. Don't make it more difficult than you need to. He placed the dot directly in the center of the back of the target's head and put a smooth, even squeeze on the trigger. The .233 round spat from the end of the silencer. The weapon jumped an inch and then the big square viewfinder came back to level, just in time to see a cloud of pink mist erupt from the man's head.

"Fire," Karim said, as he moved his rifle back toward the bunkhouse. Just as he was putting his next target in the crosshairs the man went down. At the same time the plane screamed in low overhead. With both eyes open, Karim saw there were two more men, but by the time he could get to either of them they were both taken care of. By his own count five men were outside and that left two more inside. As per the plan, the men switched to fully automatic and began pumping rounds into the bunkhouse. Karim expended his first thirty-round magazine and moved to reload. That was when he noticed someone screaming from inside the bunkhouse.

Without hesitation Karim chambered a fresh round and stood so he could shoot level with the floor of the bunkhouse. The other seven men did the same. They marched out of the jungle, closing in from two sides until they were no more than ten meters from the structure. Karim burned through another magazine and paused to look at his men. They were firing away, sweeping their rifles back and forth, taking care of their assigned areas. He was proud of their discipline. Two perfect skirmish lines doing exactly as he had told them. The opponent may have been weak, but his men had performed exactly as instructed. He felt great pride in how far they had come, and allowed himself for one brief moment to think of the legendary status he would obtain after he had struck at the heart of America.

CHAPTER 27

BETHESDA NAVAL HOSPITAL

NASH caught the tail end of rush hour as he crossed the Chain Bridge. The Little Falls to the north wasn't so little. Heavy spring rains had the Potomac as swollen as he'd seen it in years. For all of the things that were wrong with Washington the vistas were not one of them. Nash rolled down his window and listened to the roar of the rapids. His headache eased a bit. When he reached the far bank his thoughts turned to Stan Hurley. The man was everything that epitomized the old CIA. An outsider might think it odd that Hurley, at seventy-eight, and officially retired from Langley for nearly thirty years, was on the mind of the CIA's director on this media-crazed morning.

For those who knew Hurley, however, it was far less a surprise that Kennedy had ordered Nash to go see the old man. In the business world, there is a top cadre of lawyers that high-powered people turn to when they get in trouble. These lawyers are experts at manipulating the system, and working behind the scenes to make their clients' problems simply go away. In the insular world of espionage, Stan Hurley was such a man. Brave, brash, and although one would never know by his appearance, fabulously wealthy. Unlike those high-powered law-yers, though, Hurley was as rough as a street fighter from the South Side of Philly.

He was a man who could, with a simple expression, send a chill down your spine, or bring a tear to your eye. There was no one else quite like him. Nash supposed Rapp was the closest thing he'd ever encountered, but Rapp was more of a single-minded force of talent and sheer determination. Hurley was whatever the situation dictated. He was a magician, an entertainer, a philosopher, an assassin, and a man with passions that at times could seem insatiable. He was without question the most colorful person Nash had ever met. He somehow always found a way to bring out in you the things you least wanted to discuss. This was both his gift and his curse. He forced you to confront your problems.

As Nash worked his way through the District toward Maryland, he asked himself what it was that Kennedy felt Hurley could do to solve his crisis. He either knew something that could help him out, or he had an idea that would more than likely keep him awake at night. That was another thing about Hurley. He was old-school and was not above using the most unsavory tactics to win his battles.

Hurley made him nervous and Nash wasn't afraid to admit it. It wasn't that he didn't like the man. He absolutely did. His wife adored him, his kids got a kick out him, and Nash himself couldn't help rever-ing some of the man's accomplishments in the world of espionage. But the two men had chosen significantly different paths in life. Nash didn't like the fact that, with everything that was going on this morning, Ken-nedy wanted him to see Hurley. Hurley was the emergency brake. The ejection handle. The guy they went to when the options were slim and the problem was big.

It could be that Kennedy was losing her nerve, or, more accurately, her calm. There was no denying the fact that she had changed since the attack on her motorcade in Iraq the previous fall. She had been an extremely intelligent and capable boss who under the right circumstances might crack a smile, but would never under any circumstances show anger. Her patience, more than anything else, had amazed him. She was surrounded by passionate field operatives like himself, O'Brien, Ridley, and Rapp. Cowboys who were not afraid to speak their minds in a very forceful and sometimes uncouth manner. Even with all the big egos and big dicks speaking their minds, she'd keep her cool.

Things had changed since the abduction, though. She was far more prone to letting her displeasure be known, and her hallmark patience was all but gone. The thing that worried Nash the most was her new aggressive behavior. For years Nash and Rapp had been pushing for bolder operations. It was Kennedy who challenged their every idea and dissected their every move. She would patiently listen to their often harebrained schemes and then methodically shred their plans and expose the myriad of pitfalls. Her constant pushback made them sharper and their plans better. The ones that truly sucked never got off the ground, thanks to Kennedy's ability to extrapolate—to look at things from every conceivable angle and project them to the end.

Those days seemed to be gone. She was no longer challenging them. Nash feared that the war had gotten personal for her, and in her zeal to take the fight to the enemy, she was making careless decisions. Things were out of balance, and Nash couldn't shake the feeling that some eight-hundred-pound gorilla was about to jump all over him. He'd seen far too many good men and women get caught in Washington's incessant political cross fire. Real lives and national security were trashed for political and personal gain, and it was never pretty.

Nash pulled up to the main gate at the National Naval Medical Center and flashed his government badge. The guard signed him in and waved him through. After parking in the visitors' lot, Nash began what ended up being a twenty-minute search for a seventy-eight-year-old man who was supposedly laid up after his surgery. Nash eventually found him sitting in a wheelchair under a shady tree with a well-fed nurse fawning over him.

Nash's first observation was that the two looked a little too cozy. As he approached, he saw Hurley reach out and place his hand on the nurse's ample upper thigh. The nurse playfully slapped his hand away and started giggling.

Anyone else, Nash might have been surprised, or thought he was reading more into it than was wise, but not with Hurley. The man was a legendary pussy hound. He loved women and he loved to chase them. Eight feet away Nash stopped and cleared his throat. "I hope I'm not interrupting something."

D.C. had thousands of federal law enforcement officers who worked for everyone from the FBI to the U.S. Postal Service. Many of them fit a pretty basic description. Short hair, athletic build, dark, boxy suit, and bulges on each hip—one from mobile phones and the other from a government-issue sidearm. Mike Nash fit the bill perfectly.

Nash watched the nurse blush and said, "Miss, do you know you are associating with a known felon?"

Hurley roared with laughter. "Beatrice, darlin', don't listen to a word this moron has to say. Based on what I read in the paper today, I'm not the one who has to worry about going to jail. Now, honey, why don't you run along and give me a few minutes alone with my friend here. But don't go far, I want to be able to keep an eye on you. I don't want you flirtin' with any other patients."

"Oh . . ." She slapped him on his good leg. "You are just horrible." The nurse stood and retreated up the path.

"Wait till you get me in bed," Hurley said under his breath. "Then you'll see that I'm downright nasty."

The nurse looked back over her shoulder and asked, "Did you say something?"

"No, darlin'. I was just admiring that gorgeous figure of yours."

Nash unbuttoned his jacket and looked at the nurse's pear-shaped butt. She had to weigh as much as Hurley, if not more. "You are unbelievable."

"Use it or lose it, buddy."

"Yeah, right." Nash sat down on the bench. His shoulders slouched.

Hurley looked at him with the eyes of someone who'd spend a life studying people. "Everything all right with Maggie and the kids?"

Oh fuck, Nash thought to himself. *Here we go.* He was afraid to look the old spook in the eyes. There were times like now when he'd swear the man was a mind reader. "Sure . . . everything's great. They love the fact that they've seen me for a total of about eight hours in the last two weeks."

Hurley grabbed a mobile phone out of his robe pocket and pressed a few buttons. The device was equipped with anti-eavesdropping measures to frustrate anyone who might try to listen in on their conversation. "What's going on?"

"You know how it is. I'm flying all over the place, and when I'm not flying and I'm supposed to be with them the damn phone is ringing."

"It's not easy. I fucked up three marriages. Two kids talk to me . . . three don't."

"And then there's all the ones you don't know about."

Hurley nodded. "And then there's those. Shit, I bet I got another half dozen running around."

"At least."

"Who knows?" Hurley got a faraway look in his clear hazel eyes. "God, I had a lot of fun. That's one thing I can never complain about. I bet I bagged more ass than any spy in the history of the country."

"I bet any country. I'm amazed your pecker hasn't fallen off."

"Speaking of peckers . . . is everything okay between the sheets?"

The question caught Nash so off guard he was unable to play it off as nothing. His brain raced off in multiple directions wondering in quick succession; how Hurley could know, was it a lucky guess, did Maggie talk, or was his house bugged? His job was more conducive to fits of paranoia than perhaps any other occupation in the world, and now it had caused his brain to freeze half a second too long. Just long enough for Hurley to notice.

"Kid," the old spook said in a sad voice, "once you stop sleeping with each other, you're screwed."

"Okay, Yogi."

Hurley scooted forward, ignoring the reference to the great Yankees catcher and all of his upside-down sayings. "Kid," he said, "take those glasses off."

"Why?"

"Because I want to look you in the eyes."

Nash reluctantly took off his glasses.

"You've got the weight of this damn ungrateful country on your shoulders. I know because I've been there."

"You're still there."

"Not anymore. Shit, I was never in as deep as you are. Back in the day I could count on any one of a couple dozen senators and a good fifty congressmen to support what I was doing. And by support I mean a lot more than money. They understood that we had to operate in the shadows. That we were going to get our hands dirty and occasionally shit was going to blow up in our face. This new generation . . ." Hurley shook his head. "They're worthless."

"You're not going to get an argument from me."

"This shit festers. It all gets thrown into the pot whether you want it there or not. It's your own little personal goulash. You might not think one thing is going to affect another, but listen to me when I tell you it does."

"Yeah . . . I know."

"So tell me," Hurley said with genuine concern, "what's wrong with you and Maggie?"

"I didn't come out here to talk about my marriage."

"I know you didn't, but right now you're one of my starting pitchers and I need you to get your head screwed on."

"My arm feels great."

"Bullshit. I spoke with Irene before you got here."

"So?"

"She told me you lost your cool in front of Glen Adams."

"Big deal."

"She said Adams already filed an official complaint claiming that you physically assaulted him."

"All I did was grab him by the arm."

"You need to act like a professional. Especially around clowns like Adams."

Nash looked across the lawn and nodded. "Message received. What else?"

"I called Maggie."

"You called my wife?" Nash said in shocked voice.

"Yes. I've been hearing rumblings that you haven't been yourself lately, so I called her up. She's worried about you."

"She's always worried about me. Who wouldn't be?"

"Listen to me," Hurley said with a biting intensity. "We've got a lot in the offing right now, and you've got a ton of crap you need to attend to, so I'm going to cut through all the bullshit and put my cards on the table. I know you've had some difficulty raising the old flagpole lately . . ."

Nash didn't hear another word. He felt as if he'd just been tossed into a deep, dark pit. His own personal hell here on earth. This conversation was out of bounds in so many ways, all he could manage to say was "We're not going to talk about my personal life." Nash started to stand, but before he got far, Hurley reached out and with surprising strength yanked him back down.

"Yes, we are, and so help me God, if you so much as raise your voice at Maggie, I'll kick the piss out of you. You need to get your head screwed on and that means you need to make love to your wife and you need to do it quickly, boy. You're a goddamn ace. You know what an ace gets paid in the majors? The good ones are pulling in twenty million a year. How do you think those guys would perform if they got up on that mound and knew they couldn't get a hard-on? They'd get shelled. Their confidence would be shot."

"Stan, I hardly see what . . ."

"Just keep your piehole shut for a minute, junior. This job fucks with your head bad enough, you throw something like this on top of everything else and you can become a liability real quick."

"I'm fine. It was a onetime thing."

"Then explain to me how you let some worthless suit like Glen Adams get under your skin this morning, because that's not the Mike Nash I know. The Mike Nash I know would never lose control like that."

As much as Nash hated to hear it, he knew Hurley was a little too close to the truth. With more attitude than was wise he asked, "So your point is?"

"My point is, numbnuts, that while you are diddling around with your dick, Rome is burning. That's the problem with this whole country. Fucking vast prosperity. No one has any real problems anymore. Ninety percent of the damn politicians in this town either think there's no war on terror, or if we'd just be nice to these zealots they'll leave us alone. Well, that ain't going to fucking happen. The Huns are circling, and we're sitting around arguing about gay rights and prayer and guns and global warming and all kinds of bullshit. These idiots will eventually wake up to the threat, but by then it might be too late." Hurley looked over both shoulders to make sure no one was nearby and then said, "You need to get laid, boy, and then you need to find out who in the hell is leaking your operations to this fucking reporter at the *Post*, and you need to put a bullet in his head."

"Come on, Stan. You can't be serious."

"About which part?"

"I'll take care of my love life, all right? Let's just take that one off the table."

Hurley ran a hand over his wrinkled face and said, "Kid, if someone at Langley is leaking shit to reporters, they're a traitor, and traitors in our business get taken out back and shot. At least they used to until all these PC pussies got involved and everyone lost their nerve."

"You want me to kill a fellow employee of the CIA?" Nash asked in near disbelief.

"You've killed plenty of men before. Don't tell me you're losing your nerve."

"I've never killed a fellow American."

"Well don't think of them as an American. Think of them as a traitor who is exposing an intelligence operation that has done more to protect this country than anything else we've done around here in a good twenty years. And now we've got confirmation that a third cell is out there. What the fuck do you want to wait around for? You want a grade school full of kids to be taken hostage and slaughtered? You want to see a damn mushroom cloud over the Capitol?"

"No." Nash shook his head. These were the nightmares he'd lived with since 9/11.

"Then get your head screwed on, and get out there and get these fuckers before they get us."

CHAPTER 28

BAGRAM AIR BASE, AFGHANISTAN

LELAND walked through the mess line sliding his tray along as he went. Since he couldn't use his right arm he chose the pasta Alfredo over the meat, which was difficult to cut even with two good hands and a sharp knife. He skipped the salad bar, grabbed a piece of blueberry pie, and then came the hardest part of all. He turned and looked out across the huge dining hall. This part was never fun, trying to find an open seat, preferably next to someone he actually liked.

The place was barely a third full. Leland looked around for a familiar face but found none. He was usually on duty at this time, but Garrison had given him the night off. Not feeling like making small talk, he picked an empty table, set his tray down, and headed over to the beverage station. He grabbed a glass and filled it with ice and then Diet Coke. Back at the table he sat and took a sip. He thought about his CO and the advice he had given him—to wait forty-eight hours before writing his official report.

Leland was tempted to go over Garrison's head on that point alone, but he didn't know whom he could trust. The whole thing was wrong on so many levels, his head ached just thinking about all the compromises he was being asked to make. And then to make matters worse, Garrison had asked to have a word alone with him. Off the record. Academy grad to academy grad. The words stung him more than the brutality he'd suffered at the hands of the fascist from the CIA. Garrison told him that he had a reputation for being difficult. And it wasn't just his assessment; the previous CO felt the same way. He'd already been passed over once for promotion to major. Garrison explained to him that it came down to the fact that he was not liked by either his superior officers or those he commanded.

Garrison very firmly told him if he ever wanted to live up to his abilities and become a flag officer, he was going to need to stop being such an inflexible prick. *The audacity,* Leland thought, *to turn this into a popularity contest.* It flew in the face of everything they'd been taught. This was not high school. Promotions were not based on popularity. They were at war, and during combat it was about results. Talent and results. Who could get things done, and Leland got things done.

There were a couple of ROTC guys who were his same age who had received the bump. Leland took it personally, and wrote it off to the fact that his CO didn't like him, and here he was again with another CO who didn't like him.

Leland stabbed his fork into the creamy noodles and found a piece of chicken. He tried to twirl the fork, but couldn't. He was self-conscious due to his lack of dexterity and looked around to make sure no one was watching him. Satisfied he was safe, he leaned forward and shoveled a forkful into his mouth. He could feel a dab of creamy cheese sauce on his chin and grabbed a napkin. As he wiped his chin, he thought of his previous CO. The man was not an academy grad, so the fact that he didn't like Leland was understandable. Leland had always felt there was a strong animosity in the officer ranks among those who had learned their skills at lesser institutions. Garrison, however, was an academy grad. *Was he one of those officers who bent over backward not to show favoritism?* Leland wasn't sure, but he was thinking that was more than likely the case. Either way, the man was not living up to the standards and ideals of a commanding officer.

The whole situation was so entirely wrong, Leland felt almost disembodied. His wrist throbbed, his eye ached, but worst of all, his honor had been assaulted. Bending the rules was one thing, but this was far worse. These men were snapping, breaking, and trashing the very rules that were the backbone of the United States Air Force. Leland had never felt so isolated, even during the horrible hazing he'd suffered at the academy his freshman year. None of it was fair. He'd done everything by the book. He deserved his promotion to major, but he didn't want it this way. He wanted his talent and effort to be recognized. He told himself that on a much deeper, selfless level, he wanted justice. The offer of any posting and being fast-tracked for colonel was nothing more than a bribe. Did they really think him so unprincipled?

Leland wasn't paying close enough attention to his food and he ended up dumping most of a forkful down the front of his uniform. He swore to himself and set the fork down. As he went to wipe his uniform he heard laughter from a nearby table. He looked up to see a major and two nurses laughing at him. He knew the major well enough to dislike him. His name was Cliff Collins. He was a graduate of the University of North Dakota Air Force ROTC program. He was athletic, handsome, witty, and far too full of himself. In fact, he was pretty much the poster child for what was wrong with the promotion boards. In Leland's opinion, the man was proof that it was more about being popular than having talent.

The stress of the last few days had worn away his patience. He glared at Collins and said, "You find this amusing, Major?"

"Sorry, Captain," Collins said with an insincere grin.

"You don't look very sorry, Major." Leland fixed a laser stare on the man.

Collins changed his expression as well, the jovial smile vanishing.

"I'm glad you find humor in another man's pain," Leland added.

Collins nodded. Seemed to hesitate for a second and then said, "Yeah . . . well, it couldn't have happened to a nicer guy. Enjoy the rest of your meal, Captain. Ladies, let's go catch the movie." Collins and the two women got up and left.

Leland silently watched them leave, his insides slowly turning over, his gut twisting tighter and tighter. *What did he mean by that? Did Collins know what happened, and if so, how many others knew?* Leland felt his face flush with anger. Military bases were as filled with gossip as an American high school. The thought of others whispering about this behind his back made him want to vomit. *They were all so undisciplined.* Leland thought of something that had been given to him back at the academy. It was a guide that he went back to from time to time, to help remind him of who he was and what it all meant.

He left the tray on the table and headed straight back to his room. It was located near the bottom of his footlocker and after a few minutes he found it safely tucked away in the pages of his King James Bible. Leland looked down at the Little Blue Book and read the words aloud. "United States Air Force Core Values. Integrity first. Service before self. Excellence in all we do." The words still had heft after all these years. If anything, they meant more to him today than when he'd first read them as a cadet more than ten years ago. Why couldn't General Garrison understand their importance? Leland continued to scan the pamphlet that had been given to him back at the academy. He found the quote he was looking for on the second page.

It read:

In 1965 I was crippled and was all alone (in a North Vietnamese prison). I realized that they had all the power. I couldn't see how I was ever going to get out with my honor and self-respect. The one thing I came to realize was that if you don't lose your integrity you can't be had and you can't be hurt. Compromises multiply and build up when you're working against a skilled extortionist or manipulator. You can't be had if you don't take the first shortcut, of "meet them halfway," as they say, or look for that tacit deal, or make that first compromise.

—*Admiral James B. Stockdale*

Leland ran his fingers over the words and recited them again, this time with tears in his eyes. When he was done he told himself that he would not take the first shortcut. He would not meet them halfway. He would not make that first compromise. He would stand up to them. He would show them what it was like to live life with integrity and honor.

He closed the booklet, placed it back in his Bible, and began reviewing his options. If he did not handle this properly, he could easily ruin his career. If done the right way, though, this could catapult him to great heights. But where to go first? He was isolated on this base, thousands of miles from those who were most sympathetic to his cause. Whom could he call? Whom could he turn to? There was the Office of Special Investigations, of course, but that presented a whole other set of problems. A great many people would think of him as a rat, and the old boys' club that still ran the air force would likely never trust him again. His name would forever be attached to the scandal that was sure to follow. He needed someone else to blow the whistle. To sound the alarm and show him as the true victim in this travesty of justice.

Leland paced nervously from one end of his small room to the other. He went through a mental list of all the commanding officers he'd had and none of them fit the bill. *Who would be willing to lock horns with the CIA?* Leland asked himself. He suddenly stopped, thought back to earlier in the week, and said, "Of course."

Leland raced over to the tiny desk he shared with a fellow officer. He moved a stack of magazines and a pile of opened envelopes and letters and pens and junk and then finally, there it was. A beautiful embossed card with a gold eagle smack in the center. Leland snatched the card off the desk and held it up as if it were a winning lottery ticket. He ran a finger over the embossed name and wondered if the person would remember him. After a brief moment Leland decided he would. This was his way out. He would call Washington and sound the alarm and then that arrogant imbecile would have to answer for what he'd done.

Leland grabbed one of his prepaid phone cards that had been sent in a care package and then tried to think of the safest place to make the call from. It was mid-morning in Washington. Probably the best time to call. Leland started for the door. For the first time in days a smile spread across his face. As he raced down the hallway he thought of Rapp and said to himself, "We'll see how smug you are after I'm done with you. You're going to wish you'd never laid a hand on me."

CHAPTER 29

TRIPLE FRONTIER

I T was fast approaching noon. The sun high in the sky. The valley turning into a soupy mix of heat and humidity. Karim waved away a large bug that almost flew up his nose and then mopped his brow with a drab olive bandana. He looked over at the white and blue plane. It was a Basler BT-67. Basically an old DC-3 that had been refurbished with two Pratt & Whitney turboprop engines and a new skeleton and avionics. It sat a mere fifty feet from the ramshackle warehouse, its two propellers glistening in the sun.

The tractor had been retrieved from the edge of the jungle, and the bucket had been removed and replaced with a set of forks. The two pallets of cocaine were then eased out of the warehouse and positioned as close to the plane as possible. Four of Karim's men formed a line, passing the bricks of cocaine to each other and into the cargo hold. They'd been working steadily for an hour. One pallet was loaded and they were about halfway through the second one. Unlike the men they had just killed, these men worked without complaint and were far more efficient at their task.

Karim glanced at his watch and thought about the pickets he'd placed on the two main trails. It had been nearly thirty minutes since they'd last checked in. He thumbed his radio and asked for a situation report. They both reported back that the trails were quiet. Karim felt his chest tighten and his pulse quicken. He was caught in a no-man's-land between two conflicting thoughts. The first was that he simply wanted to get out of this horrible place, and the second was that he hated to fly. New engines or not, this plane looked to be of a very old design. His friend Hakim had told him that it was indeed an old design. Nearly a hundred thousand of them had been made in the 1930s and then during World War II, but that was a good thing. The fact that they were still being refurbished and flown after all these years was a testament to the plane's simple and robust design.

Karim looked nervously over his shoulder at the plane and wondered if his childhood friend knew what he was doing. Not in terms of flying. He was more than capable of that. Hakim had been flying since he was sixteen. Helicopters, planes, jets, gliders—pretty much anything he could get his hands on, and besides, he'd got the thing here and landed it with only one tiny bounce. Karim's more immediate concern was how they were loading the plane. He didn't know much about such things but it seemed there would have to be a science to it. The two men had met at the age of seven. They lived only a few short blocks away from each other and attended the same school. Karim knew that his old friend had many talents, but academic proficiency was not one of them. Hakim had never been a good student, and the thought that he was now trying to load more than a thousand pounds of cargo onto a plane made him extremely nervous.

Karim marched over to the plane and told his men to take a quick five-minute break. All four of them were dripping with sweat and could use a drink of water.

Hakim poked his head out the door, flashing his smile with a slight gap between his top two front teeth. "Karim, you are a genius."

Karim glanced nervously over his shoulder at his men.

Hakim saw the concern and moaned, "When are you going to get over it?"

"Maybe never."

Lowering his voice so the others wouldn't hear, he said, "Then you are a fool."

If any other man had spoken to him this way he would have considered killing him, but it was his old friend so he let it pass. As a devout Muslim he abhorred drugs, but his options were limited.

"I love you like a brother, but you are so naive to the ways of the world."

Karim was proud of the fact that he was naive to such ways. They were ways that led one to stray from the path. Three years earlier he had convinced Hakim to come fight in the holy war and the two had made the journey to Pakistan together. Only a year out of graduate school, Karim had seen little of the world. Drugs were nonexistent in Makkah, the town where they had grown up. After college his parents had tried desperately to find him a wife with the hope that it would prevent him from running off and fighting in Afghanistan or Iraq. In his mind Iraq was never a consideration. The Muslim world was a better place without Saddam Hussein, and he did not want to give his life fighting for Baath party thugs so they could once again turn on their Saudi neighbors and repress their fellow Muslims.

So it was off to Pakistan to join the fight with al-Qaeda and the Taliban. Karim had prepared himself for all of the mental and physical challenges, but he could never have guessed the role that the heroin trade played in the struggle. Opium was everywhere. It was cultivated and collected and sold and distributed. Many of the foreign fighters were addicted to it. For them it was the best way to cope with the hardship of the mountains and fighting an unseen enemy who could strike at you from over the horizon any time, day or night. For the Taliban it was their lifeblood.

Karim did not worry that he would fall under the spell of the highly addictive heroin, but he worried about his friend Hakim. Even more troubling, though, was the complete lack of judgment by the al-Qaeda leadership. That they would lower themselves to the status of common drug dealers was beyond belief. That they would so willingly participate in something that the prophet was so against was an affront to their very faith, and it deeply affected his willingness to volunteer on their behalf.

Karim looked at the half-loaded pallet, shook his head sadly, and said, "I don't know if he will forgive us for this."

"Oh," Hakim moaned, "there are times when I would like to choke you." He jumped out of the plane and walked over to the pallet, where he picked up one of the bricks. "Do you have any idea how much this is worth?"

"You told me if we were lucky we could get a million dollars for it."

"Yes," laughed Hakim, "but you never said there would be this much. You were talking about loading several duffel bags. This . . ." Hakim backed away, held out his hands, and spun in a circle. "This is worth . . . I'm not even sure . . . ten million, maybe more."

Karim could not hide his surprise. "Ten million?"

"Yes. Maybe more."

"I had no idea . . ."

"Now how do you feel about drugs?" Hakim grabbed his friend and put his arm around his shoulder. "I told you this would work. Think of what you can do with that type of money. You will never again have to ask them for permission. You will be able to fund and run your operations."

Karim smiled ever so slightly. He would never forget what his friend had told him nearly two years earlier while they were sitting by the campfire one night. Karim had been in a particularly pious mood that night and was angry with Hakim for spending too much time with the drug-dealing Afghanis. The argument had started with a simple premise on Hakim's part: How was opium any different from oil? Karim was shocked by the stupidity of the question, but not for long. Hakim stated his case very clearly, that opium was a resource no different than any other commodity. When Karim tried to argue that oil did not destroy people's lives, Hakim had laughed at him. What good had all of the oil profits done Saudi Arabia? They had discussed this many times while in college. That oil was corrupting their country. Hakim furthered his point by saying that Karim was a hypocrite. That he willingly took oil money to wage their jihad, but somehow the profits from the local crop were not good enough for the cause.

That night they had gone to bed as mad at each other as they had ever been, but later Karim began to ask himself what Allah would want. He wanted them to win, that was for certain, but at any cost? Karim wasn't sure, but as the al-Qaeda and Taliban leadership proved increasingly inept, he'd been looking for other ways. Other avenues to carry the fight to the enemy without the aid of al-Qaeda. Karim left them not long after that. He wanted to make his own money. Money he would never be able to make in Saudi Arabia, for there was no upward mobility. The royal family and their friends had a monopoly on power and wealth.

When Karim laid eyes on the airstrip and the drug operation the first person he thought of was Hakim. Over the next month he thought more and more about having a backup plan and isolating himself from al-Qaeda. In a coded e-mail he sent the idea to Hakim, who immediately embraced it. When the other two cells disappeared, Karim made up his mind that he would have Hakim fly them out.

"This is a very good day, Karim."

"Yes, it is."

"Are you going to smile? At least show you are happy."

"Allah likes us to be humble."

"Allah also wants you to be happy and today is a day for you to be happy."

Karim allowed himself a brief smile, and then he remembered what lay ahead. His expression turned solemn and Hakim asked him what was wrong. Karim looked at his men, sitting on the ground, drinking from their canteens. Within a week or two they would all be dead. Those perfect young bodies so full of life would be smashed and broken. Probably riddled with bullets. His only consolation was that they would make America feel pain. Real fear, and then there would be the second act and the third and the fourth. After their success, many more would step up to take their place. They would hit America with wave after wave. He would lead a real jihad. Not one grand attack and then sit back and do nothing. The current leadership of al-Qaeda disgusted him.

"What is wrong?" Hakim asked.

"When we begin killing Americans, I will allow myself to smile. Until then, there will be no celebration."

CHAPTER 30

WASHINGTON, D.C.

N ASH hopped on the Beltway and circled back around the city in a counterclockwise motion. He'd made three seemingly random stops: a gas station, a coffee shop, and a drugstore. Both his phones were turned off and the batteries removed. The internal GPS computer on the minivan had been disabled long ago. This way if they ever tried to pull his records there would be no record of his stopping at these various locations every week. In the immediate aftermath of the attacks on New York and D.C., none of this had been necessary. In Saudi Arabia and Syria, yes. He was used to being followed when he operated over there, but not here in America.

When they'd decided to launch their own operation in America, though, everything changed. For political reasons, the FBI wasn't exactly thrilled with the idea of sending deep-cover operatives into mosques. The idea had been suggested by many people, more times than anyone could count. The folks at the bureau knew it was the right thing to do in terms of national security, but they also knew whoever signed off on it would be crucified up on the Hill, so the bureau found a middle ground. Their solution was to stay out of the mosques and instead focus on Muslim charities. It was a good start and early on they had a lot of success, especially on the money side. That's what the bureau was really good at. They could investigate the hell out anything. Throw a hundred bright and motivated agents at a problem and inhale it. Collect every little bread crumb until they'd pieced together an amazing picture of what was going on.

With the charities, they found out that a lot of these seemingly innocuous organizations were actually fronts for more militant terrorist groups like Hezbollah, Hamas, and al-Qaeda. Just like organized crime, the groups adapted. They changed the way they did things and slowly withdrew behind the walls of their mosques, and the FBI stopped at the imaginary line. A line shrouded in the First Amendment. The right to practice one's religion, to say what you'd like, and associate with whomever you saw fit. They'd beat this one to death—"they" being all of the men and women who staffed the National Counterterrorism Center, or NCTC. The nerve center of the fight against terrorism in all its emerging forms.

The few who dared to speak out said that this was not about the First Amendment. The decision to stay away from the mosques was political correctness at its apogee. It was a fear of being painted bigots for spying on minorities practicing a minority religion, and it was born out of the illogical, emotion-based, feel-good philosophy of the sixties. Because Islam was different, they dared not criticize it. One of Nash's counterparts at the FBI summed it up best one time when he said, "If four abortion clinics were blown up tomorrow, killing hundreds of people, and a group of white men who were all part of a Southern Baptist antiabortion group took credit for the attacks, do you think we would hesitate for a second to send undercover agents into their churches?"

The question was never answered. The word came down from on high that they were to continue investigating the charities, but they were to stay away from the mosques. That had been nearly two years ago and that had supposedly been when Kennedy, Stan Hurley, and a few select senators got together and agreed that something needed to be done. They pulled Rapp and Nash in and gave them their walking orders. Everything would be funded off the books. A budget of ten million was provided to start with. The initial million was culled from safety deposit boxes at an old bank in Williamsburg. More was flown in from overseas and not a single receipt was kept. Everything was shredded every step of the way. Kennedy had placed her trust in Rapp and Nash that they would spend the money wisely, and they did. The hardest part had been recruiting the agents. They started with four and hooked them with service to their country and a pile of cash. One million per guy, all tax-free, and they could choose to keep as much or as little of it offshore as possible.

They targeted four mosques. One in Washington, one in Philadelphia, and two in the New York area. They were now up to eight agents, and the intel was pouring in. It was where they'd first learned that al-Qaeda was training commando teams to send to America for coordinated attacks against individuals and infrastructure. The last six months had been an intelligence bonanza. They were steadily connecting the dots of a terrorist network that was being built to help fund and support jihad in America. Two cells had been intercepted and a third had finally been confirmed. And now he was being asked to pull the plug on the entire thing. Roll it up and make it go away. Get ready for the investigation.

Nash pulled through the security checkpoint at the NCTC and parked in the underground garage. He didn't know what he dreaded more, going upstairs or having to go before the Intelligence Committee later in the afternoon. At least with most of the people on the Intelligence Committee he knew where he stood, which was pretty much that he didn't respect three-quarters of them. Upstairs was filled with people he liked. People he respected and people he was going to have to lie to yet again. The internal conflict was wearing on him, which made him think of Hurley and his comments on how it was all tied together.

Nash put his phones back together, turned them on, and headed for the elevators. When the doors opened on the sixth floor, he forced himself to get out. He walked across the carpeted hallway, held his card up against the black pad, and waited to hear the click that would allow him to enter the bullpen. It came and he opened the door and stepped into the big room. Men and women from virtually every federal agency that had anything to do with law enforcement, intelligence gathering, and the military were present. They were sprawled out across the gymnasium-sized room in working pods designed to make them more efficient. On the far wall was a massive screen the size of a neighborhood movie theater. It was flashing images from eight different news organizations.

Nash didn't look at them, but he could feel the hush spread through the buzz of the room and knew that one by one they were turning to note his arrival. Nash had spent much of the day bracing himself for what was about to happen. His voice mail was full, and he hadn't bothered to clear it. He figured he'd wait until he could sit down at his desk and call it up on speakerphone. Besides, the people who really mattered knew not to call that number.

Nash broke left and headed down the side of the room. He passed several glass-walled offices and kept his chin down. He'd made it to within a few feet of his own office when he heard his name barked by an all-too-familiar voice. Nash slowly turned and faced Art Harris. The forty-two-year-old was the bureau's deputy assistant director of their CTC division. He was almost six feet tall, had receding close-cropped hair, and mocha-colored skin. He was extremely fit for a man who spent his days behind a desk.

Harris had one hand resting on the hilt of his 357 Sig and the other held a copy of the *Post*. "You want to tell me what in the hell this is all about?"

"Good afternoon, Art."

"Don't good afternoon me. Explain this."

"There's nothing to explain."

"Bullshit."

Nash pointed at Harris's hip. "Are you gonna draw on me, cowboy?"

Harris, feeling slightly foolish with everyone watching, took his hand off his gun. "Don't change the subject. I asked you a direct question."

"I wasn't aware that I answered to you, Art."

"Don't play games with me, Nash. I'll have your ass transferred out of here by sundown."

"Please do. Although I might miss watching you play wet nurse."

Harris shook the paper. "Stop dodging my question."

"It's all bullshit, Art."

"Fiction?"

"Yep."

"You know I'm no fan of the *Post*. They usually manage to put their little spin on most of the propaganda they put out there, but I don't recall them being in the business of just making shit up whole cloth."

"I don't know what to tell ya."

"How about the truth?"

Nash sighed and said, "Art, I don't know how to say it any other way. I have no idea what that reporter is talking about."

"If I find out that you're lying to me, I'm going to nail your ass to the wall."

"You arrogant prick." Nash took a couple of steps toward Harris. "You gonna start investigating people based on what's printed in the *Washington Post*? Because if that's the case, maybe we should investigate you guys for being a bunch of nutless pussies."

Harris took three quick steps forward and got right in Nash's face. "You want to take this down to the parking garage?"

"You wouldn't stand a chance, and you know it."

"Don't be so sure."

"I'm sure," Nash said as he backed away. "Why don't you call that reporter and find out why he's printing lies about the CIA. Maybe you could indict him for treason." Nash slipped into his office and slammed the door. With a smile on his face, he walked over to his desk and looked down at a printed call list. The damn thing was a page and a half long. His wife had called three times. Nash quickly picked out which ones were the most important and then checked his watch. He had about an hour before he'd have to leave for the command performance with the Intelligence Committee. He would have done almost anything to get out of it, but he knew he had no choice. He'd have to sit there and take their pompous shit, and then lie to them, and thank them for their thoughtful and patriotic stewardship.

CHAPTER 31

SENATOR Lonsdale stared up at the vote total on the board and looked around for someone to choke. She'd waited sixteen years for her party to get control of the Senate, and now with a five-person majority they couldn't even pass a simple spending resolution. She scanned the well of the Senate in search of the majority whip. She'd never liked the little pudd from Illinois and had led a very vocal opposition to his being given the post. Her dark brown eyes zeroed in on him, and she began muttering a few profanities under her breath.

Then, just as quickly as she'd started, she stopped. A placid expression washed over her face as she remembered the admonishment she'd been given by her entire staff a little over a month ago. Something about her looking old, angry, and constipated. It had taken the little pussies two full weeks to work up the courage to tell her that someone had started a Web site dedicated to her declining looks. It had been a full-blown intervention with eight of them filing into her office with a slide show from the Web site. Her chief of staff, Ralph Wassen, who had not been involved in the conspiracy, stumbled upon the intervention and was appalled. Upon seeing several of the enlarged still images of her deeply lined and contorted face, he announced, to the utter delight of all, that she looked like an angry lesbian. Wassen, in addition to being her closest advisor and friend, was also a queen. His sexual preference gave him the cover to say all kinds of politically incorrect things.

As much as it pained Lonsdale to admit it, they were right. It was as if Mother Nature had sucked all the moisture from her beautiful skin and carved deep lines all over her face. That night she'd gone home and looked through a string of recent photographs and was further depressed. It was as if turning fifty-eight had suddenly aged her a full decade. She'd put on at least five pounds, if not ten. She was getting lazy. Lonsdale was not the type to sit around and feel sorry for herself for very long, so the very next day she went on a crash diet, doubled the number of cigarettes she allowed herself from four a day to eight, and began walking and taking the steps every chance she had. She made an appointment with a dermatologist and had already completed two dermabrasion sessions that hurt like hell, but they appeared to be helping.

A month later she'd lost five pounds and was set on losing at least another five. She'd talked to her dentist about getting some veneers for her teeth and was finally convinced it was time to have a little minor face work done. Just around her eyes. None of that Botox stuff, though. She'd come across one too many of those crazy bitches at fund-raisers. They looked like freaks, walking around with that stupid, wild-eyed permafrost expression. She wasn't going to complain to her colleagues about it, but there was no doubt it was much more difficult for a woman to do this job.

As Lonsdale slid her feet into a pair of black pumps, she reminded herself to keep that placid expression on her face. Slowly but surely she was reprogramming herself to be more self-conscious about the faces she made. She stood and grabbed the bottom of her silver jacket, giving it a tug. Down the aisle she went, tucking first her shoulder-length raven black hair behind her left ear and then her right. As she reached the well, she turned right and slowed as she passed her party's leader-ship table.

"Wonderful job, gentlemen," she said with false sincerity. She stopped in front of the senior senator from Illinois and bent forward. With a congenial smile on her face she said, "Get your shit together, Dickie. You're embarrassing all of us."

Lonsdale left the floor and entered the cloakroom. Two of her staffers were waiting for her. A man and a woman, or more accurately, a boy and a girl. The girl had her burgundy leather briefing folder clutched tightly against her perky breasts, and was wearing a short-sleeved ivory cashmere sweater. Lonsdale suddenly resented the wom-an's youth. That and the fact that she was pissed about losing the vote caused her to ask a bit impatiently, "What now?"

The woman, in her early twenties, tilted her briefing folder for-ward and scanned her notes. "You have a photo opportunity with the Pipefitters Union . . ."

Lonsdale listened as her aide spoke excitedly about the day's re-maining events. It was an entirely boring litany, and she unfortunately had no choice but to attend each and every one. The boy stepped for-ward. His name was Trent or Trevor or something like that.

"Wade Kline is waiting for you in your office."

"Which one?" Lonsdale asked, trying to sound uninterested.

"Upstairs."

As the senior female senator in her party, Lonsdale had an office in the Capitol as well as her larger one in the Dirksen Senate Office Building.

"Did he say what he wants?"

"No."

Without wasting another moment, she turned and left the cloak-room. She took one step toward the stairs and then headed for the el-evator. Her heart was beating fast enough over the prospect of seeing her favorite Justice Department employee. She didn't want to show up flushed and out of breath. Paula or Pastel or Pearl or whatever her name jumped into the elevator along with Trent. She waited to see which button her boss pressed. Down meant the tram over to Dirksen and the Pipefitters and up meant the handsome lawyer from the Justice Department. Lonsdale pressed the button for the fourth floor and the aide immediately began pecking an e-mail on her BlackBerry that would alert the rest of the senator's staff that she would be late for the photo op.

Lonsdale's Capitol office consisted of five rooms: a reception area that was staffed by two receptionists, a conference room, a bullpen stuffed with five legislative assistants, a good-sized office for her chief of staff, and a massive office for herself with a veranda that looked out over the Supreme Court, the Russell, Dirksen, and Hart Senate Office Buildings, and Union Station. Lonsdale knew Kline would be waiting in her office. She walked past her receptionists, ignoring their pleas for a word, and she continued straight into her office, closing the door behind her.

Kline didn't bother to stand. He was sprawled out on the leather couch, his suit coat open, his narrow waist and lean chest on display. He looked at the senator from Missouri and said, "You look fantastic. What is that, Donna Karan?"

"It is, as a matter of fact." Lonsdale placed the toe of her left foot out in front of the other foot, bent her knee, and held out her arms, striking an elegant pose. Her silver jacket and matching skirt were accessorized with a black belt, black blouse, and black pumps. She did not look fifty-eight.

"You've lost weight."

"Please." Lonsdale spun and walked over to her desk. She was extremely pleased he'd noticed.

The office looked like a European drawing room with its fifteen-foot gilded plaster ceilings, massive stone fireplace, and large oil portraits of well-fed men from centuries before. Lonsdale opened the top left-hand drawer of her desk and pulled out a pack of Marlboro Lights. She held the pack up for Kline to see.

"Care to join me?"

"Why do you think I'm here?" Kline smiled. "Other than to see you, of course."

The two headed out onto the veranda, like high school kids sneaking a smoke at lunch. It was a gorgeous afternoon. The sun was out, there was a hint of humidity in the air, and the flowers were blossoming. Lonsdale looked into Kline's eyes as he lit her cigarette and she felt herself stir. She looked away and exhaled a cloud of smoke. *It was his damn eyes,* she told herself. They were this crazy blue gray that sucked you right in. If you looked at them for too long you'd begin to think of things that you shouldn't be thinking of in the middle of the afternoon.

"That thing you wanted me to dig into," Kline said as he finished lighting his own cigarette.

The spell was broken, and Lonsdale was momentarily confused. She shook the flustered look from her face. "What thing?"

"These black-bag guys over at Langley. Rapp and Nash."

"Oh, those two," moaned Lonsdale. "Please tell me you're getting ready to indict them."

"I wish, but at the rate things are going, we'll both be retired by the time I actually get a chance to question them."

"They're stonewalling you?"

"I wouldn't even say stonewalling. I can't track them down. For a month straight I've been requesting meetings with them and I've got nothing. I finally got Director Kennedy to show up on Friday. What a coldhearted bitch she is, by the way."

"Not my favorite person in Washington."

"Well, she and I locked horns and it wasn't pretty. I pretty much told her that if she didn't put Rapp and Nash in front of me by this Friday I'd start serving subpoenas."

"And?"

Kline took a drag and shrugged his shoulders. "The woman's a coldhearted bitch. I don't know what to tell you. She just sat there and stared back at me." Kline looked off in the distance toward Union Station and after a moment said, "To be honest, she kind of gave me the creeps."

"How so?"

"I got the impression she'd like to hurt me."

Lonsdale giggled like a little girl.

"It's not funny," Kline said with a frown. "She has a lot of power."

Lonsdale covered her mouth. She was laughing because she herself would like to hurt Kline, but probably not in the way Kennedy would like to. "Sorry . . . I didn't mean to be so insensitive." She reached out and touched his firm bicep. "You're a big boy. I think you're more than capable of taking care of yourself."

"Don't get me wrong. I've put a lot of nasty people away, but these guys are different. They're not your average criminal."

"I disagree. That's exactly what they are, and that's why they need to be locked up."

"Barbara," Kline said in a tone absent frustration, "I am not lacking in conviction. I firmly believe that these guys need to be brought to justice, but ignoring the fact that they are dangerous would be foolish."

"I'll grant you that point, but now is not the time to be timid. This fictitious war on terror has dragged on for far too long. Now is the time to act. Did you see the damn *Post* this morning?"

"Yes."

"You need to get that reporter to sit down in front of a grand jury and tell you who his sources were for that article and then you need to start handing out subpoenas."

Putting reporters under oath would not work. It had been tried by a lot of prosecutors and about all it did was ensure that the reporter would get turned into a martyr and offered a big advance for a book. "It would help," Kline said, "if you could get your committees to put some pressure on them."

"Wade . . . darling, I've tried that, and I will continue to put pressure on them. Nash will be appearing before the Intel Committee this afternoon. A one-front assault against these guys will never work. We need to squeeze them. We need to catch them in their lies."

She watched as Kline looked away. He took a long pull off his cigarette and frowned. "What?" she asked, too impatient to wait for him to
speak his mind.

"The president."

"What about him?"

"I hear he and Kennedy are close. I've even heard he's fond of
Rapp."

"Don't worry about the politics of this thing. That's my arena. Just
get these bastards and make an example of them. Show the American
people that we are a nation of laws." Lonsdale pointed a perfectly manicured fingernail at him and added, "You do that, Wade, and you'll be
able to write your ticket in this town."

CHAPTER 32

CAPITOL HILL

NASH rested both arms on the table and looked up at the nine men and women sitting in judgment. The only good thing about the briefing so far was that six of the members hadn't even bothered to attend—ten, if you counted the four ex officio members—the old-timers who were granted a special status so they could keep a hand in the affairs of one of the more important committees. Nash bet if they were over in Room 216 and the meeting was open to the press, they'd all be there mugging for the cameras, showing their constituents how hard they were working. Feeding their insatiable egos.

But they weren't, they were in the Chamber, one of the most, if not the most, secure rooms on Capitol Hill. There was no ornate seal or gold script announcing to anyone who walked down the hall that this was where the Intelligence Committee met. Just two letters in caps and three numbers—SH 219. The SH stood for Senate Hart, and the 219 for second floor, room 19. The entire space was encased in steel, making it impossible for electromagnetic waves to enter or leave the room. The only people allowed access were committee staffers, the most vetted on the Hill, committee members and only their most senior and vetted staffers and those who were invited to testify or brief. The room itself was more of a suite with smaller rooms for individual briefings and a larger room for the entire committee to sit and hold a hearing in supposed secrecy.

Cell phones, cameras, and digital recorders were collected at the door. What was said in SH 219 was supposed to stay in SH 219, but more and more that wasn't the case. Nash didn't blame it on the Intelligence Committee staffers, he blamed it on the committee members themselves. While most adhered to the rules, Nash and his coworkers felt that at least half of the members leaked secure intelligence on a regular basis. Some of it was the result of idle gossip. They were politicians who were asked to speak to group after group all day long, seven days a week. When you talked that much it was hard to remember what was okay to say and what wasn't. The ones who were really dangerous, though, were the senators who held positions of power within their own party. They drank the Kool-Aid and bought into the idea that the other side was trying to destroy them and therefore it was okay to leak classified information if it made their opponents look bad.

In another time these power brokers would have been hanged or worse, but in this great democracy, this coequal branch of government closed ranks and protected itself. They saw in their opponents the same weaknesses they saw in themselves, so when a scandal broke from within their exclusive little club, they pulled their punches and let their colleague off the hook. But God forbid if anyone else broke the rules.

Nash was grateful that O'Brien had decided to show up. No one was willing to admit it, but Nash knew his colleagues were worried he was coming unhinged and didn't trust him to keep his temper in check in front of the committee. They were right because they were only twenty minutes into the session and he was thoroughly disgusted. Of the nine senators in attendance only two of them could be considered pro-CIA. Six were firmly in the anti-CIA camp and only one of the six independents on the committee had shown up. That part was surprising. They didn't want to sit through all the blustering and threats. The moderates would come in later and read the transcripts or get briefed by one of the committee staffers.

Unless one of the senators had some damaging information, nothing eventful was going to happen today. This was the game they played. The senators asked for the truth. Some of them wanted it and others didn't, but they still asked. O'Brien and Nash would look up at them and lie to the same question asked nine different ways. This was the gray area that had shrunk to almost nothing before 9/11 and had since become huge. The military had tried Don't Ask, Don't Tell, and now the Intelligence Committees had an Ask and Please Don't Tell the Truth policy. At least until the press got ahold of something and then all hell broke loose. Then they were right back to the famous "I'm shocked, shocked to find that gambling is going on in here" scene in *Casablanca*.

"Mr. Nash, there are certain members of this committee who feel that you have been less than forthright with us in the past."

Nash looked back at the senator from Vermont. The man was possibly the worst leaker on the entire committee. "Is that a question or a statement, sir?"

"Both." The man flashed Nash a smile that looked like he wanted to eat him for dinner.

Nash would love nothing more than to tell them he had lied to them, and that they all knew he'd lied to them, and that he knew that they wanted him to lie, because he was keeping them safe, but that wasn't how the game was played. He was in the business of deception and busting up terrorist networks and trying to save American lives. With that in mind, why in the world would he tell the truth to a committee of politicians who overwhelmingly had proven that they couldn't keep a secret to save their lives? But he didn't say that. Instead, he looked back respectfully at the senator and said, "Sir, if you have a more specific question, I would be more than happy to answer it."

"What my esteemed colleague is too nice to say is that he thinks you are a liar."

A minor uproar ensued as several of the committee members objected to the tone of the senator from Missouri. Nash turned and looked at Barbara Lonsdale. She was an attractive woman with deep brown eyes and a tiny little nose. She was always dressed in the latest designer clothes and took great pride in her appearance. At the moment, those beautiful eyes were locked on Nash and her perfectly lined lips were turned ever so slightly upward at the corners. She was obviously pleased that she had upset the decorum of the meeting.

When it had calmed down enough, Nash said, "Madam Senator, do *you* feel that I'm a liar?" Nash felt O'Brien nudge him under the table.

"I am a deliberate person, Mr. Nash, so I will choose my words carefully. I'm one of the members who feel that you have been less than forthright with this committee."

"In other words, you think I've lied to you?"

"If that is the word you would like to use, I am fine with it."

"Madam Senator, I can promise you that this story in the *Washington Post* is completely inaccurate. Why would the CIA launch an operation that is so clearly outside our mandate?"

"It is more than outside your mandate. It is illegal, and I promise both of you if I find out that either of you have lied to me, which I suspect you have, I will make sure you spend as much of your remaining days behind bars as possible."

"Why are we indicting these men over one article written by a newspaper that has shown a consistent animosity toward the CIA? Can anyone answer that question?"

It was Senator Gayle Kendrick from Virginia. She and Lonsdale did not get along, even though they were in the same party. Kendrick was smart enough to understand that one of the largest employers in her state was the CIA and its sister agencies in the National Security sphere. Kendrick also knew that when another attack occurred it would likely affect the people of her state more than those of Missouri.

"I have found in the past," Lonsdale said, "that newspapers like the *Post* are usually the first to break stories like this."

"I'm sorry, I know I haven't served in the Senate as long as you, but I'm a little more suspicious of what I read in the newspapers."

"I have found," shot back Lonsdale in a very authoritative tone, "that the *Post* does not print articles unless sources have been checked."

"And sources have a history of lying. If we're to believe everything that is written in the *Post*, then I'd have to believe you're currently dating a dozen or more of the most powerful men in Washington."

It was Nash's turn to kick O'Brien under the table. He leaned over and whispered, "This is going to be good."

Kendrick was every bit as good-looking as Lonsdale and ten years younger, and she was also faithfully married, or at least appeared to be. It was obvious by the constipated look on Lonsdale's face that Kendrick's jab had hit home. Before anything further happened, though, Ralph Wassen, Lonsdale's chief of staff, entered the room and slid around to whisper in his boss's ear. After a brief exchange, Lonsdale stood and followed Wassen out of the room. Before Nash could think anything of it, the junior senator from Kentucky fired a question at him.

CHAPTER 33

L ONSDALE and Wassen ducked back into her office in Dirksen using her private door so they could avoid the lobby and
anyone who might be waiting for her. As they passed the senator's administrative assistant, Wassen told him to hold all calls. Once inside
her inner sanctum, Lonsdale kicked off her shoes and sat behind her
desk. Wassen took off his jacket and pulled his tie loose. He folded his
jacket once and laid it across the armrest of the long sofa. Returning to
his boss's desk, he held up his hands palms out, but before he could say
anything further Lonsdale silenced him with a look. She opened a
drawer and retrieved cigarettes, a lighter, and a fresh tablet of paper.
She lit the cigarette, dropped the lighter, and grabbed a pen. In the
middle of the page she wrote down Mitch Rapp's name in caps.

"Slower this time," she said. "This major . . . what's his name?"

"Captain . . . Captain Leland. You met him when you were in Afghanistan last week."

"Any reason I'd remember him?"

"No. He's not handsome enough."

"But you remember him?"

"Yes."

"Why?" Lonsdale asked with suspicion.

"It's not what you think."

"It better not be. Because if I get behind this guy and the CIA finds out he's gay and my gay chief of staff is the man he went to, we could have some problems."

"Babs, I have no idea if he's gay or straight. I remembered him because he voiced some concerns to me about the CIA and their interrogation methods."

"He better not be gay."

"I don't see how it matters."

"It probably doesn't, but I want you to find out. You know I hate surprises." Lonsdale took a drag and then exhaled. "And these bastards won't go down without a fight."

"No . . . they most certainly won't."

"Please don't tell me you think I should pass on this?"

"No, I just think you should tread carefully."

"Ralph, according to what you just told me, Rapp assaulted this officer."

"Black eye and a severely sprained wrist. Possible ligament damage. The doctor told him it would have been better if he'd broken it."

"Did the doctor take photos?"

"I don't know. I'm sure he took an X-ray."

"I mean photos of his eye . . . swelling on his wrist . . . that type of stuff."

"I don't know."

"He told you e-mail was the best way to get ahold of him?"

"Yes."

"Send him an e-mail and tell him to take some photos and send them back."

Wassen took a step back and braced himself for his boss's rage. "I'm not sure he'll be willing to do that."

"Why?" Lonsdale asked tersely.

"He doesn't want this to look like he came to us. He wants us to investigate it from our end as if we'd picked up on a rumor."

Lonsdale frowned. "That's silly."

"Not really. Not if he wants to have a career in the air force."

"I think I can call in enough favors with the chairman of the Armed Services Committee to get him any job he wants."

"Posting, Babs. That's what they call it in the military."

Lonsdale ignored him. "We need to get him to make an official statement of some sort. Who do we have over there who we could trust?"

"Babs," Wassen half shouted, "you're not listening to me, and if you knew anything about the military you'd understand why he doesn't want to be the one who comes forward . . . who files an official complaint."

"Ralph, I know this is going to come as a real surprise to you, but I don't give a shit. I have been handed Mitch Rapp's balls on a platter, and I'm not going to let go. You tell this guy he either fills out an official complaint or I'll consider him part of a cover-up."

Wassen rolled his tired eyes. As chief of staff he wore many hats and one of them was to protect his boss from herself. She was a great campaigner, because like Stonewall Jackson she did not possess the ability to retreat. It was always attack and never give the enemy quarter. This, and a few other reasons, was why Wassen often fed her information one bite at a time. That way he at least stood a chance of nudging her in the most thoughtful direction. "There's something else I haven't told you."

"You did sleep with him, didn't you?" Lonsdale's brown eyes were practically bugging out of her head.

"Enough about my sex life, all right? I did not sleep with him and I will never sleep with him, and if you bring it up again, I'm going to throw your stapler at you."

"Fine," she said, as if Wassen were the one who was being unreasonable.

"Have you bothered to stop and ask yourself why Rapp would do something like this?"

"You mean hit another man? I don't need to. He's a homicidal maniac."

"I've warned you, I don't know how many times." A look of real intensity gripped Wassen. "If you are going to take Rapp and Kennedy on, you need to stop underestimating them."

"Would you like to argue the last point?"

"No . . . Rapp definitely has some homicidal tendencies, but I don't think he's a maniac."

"Well . . . let's just agree to disagree for the moment. What's this other thing you have?"

"You haven't bothered to ask why Leland was trying to arrest Rapp."

"Fine . . . why was Leland trying to arrest Rapp?"

Wassen clapped his hands together and got ready to deliver the bombshell. "Remember the two high-value targets we saw while we were over there . . . Abu Haggani and Mohammad al-Haq?"

"Yes." Lonsdale stabbed out what was left of her cigarette. "And I remember leaving specific orders that they were to be treated in exact accordance with the Geneva Conventions."

"Yes, you did, but apparently Mr. Rapp didn't get that memo, because sometime in the early hours of this past Saturday morning, Rapp and several other unidentified individuals arrived at the base disguised as officers from the Air Force Office of Special Investigations."

"You're sure about this?"

"According to Captain Leland. Rapp then went to the special interrogation facility that housed al-Haq and Haggani." Wassen stopped for dramatic effect.

"And?" snapped an impatient Lonsdale.

"He beat at least one of the prisoners and allegedly threatened the other."

"Beat?" asked an excited Lonsdale. "Define beat. Are we talking smacked, kicked, punched . . . be more specific."

"Punched and choked. Apparently there was a lot of blood."

"Please tell me this captain has it on tape." Lonsdale reached for a cigarette and allowed herself a moment of anticipated glory over releasing a tape of Rapp beating a helpless prisoner.

"They can't find the tape. Either Rapp disabled the security cameras or someone has destroyed the tapes."

Lonsdale winced at the setback and took in a deep breath before speaking. "Who else saw what happened besides Leland?"

"The base commander and several MPs."

Lonsdale quickly wrote down a few notes. "And the base commander hasn't filed a report?"

"No, in fact, according to Leland, the base commander and Stephen Roemer, the special assistant to the secretary of defense told him to sit on his official report and wait until he gets the facts straight. They've promised him any posting he'd like."

"Oh . . . this just keeps getting better." Lonsdale set her pen down. "We've got the crime and the cover-up. Now the only question is how I keep this away from the Armed Services Committee and Intel."

"That's going to be tough."

Lonsdale looked back at him. "I'll make it a straight civil liberties issue."

"For Leland?"

"Yes."

"But he doesn't want to cooperate."

"I don't give a shit if he wants to cooperate. I'll compel his ass to cooperate."

"But you need him to get the ball rolling."

"What I need is a couple of hard-nosed special agents to sit him down and get him to make a statement. Where's Rapp?"

"He's on his way back from Afghanistan. I don't know when he's supposed to land."

"One of the CIA planes?"

"I think so. Leland said Ridley went over to pick him up and they left the base this afternoon."

"Ridley is involved in this too?" asked an excited Lonsdale. "Oh, this is just fantastic." Lonsdale wrote down a few more names and then made a big circle around Rapp's. "What about Nash? Wasn't he just over there?"

"I'm not sure. Leland didn't mention him."

Lonsdale tapped her pen and took a long drag. After a good ten seconds she said, "Here's what we're going to do. I want you to find out when Rapp's plane is due to land. Then I want you to get Wade over here. We'll put him out on point for this. As the DOJ's chief civil liberties officer he'll be able to find out who the FBI has at that base and he can order them to track down Leland and take a statement from him. We'll take that statement and give it to Judge . . ." Lonsdale began snapping her fingers. "Who would be a good judge?"

"Broeder. Extremely liberal. He'll love the opportunity to get involved in something like this."

"Good. We'll use him, but we have to keep this really quiet."

"You run the Judiciary Committee. Trust me, Broeder will play ball with us."

"And we'll keep this tight. You, me, Kline, Broeder, and only one staffer. Get Kline over here immediately."

"Right away." Wassen had already stepped over to another phone and was asking one of the people in the outer office to get him Wade Kline.

Lonsdale spun her chair around and looked out the window. She was grinning ear to ear. She could see it all unfolding in her mind's eye. She'd move quietly tonight and then in the morning she would hold a press conference with Kline and drop the bomb on an unsuspecting Washington. Her fellow chairmen on Intel and Armed Services would be furious, but what could they do but get behind her and second everything she would say? This had the potential to be one of the biggest scandals this town had ever seen. It was one for the history books. She'd been warning the president and her colleagues about the CIA for years, and no one had listened. Now they would have to.

CHAPTER 34

CUBA

KARIM stood near the tailgate of one of the pickup trucks and watched as the last of the cocaine was loaded onto the two speedboats. On the flight from the Triple Frontier to Cuba they had stopped in Venezuela to refuel. There, the men got rid of their jungle fatigues and were given civilian clothes. The rifles were stripped down and packed away but the pistols were kept and shoved into the waistbands of jeans and khaki pants.

Karim half expected that when they landed in Cuba their plane would be surrounded, the drugs seized, and they'd be thrown in some hot, humid jail where they would rot for years. Hakim had repeatedly reassured him that everything would be fine. Aiding drug trafficking was a way for the Cuban military to both supplement their dismal pay and stick it to the Americans. Hakim had carefully plotted every step of the journey. He'd spent nearly a half year flying around the region, meeting the right people and gauging whom he could trust. Never did he discuss Islam or the jihad. This was about drugs, something that the United States was far more tolerant of than Islam.

Karim stayed away from the soldiers who had met them at the

airport and ordered his men to do likewise. They could all speak Spanish to a varying degree, but nowhere near as well as Hakim, who was fluent in the language. There were ten of the soldiers. All Cuban army. An officer and nine enlisted men. They were heavily armed, but Hakim had warned him in advance not to be worried. That was simply the way of the Cubans. They carried AK-47s around like most people carried a cell phone. Most of them weren't even loaded. The entire thing made Karim extremely nervous. For a man who was used to being in control, who had to be in control, this was the worst part of the journey. He had to simply trust and leave it to fate.

Hakim and the Cuban officer were smiling and laughing about something. Karim assumed it was that the man now had in his possession three times more cocaine than he had originally been told he would. The officer's take of ten percent was now worth more than a million dollars if he could unload it through the right channels. Hakim had played it perfectly. Every step of the way he had told these people that he was an advance man for a drug cartel which was looking for new trade routes to get drugs into the United States. If they knew this was a onetime deal, Hakim feared they would simply take the drugs and throw them in jail or worse. Hakim talked a big game. He told them they were not interested in a onetime deal. They were looking for partners who could help them build their business. They were going to test several routes and then begin running shipments every two to three weeks. With those kinds of numbers, any man who was not grounded in his religion would be tempted.

The Cuban officer and Hakim were now saying good-bye. Karim watched as his old friend reached out and hugged the man, kissing him once on each cheek, and then announcing for all to hear, "*Viva la Revolución!*"

The rest of the Cuban contingent repeated the chant and shook their rifles in the air. Hakim took a moment to thank the rest of the soldiers. Clasping an arm here and shaking a hand there, he went down the line flashing his infectious smile and looking each man in the eye.

Karim had always been in awe of his childhood friend's ability to charm virtually anyone who crossed his path. He was a chameleon, capable of socializing with wretches and princes alike. He was never idle and always interested in what other people were doing and how they got from point A to point B. How they made their laundry business work, how they had become a professor, how they'd started their construction business, how they took care of their fishing boat, how they became a bond trader . . . the list went on and on. If it weren't for their years of loyalty, Karim would have probably been threatened by the ease with which Hakim walked through life, but he wasn't.

Their loyalty to each other stemmed from having been childhood friends. A healthy competition that had grown into a deep respect. It also helped that Hakim was one of Karim's biggest believers. Always the better student and his equal athletically, Karim was looked up to by Hakim. It was Hakim who was the first to believe that Karim had a destiny that would make him a historic figure in the fight to save Islam from yet another assault from the West. As teens they had dreamed of greatness. They had dissected what was good and what was wrong with the various jihad groups and they had set their own course.

Hakim had been the one to first suggest setting up their own network. Both men had grown suspicious of all the infighting between the Taliban and al-Qaeda. The infighting was disgusting, and they both feared that it had led to various factions intentionally sabotaging their brothers by leaking information to the Americans. Karim had not liked the idea of sending Hakim off on his own to explore other options, but his old friend had been his usual persistent self. After Zawahiri had saddled him with his moronic nephew, Karim decided he could with good conscience turn Hakim loose.

Karim looked around the small marina and felt great pride in his friend. He had never fully understood the word *irony*. He wasn't sure, but he thought people often confused it with happenstance. Whatever the case was, he found it rather amusing that as a teenager Hakim had been completely enamored with the American author Ernest Hemingway. He so admired the man's sense of adventure that at age thirteen, after reading *The Old Man and the Sea*, he'd hitchhiked on his own to Jeddah and convinced a fisherman to take him out for a day. At nineteen he'd climbed Mount Kilimanjaro, and at twenty-one he'd fulfilled what he'd said was his greatest thrill of all, catching a swordfish off the Florida Keys. Hakim had confided in him one cold evening that the real reason why he had come to fight in Afghanistan was because Hemingway had run off to be an ambulance driver during the Spanish Civil War. He felt that a man had not lived until he had experienced the raw thrill of war.

Hakim ambled over with his disarming grin. He placed an arm on Karim's shoulder and said, "That wasn't so bad now, was it?"

"You amaze me."

"Even after all these years?"

"Yes, even after all these years." Karim looked nervously back over his shoulder at the soldiers. "So we are free to go?"

"We are encouraged to go." Hakim made a motion toward the men in the boats and they fired up the engines. "They do not want us to loiter."

"Good, so we are leaving?"

"Yes." Hakim pointed west at the setting sun. "I have rations on the boats. We will leave now and sail around the western end of the island out into international waters. Then we'll set course for the Florida Keys."

The two men stepped onto the old wood dock, careful where they put their feet since the planks were rotten and uneven. "Are you sure that this is the right spot?" Karim had always thought they should try to enter the country farther north. Up toward Tampa or even the Panhandle.

"I've told you before, my friend. It is a numbers game."

"I know . . . more coast, more boats . . ."

"Yes. They can't tell the difference between drug runners and fishermen. We take our time tonight and then in the morning we meander out into the Keys."

"And if their Coast Guard shows up?"

"Then we run like hell." Karim pointed down at the two dull gray fiberglass boats. Each vessel had three 250 hp Mercury outboard motors on the back. "These boats are as fast as anything they have."

"As fast but not faster?"

"No, but don't worry. We have a secret weapon."

The creases on Karim's forehead deepened. "What secret weapon?"

"You and your men. They are not used to being shot back at." Hakim laughed and pointed at the second boat. "Stay two hundred meters back and follow in my wake. Everything is programmed into the GPS, and if you have any questions, just call me on the radio."

Karim reached out and stopped his friend. "Wait. That is the extent of your plan? We run?"

"Essentially, yes."

Karim felt the symptoms of one of his anxiety attacks. "After all we have been through . . . after all the preparation . . . this is what it will all come down to?"

"No, my friend, it will come down to more than just this, but we cannot control everything. At some point we must make our leap of faith." Hakim could see his friend's agitation. The eyes darting from left to right, focusing on nothing. His breathing becoming quick and shallow. "Would you rather try to fly into the country with all your weapons?"

Karim did not answer.

"You wanted me to find a way to get us into America with all the weapons and your detonators. There is no easy way, my friend, and you knew that going in. At some point we must put our faith in Allah and move forward." Hakim reached out and grabbed him by both shoulders. "Look me in the eye. Take a deep breath. Trust me to get you through this part of your journey. We are so close. America lies just beyond the horizon. When the sun comes up, I will have you there."

"But what about . . . ?"

Hakim cut him off, saying, "Now is not the time to hesitate . . . to question. Now is the time to act. Remember, you have always told me that victory favors the brave. Now is our moment to be brave. Trust me. Get in your boat and follow me. I will lead you on this leg of your crusade, and I will not fail you."

CHAPTER 35

ARLINGTON, VIRGINIA

NASH parked his minivan next to a beat-up Ford Taurus and walked into the Safeway Food and Drug. He grabbed a cart and began to amble through the produce section. The only thing he really needed was milk for Charlie, but he had other reasons to be at the store. He grabbed a half dozen bananas, two large grapefruits, and a cantaloupe. A few aisles down he grabbed some peanut butter because he'd learned in the past that they could never have enough peanut butter. In the next aisle he saw the guy he was looking for waiting for him in front of the taco shells. His blond hair was poking out from under his Washington Nationals baseball hat.

Nash pulled up beside him and looked back down the aisle to make sure the other shoppers were out of earshot. Keeping his eyes on the taco shells, Nash said, "How are you, buddy?"

"Better than you." The man was about the same size as Nash, although maybe a little thinner and a decade older.

"No doubt," Nash said as he remembered Monday night was taco night. He took a box just in case.

"How are the kids?"

"Good."

"Charlie?" he asked as he read the back of a box.

"He uttered his godfather's favorite word this morning."

The man turned his head and looked at Nash. "You fucking kidding me?"

"I wish I was."

"That's great."

"No, it isn't," Nash said seriously bothered. "He's only a year old."

Scott Coleman began laughing silently to himself. He'd known Nash for a little more than seven years and they'd grown very close. Coleman had been the one who brought Nash to the attention of Rapp. That was back when they were running around the mountains of Afghanistan having the time of their lives hunting Taliban and al-Qaeda. Now the pussies were hiding on the other side of the border and the Pakistanis wouldn't let them come over and finish the job.

Smiling and talking out of the side of his mouth, Coleman said, "You need to lighten up, buddy. I've told you before, the key to this shit is to never take it too seriously. The moment you do that, you lose your edge, you lose your nerve, and then you're going to fuck up."

Nash had heard the lecture many times before. Coleman, almost ten years his senior, was a former SEAL, and had been running his own security and consulting firm in D.C. since just before the attacks. The deluge of money that had been pumped into security firms had made him a wealthy man, but not as wealthy as he could have been. Coleman made the conscious decision to stay small. He had no interest in running a big company and managing hundreds of people.

Nash asked him, "You read the paper this morning?"

"Yeah." Coleman grabbed a box of shells, set them in his cart, and started moving. "You'd better hope those pricks on the Hill don't dig too deep, or you're fucked."

"I just left a hearing with the Intel folks. It was a real joy."

"Any idea how this Commie reporter got his info?"

Nash turned the corner and grabbed a bag of Doritos. "I have a short list."

"Let's hear it."

"In a moment. This reporter . . . Joe Barreiro . . . you have any problem setting up passive surveillance on him?"

Coleman scanned the next aisle and said, "Nope."

"Good. Check the nearby pay phones first and then the e-mails. You still have your back door into the *Post*'s server?"

Coleman laughed.

"What?" Nash asked wondering what he'd done wrong now.

"Look at you. All grown up and telling me how to do my job."

Nash looked embarrassed. Maybe even a little beaten. "Sorry, I know you know what you're doing. This is more for me, so I can just cross it off my list."

"Fair enough. I don't want you to burn out."

"Scour his hard drive as well as his editor's, and check the people who sit by him just to make sure. And his kids . . . don't forget to look at their phones."

"If you give me the list of suspects it'll be quicker," Coleman offered.

"Let me think about it," Nash said, his eyes narrowing.

"If they've met face-to-face, I can look at the cell tower records and find out if they overlapped at all in the last month."

Nash thought about it for a moment, weighed the pros and cons, and decided he really didn't give a shit. He needed to unload some of this stuff, and who better to trust than Coleman. In a voice barely above a whisper he said, "Glen Adams."

Coleman nodded slowly at first and then more enthusiastically. "It figures. The fucking narcissist. He'd hate anyone who was good at your job. He wasn't worth shit back when he was operations."

Nash agreed and said, "I need you to move quickly. I need to know how much they know and how they know it."

"I'll get on it tonight. You going to be around for Rory's game on Saturday?"

Coleman was referring to Nash's fourteen-year-old son. "If I'm not in jail."

"Come on . . . don't be so morose. Your one-year-old son is well on his way to mastering the greatest word in the English language."

Nash smiled. Thought of Charlie dropping the F-bomb at the breakfast table. The look of absolute horror on his wife's face. "I'll tell you the story about it some time over a beer. It's pretty funny. If you're in the neighborhood this week, stop by for a drink."

"I don't know, things are pretty crazy and now you want me to get on this . . ."

"Maggie and the kids would love to see you."

Without missing a beat, Coleman said, "I know Maggie would."

"Why are all you SEALs such pigs?"

"Oh, and you Marines are such a dignified lot."

Nash grinned. "We are charming bastards, aren't we?"

"You look good in your dress blues, but that's about it." Coleman turned down the next aisle and over his shoulder said, "Keep your dobber up."

Great, Nash thought as he stared at Coleman wheeling his cart down the aisle. *Just what I need, another reminder about last night.*

CHAPTER 36

DULLES INTERNATIONAL AIRPORT

THE Gulfstream G500 dropped through the clouds at 6,100 feet; the hydraulic landing gear whirled into the down position and then locked with a slight thud that woke Rapp from what had been an unusually deep sleep. He turned his head to the right and lifted the shade on the window. Thousands of lights greeted him. Of all of the airports the world over this one was probably the most familiar to him. It had been built before he was born. They'd stuck it out here where the edge of Fairfax County met up with Loudoun County. Back then it had been nothing more than farmland and horses. Now it was built up with highways, roads, parking lots, malls, businesses, hotels, apartments, and housing developments. Urban sprawl at its finest.

Rapp watched the cars driving up and down Sully Road past the old plantation, and as he had done so many times before, he felt a tinge of envy. He wondered what it would be like to switch places with them. To lead a life not knowing the things he knew. What it would be like to wake up and kiss his wife and kids good-bye and just go into an office like so many of the friends he'd grown up with. He never dwelled on it for more than a few seconds, and he never felt even remotely sorry for himself. The truth was he loved what he did. It had taken him many years to come to that realization, and more than a few hardships, but it had finally sunk in.

Strangely, it was the murder of his wife and unborn child that had finally got him to admit it. Not at first, of course. They had placed a bomb in his house out on the Chesapeake Bay that had been meant for him. Once again, he had cheated death, but this time paid for it with the loss of the woman he loved and the child he so badly wanted to meet and hold and raise and be a father to. He thought of that blissful, brief time that they'd had together after she'd told him she was pregnant. It was only a week, but he could still taste the emotions as if it were all happening at this very moment.

Lovely Anna, with her emerald green eyes, had taken on a radiance that made her look like something out of a dream. He'd have never thought she could be any more beautiful, but somehow the pregnancy had done it. Her already flawless skin glowed and her eyes sparkled with even more life than normal. She was filled with excitement, and was all the more elated knowing that this was something her rough-and-tumble husband so badly wanted. To give him the ultimate gift of a child, she knew, would be the final piece of leverage to get him to walk away from his dangerous profession. She had said to him once after making love that he'd given enough to his country. He'd been shot, stabbed, hunted, and tortured, and it was time for him to let go. To let someone else step into the breach and fight the battle.

For all of her liberal leanings, Anna was not a head-in-the-sand liberal. She'd seen firsthand what these fanatics were like, and she never for a moment questioned the fact that when you stripped it all away her husband's job was to hunt them down and kill them before they had the chance to incite more hatred and kill more innocent people. She'd never admitted it to him, but he knew now that she had been secretly proud of what he did. Her brother had confided to him after her death that Anna thought him the most noble man she had ever met.

After she'd been taken unexpectedly from him, his immediate reaction was predictable. He took his pain and anger and devastating
anguish and he stuffed it deep down into the furnace of his belly and
he used it to fuel his hunt for those who were responsible. He methodically tracked them down and got his vengeance. Two of them he
had allowed to live. The reasons were complicated, but he knew ultimately it was what Anna would have wanted. With the retribution
taken care of and reality staring him straight in the face, his entire
world had then came crashing down around him. His moral compass,
his sense of right and wrong, had been demagnetized and he found
himself awash in a sea of guilt and self-recrimination.

Having spent his life so sure of himself and his actions he took the
only avenue that made any sense to him. He simply walked away. No
one knew where he was for more than six months. Not his brother, not
even his handlers at Langley. When he reappeared he was a changed
man. Broken, but not shattered, he was more aware of his faults. More
understanding of his shortcomings and how they would affect his job.
In the end he would blame himself forever for thinking he could have
a normal life, and he carried with him the guilt of her death every day.
A quick prayer to her every morning and every night apologizing for
getting her involved in his nasty world. Sometimes he would admit to
himself that she was a willing participant. As strong-willed as anyone
he had ever met, no one ever talked her into doing anything she didn't
want to do. She came along because she loved him, and in the end that
was the one glorious thing that brought him solace, a bit of happiness,
and even an occasional smile to his face. She believed in what he did
and she loved him.

It had taken him somewhere between a year and half to two years
to get to that point, and when he did, it was as if the wound magically
began to heal. Not all the way, of course. There was still a scar that ran
deep and wide, but at least it wasn't being torn open every day as he
rode a sea of guilt, anger, and self-pity. He would never be entirely
whole again, but he had his confidence back. His sense of purpose was
restored and he was far wiser than he'd been before the tragedy.

There was also something else. It was an awkward thing for a man who was well into his second decade of living a life of secrecy, most of it operating alone, in foreign countries for months at a time. A life of deceiving everyone around him, even his fellow countrymen. Rapp now felt a massive sense of responsibility for setting things right. He had confided only in Kennedy about the first part. Because of his job and its solitary nature, Rapp had been trained to survive by thinking of himself first and foremost. But now he looked around at people like Mike Nash and his family and he realized what was at stake. In a suddenly immediate sense, Rapp felt the need to protect these people and set things right.

In the waning light of the attacks that had briefly awakened America to the threat of Islamic radical fundamentalism, the politicians had gone back to their old ways. They had turned on the very people they had asked to secure the country from attack. It always amazed Rapp that these were the very same people who in the year following 9/11 repeatedly asked the CIA if their measures of interrogation were tough enough. Now they were denying ever saying such things. They were on the attack. They smelled an opportunity and sooner or later they were going to begin destroying the lives of the men and women who Rapp now felt responsible for. Good men and women who had sacrificed for their country when their country needed them most. And now an ungrateful Senate and House of Representatives were circling like sharks looking for an opportunity to boost their political fortunes into a still higher orbit.

The plane floated downward and gently set down on the runway. Ridley woke up on landing and after stretching for a second pulled out his phone and began checking messages. Rapp continued to look out the window as they continued past the big terminal toward the private aviation section, where Langley kept a hangar. As they pulled parallel to the hangar he noticed a couple of police squad cars and another half dozen government sedans. Langley liked to keep as low a profile as possible, so this was not the normal welcoming party for a couple of spooks coming back from Afghanistan. Ridley was too preoccupied with his messages to notice and Rapp decided not to bother him.

When the plane finally stopped, Rapp grabbed his bag and thanked the crew member and the pilots as he headed out the hatch. There on the tarmac were nine men and one woman. Rapp could tell they were Feds without having to ask. They all had that "uptight, take-them-selves-too-seriously" look on their faces.

One of the agents stepped forward with a piece of paper in his hand and said, "Are you Mitch Rapp?"

Rapp considered a smart-ass comment, but decided against it. "Yep."

"I have an arrest warrant for you. Would you please drop your bag, lay down on the pavement, and place your hands above your head."

Rapp looked at the man incredulously. "I'll tell you what. You show me which car you'd like me to ride in, and I'll mosey on over with you . . . we'll toss my bag in the trunk, and I'll get in the backseat."

The agent moved his right hand to the hilt of his pistol. "I'm not going to say this again. Drop your bag . . ."

Before the agent could finish his sentence, Ridley's head popped out of the plane and he yelled, "What in the hell is going on here?"

The agent's eyes darted from Ridley to Rapp and then back to Ridley. "Sir, I have an arrest warrant in my possession for this man right here. I'll need you to step aside."

Ridley charged down the steps, past Rapp, and to within three feet of the agent. "FBI?" Ridley barked.

The man was half a head taller than Ridley. He looked down at him and said, "Don't make me use force."

"Don't give me a reason to kick your ass off my property, junior. I'm the deputy director of the Clandestine Service out at Langley and you are standing on my turf. So before you put one of my people under arrest you are going to explain to me just what in the hell is going on."

The agent took a half a step back and said, "I'm only doing my job, sir. I have been ordered to place that man," he pointed at Rapp, "under arrest. I wasn't told why, I was simply told to do it."

"Who at the Justice Department?"

"Wade Kline."

"You've got to be fucking kidding me. Let me see the arrest warrant." Ridley stuck out his hand, the agent hesitated, and Ridley said, "You want me to call Director Powel?"

The agent didn't like the sound of that, so he handed over the warrant.

Ridley unfolded it, gave it a quick read, and handed it back to the agent. "You know who this is?" Ridley pointed his thumb over his shoulder at Rapp.

The agent shook his head.

Ridley stepped in closer and lowered his voice so only the agent could hear him. "He's a damn American hero, and this," Ridley snatched the warrant out of the agent's hand and waved it around, "is a bunch of PC bullshit. Now, I can't stop you from arresting him, but I'll tell you right now, Special Agent whatever the fuck your name is, if you make him lay down on this tarmac like some common criminal I will fucking ruin your career. I will call in every favor the bureau owes me to make sure your fucking ass ends up in Yemen searching cargo containers for next three years. So what's it going to be?"

The agent took a long moment to consider his options and then finally said, "He's one of your boys?"

"He ain't my boy. About the only two people he answers to in this town are the director of the CIA and the president, and he doesn't even answer to them most of the time."

CHAPTER 37

FLORIDA KEYS

THE sun rose brilliantly, casting its rays across the vast expanse of blue water. All nine men were on deck to witness the glorious power of Allah as another day of their blessed journey began. They'd spent the night lashed together, the two boats gently rolling in the shallow swells. Even with the calm water, though, four of the men had vomited. Hakim took a bit of perverse joy in seeing these land-loving freedom fighters buckle so easily to the gentle motion of the ocean. Even more joy knowing that it bothered his old friend Karim that he had failed to prepare them for this relatively short jaunt.

When they were done praying, rations were handed out and the men were encouraged to drink plenty of water, especially those who had thrown up. Hakim checked their position again and then climbed out onto the long bow of the fast boat. He looked through a pair of binoculars at a speck on the western horizon. They were sixteen nautical miles almost due east from Marathon, Florida. To the north an almost equal distance was the U.S. Coast Guard Station at Islamorada. Farther to the south and the west was the Coast Guard Station at Key

West. Both bases were equipped with enough air and surface assets to make this a miserable morning, but it was Key West that he feared most. That was where the command center for the new Helicopter Interdiction Tactical Squadron was located. The farther north they went, the more they could mix in with the pleasure boaters and sport fishermen coming out of Miami and the day trippers crossing back and forth from southern Florida to the Bahamas.

Hakim scanned the surface first and then tilted the binoculars skyward. There were a few contrails from commercial planes flying at higher altitudes, but no sign of any helicopters at the moment. From his past excursions Hakim knew they were most active in the dead of night and then later in the day when the boat traffic picked up. The boats didn't worry him as much. There were only a few that could keep up with them and they weren't armed with the bigger guns of the cutters and coastal patrol boats. The problem would be the helicopters. They were faster than his boats, and worse, they could keep an eye on them from a distance and radio for help. If they weren't careful they could end up with a bunch of police units converging on them when they reached shore.

This had been the most difficult aspect to plan, but Hakim thought he had it figured out. Karim joined him on the bow, and Hakim asked, "Are you nervous?" He asked the question knowing how his friend would answer.

"Only fools and liars say they aren't."

"Well, my friend, then which one am I?" Hakim continued his search of the sky, now turning back toward Key West.

"You are not nervous?" Karim asked with concern.

"No. Not in the least."

"Why do you tempt fate like this? You know you shouldn't say such things."

Hakim laughed. "I am excited. Why aren't you excited? This is what we have been working for. This is a great day." Hakim pointed toward the spit of land on the horizon. "There, my friend, is the great Satan. In a few minutes we will fire up these engines, and we will penetrate their defenses. Defenses they have spent billions on, and there is nothing they can do to stop us."

Karim frowned. "You are assuming they will not stop us."

"Yes, I am." Hakim lowered the binoculars. "When will you begin to have faith in your destiny? I have been telling you for years that this is what awaits you." Again he pointed toward the shore of America.

"Allah prefers us to be humble."

"Then you can be humble, but I will be excited. This is something they will write about. In a few days the entire Arab world will be talking about these new lions of al-Qaeda and their leader, the great Karim Nour al-Din, who have struck at the heart of America."

"We have done nothing yet."

"Is it wrong to hope?"

Karim made a brooding face and finally said, "I suppose not."

"And think of the faces those old women will make when the news finally reaches them in the mountain hideouts. Zawahiri will be furious that he and his millionaire boyfriend do not receive the credit."

"Do not speak of him that way," Karim said angrily.

"I'm sorry, but you know I think Zawahiri has poisoned him."

"He still deserves our respect." Karim was disgusted with the al-Qaeda leadership, but his fellow Saudi Arabian did not deserve to be spoken of in such a manner. "So," Karim said, "tell me of your grand plan. Do you really think we will just sail ashore and unload your drugs?"

"That all depends on the Coast Guard."

"And if they show up?"

"We will outrun them."

"What if it is a helicopter? Like you mentioned last night."

"You keep going straight, and I will worry about the helicopter."

"That is it? That is the extent of your grand plan?"

Hakim showed off his bright white smile. "No, I have a few tricks."

"Ahmed?"

"Yes, he is one of them, in fact now is the perfect time to show him the present I brought along for him." Hakim climbed around the windscreen and went below deck. A moment later he appeared with a long, black rectangular case. He looked into the other boat and said, "Ahmed, I have something for you."

The twenty-four-year-old Moroccan hopped from one boat into the other as the others came to the edge. Hakim set the case on the flat cushion just aft of the cockpit and popped the clasps. He swung the case open to reveal a very large gun.

Ahmed gasped as he said, "A Barrett fifty-caliber. I have dreamt of shooting such a gun."

"Can you handle it?" Hakim asked.

"Of course," Ahmed said enthusiastically. "Where did you get it?"

"Nashville, Tennessee."

"Isn't that where they are made?"

"Near there."

Ahmed picked it up and looked through the Barrett Optical Range Scope. "When do I get to fire it?"

"Hopefully not anytime soon, but just in case you have to, are you familiar with the weapon?"

"There is not much to know. It is one of the finest rifles ever constructed. Robust . . . accurate . . . very easy to shoot."

"Good. There are three ten-round boxes already loaded." Hakim pointed at the case.

"What type of ammunition?"

"Fifty-caliber BMG, armor-piercing incendiary."

Ahmed tore his eyes away from the gun and said, "Only NATO troops have that ammunition."

"And you." Hakim laughed loudly.

"Where in the world did you get . . . ? "

"I'll tell you on the long drive to Washington. We'll have plenty of time, but now we must get moving." Hakim turned and looked up at his old friend, who was standing on the other side of the windscreen. "Are you ready, my friend?"

"Yes."

"Good," Hakim said with unbridled enthusiasm. "Just like we practiced last night. Everybody get in your proper place and we will start the engines." The men started scrambling into their assigned boats. "Remember," Hakim said, "keep your weapons hidden unless Karim or I tell you to get them out." He then turned to Ahmed and whispered, "Stay close to me, and make sure your new toy is ready to use."

Hakim started his engines one at a time and waited for his friend to do the same. After another minute Hakim ordered the lines to be undone and then got under way at a leisurely fifteen knots. With the wind whipping over their heads, Hakim turned to Ahmed and asked, "Are you familiar with the MH-65C Dolphin helicopter?"

Ahmed shook his head.

"Not to worry." Hakim popped the small glove box on the dashboard and retrieved several pieces of paper. "Here are the schematics. I've circled the three places where it is most vulnerable. If we come across one it might be useful information."

CHAPTER 38

WASHINGTON, D.C.

R APP had to laugh at the irony of the situation. Here he was in
an orange prison jumpsuit shackled to a metal table in a room
that reeked of urine. The cinder-block walls of the ten-by-ten-foot interrogation room were covered with a variety of body fluids that Rapp
did not want to attempt to identify. The fact that America treated terrorists better than its own citizens was just another example of how
upside down things were. He was in the Central Detention Facility, or
D.C. jail, as it is more commonly known. A place located in one of the
most run-down, crime-ridden neighborhoods in America. Every year
for the last thirty, Southeast D.C. helped the capital city finish in the
top five for most murders—usually number one. The jail was filled
with gangbangers and crackheads and every other kind of reprobate
that roamed the not-so-safe streets of the nation's capital.

It was obvious that the political forces behind his arrest thought
they could somehow unravel him by sticking him in this place, which
was proof that they were either very stupid or very petty or probably
both. When they'd finished fingerprinting and photographing him,
they took away all his clothes and gave him the orange jumpsuit and

the paper slippers and stuck him in general holding. No lawyer, no phone call, just Ridley standing there, doling out threats like a kindergarten teacher on a field trip. Ridley warned them it was a mistake. Told them over and over not to dump him in general holding, but the jailers stuck with their official line that everyone gets the same treatment.

Rapp lasted less than five minutes in the big thirty-by-ten-foot cell. A wiry black perp, all strung out on drugs, got in his face almost the second he walked in the door. Rather than engage the man in conversation, Rapp hit him with a quick jab to the solar plexus and sent him to the floor, where he lay gasping for air like a fish out of water. Two slightly larger and younger black men took umbrage at this and strolled across the cell hooting and hollering about all the hurt they were going to put on their new bitch. In five seconds Rapp sized them up, drew them in, and dismantled them. The man on the left got a half a step ahead of the other guy and threw the first punch. Rapp moved his head a mere six inches and let the fist sail past. With a slight pivot he brought up his right leg and then sent his foot crashing down on the outside of the man's right knee. Having thrown his punch and missed, the man was left for a second with ninety-five percent of his weight resting on that front foot. When Rapp's foot made contact and pushed through the target, the man buckled as if he'd been walking on a pair of flimsy stilts.

The second guy was on him almost immediately and actually got ahold of Rapp's jumpsuit for a second, before Rapp broke free with a series of quick rabbit punches to several vital organs. He then took the man by the wrist, twisted the hand 180 degrees, and straightened his arm so that his elbow was in a locked position pointing directly up at the ceiling. One quick kick to the stomach sent the man to the floor. There was a moment where the entire room was still. Rapp looked across the cell at the other gangbangers and tried to gauge their mood. They were all paying rapt attention, and a few looked like they might join in. Rapp decided that the easiest way to stop the violence was to make an example. With the perp's arm still in a straight and locked position, Rapp dropped to his right knee, brought his left arm up above his head, and brought his elbow smashing down. When the blow struck, the other man's elbow socket exploded, sounding like a two-by-four snapping from too much weight.

When the guards showed up, the first perp was just regaining his ability to breathe, but the other two were rolling around on the ground screaming in pain with limbs pointed at very unnatural angles. The guards had a quick conference and decided to move Rapp to one of the interrogation rooms. That was where he had been sitting from roughly one in the morning until now. He was shackled around his wrists and ankles and chained to the metal table. The cinder-block walls were blank. With nothing to look at and nothing to do but wait, Rapp rested his head on the table and tried to sleep. He lost track of time but it felt like he'd been in the room for close to ten hours, which meant it was probably closer to five. Alone with nothing but his thoughts, he wondered how Kennedy was taking things. There was a good chance that she was raising holy hell, but one never really knew in this town.

When the door finally opened, Rapp looked up and saw a man roughly his age, wearing a blue suit and a mint green and blue striped tie. He was handsome, but not in a masculine way. He was too perfect, too deliberate. Like he put a lot of effort into his grooming and appearance. He entered the room holding a cup of coffee, a scone, and a leather briefing folder under one arm. He kicked the door closed and sat down across from Rapp.

After straightening his tie and taking a sip of coffee he said, "You have managed to get yourself into a lot of trouble."

Rapp stared back at him with his brown eyes that were so dark they were almost black and said nothing.

"Striking an officer of the United States Air Force is a very serious crime." He glanced at Rapp with his most serious expression and flipped open the briefing folder. "Not to mention this part about you donning the uniform of colonel and sneaking around a United States military installation without authorized access. I would say you've finally run out of luck, Mr. Rapp."

Rapp said nothing. He stared back at the man and wondered if he really thought he was going to somehow scare him.

"You're looking at ten years . . . maybe more."

Rapp chuckled.

"You find this funny?"

"I find your theatrical bravado funny."

The man took a sip of coffee and in a morose tone said, "I don't think you're going to be laughing when you're sitting in a federal prison getting buttfucked by a bunch of hard cons."

Rapp's eyes narrowed, the creases in his forehead deepening. He sensed something in the man across the table. Something he should be leery of. "Who are you?"

The man straightened his tie and said, "I'm Wade Kline . . . Department of Justice Chief Privacy and Civil Liberties Officer, and I'm your worst nightmare, Mr. Rapp."

"Really?" Rapp asked in a not-impressed tone.

"Yes. I'm incorruptible, and I don't like people who think they don't have to play by the rules."

Rapp nodded. "Speaking of the rules," Rapp glanced up at the camera in the corner, "would you mind telling me why I haven't seen my attorney?"

Kline grinned at Rapp and with an arched brow said, "Sometimes it's hard to track down a lawyer in the middle of the night. I'm sure he'll be along in time for your arraignment."

"Well, it is very considerate of you to come in here and talk to me without my lawyer present, but I think I'll pass."

Kline plucked a chunk of the scone from the wax paper and popped it into his mouth. "What if I were to tell you I could make this all go away?"

"How?"

"You cooperate with my investigation. You talk to me about your superiors at Langley. You fill me on your illegal domestic spying operations. It's your only chance."

"You're joking, right?"

"Mr. Rapp, do I look like the type of person who jokes around?"

Rapp thought to himself that it was a valid point. This guy took himself far too seriously to screw around. "You know what I think, Kline? I think there's a real shit storm brewing outside this room right now. I think there's a lot of pissed-off people at the Pentagon and the White House."

"Really?"

"Yep . . . I think you got wind of this little misunderstanding between Captain Leland and myself and you decided to run with it before checking in with your superiors. I think the attorney general has had his ass reamed by the president, which means the AG has now turned around and reamed your ass, and since you're a desperate type of fellow and you hate to lose, you've now decided the only way you can save face on this deal is to try this lame-ass Hail Mary attempt . . . promising you'll go light on me in return for me telling you about all the nasty shit I've seen the CIA do over the last eighteen years."

"I can promise you, Mr. Rapp, I don't make empty threats," Wade said seriously. "I've spent too many hours in a courtroom to say something I can't follow through on."

"Then help me understand your situation, because you don't have a case against me. This little scuffle between Captain Leland and myself . . . there's two sides to how that went down and even if you believe everything he's telling you, which would be a mistake, all you've got is a misdemeanor assault. You and I both know I'll never see the inside of a jail, let alone have to endure all these boyfriends you're talking about. And as far as me putting on the uniform of a colonel"—Rapp shrugged—"that's what we do in the Clandestine Service. So unless you've got something you're not telling me, you're wasting my time."

"Well," started Kline with a big smile, "there is this other matter."

"And what would that be?"

"The part about you beating and torturing a bound prisoner."

A small grin spread across Rapp's lips. He was waiting for this card to be played. "I don't know what you're talking about."

"Sure you do. Captain Leland and General Garrison have already filed their official reports." Kline consulted his notes. "The prisoner's name is Abu Haggani. We have photos of his cut and bruised face attached to the report."

"Didn't happen."

"I have a security tape that says different." Kline stared unflinchingly at Rapp. "You'd better make this deal with me or you're going to get caught up in a media firestorm that is going to make Abu Ghraib look like a twenty-four-hour scandal."

If Rapp hadn't already spoken to Marcus Dumond, who had assured him that all recordings had been destroyed, he might have been slightly anxious, but even if Kline did have the tape he would never flip. Rapp glanced down at Kline's notes and said, "Show it to me."

"What?"

"The tape."

"The FBI," he said calmly, "is analyzing it for evidence."

"Sure they are." Rapp smiled and gave Kline a look as if they were both on the inside of a joke. "You don't have shit, Kline."

"I do, and you're going down . . . and you're going to bring the rest of that den of rats down with you."

"You're a big talker, Kline," Rapp said in a confident voice. "I've seen your type come and go every few years. You've got your righteous gung-ho attitude. You talk tough about cleaning up crime and defending Lady Liberty, but we both know why you do it."

Kline looked amused. "I can't wait to hear this. A knuckle-dragger from the CIA is going to impart a pearl of wisdom."

"It's your ego. It's not a sense of duty. You want to make a name for yourself. You want to climb the ladder of success. Maybe run for office someday or open your own law practice. You're nothing but a big pussy in a suit. You wouldn't last a day out there doing what we do."

"I would never stoop so low as to do your work."

"You mean killing terrorists and saving lives. Of course you wouldn't, because you're a selfish little prick."

"You know what I think?" said Kline hotly. "I think you're a sick man. I think you get off on beating defenseless men." Kline circled around and whispered in Rapp's ear, "I think it's a real thrill for you." He placed his hand on the back of Rapp's neck and began to squeeze.

"I'm only going to say this once," Rapp said in a firm voice. "Take your hand off me, right now."

"What?" Kline laughed loudly. "You can dish it out, but you can't take it."

In an almost disembodied voice, Rapp said, "You have no idea who you are dealing with."

"I'm dealing with a guy who gets his jollies slapping around men who are handcuffed." Kline playfully smacked Rapp across the back of the head with an open hand.

"Is that all you've got?" Rapp asked, his anger building.

Kline slapped him harder and then grabbed a handful of Rapp's thick black hair and yanked his head back. "Why should I play by the rules when you don't? Huh, Mr. Tough Guy?"

"Because I got out of my handcuffs, you idiot."

Kline's eyes froze for a moment and then moved from Rapp's face down to his lap, where he saw the handcuffs and chains lying in his lap.

Before Kline could move, Rapp's right hand shot up and grabbed him by the tie. Spinning out of the chair, Rapp stood and drove the Department of Justice employee back into the corner and delivered a quick knee strike to the groin. Then, grabbing Kline's tie with both hands, Rapp began to cinch the knot tighter and tighter.

As Kline's face began to turn purple, Rapp asked, "Who's the tough guy now?"

CHAPTER 39

FLORIDA KEYS

HAKIM turned on the surface radar, noted the location of several vessels sitting just on the other side of U.S. territorial water, and then turned the radar off. Everything seemed normal, at least compared to the other three test runs he'd taken with the boat. He'd decided months ago that they would make their run on a Monday. For the Coast Guard down in the Keys, every weekend was a pain. Thousands of boaters took to the waterways, and while the vast majority were respectful and law-abiding, there was still a significant number who drank too much, acted like idiots, and caused a lot of trouble. So the Coast Guard was always a little slow to start after a busy weekend.

Now came the part that his friend would never understand. Karim was far too rigid. In many ways it was what made him such a great leader, but his lack of trust and inflexibility had also made things almost impossible. At some point they needed to move outside their group. Without help from within America, Hakim knew it would be impossible for them to succeed, so he had acted unilaterally.

Pretending as if he'd dropped something, Hakim bent over and withdrew his mobile phone from his cargo pocket. He quickly punched in the number and held the phone to his ear. He counted the rings, each one making him more nervous. On the sixth, the person on the other end answered.

"Hello."

"Mike," said Hakim, "it's Joe. How are you doing?"

"Good."

"Are we still on for breakfast?"

"Yes. I'm here waiting for you."

"Good. I'll be there in twenty minutes."

"I'll be waiting."

Hakim stuffed the phone back into his pocket and stood. He looked over at Karim and gave him the thumbs-up signal. Karim, looking as serious as ever, gave him a slight nod. Hakim had a moment of hesitation. Not for himself, but for his friend. For all of Karim's drive, intellect, and talent, he lacked polish. He was too stiff, and in a relatively laid-back country like America, Hakim feared he would stand out too much. He had a plan for that as well. At least to get them as far as D.C.

Hakim grabbed the large headphones off the dash and held them high above his head. He waved them back and forth until Karim saw what he was doing and then he put them on his head. Once they started the engines it would be the only way they could hear each other. Karim put on the headphones as well, and after a brief radio check they turned the powerful outboard engines on. One by one they rumbled as the pistons started cranking. Outside of the offshore racing circuit these boats were about as fast as you could get. Even so, they could never outrun the helicopters the Coast Guard used.

A gust of wind blew across the bow, forming ripples on the calm water. Hakim cranked his head around and looked to the east. The seas still looked pretty calm, but it wasn't likely to last. Weather was one thing he did not want to have to contend with. If they had to open up the boats to near full throttle in rough seas, they were in trouble. Karim was nowhere near a good-enough seaman to contend with big swells.

Thumbing the transmit button on the headset, Hakim said, "Charlie, I'll race you in for breakfast." Hakim had gone over the plan the night before. This was just like Afghanistan, where you had to assume the Americans listened to everything. "Remember, don't stop for me." He looked across the water at his friend, who gave him the thumbs-up.

Hakim pushed the three throttles forward a fifth and marked his heading. He'd done this exact run before. Point the boat straight at Marathon and head in at a steady 20 mph. Karim fell in behind him, fifty meters back. Two minutes later, Hakim turned on the surface radar and left it on this time. As they prepared to leave international waters, Karim called down below for Ahmed. He handed the young Moroccan the binoculars and told him to start scanning the sky for helicopters.

All of the drugs had been transferred onto Hakim's boat, and all of the men, except Ahmed, were now on Karim's boat. Hakim had revealed this part of his plan while they were at sea during the night and Karim had been none too pleased. He hadn't realized until they had left Cuba that all of the cargo and all of the men could have easily fit onto one boat. Karim had learned firsthand in Afghanistan that the more simple the plan, the better chances there were of success. The idea of using two boats, when one would suffice, made no sense to him. Hakim explained his reasoning, but Karim, stubborn as always, held his ground and disagreed.

"Why can't we simply transfer everything onto one boat and set the other adrift?" he had asked.

Hakim wanted to strangle him. They had ended up out on the bow of Hakim's boat arguing in hushed angry tones. It finally ended when Hakim told his old friend he was acting like one of those overfed Taliban commanders who never ventured to the front, but claimed to know everything. Karim, having spent months without a soul questioning anything he said, almost threw his friend into the water. With great restraint, he calmed himself down and consented to allow Hakim to continue to run this part of the operation.

The two boats crossed into American water without fanfare. Knowing that his friend was a bit overwhelmed with the task of staying on course, Hakim doubted he even noticed the significant event. They continued on for two more miles, heading directly for Marathon. This was the trickiest part. The American Coast Guard was very well funded, and had some of the best equipment that money could buy, but there were limits. With thousands of vessels coming in and out of the Keys every day, the Coast Guard had to deploy its assets judiciously. If a vessel were on course to enter port at a decent-sized city like Marathon, the Coast Guard would deal with it when it got there or send one of its many vessels out to inspect. The helicopters were expensive and far more rare than the hundreds of patrol boats that were used to keep the waterways safe.

At the five-mile mark, Hakim's pulse began to quicken. He looked at the surface radar and then scanned the horizon. With the wind whipping through his hair, he noted the location of a half dozen contacts, none of them close enough to identify as Coast Guard or not. The sky was thankfully clear.

As they neared the three-mile mark, Hakim could feel the adrenaline coursing through his veins. This was what it was like to live, to really experience the grand thrill of blazing a trail through life. Hakim laughed loudly as the wind buffeted his face. He looked over at his friend, who was hunched behind the windscreen frowning with intensity. Hakim laughed louder. His friend had never understood his fascination with Ernest Hemingway, but then again, Karim was anti anything American. Especially someone as American as Hemingway. But Hakim had read everything the man had written as well as a few biographies. He'd been to the house in Key West as well as the one in Cuba, but he couldn't bring himself to visit the home in Idaho where he'd blown his head off with a shotgun. Hakim didn't like to think of him in that phase of his life. He preferred the younger version of Hemingway who seemed to be running off on grand adventures every other month.

Hakim glanced down at the navigation system. The turn to the north was a mere twenty seconds away. He was not sure if he had ever been this excited about anything in his life. He flipped the transmit button on his bulky headset and counted the seconds. At zero he began the turn. Karim stayed back on his port side and executed the turn as he'd told him so he was now the boat closest to shore.

Hakim tapped Ahmed on the shoulder and shouted, "Get down below and get the rifle ready." Hakim saw the Moroccan look nervously to the north. "Don't worry, I haven't seen them. I just want to be prepared."

Ahmed grabbed the railing and went down the four steps into the cabin. A moment later the triangular muzzle break of the .50-caliber rifle appeared. Ahmed adjusted the legs on the bipod and got behind the scope. When he was satisfied that he had a comfortable shooting position he set the butt stock of the rifle on the carpet and picked the binoculars up.

Topside, Hakim gave Karim the signal to increase speed and then began to push his own throttles forward at a slow, even pace. The three Mercury Pro XS 250 HP outboards came to life, growling with power. The boats responded immediately. In less than five seconds they were slicing through the water at close to 60 mph. Five seconds after that they reached 80 mph and, as per the plan, eased back on the throttles and held the speed. The boats settled into a side-by-side tack, Hakim allowing his friend to take a half-length lead as they raced on a northeasterly heading.

Hakim settled into a pattern. His eyes steadily swept from right to left 180 degrees, and then checked the surface radar before scanning skyward. The Coast Guard helicopters topped out around 150 mph, but tended to cruise close to 100 mph. Because of that he was less concerned that one of them would catch them coming up from Key West. The problem was straight ahead at Islamorada and even they were quickly running out of time. The navigation system ticked off the distance to the next course adjustment. It was now a mere four miles and the sea was still calm. If need be they could easily increase their speed.

Hakim was half regretting that they wouldn't have a run-in with the Coast Guard when he spotted the speck on the horizon. He almost missed it, but the sun caught the windscreen just right. The quick flash of light brought his head back around and he focused on the speck. They were so close, but now, if they got their next turn too fast, the helicopter would be able to report their new course heading, and he didn't want that.

Hakim made a quick decision and hit the transmit button on his headset. "Charlie, slow it down to forty miles per hour." Hakim pulled back on the throttles and watched the helicopter come into focus. He could now make out the bulbous black nose, the windscreen, and the red housing that covered the engines. He'd considered his next move with great care. It was risky, but with the Coast Guard's advantage in manpower, it was his best tactic.

"Slow down to twenty miles per hour," Hakim said.

"But you told me to keep going," said Karim in surprise.

"I know, but I have changed my mind." Hakim glanced over at this friend and smiled. "Trust me."

The helicopter was closing fast. So fast that Hakim thought for a moment that it might continue straight past them, but then it altered course a few degrees and Hakim knew it was preparing to loop around for a closer look.

"Ahmed," he shouted, "remember, you will probably only get one shot at this."

The helicopter changed from a nose-down attitude to a slightly nose-up attitude, another sign that it was slowing. Hakim watched it begin to slide to his starboard. He didn't bother turning on his marine radio even though he knew they were trying to hail him. The chopper was now a quarter mile ahead and off his starboard side. Hakim held his course and waited for the chopper to do the move he'd heard about. As the two boats closed to within a few hundred yards, the helicopter started to loop around.

Good, Hakim thought. *Just like I was told. Keep coming . . . keep coming.* He started to wave at the helicopter but made no effort to reach for the throttles. There were plenty of idiots on the water in Florida, and the Coast Guard dealt with them every day. They would not open fire unless they tried to run, which Hakim was not ready to do just yet. The chopper slid sideways through the air, keeping pace with the boats. A voice came over the loudspeaker and even though Hakim could hear it, he pointed at his headphones and shook his head. It would all happen in the next few moments. Karim silently urged them to circle around to his aft and take a look at his engines. Moving slow like this they could call in patrol boats easily and they'd be trapped.

The HH-65 Dolphin was the king of these parts, though, and as long as they were here they might as well take a thorough look. The sleek red helicopter began to slide around to get in behind the two boats. Karim continued to wave and smile, and above the rotor wash, he yelled, "Ahmed, they will be coming into view from the starboard side!"

As the boat moved past the helicopter, Hakim saw that they had a gunner with a sling-mounted machine gun sitting in the open doorway. He was wearing a flight suit and a helmet and was holding the weapon in both hands, but did not have it pointed at them.

"Remember," Hakim screamed, "the engines first."

He watched as the helicopter hovered at fifty feet and moved from four o'clock to five and then finally six. Hakim didn't dare look down, even though he desperately wanted to. The first shot, though, almost caused him to leap out of the boat as the hot gas from the muzzle break swept across his feet and legs. With every ounce of control that he could muster he kept his eye on the helicopter, so he could count the hits. He was sure the first three struck the starboard engine of the twin-engine helicopter and possibly had torn through and hit the port-side engine as well. The big armor-penetrating rounds would burn at 3,000 degrees and pretty much slice through anything on the helicopter, including the engines.

One more round hit the engine housing and then as the helicopter began to lose power and yaw, holes were punched, one after another, down the tail, and finally the fan blade on the rear stabilizer exploded. It was as if the hand of Allah came down and tossed the helicopter through the air. The nose lurched downward and then the tail whipped end over end, slamming the helicopter into the sea, and breaking it into dozens of pieces.

Hakim was stunned. He turned to look at Karim and the two of them shared a brief smile. Then the moment passed and they both realized they needed to get moving fast. Hakim leaned on the throttles and tore off. Karim followed suit and seconds later they were racing again across the sea at speeds approaching 100 mph. Hakim glanced down at surface radar and was relieved to see that the closest contact was more than a mile to the north. With any luck they would be off the water before the Coast Guard confirmed that their chopper was down.

CHAPTER 40

ARLINGTON, VIRGINIA

N ASH'S Tuesday morning started out pretty much the same way his Monday morning did. He woke up with a screaming headache, grabbed Charlie from his crib, and went downstairs. Fortunately, there was no front-page story in the *Post* about his illegal activities, but there was another problem looming. Once again, his wife had decided to ignore him and had turned off his work phones. Nash's sleep patterns were predictable only in the sense that he slept like shit most nights, but every three weeks or so the exhaustion would catch up and he would sleep for nine or ten hours straight. Last night had been one of those nights.

Nash had put his ten-year-old son Jack to bed shortly after nine and had fallen asleep with him while they were reading a story. Sometime around midnight he made it into his own bed and went right back to sleep facedown. A few minutes before seven he'd awoken to Charlie's morning wrestling match and it wasn't until he had him settled in his high chair that he discovered his phones were off, as well as the ringer on the home phone. She came floating into the kitchen a few minutes later and when asked about it her response was that he was no good to his family or his country if he was run-down.

Nash turned on both phones and watched the message indicators begin to climb. There were sixteen voice mails and forty-seven texts and e-mails. The first two messages were nothing too important, but the third kicked his headache into overdrive. The subsequent messages only made it worse. Half of them were from Ridley, asking for help. Nash felt like a fool. While all of this was going down he was sleeping peacefully in his bed.

He raced to get ready and cut himself shaving, bad enough that he had to stick a wad of toilet paper on his Adam's apple to stem the bleeding. By 8:00 he was backing out of the driveway in the minivan. At the end of his street he stopped to make a right turn and stopped cold. His foot stayed on the brake and his eyes stayed fixed on a sign. There, stapled to a tree, was a piece of bright yellow paper with the words *Lost Dog* printed in big block letters. Nash stared at the paper for a good five seconds. Why this morning? Why at all? The whole damn thing was supposed to be shut down.

Nash racked his brain for the procedures they'd set up. He knew yellow was urgent, but it was a Tuesday and he couldn't remember at first how that affected the schedule. After a moment it came to him, the Java Shack on Franklin. He slapped the turn signal down and gunned the gas. It would take about five minutes to get there. He considered calling Ridley or O'Brien to see what was going on with Rapp, but decided he didn't want to talk to them until he tied up this loose end.

He drove past the place once to scope things out and then found a meter around the corner. Nash stepped out of the car and plugged four quarters into the meter. He adjusted the .45-caliber Glock on his right hip and took note of the people and cars across the street at the tire store. Casually, he buttoned his suit and started down the sidewalk. It was a slightly overcast morning, but the temperature was already in the mid-sixties. When he reached the coffee shop he scanned the outdoor tables but didn't see whom he was looking for.

Inside, he stepped up to the counter and ordered a cup of black coffee from the woman behind the counter. He counted three patrons. Two of them weren't his guy, so he focused on the third, who was hiding behind the Metro section of the *Post*. Nash walked over to the guy's table and said, "You mind if I take a look at the sports section?"

The man lowered one corner of the paper and looked back at Nash with angry eyes, but in a polite voice said, "Help yourself."

Nash grabbed the section and sat down facing the door, just like the other guy. He took a sip of coffee and picked up the paper.

The man next to him whispered out of the side of his mouth, "Who the fuck ratted us out?"

Nash held up the paper and pretended to read. "I'm working on it."

The man drummed his long black fingers on the table. "Do you know how long it's been since I've had a beer?"

This was a subject he had no desire to revisit, but knew that his operative had been under a great deal of stress. Nash had found Chris Johnson near the end of his second tour in Iraq while serving with the 101st Airborne Division. Letting him vent for a minute was probably not the worst thing.

"One hundred and eighty-four fucking days," the man said, answering his own question.

"Trust me," Nash said, "I'm not happy about it either."

"I haven't watched a football game or a basketball game in almost a fucking year. I haven't been with a women in seven months . . . hell . . . I haven't even looked at porn."

"Calm down," Nash said in a slow, steady voice.

"You want me to fucking calm down," the other man hissed. "I've lived in that fucking stinky mosque every day. On a good week they might take one shower."

"No one is saying you didn't do a good job," Nash said in an easy voice.

"That's not the point. The point is, I've put in a shitload of time.

I've spent the better part of a year of my life that I ain't gettin' back, by the way."

"I know."

"I've eaten their shitty food, I've had to put up with their anti-Semitic remarks, their bigotry, the way they treat their wives and daughters . . . and now when I've finally earned their trust . . . you pull the plug."

"It wasn't me. It came down from the top."

"Well, fuck that."

Nash turned and looked his man in the eye. "Lower your voice, and that's an order."

The man sat back and took a frustrated breath. After a moment he said, "I'm going to kill someone."

Everybody is losing their mind, Nash thought. "No you're not," he said to the man. "You're going to casually tell one of them that your mom is sick and you have to go back to Atlanta. Then you are going to pack up and lie low until I say different."

"I can't believe this is happening."

"Believe it. Shut it down, and I mean yesterday."

"I can't."

Nash looked at the young former Army Ranger and said, "You can and you will."

"I'm too close," the man said, shaking his head.

Nash was getting mad. There wasn't a single one of them in the Clandestine Service who didn't have a healthy streak of insubordination in them, but this was pushing it.

Lowering his newspaper, Nash gave up the pretense of a clandestine meeting and in a very clear voice said, "I am giving you a direct order to shut it down. Do you understand me?"

The man thought about it for a second. Someone entered the coffee shop and his eyes darted to the motion at the front door. He flipped his newspaper back up and said, "Something started happening a few days ago."

"Don't do this."

"Do what?"

"Start making shit up."

"I'm not. Some boxes arrived."

"Big deal," Nash said, suddenly bored. He needed to end this thing and get his ass into the office. "The place must get three or four deliveries a day."

"True, but this delivery didn't come during normal hours."

"Come on," Nash said in a tired voice. "You're clutching at straws."

"Just hear me out for a second. The boxes arrived during evening prayer two days ago. They never do shit during evening prayer except pray. Six of the younger more radical guys weren't around, so I snuck out to see what they were up to."

"And?"

"I saw them carrying these boxes down to the basement."

"What's in the boxes?"

"I don't know. They put them in a storage room and put a couple new padlocks on the door."

"That's awfully thin."

"Just give me forty-eight hours. I've given you a year of my life. You can give me forty-eight hours."

Nash grabbed his coffee and took a sip while he thought about it. The truth was that only two people other than himself knew the real identity of the man sitting next to him and they weren't about to run to the FBI.

While Nash was thinking about it the man asked, "Did you ever get a photo of the guy I told you about?"

"No. I couldn't get someone up there fast enough."

"Well," the man said in an I-told-you-so voice, "he's is supposed to be coming back in town today or tomorrow."

Nash figured he could waste the whole morning going back and forth like this, but he didn't have the time. *One year of his life.* The words rang in Nash's ears.

"Nobody even knows I exist. Two more days is all I ask and then I'm done. I'm going to walk into the first sports bar I can find and order a big fucking Budweiser. One of those thirty-six-ouncers. I'm gonna get smashed and then I'm gonna get laid."

"Can I at least debrief you first?" Nash said with a grin.

"If you bring the beer."

Nash nodded. "Toss out the normal protocols. Text me at this number." Nash wrote the number down on the corner of the newspaper. "Ten and ten. You got me?"

"Yep. Twice a day."

"Don't miss your fucking check-in."

"Yes, sir," he said, satisfied he'd gotten what he wanted.

"There ain't no cavalry to come save your ass. You're out there solo. You don't even exist."

"I didn't come this far to lose. I'll get the goods on these assholes."

"Two days. That's all you've got and then I want you out." Nash leaned forward so he could look him in the eye. "You hear me?"

"Loud and clear."

Nash folded up the sports section and handed it back to Johnson. Without saying another word he got up and left the coffee shop.

CHAPTER 41

CAPITOL HILL

THE wide hallway outside the Senate Intelligence Committee's meeting room was crowded with staffers. Some actually appeared to be in transit from one point to another, but a surprising number were simply loitering—leaning against walls and clogging doorways, standing with their politically like-minded coworkers. Nash knew he shouldn't have been surprised. This was entertainment for a group of underpaid partisans, men and women who worshipped either the senator they slaved for or the party, or both. This afternoon's little event was one of the reasons they worked for scraps. Most of them could walk across the street and within a few hours land a job in the private sector making double what they were already making. This was what kept them from leaving—the proximity to power. The draw of powerful men and women meeting in secret to discuss things that would have far-reaching implications.

Nash stopped at the door for a moment and looked at the faces of the conservatively dressed staffers. Most of them looked to be no more than a few years out of college. Nash felt a pinch of rage at the entire system. None of them should be here. Nothing that was said inside

SH 219 should ever be shared with these people. They were too young and too politically motivated to ever be trusted with national secrets. But they would be. The hearing was likely to last into the dinner hour, and the more senior staffers who were read in would come and go over the next several hours, relaying messages from the bosses back to their offices and slowly but steadily the leaking would start. It would start out innocently enough.

Moods would be reported, who was upset and who was trying to calm people down. From there the facts would start to trickle out. Maybe only ten to twenty percent of what was actually going on. That's what you could count on the staffers to do. The real damage would come from the senators themselves—men and a few women who were schooled in the nastiest game of all—politics. In the public relations arena they were the ultimate street fighters, in many cases willing to do whatever it took to win. There was a block of six or so who would uphold their end of the bargain, and another six who would hold their fire until someone else leaked first. That left two or three senators, depending on the issue, plus the four ex officio members who were the worst offenders of all. That was who Rapp was planning to meet head-on and none of them with the exception of Kennedy thought it was a wise move. Nash couldn't figure that one out, what was going on with her, but the whole thing was making him nervous. He could feel something bad just around the corner. What it was, he had no idea, but it was twisting his gut. The last time he'd felt it this acutely was right before the mission in Afghanistan when he'd almost died.

Nash shook the thought from his head and entered the room. He took both of his mobile phones out and handed them over to a staffer who stuck them in a numbered cubbyhole for him to retrieve when he left. No electronic devices were allowed inside the secure chamber without special authorization. As a precaution to prevent someone from pulling up his call list, e-mails, and address book, Nash had already removed the SIM cards and the batteries from each phone.

Nash walked up the small ramp and entered the secure portion of the committee room. He squeezed by a few people in the narrow inner hallway, opened the glass door to the main committee briefing room, and was hit with a wall of noise. The raised portion of the room where the senators sat was packed. Sixteen of the nineteen seats were filled and the area behind the senators was crawling with committee staffers and senior staffers from the office of each senator. There were at least two people for every senator and maybe a few more. And people wondered why they couldn't keep secrets.

In front of him were two rows of chairs and a long table where six people sat. Nash knew four of them intimately and the other two only in passing, and hoped he had no reason to get to know them any better. They were the CIA general counsel and his deputy. The two men flanked Kennedy, who was sitting in the middle of the table. Charles O'Brien, the director of the National Clandestine Service, was there as well as his deputy, Rob Ridley. Rapp was the last one, and he was sitting all the way to the left. Nash grabbed a chair behind Rapp and squeezed his shoulder.

Rapp turned around and gave Nash a confident smile. He was in a dark blue pinstripe suit with a white shirt and light blue paisley silk tie. "Glad you could make it."

Nash leaned forward. "Are you sure about this?"

"Absolutely," Rapp said in an upbeat tone.

"But you know"—Nash glanced up at the men and women who represented nearly one-fifth of the United States Senate—"they're nasty fuckers, Mitch. They won't play fair."

Rapp laughed casually and said, "I have a few tricks up my sleeve. Just sit back and keep your mouth shut. You're only here because they asked for you."

"I don't like you taking all the heat."

"I don't give a shit what you like," Rapp said with a grin, "you're not running the show. Just be a good Marine and sit there."

The background noise reached a crescendo as the last two senators entered the room. Bob Safford, the chairman of the committee, and Evan Whaley, the vice chairman, tried to get to their seats but every few feet they were stopped by a colleague or a staffer. Nash had been told by Ridley that there had already been a great deal of fighting between the two parties, and various factions within the parties, over not just how this hearing should be handled, but whether or not the Intelligence Committee should even get the first bite at the apple. The Armed Services and the Judiciary Committees were both trying to stake a claim, and then there was the House of Representatives to deal with. There was a very real chance that they would all spend the better part of the next year testifying in front of all these committees and quite possibly a special prosecutor and a grand jury as well.

Safford gaveled the hearing to order, and the next five minutes were taken up by motions and a variety of procedural issues that had very little to do with any of the people who were called on to testify. It was simply the nature of the Senate. When all of that was sorted out, Safford took a final look at his notes and then flipped his reading glasses up onto his forehead, which was his habit when the cameras weren't around.

"Director Kennedy, I would like to say that I am deeply disturbed by the accusations that have been leveled against one of your employees." Safford's deep-set eyes floated over to Rapp.

Rapp raised his hand in case anyone had any doubt as to which employee the senator was referring to. Nash cringed. He could tell Rapp was in one of his insolent "I don't give a shit" moods.

Safford's lips curled into a sneer, but he didn't engage Rapp. That would come later. Addressing Kennedy, he said, "There has been a great deal of maneuvering in the Senate today. There are several chairpersons who feel that this issue of Mr. Rapp's potentially illegal and definitely unprofessional behavior would be better handled in their committees in a more open manner. Senator Whaley and I have managed to persuade them that for now this issue should be handled by this committee."

"I would like the record to show," Senator Lonsdale said forcefully, "that as chairperson of the Judiciary Committee I strongly disagree with your decision and plan on holding open hearings as soon as tomorrow to get to the bottom of this."

"I'm sure you will," was Safford's tired response.

"And I would also like the record to show"—this time it was Senator Russell Sheldon—"that as a former air force officer and prosecutor and current member of the Armed Services Committee I am deeply disturbed by what looks to be an attempt at a cover-up by the CIA and certain sympathizers at the Pentagon. I am shocked at the lack of professionalism exhibited by Mr. Rapp and expect to see him prosecuted to the fullest extent of the law."

With hunched shoulders Safford looked from one end of the curved table to the other and said, "Is everybody done, or are we going to have an open mike this afternoon?"

There were a few snickers from the older senators who were proud that one of their fellow bull elephants had put the young ones in their place.

"Because," Safford continued, "I'm not going to put up with this. Everybody knows the rules. Each member will get fifteen minutes to question the panel. Make your complaints verbally . . . file them in writing . . . I don't care. Just wait your turn. Are we all clear?"

A smattering of senators nodded, but most simply ignored the chairman.

"Now, Director Kennedy, is there anything you would like to say before we get started?"

Kennedy leaned forward and in a respectful but distant voice said, "No, Mr. Chairman."

Safford looked to his right and gave the okay to begin questioning.

CHAPTER 42

BRUNSWICK, GEORGIA

HAKIM clenched his jaw and looked down at the body with a seething anger. The bullet hole was clearly visible in the back of the head. A neat little pucker mark no bigger than a nickel. Thank Allah the man had been dumped facedown, because Hakim did not want to see what the heavy-caliber bullet had done to his face. So much matter had exploded from the other side that Hakim imagined a gaping hole encompassing what used to be the mouth and nose.

"What a waste," he told himself.

They had traveled nearly five hundred miles in just under eight hours, from the southern tip of Florida all the way up and out of the state. That had been Hakim's goal and they had achieved it, and this was their reward. He looked down at the body again and didn't know if he should cry or laugh. Cry for the boy whose only crime was that he had helped them, or laugh because he didn't want to cry. He called into question for perhaps the first time the heart of his friend. It had been Karim, of course. Something had changed in the man.

Hakim thought back on the day. How it had started with the magnificent destruction of the Coast Guard helicopter and the mad dash to shore. The exhilaration of cutting through the sea and the wind at a hundred miles an hour, knowing every second might count. Karim had been happy then. Hakim had looked over and saw him smiling like he hadn't seen him smile in years. Unfortunately it didn't last. His mood instantly soured when they landed the boats in the tall grass at Long Key State Park. The men from the drug cartel were waiting with their four-wheelers to off-load the drugs and Karim was livid. He'd had it in his mind that they would simply leave the boats and not be seen by anyone. He was ranting and raving about operational security and a bunch of other things that Hakim guessed he had read in one of his U.S. military manuals that he was always studying. The man couldn't get it through his head that American Special Forces had near unlimited assets to get them from point A to point B. Billion-dollar aircraft carriers, billion-dollar submarines, stealth planes, and the best helicopters and pilots in the world. They, on the other hand, this little offshoot of al-Qaeda, had nothing but themselves, and Karim was delusional if he thought they could so closely mirror the American model—just the nine of them.

They had almost come to blows over it, and if it weren't for the fact that the Puerto Ricans were so well armed, Hakim had no doubt that Karim would have executed all of them on the spot. Hakim took charge and ordered the men to help off-load the cocaine bricks. Karim tried to countermand the order until Hakim snapped at him and asked him how he expected to pay for everything that they were about to do. And then in a much quieter voice, he asked him how he expected to get out of the country when they were done wreaking havoc.

Karim was on unsure ground here, and Hakim pressed his slight advantage by telling him that it was going to be very expensive to buy safe passage out of the country. As if on cue, one of the Puerto Ricans handed over a duffel bag filled with a million dollars in cash and Karim was silenced. The rest of the money, some eight million dollars, would be transferred to a bank account in Dubai. The men from the drug cartel were well schooled in the drill. The first eight bricks of cocaine were taken off the boat and put into the saddlebags of two motorcycles, which immediately left. This way the cartel covered its costs should the rest of the drugs be seized.

In just under ten minutes the drugs were unloaded, and then came the next big surprise for Karim. They completed the hundred-meter hike through the tall grass to a waiting passenger van. Hakim introduced Karim to Mohammad, a Libyan grad student at the University of Miami who he had recruited months earlier. This sent Karim into an apoplectic rage. He was furious that someone had been brought in to help without his approval. If it weren't for the fact that they heard a helicopter drawing closer it might have happened right there, which really would have been stupid.

This, Hakim thought to himself now as he looked down at the body, *was just a waste. An utter waste of talent and human life . . . and for what?*

All ten of them piled into the fifteen-passenger van and headed north on U.S. Highway 1. The windows in back were heavily tinted, so it was easy for the men to change. Each man had a duffel bag that Hakim and Mohammad had filled with T-shirts, socks, sweat suits, and baseball hats. Everything except the socks were a combination of blue, white, and red and sported the eagle logo of American University in Washington, D.C. All of it had been purchased online and in person at the school's bookstore. The van also had District of Columbia license plates and school bumper stickers. If they were stopped by the police, their story was that they were returning to school from a track meet at Florida International University.

They made it through Miami just as the morning traffic was starting to pick up. Interstate 95 was crowded but the cars moved along all the way to the Palm Beach exits and then things thinned out. They kept the radio tuned to an all-news AM station and stayed five miles over the posted speed. Karim had questioned this, but they pointed out that most of the cars were going ten to fifteen miles over the speed limit. Otherwise, Karim didn't speak and the mood in the van was tense. The van had two twenty-five-gallon tanks, and they stopped for gas only once, south of Jacksonville. The only person who got out of the vehicle was Mohammad. That was when Karim leaned forward and hissed his admonishment in Hakim's ear.

Back on the road Karim asked for a map, and an hour and a half later he told Mohammad to pull over at the next exit. It was time for the men to stretch their legs. They exited I-95 at Hickory Bluff and entered Blythe Island State Park. The towering pines at the entrance gave way to mangrove trees and Spanish moss as they neared the water. Hakim had an uneasy feeling as they went deeper and deeper into the park, but he didn't say anything. They came upon a rutted dirt road that appeared to simply disappear into the dense woods. Poor Mohammad was the one who saw it and asked if he should take it. Karim told him yes.

A few hundred meters later they stopped. The men all piled out of the van. Karim gave them a series of subtle hand signals and without a word they began to spread out. Two of them headed back down the road to keep an eye out in case someone stumbled upon them. Two more headed farther down the road and the other three spread out around the van. Karim casually joined the young grad student and Hakim at the front of the van. After only a few seconds he pointed over Mohammad's shoulder into the woods and said, "What is that?"

Hakim saw it all happen in slow motion. Karim drew his .45-caliber Glock from his waistband. A stubby four-inch suppressor had been screwed onto the end. Karim placed the tip of the suppressor no more than a few inches from the back of the young man's head and squeezed the trigger. The heavy round left the gun with a clank and then a pink mist of flesh, blood, and bone exploded from the other side of Mohammad's head. In a strange way Hakim thought it looked as if Mohammad had vomited off his own face.

With the gun still extended, and the lifeless body tumbling to the ground, Karim asked, "What were you thinking?"

The words seemed distant, like someone was talking to him from the other side of a heavy fabric. Hakim slowly lifted his head and looked at his childhood friend. For the first in his life, he felt like he didn't know the man he considered a brother. Slowly he turned away from the contorted body and addressed his friend with near disgust, "What is wrong with you?" Hakim asked.

Karim ignored the question and said, "You should have never recruited him."

"How would you know? You never asked him a single question."

"It doesn't matter. He is an outsider. We cannot trust him."

"You think he's working for the FBI?" Hakim pointed at his own head.

"You never know. That is the problem."

"The problem is that you have become a paranoid, angry zealot."

"Do not speak to me in such a manner."

"Or what? Are you going to shoot me like you shot him? Like you shot Zachariah?"

"I just might."

Hakim scoffed at him. "Think about this! You were always the better student. If he was working for the FBI don't you think they would be swooping down out of the sky right now?"

"They might want to see where we are going first."

"Look at you . . . you don't even believe yourself. You think they would let four dark-skinned men shoot down one of their helicopters and then begin driving north toward Washington and New York?"

"That is not the point."

"Then what is the point?"

"No one can be trusted." Karim matched his volume. "I have told you this from the very beginning. Only the people we have fought alongside in Afghanistan can be trusted."

"And how many of those people are here in America?"

"That is my point!" Karim yelled. "I gave you specific orders. You are the advance element. Your job was to go in first and pave the way for us."

"And what in Allah's name do you think I've done?"

"You have compromised our entire operation by recruiting a student." Karim looked down at the dead body with disgust. "If you were not my friend I don't know what I would do."

"And if you weren't like my brother, I would beat your brains out." Hakim balled his fists in anger.

"I will not warn you again. Do not speak to me in such a tone."

Hakim brought his nose to within inches of Karim's and in an angry whisper said, "I think you are the one who should be warned. I think you believe a little too much in your destiny. I think it has gone to your head."

Karim shoved his friend. "I am ordering you to get in the van . . . right now."

Hakim didn't move. "No one has been more loyal to you. No one has more faith in you than me and this is how you repay me." Hakim pointed at the lifeless body.

"You are a fool."

"Careful what you say, Karim. I am not one of your robots who you have brainwashed for the last six months in the jungle."

"These men are elite warriors."

"They might be, but they have proven nothing yet. It has been my skill and ingenuity that have gotten you this far, and the help of a twenty-two-year-old student."

"We do not need your help."

"Hah!" Hakim scoffed at his friend's outrageous statement. "Then why did you send me here?"

Karim refused to answer the question, instead saying, "It is time to leave." He looked at one of his men and flashed a hand signal.

Hakim grabbed him by the front of his sweatshirt and yelled, "You sent me here because you couldn't do it yourself, and you hate to admit it, because you think so highly of yourself. I am not one of your soldiers, Karim, I am your equal."

Karim jabbed his gun into the belly of his friend, "I will kill you right here and now if you do not let go of me."

Hakim's eyes searched Karim's for a sign that he was bluffing but he saw none. Hakim let go and stepped away. "Fine, have it your way, but when we get to Washington, I am done. Since you and your men are so talented, I'm sure you will have no problem completing your mission without me."

Hakim started for the driver's door and under his breath added, "Good luck finding your way back to Pakistan."

CHAPTER 43

CAPITOL HILL

NASH sat in silence and watched as one senator after another peppered his bosses with questions. Rapp was taking most of the heat, followed by Kennedy, and they were holding their own against the considerable combined intellect of the committee's members. Normally loath to pay the group of windbags any compliment, Nash had to admit that this was no collection of dummies. They had their faults, to be sure, but not when it came to verbal combat.

For the better part of two hours he had watched them maneuver and attempt to punch holes in Rapp's and Kennedy's stories. Kennedy's narrative was fairly easy to stick to. As part of Rapp's arrangement, the only thing she had to do was deny any knowledge of the operation. This would seem easy enough, if it weren't for the fact that she was in charge. Thirteen of the nineteen members had law degrees, and two of them had been prosecutors. Without a gallery of reporters to play to, they were quick and to the point. Nash also thought he noticed them treading more lightly than normal.

The first group of senators focused on getting Rapp and Kennedy to make statements under oath, and then as their version of events became record, the senators who followed looked to point out inconsistencies and try to get them to contradict themselves. Again, for Kennedy, this was not difficult, although several senators tried to make Rapp's history of insubordination an issue. They hammered Kennedy for her lack of leadership and accountability. One senator went so far as to actually say that he had been warning Kennedy for several years that she needed to keep Rapp on a shorter leash.

It was the only time that Kennedy bristled at her questioners. In a tone that bordered on rebellious she admonished the committee for referring to her most decorated clandestine operative in such a demeaning way. "Regardless of your personal feelings," she told them, "you should respect the sacrifice this man has made to defend this country."

Most of the senators took Kennedy's words in a sober manner, but a few couldn't help snickering and whispering derisive remarks to each other. The day dragged on, and the dinner hour approached. With nearly a third of the members still having to get their time, the chairman suggested they take a quick fifteen-minute break and then push through. The five of them went into one of the smaller secure briefing rooms and gathered themselves together, while the two CIA lawyers went off to try and get a word in with the chairman. Kennedy's mood was as usual unreadable, while O'Brien and Ridley looked like tired old warriors who knew they were in the middle of a battle that was already lost. Rapp, on the other hand, was upbeat, bouncing around the room clapping his hands and rubbing them together like he couldn't wait to get back out there.

He must have noticed the dire expression on Nash's face, because he grabbed him by the shoulder and said, "Cheer up. The fun's about to start."

"It doesn't look real fun out there."

Rapp laughed. "I haven't had such a good time since I drowned that little prick down in . . ."

"Mitch!" Kennedy screamed from across the room, stopping him from providing any more details to a murder that only the two of them knew about.

"Relax," Rapp said as he looked around the room. "You guys are way too uptight."

Kennedy picked up a phone and dialed the office. Ridley joined Rapp and Nash and said, "Seriously, Mitch, what in the hell do you think is going on out there? We're getting our asses kicked."

"No," Rapp replied, "I'm getting my ass kicked."

"You don't think this is going to affect the rest of us?" Ridley said.

"I never said that."

"Well, it is going to affect us, and it is quite possibly going to affect our ability to do our jobs."

"By jobs, do you mean running up here five times a week to hold their hands and fill out all your forms in triplicate, or do you mean going out there and busting up these terrorist cells before they hit us?"

"You know what I mean."

"I'm not sure I do sometimes, Rob." He gestured to Nash and said, "Look at you two. You look beat. You look ashamed."

"We're worried," Nash said.

"Well, don't be," Rapp replied, "I've got it under control."

"It sure the hell doesn't look like it." Ridley turned and walked over to O'Brien.

Looking at Nash, Rapp said, "What in the hell is wrong with him?"

"Mitch," Nash said in a tired voice, "you just don't get it sometimes."

Rapp looked slightly taken aback. "Now I'm getting it from you too, junior."

Nash put his right hand on his hip and looked at the ground. "It doesn't look good out there."

"Everything is going exactly the way I thought it would."

"Does that include you going to jail?"

"I'm not going to jail. I can promise you that."

"What about us?"

"You don't see them asking you any questions, do you?"

"Not yet. That's the problem with these things, Mitch. They have a way of growing. You said it yourself. Before this is over there'll be another five committees looking into what happened."

"Let 'em."

"And you don't think that's going to take a toll on us? Both personally and professionally?"

"I'm the one they're after."

"There's no doubt about that," said Nash dully, "but this isn't going to be a precision air strike. It never is, with these guys. They're gonna carpet-bomb us and you can't guarantee that a few of us won't go down in the process."

Rapp sighed, "So that's what you guys are so glum about?"

"Yeah," Nash said in hushed voice. "We have families, Mitch. Maggie is scared to death that Feds are going to show up one day and take me away in cuffs. Right in front of the children. Right in the middle of frickin' dinner. She has the nightmare once a week at least. There're countries I can't go to now because that goddamn rendition program got leaked. Italy! We went there on our honeymoon and now we can't go back. This shit is wearing on our families. You look at Rob over there." Nash pointed to Ridley. "He's got three kids he has to put through college. How in the hell do you think he's going to do that if these asses get him fired and take away his pension? How in the hell do you think he's going to afford the attorneys he's going to have to hire to try and keep his ass out of jail?"

Rapp nodded as if he finally understood this for the first time, but he didn't. This was central to why he was forcing the issue. He turned to O'Brien and Ridley, who were talking in the other corner. "Guys, come here."

The two men shared a few more words and then joined Rapp and Nash.

"Gentlemen, maybe I haven't been clear enough with you. Chuck,"

Rapp said to O'Brien, "I think you probably understand this more than these two because Irene has been keeping you in the loop." Rapp grinned and added, "Your kids are all out on their own, and being the salty prick that you are, you've put in enough time that you can tell every one of those senators to stick it right up their ass if you feel like."

"That's right," O'Brien said without smiling.

"So my comments are more directed at these two, but I think you'll want to hear them as well." Rapp looked at Nash and then Ridley and said, "We've spent the last six years avoiding this fight. And I mean this shit right here." Rapp pointed at the ground. "This committee. We're like an invading army that keeps bypassing cities because we know things are going to get ugly if we go in and try to clean the rat bastards out block by block. We've avoided the problem, and now because we didn't do it right the first time we have this insurgency on our hands. Our supply lines are all fucked up and our confidence is shot. We spend every day looking over our shoulders wondering if our government is going to ambush us." Nash and Ridley shared a sad knowing exchange and nodded.

Rapp leaned in a few inches and said, "Well, I'm done fucking around. And as two retired Marine combat officers you two should understand this better than most. This fight with the Hill has been coming regardless of whether or not we want it. You know the tactics . . . if a fight is unavoidable then you might as well pick the time and the place. Take some of the guesswork out of the equation and take the battle to the enemy. As to why I decided to force the issue now . . . you guys both know the answer to that. This third cell we've been worried about . . . we've hit a wall. We don't know where to even start looking for these guys."

"So what is all this going to accomplish?" Nash asked. "You trying to put yourself up on the cross? I don't get it."

"I'm not into the martyr thing," Rapp grinned. "You know that. What I'm trying to do is bring this thing to a head."

"Why?" asked Ridley. "Why now?"

"Because I think we're going to get hit. And I just told you, I'd rather choose the time and place of the fight. Have you noticed that not a single senator has bothered to ask me why I would take such a gamble running an op like this?"

The other three men shared a look and said, "No."

"It's because they're so stuck in their own world. We've allowed them to depict us as a bunch of goons who smack prisoners around because we get some sick, sadistic thrill out of it. They hold us accountable, but we never hold them accountable."

"How in the hell are we going to hold them accountable?" O'Brien asked in his raspy voice.

"By telling them about these other two cells and letting them know the third one is on the loose."

"And what are you going to do when they ask for the details about this plot? The whole damn reason we haven't told them so far is because they always want to know the details. Are you going to tell them the Brits farmed it out to the Thais—and they tortured the shit out of them?"

"You'll see when we go back in there."

"What are you waiting for? You've already gone through two thirds of them."

Rapp smiled. "I'm waiting for Lonsdale."

"Why her?" Nash asked.

"Because she chairs Judiciary, and that's where this whole thing is headed."

One of the committee staffers poked their head in the door and told them it was time. Rapp said they'd be right along, and then as soon as the door was closed, he looked each man in the eye and said, "You guys all have deniability, so stop looking so damn defeated when you're in there. You're warriors . . . be proud of what we do."

CHAPTER 44

SENATOR Lonsdale hurried down the hallway as quickly as her black leather Marc Jacobs pumps could carry her near perfectly proportioned frame. Her rail-thin chief of staff was galloping beside her, his long, lanky stride doubling his boss's. They crossed over from the Hart Senate Office Building to Dirksen. Technically they were two buildings, but they existed as one, with every floor of the two buildings connecting. Lonsdale and Wassen went through the senator's private door. Wassen stopped to have a word with the two executive assistants, but the senator kept moving.

She went straight into her large office and closed the door. This one was drastically different from her office in the Capitol. It was almost as big, but where the other one was ornately decorated, this one was utilitarian. There were no marble or plaster reliefs, just Sheetrock and carpeting. The furniture reflected the space. Everything was very linear and slightly modern.

Lonsdale kicked off her pumps and grabbed her pack of cigarettes and lighter from her top-left desk drawer. She flicked the switch on the

special ventilation unit she'd had installed and fired up her first cigarette. The smooth, warm smoke filled her lungs and she felt herself
begin to relax. It took every bit of her reserve to sit there silently for
two hours while her colleagues maneuvered. There was Joe Valdez,
whom she had never been impressed with, serving up one retarded
question after another. She could see that, as chairman of the Foreign
Relations Committee, he was going to try and get a piece of the action,
but the way she had it figured he was fifth on the list, and she wasn't
going to give him jack shit.

A couple puffs later she looked down and scanned her call sheet.
Most of the names weren't important enough to call back today, but
there were a few she would have to get to tonight when they wrapped
things up. For now she wanted to get herself in the right frame of mind
for her shot at the den of liars. Pretty much everyone had gone over
their allotted fifteen minutes, and Lonsdale planned on doing the
same. She figured as chairman of the Judiciary they would all expect
her to go after them, and fifteen minutes wasn't nearly enough to question the five of them.

An unmarked manila folder lay on the desk. She opened it and
began reading the list of potential questions her staff had put together
for her based on the first round of questions. By the time she'd finished
reading them, she was finished with the cigarette. She stabbed it out in
the crystal ashtray, where it sat there crooked and tattooed with red
lipstick. Lonsdale hesitated and then decided to grab another one.
She'd just finished lighting it when Wassen entered the room. As always, he closed the door behind him.

"Five minutes."

She nodded and exhaled a cloud over her shoulder toward the
ventilation machine.

"Second one?" Wassen asked with a curious eye.

"I didn't know you were counting."

"I've noticed an *uptick* lately," he said in a disapproving voice.

Lonsdale's pretty little nose scrunched up, and it looked for a moment like she might stick her tongue out at him. Wassen unnerved her

at times, probably because no one knew her better. Since the death of her husband thirteen years ago, he had been her constant companion. He was like a father, husband, and girlfriend all rolled into one.

"Big deal," she said as she took another drag. "I'm still only smoking a pack a week."

Wassen knew it was closer to two, but there wasn't time to argue about it right now. "Did you review the questions?"

"Yes."

"And?"

"They're fine."

"Any idea who you're going to start with?"

"Kennedy," she said as she turned and looked at herself in a full-length mirror on the wall. "I'm going to light her up and then go after Rapp, and if I have time I'll take Nash apart."

"Sound strategy."

Lonsdale ran a hand along the front of her black Theory 'Rory-Tailor' jacket and matching pants. She spotted a few wrinkles and frowned.

Wassen read her mind and said, "Don't worry about it. No cameras."

He was right. She set the half-finished cigarette in the ashtray and grabbed a small makeup bag from the credenza behind her desk. She took a brush with powder and began dabbing her face. "Can you believe Joe Valdez is a United States senator?"

"Not the sharpest tack in the drawer."

"And then that bitch Patty Lamb. She's going to try and wrestle this thing away from me and get it in front of Homeland Security."

"Let her try," Wassen said as he checked his watch, "it'll never happen."

Lonsdale put the makeup brush away and plucked at the neck of her white spandex T-shirt to get some of the skin-colored powder off. She began lining her lips and said, "It's going to come down to Ted Darby and I."

"Yes it will, and you'll both end up holding hearings. There's no way you're going to wrestle it away from him, and there's no way he's going to wrestle it away from you."

She thought about the chairman of the Armed Services Committee while she finished lining her lips. "I suppose you're right."

"We need to get back. You don't want them to start without you and let someone else go after them as hard as you will."

Lonsdale put out her cigarette and said, "Right you are, Ralphy."

She gave herself a quick spray of perfume and put on her pumps, and they left. Her personal assistants were standing when she walked through the small lobby. Both wished her luck and told her to go get them. Lonsdale kept a pleasant yet determined look on her face and shook her fist in the air as she walked past them and into the wide hallway. As they strolled back to the committee room, more people wished her luck. This was the big show on Capitol Hill today and everyone knew she would be the one to go for the throat.

Lonsdale was in fact one of the last people to make it back to the committee room. She took her seat and peered down at the CIA employees. Her face slowly transformed into a disapproving frown and then she began to sadly shake her head. Senator Safford called the meeting back to order and before turning things over to Lonsdale reminded the witnesses that they were still under oath.

"Senator Lonsdale," Safford said as he slid his reading glasses up onto his shiny forehead, "you may begin."

Lonsdale thanked the chairman and took a moment to look down at her notes even though what she was about to say was not written down. She deliberately removed her stylish black reading glasses and said, "Director Kennedy, I think that your performance as director of the Central Intelligence Agency has been an embarrassment to this country from the day you took over. Your tenure has been one disaster after another, and for the life of me, I can't understand why you won't simply resign."

The objections erupted from the other side of the table. Even Lonsdale's fellow party members were shaking their heads and mumbling to each other. Safford banged his gavel until silence was restored and then admonished Lonsdale. "We are here today to gather information, not to indict and convict on incomplete evidence."

Lonsdale stayed on the offensive, saying, "I'm not even talking about illegal activities. I'll get to that in a minute. I'm talking about gross incompetence. This is not our first go-around with Mr. Rapp. This committee has been telling Director Kennedy for some time that she needs to keep Mr. Rapp on a shorter leash. Apparently she has intentionally ignored us, or she is incapable of managing her people. You choose," she said, looking directly at Kennedy. "Either way, she needs to go."

The objections erupted yet again, with Senator Gayle Kendrick leading the charge, "I would like to remind my colleague from Missouri that Director Kennedy has devoted nearly twenty-five years of her life to the service of this country and she deserves to be treated with respect, regardless of one's political beliefs."

"So you want us to just blindly respect people because they've been a bureaucrat for twenty-five years without taking into account the abuses and illegal activities they've condoned and participated in?"

"You see," Kendrick said to the chairman and vice chairman, "this is what she's going to do when she gets this in front of her committee. She's going to turn a hearing into a trial, and she's going to act as the judge even though she already has her mind made up."

"That's not true," Lonsdale said without much conviction.

"You know it is. All you want to do is crucify her in front of a nationally televised audience."

"My committee will go where the facts take us," Lonsdale replied with a steely look.

"You will do great harm to an organization that is trying its best to protect us from our enemies."

"I would like to remind the senator from Virginia that we are a nation of laws. And it is our job to make sure those laws are obeyed."

"And I would like to remind the senator from Missouri that

nowhere in the Constitution does it say we should go out of our way to afford those protections to our enemies."

The committee members erupted again with the two sides shouting at each other. Safford gaveled the room back to silence, and then without being told to proceed, Lonsdale said, "I think we can all agree that striking an officer in the United States Air Force is a crime. Now, Mr. Rapp, would you agree with that statement?"

A faint smile formed on Rapp's lips.

"Do you find this humorous, Mr. Rapp?"

"No, ma'am. I find your directness rather refreshing."

"I would appreciate that same directness from you when you answer my questions."

"I'll do my best, ma'am."

"Crimes committed," Lonsdale, repeated, "are you in agreement, Mr. Rapp, that you have broken several laws?"

"We are not in complete agreement, but I can respectfully see where you would think that I have committed a crime, or several crimes."

Lonsdale was slightly surprised by Rapp's apparent willingness to answer her. "Well, let's just start with the first one. Striking a United States Air Force officer . . . is that a crime?"

Rapp had already denied striking Captain Leland but answered Lonsdale's question anyway. "I agree that it is a crime, but I did not strike the man."

"If I call you before the Senate Judiciary committee, will you answer that same question, or will you plead the Fifth?"

Without hesitation, Rapp said, "I will honestly answer your questions, Madam Senator."

There was a quiet rumble of voices as Lonsdale's colleagues shared their surprised opinions. "So," Lonsdale pressed, "you will not take the Fifth."

"I have no desire to take the Fifth, ma'am."

"Let's leave desire out of this," Lonsdale said. She was used to working with lawyers and got the feeling the word would provide Rapp with some wiggle room. "You're telling me right now that you will freely testify before my committee and will not invoke your Fifth Amendment rights?"

"Yes, I am."

The shock caused by Rapp's openness swept over all of them. Every senator took a moment to look at each other and share their surprise. No one was more astounded than Lonsdale. She'd had it in her mind for some time now that she would have to drag Rapp before her committee and beat his brains out while he stubbornly refused to incriminate himself, which in a way was just fine with her. CIA employees had a nice history of looking guilty while they pleaded the Fifth. This sudden change, however, was even better.

Lonsdale directed her glare at Kennedy and said, "How about you, Director Kennedy? Will you testify before my committee or will you be exercising your Fifth Amendment right?" Her voice dripped with disdain.

"Like any American citizen I will reserve my right to exercise the Fifth Amendment."

Lonsdale shook her head in an overdisappointed manner. She looked back to Rapp. "So, Mr. Rapp, if I ask you about your interrogation of Abu Haggani, an Afghani in the custody of U.S. forces, you will not take the Fifth Amendment?"

"I will answer your questions, ma'am."

Rapp's responses were so unexpected that Lonsdale wasn't sure where to go. Sensing this, her chief of staff leaned forward and touched her shoulder. Lonsdale turned toward Wassen, who cupped a hand over her ear.

"No sense in bringing anything up here where they can classify it. Keep your powder dry until you get them in front of your committee."

Sound counsel as usual, Lonsdale thought to herself. She nodded and then looked over at Bob Safford and said, "No, further questions, Mr. Chairman."

CHAPTER 45

ARLINGTON, VIRGINIA

NASH homed in on the tennis ball hanging from the rafters of the garage like an F-18 pilot focusing on a rain-swept carrier deck. The garage was designed for two cars, but not two cars, three bikes, a couple of strollers, an old trike, scooters, razors, skateboards, and every stick and ball known to mankind. The tennis ball kissed the windshield and Nash threw the gearshift into park. *Safe in my garage,* he thought. *Maybe I'll just stay here the rest of the night.* But as much as he'd like to just check out for a few days, he wanted to see the kids.

He climbed out and went around and got the groceries out of the back. At the back door he set one bag down and checked the handle. It was unlocked. His blood started to boil. He'd told the whole damn family a hundred times that the doors were always to be locked. He opened the door and carried the groceries through the mudroom and into the kitchen, where he found his ten-year-old son sitting a mere foot from the TV eating a bowl of cereal. Nash set the groceries down and went back to the mudroom, where he closed and locked the door and then opened his pistol safe. He pulled the black paddle holster and gun off his hip and stuck it in the safe.

By the time he got back to the kitchen his fourteen-year-old daughter, Shannon, was waiting for him with Charlie in her arms. She looked just like her mother. Beautiful ivory skin with thick, shiny black hair. "Hi, Dad."

Nash kissed her on the cheek and asked her how her day was. Rather than answer him, she extended her arms and handed him Charlie. "Mom was supposed to be home twenty minutes ago. I'm late for play practice."

Just like that, she was gone with her backpack out the mudroom door.

Nash looked into the smiling eyes of young Charlie and from across the room heard, "I think he has a bomb in his pants."

Nash looked over at the ten-year-old, who was glued to the TV. Reluctantly, he turned Charlie around and sniffed his backside. With a sour face, Nash said, "Oh God, that stinks."

"I told you," the ten-year-old said after downing another spoonful of cereal.

"Your mother teach you how to change a diaper yet?"

"Nope"—Jack shook his head—"that's women's work."

Nash wanted to laugh, but resisted the urge. "You better not let your mother hear you say that."

Jack slowly turned toward his father, his mouth half open. "Who do you think I got that line from?"

"Doesn't matter. You're ten. You talk like that around your mother, and you're likely to get your butt swatted." Then under his breath he said, "And I'll really get in trouble."

"I learned it from you, Dad."

Nash carried Charlie through the kitchen and as he passed, his ten-year-old mumbled, "I'm surrounded by traitors." He continued into the living room and set Charlie down on the floor. Kneeling next to him, he grabbed some wet wipes and a fresh diaper from the bookshelf. Charlie lay on his back with his feet up making motorboat noises with his lips. Nash laughed at his little tuft of fine blond hair. Other than that, he was pretty much bald. Nash got everything ready and then went in. He unsnapped the inseam on the kid's bib overalls and undid the old diaper. A heinous mix of rotten vegetables and diarrhea wafted out from under the freed diaper.

Nash turned his head away and snatched a breath of fresh air. "Now, this is torture." He looked back down at Charlie and said, "What are they feeding you, little buddy? This is horrible." Turning his head back toward the kitchen, he yelled, "Jack, get in here."

A moment later the sandy haired, flat-topped ten-year-old appeared. "Yeah, Dad?"

Nash finished wiping all the crevices and then rolled the old diaper up tight and sealed it. "Throw this in the diaper pail." He saw his son's apprehension and added a "please" for good measure. His wife claimed the kids would be more open to helping out if everyone around the house was a little more polite. Nash countered that he'd gotten a lot of shit done in the Marine Corps, and so did his men, and no one ever said please to anyone. Maggie countered that he was no longer a Marine, nor were any of their kids.

Nash held out the softball-sized diaper.

The ten-year-old held his ground. "You're three weeks behind on my allowance."

"Yeah . . . well, you're ten years behind on rent, so unless you want to end up sleeping in the diaper pail, get your butt moving."

The kid lifted his Boston Celtics jersey over his nose and mouth and grabbed the diaper with two fingers like it was a hunk of radioactive waste. The smell still lingered, so Nash decided to give Charlie a bath. He carried him into the mudroom and started to fill the laundry tub. Jack came back in from his trip to the garage as his father was sticking the stopper in the bottom of the tub.

"How was school today?"

"Good . . . how's your back?"

"Better, thank you."

"And your melon." Jack pointed at his own head.

Nash smiled. Jack was the family comedian. "The melon is okay today. Not great, but okay. Did you have a test today?"

"Quiz."

"How'd you do?"

"Twenty-five out of twenty-five."

"Congrats," Nash said as he added some soap to the water. "Did you finish your homework?"

"When was the last time I didn't do my homework the minute I got home from school? It's your other son you need to worry about . . . the troglodyte."

Nash gave his third child a hard stare. "That's a big word for a ten-year-old." He set Charlie in the tub. "Do you even know what it means?"

Jack started dancing around like an ape. With his jaw stuck out, he said, "Caveman."

With a fatherly look of disapproval he grabbed a washcloth for the baby. Rory, the second child, struggled in school, but excelled in sports. He was thirteen and a half and on the verge of shaving. "Jack, let me give you a little advice. Don't say that to your brother."

"He calls me girlie boy all the time."

"That's what older brothers do."

"I don't do it to Charlie."

Nash looked down at the one-year-old, who was happily splashing away and sucking on the soapy washcloth. Looking back at Jack, he said, "Go ahead. Call him a girlie boy, if it'll make you feel better."

Jack smiled, got close to the tub, and said, "Girlie boy. Charlie, you're a little girlie boy."

Charlie looked up at his older brother and let loose an ear-splitting squeal. They all started laughing and Jack tried it again. Nash reached out, put his arm around Jack, and kissed him on the top of the head. "I'll talk to him, Jack, but you have to remember, Rory's going through a tough time right now. School isn't as easy for him as it is for you."

"So . . . I'd rather be good at sports like him."

"Buddy, you haven't even hit puberty yet."

"Rory was good at everything. Even before puberty."

"We all have our God-given gifts, son. I was a good athlete, and right now I'd rather have your brains than my brawn."

Just then, Maggie walked in the door, her hair pulled back in a high ponytail. She looked lovingly at her husband with his arm around her third child and the soapy head of her baby just barely visible over the top edge of the laundry tub.

"Oh . . . isn't this a nice picture? Look at Daddy and his little helper and my precious baby."

Charlie had been preoccupied with something beneath the water-line, but when he heard his mother's voice, his big brown eyes darted up to find the most important person in his world. A huge smile spread across his face and his little fingers reached out for the edge of the tub. He grabbed ahold of the lip and with considerable effort pulled him-self to his full height of twenty-seven inches, and blurted out the word that he had so proudly yelled nearly twelve hours earlier while eating his breakfast.

Maggie froze, Nash tried not to laugh and Jack blurted out, "I swear I didn't teach him that word." Neither parent responded, so he added, "I bet it was Rory."

"It was your mother," Nash said with no lack of joy.

Maggie snapped at her husband, "Like you don't walk around here swearing all the time."

"Jack," Nash said, "who swears more, me or Mommy?"

Jack looked back and forth between his two parents and then proved just how smart he was by darting past his father and into the kitchen. "No way am I getting in the middle of this," he yelled over his shoulder.

Maggie defiantly folded her arms across her chest and stared at her husband. "I'm sure he's heard you say it before."

Nash nodded, dipped a hand into the soapy water, and came up with the washcloth. He started wiping down Charlie's backside. "You do whatever you need to do to make yourself feel better about this one, princess."

Charlie looked up at his mother. The happy look was gone, replaced by a look that mirrored the concerned look of his mother. In a much softer voice this time he muttered the word that was causing his mother's distress. Nash couldn't take it anymore and burst out laughing.

Maggie, trying to hold her neutral expression, said, "Michael, you have to ignore him."

Charlie smiled at his dad and repeated the word two more times. Nash began laughing harder. Charlie reacted with equal vigor and started throwing the word out in quick repeated bursts. Nash completely lost it, and started howling.

"Stop it!" Maggie yelled at him. "All you're doing is reinforcing his behavior."

Nash tried to stop, but it only made it worse. Maggie, not thinking that any of it was funny, whacked her husband across the shoulder and yelled, "Goddammit, Michael, this isn't funny."

Charlie suddenly stopped saying the word. He looked up at his mother and then his father, the dark brown orbs that dominated his eyes growing seemingly larger. He zeroed in on his mother's less-than-happy expression, and then the bottom lip started to tremble, the big brown eyes filled with tears, and then it all came pouring out.

"No, honey," Maggie said in a soothing voice. "Mommy and Daddy love each other."

"Most of the time," Nash said under his breath.

Maggie craned her head around and shot him a look that caused him to cover his groin with his dry hand. Charlie was now wailing. Maggie stroked his cheek with the back of her hand and said, "Look . . . Mommy and Daddy love each other. Look up here, honey."

Maggie cupped her left hand around her husband's neck and pulled him close. Nash kept his family jewels covered on the off chance she was luring him in for a knee to the groin. Maggie laid a big exaggerated kiss on her husband replete with sound effects. She turned back to Charlie, who was still crying, and said, "See, Mommy and Daddy love each other." He was still crying so she went back to kissing her husband.

Nash decided she wasn't going to hurt him, so he joined in with gusto. Ten seconds later the two were still locked in a passionate kiss that was suddenly much more than acting. Nash's hands began to wander over his wife's body, and he pulled her in close. Charlie slowly stopped crying, but they kept going. Maggie reached her hand down below his belt and gave him a soft squeeze.

She moved her lips away from his and offered her cheek. "It appears everything is working just fine down there."

Nash nodded enthusiastically. "Let's go upstairs."

"You're going to have to wait."

Nash let out a long groan. "I love you," he moaned.

"I love you too."

Charlie began to giggle and smile.

"That's right," Maggie said. "Mommy and Daddy love each other."

Charlie said the word again, although this time in a soft and sensitive voice.

Nash looked down at him and said, "That's right, buddy."

Maggie finally broke down and started laughing. "You are horrible."

"I know."

"How was your day?" she asked with a touch of concern.

"It was interesting?"

"But you can't talk about it."

"No."

She stiffened a little. The happy moment was gone and the stress of his job was back in the happy little home. "Just promise me you'll tell me yourself. I don't want to wake up one morning and read it in the paper."

Nash kissed her forehead. "I promise."

CHAPTER 46

CAPITOL HILL

SENATOR Lonsdale stepped quietly out of her Capitol office and onto the veranda. She stood still and took in the beautiful sight before her. The setting sun was bathing the alabaster columns of the Supreme Court in a brilliant orange glow, but it was lost on her. She was frozen like a love-struck teenager staring at Wade Kline as he stood with his back to her, one hand on the stone railing and the other holding a cell phone to his ear. She'd never seen him with his suit coat off, and her eyes worked their way from his broad shoulders down to his narrow waist and finally his backside. Lonsdale took in a slow breath as she bit down softly on her bottom lip. She may have had crushes like this as a teenager but never such erotic thoughts.

Since her husband's death she'd had her fair share of lovers, but none this young. *This*, she told herself, *would have to be handled very discreetly.*

Kline turned around and greeted Lonsdale with a smile as he held up a finger. "I have to go," he said. "The senator is here. I'll call you later."

Something about his tone told Lonsdale that it was a woman. "Who was that?" she asked as casually as possible.

Kline hesitated and then said, "My wife. She's up in New York."

"Oh," Lonsdale said as she noted that he didn't tell her he loved her before hanging up. "Do you commute?"

"Yes and no," he said a bit sheepishly. "I have an apartment down here, but my workload is pretty heavy, so I'm lucky if I get back every couple weeks."

"Well," she said as her eyes danced over his body once again, "you obviously find time to work out."

"It's the only thing that keeps me sane."

"Just remember, life can be short. I found that out the hard way with my husband. He worked seventy, eighty hours a week, building his family business and he ended up dropping dead at age forty-five."

"I'm sorry to hear that."

"It's all right," she said in a lighthearted voice. "He gave me a beautiful daughter and a lot of financial security."

"I'm sure the beauty comes from you," Kline said with a smile.

"Well, thank you." Lonsdale had learned long ago how to take a compliment. "Are you in the mood for a drink, or just a smoke?"

"I'd love both."

"Good." Lonsdale walked back inside. "I'm having a vodka on rocks with a lemon twist. What would you like?"

"The same, but let me get them. Just point me in the right direction, and I'll take care of it."

Lonsdale got him started and then retrieved her cigarettes and lighter and met him back out on the veranda. Kline gave the senator her drink and said, "God, I need this."

Before he could get it to his lips, she stopped him and said, "A toast." She extended her glass and said, "To living a life without regrets." Lonsdale gave him a little wink and then took a sip.

"I'll drink to that."

"So how was your day?"

"Pretty shitty," Kline said in a matter-of-fact way. "In fact . . . I'd say it was one of the worst days I've had in a long time. Maybe ever."

Lonsdale set her drink down on the small black bistro table. "You're serious."

"As a heart attack."

"What happened?"

He thought back on the day, regretting rather intensely that he had given in to his more basic instincts and even worse that he been so foolish in underestimating Rapp. When you stripped it all away the man was a Goddamn professional killer. Even if only a third of the rumors were true, he had pulled off some pretty amazing shit. Who were they to think that they would be the ones to take him down? And it would be one thing if they could confine the fight to the justice system, but he'd been foolish enough to cross the Rubicon with Rapp and enter his arena of violence. He thought back on what had transpired in the cramped interrogation room and knew he was going to have nightmares about it for a long time.

He was lucky the psycho didn't kill him. After choking him unconscious, Rapp had put his handcuffs back on and called for the guards. Kline awoke to find himself in the ridiculous situation of having to say he didn't know what had happened. Kline had been in a couple of fights in his life. More like scuffles, really. One was in college and one was in his mid-twenties. Both times had been to defend the honor of his hot dates. There were some torn shirts and some minor scrapes, but that was it. No punches connected and the bouncers broke things up before they got out of hand. He remembered going home with his dates, though, and being rewarded for his bravado. There would be none of that this time, although, he had no doubt he could bed the woman standing before him if he so chose. She was gorgeous, elegant, and one of the most powerful women in America, and there was something about the age difference that for the first time in his life turned him on. It would all have to wait, though. It was far too valuable a card to play so carelessly, and so early in this game.

His thoughts jumped to the moment when he looked down and saw Rapp's cuffs lying in his lap. The absolute terror that he'd felt at that moment was unlike anything he had ever experienced in his life. Primal fear gripped him with the sudden knowledge that he was stuck in a ten-by-ten-foot cell with a predator as dangerous as any he'd find in the wild. If he had known Rapp was uncuffed, he never would have poked and prodded him the way he did. He couldn't believe he had been stupid enough to think he could fuck with him.

And then it was all a jumble of movement and pain. Rapp was on him like one of those big fucking lions that you see on the National Geographic channel late at night, and he was helpless. Looking back on it, he couldn't say whether it was due to his own incapacitating fear or Rapp's skills, or both, but the bottom line was that he was completely and utterly feeble. Kline considered himself to be in better shape than 99.9 percent of the people out there, and he'd taken kick-boxing classes and even done some sparring, but it had all failed him when he needed it most.

Rapp was choking him with his own tie and speaking to him in his deep, confident, deliberate voice, and what did he do? He wet himself. He wanted to believe he did it after he'd passed out, but he knew he'd done it while he was still conscious, because he remembered the warmth spreading down his leg and thinking that Rapp had stabbed him and it was his blood. Then when he'd come to, he'd felt the wetness and saw the expression on Rapp's face. It was a look of utter contempt. A look that said, "I had no idea you were that big a puss." Kline had never felt so emasculated in all his life. He shuddered at the memory.

Lonsdale saw him shake and asked, "What's wrong?"

Kline shook it off and said, "Nothing, it's just been a really bad day." Actually, it probably really had been the worst day of his life, but he didn't want to appear so weak in front of the woman who held so much sway over his future.

"What happened?"

He skipped over how his day began and jumped ahead a few hours. "It started out with the deputy AG chewing my ass out for a good thirty minutes, and then the assistant AG for the criminal division read me the riot act, and then the director of the FBI called and told me to pull my head out of my ass, and then shortly after that, the AG himself called me and reminded me in extremely unpleasant terms just exactly who I worked for. Secretary of State Wicka's office left a message for me and finally Secretary of Defense England himself called."

Lonsdale expected a little heat to come down from within the Justice Department, but not from other Cabinet members. "What did England say?"

Kline looked over the top of his glass as he took a drink and said, "He called me your butt boy."

"My butt boy?" she repeated, somewhat shocked.

"Yep. He said he knows damn well who was behind this stunt, and he's not going to put up with some PC attorney from the DOJ sticking his nose in something that was already being handled."

"I hope you told him it wasn't being handled."

Kline picked up the cigarettes. "I don't think he was in the mood," he said as he lit the first cigarette and then handed it to Lonsdale, "to hear what I had to say."

Lonsdale took the cigarette, thrilled by the prospect that it had just touched Kline's lips. "You have nothing to worry about."

"From where I'm sitting it seems like I have a lot to worry about."

Lonsdale set down her drink and reached out and grabbed his arm. "You have to trust me on this, Wade. They're trying to scare you off this, hoping that it will simply go away, but it isn't going to go away. This whole sordid mess is going to be in front of my committee the day after tomorrow, and then you are going to look like a hero."

Kline was silent for a long moment and then after looking around he started laughing.

"What's so funny?"

"I don't know," he said. "I just thought of something my dad said to me years ago."

"What's that?"

"He was a lawyer too, and he used to rattle off all the great attorneys in New York, and he used to say to me, 'Son, do you know what they all have in common?' And I used to say, 'They're all smart,' and he'd laugh and say, 'They're all smart, but what they really have in common is that everyone hates them.'"

"The old adage that you can't be successful without people hating you," Lonsdale agreed.

"I suppose."

"Don't worry, I'll stick to our deal," she said. "The Criminal Division is yours."

"Not if the White House has anything to say about it."

"If the president wants to get any of his judges confirmed he'll go along . . . trust me."

Kline took a big gulp from his drink and said, "So what's next?"

"How about dinner?"

"Oh," he said, trying to buy a second to think, "I'd love to, but I have plans. In fact I really should get going."

Lonsdale looked up into his damn blue/gray eyes and thought about kissing him. "But I just got here."

"You were forty-five minutes late," he reminded her.

"But I'm a senator." She smiled. "I have a busy schedule."

Kline took a step back and laughed in a carefree way. He held his glass up and said, "The most beautiful senator on the Hill."

Lonsdale blushed. "Flirting will get you everywhere."

"I'll have to remember that, but I'm going to have to take a rain check on dinner."

Lonsdale's euphoric mood plummeted, but she didn't let him see the disappointment she was feeling. "I know," she started, "I have three more functions to attend to this evening, but I would have loved some company."

"Next time," he said in a rush. "I promise."

"Good." Not wanting the rejection to drag on any longer than it already had, she offered him her cheek, and said, "You'd better get going."

Kline kissed the smooth skin just beneath her high cheekbone and then retreated. Lonsdale watched him walk back into her office and when he was finally gone, she let loose an emotional exhalation and began fanning herself with her free hand.

CHAPTER 47

RALPH Wassen entered the expansive office and eyeballed the dejected look on his boss's face. He had just passed Wade Kline in the hallway and guessed correctly that Lonsdale's consternation was due to the handsome boy wonder from the Justice Department. Never one to beat around the bush he blurted out, "You want to sleep with him, don't you?"

"Excuse me?" Lonsdale said, genuinely stunned.

"Don't act so shocked."

"Ah . . ." she stammered.

"I knew it."

She smiled, "It may have crossed my mind."

"I'm going to win so much money."

Lonsdale grabbed his arm. "What?"

"We started an office pool," he said in an exaggerated noncha-lant way.

"You're full of shit."

"Of course I am." Wassen turned and went to the bar. As he started to pour himself a scotch on the rocks, he asked, "Well . . . why don't you?"

Lonsdale plopped down on the silk Empire sofa and kicked off her pumps. "You know why?"

"No, I don't."

"For starters . . . he's a little young."

"That hasn't stopped you before."

"This one is different."

"How?" Wassen asked as he collapsed into one of the parlor chairs.

"He owes me his job."

"Who cares? People do it in this town all the time."

"He's married."

"That hardly matters these days."

"I thought you were supposed to look out for my best interests?" she asked with a curious eye.

"I am. It's just that I think you're in a bit of a funk lately."

"A funk?"

"You know . . . a little bitchy." He took a sip of his drink.

"So I should sleep my way out of it?"

"Basically. No one is going to hold it against you. At least not your base. The jackals might take a swipe at you, but then again it might help your image. The two of you make a striking couple."

"I'm old enough to be his mother."

"Technically, yes, but you don't look twenty years his senior."

"Thank you." She smiled.

"At least not with your clothes on," he added quickly.

"You are terrible," Lonsdale said with a scowl.

"Teasing," Wassen announced as he held up his drink. "You know my motto . . . You only live once. So, start living. Sleep with him, get it out of your system, and drop all this nonsense with Rapp and Nash."

Lonsdale was startled. "Where in the hell did that come from?"

"Everybody in the office is talking about it."

"About Rapp?"

"No, that you need to get laid."

"Cut the crap for a minute. Why in the world do you think I should let the CIA off the hook?"

"I don't know," Wassen shrugged, "because maybe they're doing the right thing?"

Lonsdale sat there for a long moment and stared at her longtime advisor. "You can't be serious."

"I am, and I don't know why you've decided to make this your cause. There's plenty of things to get upset about in this town."

Lonsdale set her drink down. She was used to Wassen's pranks, but this was different. Without the slightest hint of humor she asked, "You're not playing devil's advocate, are you?"

"No, I'm one hundred percent serious."

"Well, I think you're wrong."

"Have you ever looked at the polls on this issue?"

"Yeah . . . over ninety percent of the country is against torture."

"And over seventy percent of the country thinks child molesters should be castrated."

"The number is not that high."

"It is if you phrase the question properly."

"You can do that with any poll," Lonsdale said dismissively.

Wassen pointed at her and said, "And that's how they get the ninety-percent-against-torture number. They ask the question in a vacuum. Yes or no, are against torture?" He frowned. "I mean . . . who the hell is pro-torture?"

"You'd be surprised."

"Did you ever read *A Time to Kill* by Grisham?"

"Yes."

"Remember . . . the little girl got raped by the two rednecks and the dad ends up killing them? Would you convict the father or set him free? And stop being a politician for a second. When you were reading the book, did you want the father to be convicted or set free?"

"Set free, of course. But that has nothing to do with . . ."

"It has everything to do with what is going on!" Wassen said force-fully.

"Are you drunk?"

"I wish." He took a big gulp. "Ask yourself something. Why is Rapp willing to go before your committee?"

"Because he has no choice."

"B.S. You know he could spend months screwing with you on this."

"So?"

"So he's chosen not to." He watched his boss shake her head in disagreement and sat forward. "Let me help you understand some-thing. Terrorists are like pedophiles."

"Excuse me? When the hell did you become a right-wing whack job?"

He shook her off and pressed on. "You ask a hundred people if they're for torture . . . you're only going to get a handful who say yes. You ask a hundred people if they think pedophiles should be castrated . . . same thing." Wassen drained his drink, grabbed his boss's empty glass, and walked over to the bar, saying, "Now you show them a pic-ture of little five-year-old Suzy Jones, and you tell them how she was plucked from her bed in the middle of the night, dragged to some musty basement, and repeatedly raped by this hairy disgusting forty-five-year-old guy who's already been convicted twice for sexual assault on a minor." Wassen tossed a few more cubes into each glass. "You tell them how the government has spent hundreds of thousands of dollars trying to rehabilitate this scumbag. You explain to them that the re-cidivism rate for pedophiles is less than five percent, and then you ask them if they think the piece of human refuse should have his balls cut off." Wassen put a few ounces of booze into each drink and walked back to the seating area.

As he handed Lonsdale the drink he said, "The numbers flip-flop. Ninety percent say cut his balls off." He sat in his own chair and put his feet up on the coffee table.

"Your argument makes no sense. People are disgusted by torture."

"You're confusing the crime with the punishment. None of those people I just talked about want to actually see the pedophile turned into a eunuch. But that doesn't mean they don't want someone else to take care of it."

"But these men have yet to be convicted. It is completely wrong for one man to carry out a punishment for a man who has not had his day in court. That is what makes our country so special." Lonsdale shook her head and added, "Your argument doesn't stand up."

"You're assuming that Rapp was trying to punish this man." He took a sip and said, "I don't think that is the case. I think he was trying to get him to talk."

"This is nonsense. We are a nation of laws."

Wassen help up his hand and said, "Let me finish, before you go into one of those Jeffersonian speeches you senators are so fond of giving. You ask the people if they are pro-torture, and ninety plus percent say no. You then ask them what the CIA should do if they catch a senior al-Qaeda member who has carried out attacks in Afghanistan and Iraq that have killed thousands. You then tell them that the CIA has solid information an attack is looming and this man has information that could help stop it. You then ask them if they are okay with slapping this guy around and making him think he's about to drown and all of the sudden seventy percent of them are pro-torture.

"Now"—Wassen wagged a finger at his boss—"I can get that number to over ninety percent if you give the people a third option."

"What's that?"

"Don't tell me what's going on. Just take care of it. I don't need to know everything my government does."

"So the options are torture, don't torture, or stick your head in the sand."

"Exactly."

"That's ridiculous."

"That's reality, Babs."

She shook her head vigorously. "It's intellectual laziness."

"Maybe . . . maybe not."

"You are not serious?"

Wassen didn't respond right away. Knowing his boss as well as he did, he knew she was close to shutting him out. He chose his words carefully and then said, "You are a beautiful, intelligent woman, Barbara. People love you. You're half celebrity, half politician, and you always do well during these hearings. You come off great on TV, but I want to caution you."

She rolled her eyes in a here-we-go fashion. "Let's hear it."

"Mitch Rapp is a good-looking, rugged man. He's the type of guy Americans hope is out there keeping them safe at night."

"He's a thug."

Wassen shook his head vigorously. "He is many things, and I don't pretend to know the man's heart, but he's no common criminal. Do not underestimate him, or Irene Kennedy, or Mike Nash. These are not stupid people, and despite your personal bias, they are very likeable." Wassen watched her stand and move to put her shoes on. He had lost her.

"People are sick of this war on terror, Ralph, and when I expose these guys and their illegal ways the American people are not going to be happy."

Wassen nursed his drink for a long moment and said, "Don't be so sure of yourself, Barbara."

CHAPTER 48

WASHINGTON, D.C.

FEAR, anticipation, boredom, dread, excitement, and now an awe-inspiring elation. As the van crested a slight hill, Karim looked out across the vast expanse of lights, bridges, and monuments and felt his heart quiver. To his left he noted the large, square, white top of the Lincoln Memorial. Almost straight ahead was the dome of the Jefferson Memorial, with the Washington Monument jutting up behind it like the tip of a great sword. Farther to the right the massive Capitol sat atop a slight hill. The sheer scope and size of the building was the perfect example of American excess. Excess that had been obtained through hubris and arrogance and colonial subjugation.

Karim had experienced many emotions on his journey, especially boredom during the months of isolation in South America. It was his middle passage toward his ultimate destiny; the sacrifice great persons must make to steel themselves for the challenge that would make or break them. The boredom was gone. Now, looking out on the lights of his enemies' capital, he thought it a trivial price. He wondered if this was how the great warriors of Islam felt as they gazed out on the campfires of their enemy the night before a great battle. The swelling of pride in his chest, the joy, and the knowledge that he was about to strike a mortal blow for Allah was all too much.

Karim let loose an emotional sigh. Why was he so fortunate? Why was he the one that Allah had chosen to strike this mighty blow? To take the once great and feared al-Qaeda and return them all to their proper place as the most powerful and influential group in all of Islam. Karim felt it as deeply as he ever had before. He was ready to take his place alongside Islam's most legendary generals. This would be the beginning, the first of many cities where he would wreak havoc and spread fear and terror among the weak and godless Americans.

Everything that had come before would be a tedious preamble to how he had risen from obscurity, just as Mohammad had done, to motivate millions to fight for Islam. To once and for all banish the infidels and dirty Jews from the cradle of Islam and restore the caliphate. Restore peace and justice to their lands. Not this nonsense called democracy that the Americans were so proud of. This nonsense of government by the people of a godless country filled with nothing more than possessions and desires. They had been spoiled now for several generations and they were ripe for the taking. Karim could see it all before him as if Allah had given him the map. The Americans were in their last days of their little experiment and Karim was here to help accelerate their downfall.

The honor was almost too much to take. It rested on his shoulders to set the cause back on the proper course. Islam would once again take its rightful place on the world stage and they would cleanse their lands of the infidels. Karim's eyes slowly filled with tears, and he covered his face lest any of the others see him in such a state.

As he was doing so, he heard Hakim ask him, "Are you all right?"

Hakim handed him one of the napkins that were left over from a fast-food stop. He wiped his eyes and blew his nose, while trying to assure Hakim that everything was fine. The two had spoken very little since they had left the park in Georgia. Karim could not understand why his friend was so upset over the death of their driver. Hundreds of thousands had already died in this most recent holy war. No one man was more important than the mission. What was one more martyr?

"It is time to make the call," Hakim said as he checked his side mirror and changed lanes.

Karim looked at the clock on the dashboard. The green numbers read 10:27. They'd been on the road for nearly seventeen hours, most of it on Interstate 95. Like so much of the rest of the last year, their journey would be marked by another leap of faith into unfamiliar territory. Karim retrieved the phone from the center console and held it in his right hand atop the steering wheel. After finding the red power button on the unfamiliar phone he went to press it and then hesitated. Most people looked at a mobile phone and never thought anything beyond the convenience of what it offered them. Not those who had fought against the Americans in Afghanistan and Iraq, though. They looked at the phones as a game of Russian roulette. Every time you turned one on you were tempting the hands of fate. Zawahiri and bin Laden had not used a mobile phone in years and the rest of the al-Qaeda and Taliban leadership used them only sparingly. Dozens had been killed or captured after making calls. One minute they would be standing there talking, and the next thing you knew, a missile would come streaking through the air and blow them to bits.

"Go ahead," Hakim said as if he didn't care. "Remember . . . you're a needle in a haystack."

They had talked about this incessantly. In the mountainous border area between Afghanistan and Pakistan there were fewer than a million people spread over thousands of square miles. Very few had mobile phones, and there was extremely limited coverage for digital and analog phones. The only type of phone that worked with any real consistency was a satellite phone and that made things even more dangerous. Satellite phones were extremely expensive and rare, and they worked by using orbiting satellites that were owned almost entirely by Western telecommunications companies, and that was only the half of it. The

United States Government was rumored to have one of their billion-dollar KH-12 spy satellites in geosynchronous orbit above the region as well as a myriad of unmanned aerial vehicles and spy planes. They were all understandably gun-shy about using the devices, but here in America nearly everyone had a cell phone and the American government was not allowed to listen in on the calls without permission from the courts.

Karim closed his eyes and pressed the button. Ten seconds later the tiny screen was showing that everything was working as expected. He took a look around, and began punching in the number from memory. His hands were clammy as he held the phone to his ear and listened to the strange-sounding ring.

"Hello," a voice answered with just a hint of an accent.

"Joe," Karim said in a voice that cracked, "It's Chuck. How are you?"

There was an abnormal pause and then the male voice said, "Fine, Chuck. Are you in town?"

"Yes."

"Are you going to stop by and see me?"

"Yes."

"When will you be here?"

Karim covered the phone and asked, "How long until we are there?"

"Twenty minutes."

Karim relayed the number and then said good-bye. "He sounded nervous," he said to Hakim.

"Normal." Hakim shrugged as if he couldn't care less.

"How long are you going to stay mad at me?" Karim asked.

"I don't know. How many more innocent people are you going to butcher?"

The question was not entirely unexpected, but it stung nonetheless. "War is not without casualties."

"When you are involved, that's for certain."

"You would rather I place the outcome of this entire operation in the hands of a twenty-three-year-old boy who owes me no loyalty?"

"Back to your tribal mentality again."

"My tribal mentality is what has gotten us this far."

"No." Hakim shook his head stubbornly. "I have gotten you this far . . . me and a twenty-three-year-old boy who you rewarded by putting a bullet in the back of his head."

Karim did not want to fight. Not now. He wanted to take in this great moment as they passed through the heart of America's capital. "What is it you want me to do?"

"I want you to start consulting me, before you act so recklessly. I have spent a great deal of time in this country. I understand their culture. I understand what goes unnoticed and what gets noticed. Despite all of the tapes you have had the men watch, despite all the language lessons, they still sound stilted. They act nervous, which will make Americans nervous, which will get you noticed."

Karim did not like the criticism. "And what does this have to do with me killing your friend?"

Hakim heard the cynicism in Karim's voice and answered sharply. "It has everything to do with it. He was an ally and an asset. He could get directions, or food, or pretty much anything else without attracting suspicion. All of you"—he waved his hand toward the back of the van—"and your tightly wound demeanor and attitudes scream trouble. I haven't seen a single one of you smile once. Not once all day long. Despite what you think, people in this country are happy. They smile, and when men with dark skin and black hair walk around like robots with frowns on their faces, it makes them very nervous."

Karim was more than reluctant to agree with his friend, and even if he did, he would never show such a sign of weakness in front of his men. In a quiet and firm voice he said, "We will continue this later."

"I'm sure we will," Hakim said under his breath. As the road curved around to the left, a massive well-lit complex came into view. Hakim pointed at it and said, "There is the Pentagon. You will notice not a single sign of the attacks on nine-eleven. Within a year, the entire site was cleaned up and repaired. These Americans," he said as he glanced over at his small-minded friend, "are not all the lazy godless people you have made them out to be."

"We will see," Karim said confidently. "We will see."

CHAPTER 49

ARLINGTON, VIRGINIA

MAGGIE put Charlie to sleep at 8:00 and then got to work on Jack. The ten-year-old employed a series of delay tactics and dragged his feet more than usual. Maggie finally realized he was stalling so he could see his father before he fell asleep. Nash was gone picking up the two oldest ones from after-school activities. Jack seemed to take his father's coming and going harder than the others. Maggie knew she needed to sit down and talk to her husband about it, but she wasn't sure about putting any additional stress on him right now.

Maggie told Jack to get under the covers and that she'd be back in a few minutes. She went into her bedroom, stripped off her work clothes, and threw on a pair of pajamas. After brushing her teeth, she came back into Jack's room and told him to scoot over. Jack and Rory shared a room. Each had a twin bed with a single nightstand in between. Maggie nestled under the blankets with him and put her arm around his bony little shoulders. She kissed him on the forehead and ran her fingers through his bristly hair.

"Is everything all right, honey?"

"Yeah . . . why do you ask?"

"Because that's what mothers do. We ask, and we care, and we worry, and we get deep wrinkles on our faces, and you kids suck all the life out of us and turn us into old prunes."

Jack looked back at his mother with worried eyes and said, "I think you're beautiful, Mom."

Maggie kissed him on the forehead again and gave him a big hug. She knew she had only a year or two more at the most before she lost him. It would happen one day without warning, just as it had with Rory. She still had the bond with Shannon, but these damn boys were too much like their father. Jack would stop holding her hand and telling her she was beautiful, and then they'd start butting heads.

"You're a sweet boy, Jack."

Jack was about to ask her a question, when the doorbell interrupted him. Maggie looked at the bedside clock. It was almost 9:00. She told Jack to stay put, and she went downstairs to see who it was. When she peeked through the sidelight next to the front door, she saw Todd De Graff, whose son went to school with Rory.

Maggie unlocked and opened the door. The word *hello* got stuck in her mouth as she looked at a bloodied and battered Derek De Graff. Finally she managed to say, "Oh my God . . . what happened?"

"Your son is what happened."

Maggie's eyes moved from the son to the father. "Excuse me."

"I don't stutter, Maggie. Your son Rory beat him up after school."

"But . . ." Maggie stammered, "you and Rory are friends. Why would he do something like this?"

"That's a good question. I'd like to ask him." De Graff looked over each of Maggie's shoulders in search of her son.

"He's not home yet. Why would he do such a thing?"

"Supposedly they were screwing around, then Rory went nuts for no reason."

Maggie thought about the way he'd been acting up lately. It was entirely possible. He had way too much of his father in him. "I am so sorry. I can assure you I will deal with this the second he gets home."

Maggie shook her head and added, "That boy is going to be in serious trouble."

"I'm not spending twenty-eight thousand dollars a year so my kid can get bullied and beat up."

"Todd, I promise you Rory will be punished severely, and as soon as he gets home I will bring him over and he will apologize in person for this."

"I don't think that's a good idea." De Graff shook his head. "Kristy is really upset about this. I had to talk her out of calling the police."

Maggie was suddenly gripped by a new set of problems. Her little Jarhead in the making was going to end up with a juvenile record, and if that happened he could kiss an Ivy League education good-bye. And then she thought of Kristy Hillcrest De Graff, quite possibly the most gossipy, stuck-up mother amongst a group of women who were not the least bit embarrassed to behave like they were still in high school. Maggie felt her Irish temper coming on. She apologized to both father and son one more time and said she'd call them after she was done chewing Rory's ass out.

After closing the door, Maggie went to the kitchen and headed straight for the wine fridge. She retrieved a bottle of Toasted Head Chardonnay and wrestled with the cork. Jack appeared in the doorway, looking concerned.

Maggie looked up and said, "Back to bed, young man. You do not want to be down here when your brother gets home."

She opened the cupboard, her right hand reaching for a small Chardonnay glass and then skipping over it. A situation like this called for a big burgundy glass. After pouring nearly a third of the bottle into the glass, she took a massive drink and then leaned against the marble counter. Her mind raced off in three different directions almost simultaneously. How would her husband react to the news, how many women had Kristy Hillcrest De Graff already called, and what punishment was she going to give her thirteen-year-old monster?

She was nearly finished with the glass when she heard them pull into the garage. She waited for them in the kitchen, her anger slowly building. Shannon entered the kitchen first; she was on her cell phone, so she didn't notice the brooding look on her mother's face. Next came Rory, with his father close behind.

Nash entered the kitchen, took one look at his wife, and thought, *Holy shit, what did I do now?* Instead he said, "What's wrong?"

"Well . . . Derek and his father just stopped by." Her eyes shifted to her son. "Would you like to tell me why he has a black eye?"

Rory shifted nervously and then stammered for a second before spitting out, "He said something that wasn't right . . . and I told him to stop, but he . . ."

"Do you have any idea," Maggie screamed, "that you can be kicked out of school!"

"But, Mom, he . . ."

"I don't care what he did!"

"But he . . ."

"Did you hear me?" she screamed. "Nothing that he could have said would justify what you did to him. Do you know how much we pay to send you to Sidwell?"

Rory was shaking. "I don't care!" he yelled. "I don't even like it there!"

"Don't you dare raise your voice at me, young man! Go to your room right now!" She pointed toward the hallway. "Your father and I will discuss your punishment, but I'll tell you right now, I'm in favor of pulling you off the lacrosse team."

Rory ripped himself free from his father and ran down the hallway. "I hate you!"

Maggie yelled after him, "That's really going to help your case, young man!" She turned to her husband and said, "Can you believe this?" She snatched the bottle of wine from the counter and poured herself another third. "I have no idea how we are going to deal with this."

Nash wondered for a brief second who in the hell this woman was, standing in his kitchen. "Woman . . . what in the hell is wrong with you?"

"Me?" She pointed at herself. "Maybe you haven't been paying attention, Michael, but that school costs twenty-eight thousand dollars a year and they have a zero tolerance on fighting. He's going to get kicked out."

"Don't you think we should hear his side of the story before we get all worked up?"

"I don't need to hear his side. Zero tolerance. That's the policy. We're screwed. He's going to get expelled, and then good luck trying to get him into Harvard."

"Oh, that's what this is about."

"Don't go there with me. This is your fault. I should have never let you give him boxing lessons. It's bad enough that he has that same aggressive gene you and your brothers have."

"What are you talking about?"

"Remember . . . remember the bar you and your brothers tore apart? If it wasn't for the fact that that cop was a Marine and you were on leave you'd have a record right now."

"What I remember is you were jealous because I was talking to some girl, so you decided to do blow job shots on the bar, and if you hadn't been sticking your pretty little ass in that guy's face, he would have never grabbed it, and Sean would have never had to knock him out."

Maggie pointed at herself. "That was not my fault, and this is not my fault. This comes from your side of the family. You brother Patrick just beat up some guy in Atlantic City last month and he's thirty-five years old."

"The guy had it coming."

"Oh . . . I'm sure he did. You and your brothers . . . any excuse to fight, and now it's been passed down to our son." Maggie looked up at the ceiling and moaned. "I can't believe this is happening. He's going to get kicked out of the best prep school in Washington. Do you have any idea how many strings my father had to pull?"

Nash had heard enough. He'd never liked the idea of sending Rory to the effete prep school, but he wasn't around enough to really fight it.

"You know what, Maggie, it doesn't matter how much money your dad made, and it doesn't matter how much you make, they're never going to let you into their little club. No matter how you slice it, you're an Irish Catholic girl from Boston."

"What in the hell is that supposed to mean?"

"You tell me. I'm proud of where I came from. I'm not so sure you feel the same."

"Don't you ever!" she screamed, and held her glass up like she might throw it at him.

Nash waved her off and walked out of the kitchen, saying, "Look who's the one with the temper now."

"We are not done talking about this!" she yelled after him.

"Yes, we are."

Nash grabbed the railing and climbed the stairs. He knocked softly on the boys' door and then entered. Rory was on his stomach, his face stuffed into a pillow, sobbing. Jack was sitting in his bed reading, a frightened look on his face. Nash walked over and pulled back Jack's blankets.

"Go read in Mamma's bed. I'll come get you when I'm done."

"Is everything all right?" Jack whispered.

"Everything will be fine, buddy." Nash nudged him out the door and then closed it. He walked back to Rory's bed and sat on the edge. He put his hand on Rory's back and said, "Ror, I want you to try and calm down and then I want to hear your side of the story."

Between sobs, he managed to spit out, "What does it matter . . . Mom doesn't care."

"I care . . . so stop crying and turn over." Nash rubbed his back and added, "Son, I was in plenty of fights when I was your age. My dad used to say it takes two to tangle. Your mother doesn't understand that because she's a woman, but I do. You're a good kid. I doubt you just hauled off and smacked Derek for no reason." Under his breath he added, "Especially since he's a spoiled little shit."

Rory flipped over and composed himself enough to start the story. He said, "We were done with lacrosse . . . and were waiting for play practice to start . . . which I hate . . . and Mom made me sign up for."

Mentioning his mother elicited another deluge of tears. "Calm down," Nash told him.

"Derek was waiting to get picked up and he started talking about Shannon. He started to say . . . things."

Nash's antennae went up. "Like what?"

"He talked about how hot she was . . . and that he wanted to have . . . you know . . . he wanted to have sex with her . . . except he didn't use that word. He used that word that we're not supposed to use."

Nash felt his own anger grabbing hold. "Which word?"

"The F word."

Motherfucking little shit, Nash thought to himself. "Is that all?"

"I told him not to say it again or I was going to hit him . . . and then he started talking about Mom."

"Really." Nash said, surprised. "What did he say?"

Rory squirmed. "I'd rather not say."

"I'd rather you did," Nash said in a very firm paternal voice.

"He said . . . Mom was a . . ." Rory stopped.

"What?"

"He called her a MILF."

"He called her a MILF," Nash said in near disbelief as he thought of the acronym that stood for Mom I'd Like to Fuck. "What else did he say?"

"He said he wanted to do the same thing to Mom as he said he wanted to do to Shannon."

"And then you hit him."

Rory nodded.

"Good."

"So I'm not in trouble?" asked a hopeful Rory.

"Not from me and not from anyone else, if I have anything to say about it." Nash bent forward and kissed him on the forehead. "Let me have a word with your mother and then I'll call you down."

Nash stood and walked to the door. He stopped and turned back to his son and said, "Rory, do you like going to Sidwell?"

His son shook his head and the tears began to well up once again in his eyes. Nash felt like an absolute jerk for not being there for his son. For not putting his foot down and telling his wife the way it was going to be. His job was sucking the life out of him, and his family was suffering for it. Nash decided, at that moment, he was going to do Rory right and set things straight.

CHAPTER 50

WASHINGTON, D.C.

THE mosque was a converted corner grocery store in a crime-ridden part of town about a mile east of the Capitol, not far from the Congressional Cemetery. It was three stories of brick, chipped paint, and rotted wood. The van circled around the block once to see if they could spot any surveillance, but everything appeared to be ordinary, and besides, their contact had not waved them off by using the prearranged phrase. Hakim pulled the van into an open spot two blocks away on the opposite side of the street and handed the keys to Farid. If he saw anything unusual, or had not heard from them in fifteen minutes, they were to leave the area and head straight to a small warehouse he had leased three miles north of where they were.

Both Karim and Hakim checked their weapons before leaving the van. Karim also grabbed a radio and stuffed it in the big front pocket of his hooded sweatshirt. With a nod to each other they exited and crossed the street side by side. Hakim's gait was relaxed, while Karim's was hurried. And while Hakim casually looked up and down the tree-lined street, Karim's eyes nervously darted from one parked car and tree to the next.

"Relax," Hakim said in a slow, easy voice. "In a neighborhood like this, looking nervous is a good enough reason for the police to stop and question you."

Karim slowed his pace to match that of his friend's and forced himself to stop swiveling his head in every direction. He found comfort in the fact that they were going to a mosque. If he had not seen it with his own eyes in Afghanistan, he would have never believed it, but he had, so he did. The Americans bent over backward to stay out of their mosques. Even when fired on from the mosques they would wait for hours or days until Afghan soldiers arrived, but they themselves would not set foot in them. This had enabled al-Qaeda and the Taliban to store many of their weapons safely in mosques that were spread out across the countryside as they retreated, and then in the spring when they would start a new offensive they would simply collect them and pick up where they had left off. To Karim, it was one of the more glaring examples of how foolish and weak the Americans were.

Half a block away from the mosque they noticed a silhouette in one of the upper windows. It was a three-story building with the mosque itself on the first floor and then offices and apartments on the second and third floors. The structure occupied half of the city block, and while it was ugly, it served its purpose well. A cloud of cigarette smoke wafted out from a doorway fifteen feet ahead on the left. Both men slowed.

"Joe," Karim said in his best Americanized English.

A head popped out, and a small man with a large nose and even larger ears glanced around the door frame at them. He flashed a nervous smile and said, "Chuck." The man took one more drag and then flicked the cigarette to the curb as he stepped from the doorway. He held out his arms and said, "It is good to see you."

The two men embraced, kissing each other once on each cheek. The small man then embraced Hakim, and then the three of them went inside.

"Here, this way," the small man said as he held open a door that revealed a staircase.

They went down the creaking wood stairs to the basement and entered a big room with a low ceiling and exposed pipes. There were shelves on all the walls, and off to the left was an old delivery elevator that came up through the sidewalk. Hakim glanced at it, because a few weeks earlier he had used the elevator to unload a very important shipment. There were other storage rooms and two offices located down a hallway at the back of the space.

"Why do you look so nervous?" Karim asked the small man.

Hakim thought it a stupid question, since the man always looked nervous about something.

"There has been a development," the man they called Joe said anxiously.

"What kind of development?" Karim asked, suddenly concerned.

The man's name was Aabad bin Baaz. He was a fellow Saudi who had met Karim when they were undergraduates at King Faisal University and then had followed him to the Islamic University of Medina. Hakim not so affectionately referred to the man as the ferret, due to the fact that he looked like one. He was short, only five feet six, and he had a large hook nose and floppy ears that he tried to hide by growing out his hair.

Aabad timidly shuffled from one foot to the other and then pointed back toward the hall that led to the storage rooms and offices. Looking at Hakim, he said, "I had the camera installed, as you suggested."

Hakim could feel Karim's eyes on him, so he turned and quickly said, "After we received the shipment we put a lock on the door and I told him"—he pointed down the hall—"to install a small surveillance camera so we could keep an eye on things."

Karim turned back to Aabad. "Continue."

"I reviewed the tapes every few days," he said while rubbing his hands together. "We have a man who helps out around here. I saw him on the tape several times and didn't think much of it, and then earlier tonight . . . during evening prayer, I noticed he had slipped out, so I grabbed a few men and we went downstairs."

"The same stairs we just came down?" Karim asked.

"Yes, and we found him back in the hallway."

Karim and Hakim looked at each other and then Karim said, "He would have heard you coming."

"I think so," Aabad said nervously.

"What was he doing?"

"We found him in one of the other storage rooms, moving supplies around. While the other men were talking to him . . . asking him why he was not at evening prayer . . . I snuck into the office and reviewed the security tape."

"And?" Hakim asked, fearing that he already knew the answer.

"He was doing something with the door, so I grabbed my gun and we confronted him. We tied him up and emptied his pockets."

"Did you find anything?"

"This." Aabad held out what looked like a miniaturized version of a dental tool and three white pads in a clear Ziploc bag.

Hakim felt his heart sink. "That is a lock pick, and those little pads," he said as he closed his eyes and his voice trailed off, "are used to test for chemicals . . ."

"What kind of chemicals?" Aabad asked.

"The kind associated with explosives." Hakim took a step away and looked back at the stairs, half expecting federal agents to come barreling down with guns drawn. In a hushed voice he asked, "Have you questioned him?"

"I haven't had time."

Hakim shot Karim an *I told you so* look. He had warned him that Aabad wasn't up to the task. Karim's response was that the man was simply accident-prone. Hakim had replied that he was accident-prone because he was stupid. He reached out, grabbed Karim by the arm, and said, "We need to get out of here."

Karim pulled his arm free. "In a minute." Addressing Aabad, he asked, "Has he said anything?"

"Only that we are overreacting. He says it is his job to keep an eye on things."

"I don't like this," Hakim said.

"I don't either, but before I throw away this opportunity, I want to make sure. Have you checked for listening devices?"

Before Aabad could answer, Hakim said, "He wouldn't know where to start. I don't even trust myself. It is impossible to keep up with their technology."

Karim thought about that for a second and said, "I want to see him."

"No," Hakim said firmly. "He cannot see you. We need to leave." Pointing at Aabad, he said, "He should have given us the signal. We should have never come here."

"I am in charge here," Karim said firmly. "I will not so easily settle for our meager backup plan."

Hakim let out a sigh of frustration, knowing there would be no changing Karim's mind. Turning to Aabad, he asked, "Is anyone upstairs keeping an eye out?"

"Yes," Aabad answered nervously.

Hakim took a step toward the stairs and motioned for Karim to follow him. When the two were alone, Hakim looked at his old friend and said, "You are blind when it comes to him. You killed a man this morning who has three times the brains of that imbecile, a man who had done nothing to endanger your plan. And now you are going to tolerate him yet again."

It was far more complicated than Hakim was making it, but Karim did not have the time to debate the issue right now. "We will talk later. Go . . . take the men to the place you have prepared, and I will be in touch."

"And if I don't hear from you?"

"If you don't hear from me by seven a.m., proceed immediately to the secondary target."

Hakim did not move, so Karim grabbed him by the shoulder and sent him on his way. As soon as he was gone, he motioned for Aabad to lead him down the hallway. He sent Aabad in first and told him to send the other men upstairs to keep a lookout. He then entered the storage room by himself. He made no effort to conceal his face.

He looked down at the black man sitting on the floor. His ankles, knees, and wrists were duct-taped. Karim studied him for a long moment. He noted the man's fit appearance and stared into his eyes for a long time. He found them to be far too calm, considering the situation. Withdrawing a tactical knife from the back of his waistband, he asked, "What is your name?"

"Mohammad," the man said with a set jaw and a cautious look, like he was assessing the situation.

"Of course it is," Karim smiled as he extended the blade. He stepped forward and watched the man flinch, but noted that he did not scream. Karim reversed the grip on his knife, and with one hand, grabbed the neck of the shirt and then, taking the knife, he sliced it open along the shoulder, the cotton fabric giving way easily.

"What are you doing?" the man half shouted.

"When I fought in Afghanistan, I killed my fair share of Americans."

"Good for you," the man said. "It is an unjust war."

"Yes, it is." Karim nodded. "We would often strip their bodies and allow the local villagers to defile them."

The man named Mohammad did not answer him this time.

"Every single one of them had a tattoo." Karim saw fear in the man's eyes. Karim cut away more of the man's shirt. There was nothing on the right bicep, but there was some ink on the left. Karim moved the man roughly and smiled as he looked down at the head of an eagle with the words *Screaming Eagle* underneath.

"Ah . . . I see you were in the army."

"A lot of people are in the army."

"Do a lot of people serve in elite units like the 101st Airborne Division?" Karim waited for an answer but never got one. "What is your name?"

"I told you . . . Mohammad."

"No"—he held the knife in front of the man's face—"I mean your real name. The one you had while you were in the army."

CHAPTER 51

ARLINGTON, VIRGINIA

N ASH found his wife in the study on the first floor, checking her e-mail. He entered the wood-paneled room and closed the door. Maggie glanced up at him, the expression on her face making it clear that she was angry. He studied her profile, her determined frown, her posture she'd gotten from all the ballet lessons she'd taken as a child. He loved her deeply but at this moment it all reminded him of how much of a spoiled brat she could be at times. *Maggie's way or the highway,* was the saying her two brothers and sister were fond of using.

Nash plopped down in the overstuffed leather chair next to the fireplace and said, "Would you care to hear your son's side of the story?"

Maggie didn't bother to look up. "Save your breath. I'm sending the dean an e-mail right now. If I get out in front of this I might be able to salvage our son's educational aspirations."

"I think they're *your* aspirations, Maggie."

"If you're going to try and bait me into an argument, just leave. Go right now." She pointed at the door. "The only chance we have of salvaging this is by begging for forgiveness. Any penalty other than expulsion. I'm informing the dean as well as several of his teachers that we're going to pull him off the lacrosse team."

"The hell you are. You're not pulling him off the lacrosse team, and he's not one of your clients. You're not going to lobby your way out of this."

"Oh . . . he's done with lacrosse," she said, as if it was a forgone conclusion. "And that camp he wanted to go to this summer . . . that's gone too. Just let me send this e-mail and then . . ." She stopped suddenly and looked at her husband, who was now bent over next to the desk.

Nash found the power cord for the computer and decided enough was enough. He yanked the cord from the back of the computer and stood.

"What the hell did you just do?" Maggie screamed.

"I just saved you from embarrassing yourself."

Maggie cupped her face in her hands and stared at the screen. "You are the last person who should be trying to handle this. I'm the one with the experience in dealing with crisis situations . . ."

She continued to frantically state her case, but Nash stopped listening. He wanted to scream back at her that she didn't know jack shit about what he did for a living. He wanted to explain the complicated operations he ran against some of the most formidable organizations on the planet. He wanted to tell her that when he fucked up, people died, and when she fucked up, her spoiled clients went somewhere else with their bag of cash. But he couldn't, because at the end of the day it was his decision to stick with a thankless job that had almost killed him, might still kill him, and very likely might land him in jail.

"Maggie, I'm your husband, and I love you, and you are going to shut up and listen to me for a moment."

She stood and angrily said, "Don't you tell me to shut up."

"Derek, that little shit, told Rory that he wanted to *fuck* Shannon."

"Excuse me?" Maggie said in near shock.

"He said he wanted to fuck our daughter, and Rory told him if he said it again, he was going to hit him. So do you know what that little shit did?"

Maggie shook her head.

"He called you a MILF."

"A MILF."

"Yep, a Mom I'd Like to Fuck."

Maggie's eyes opened in shock and her jaw hung loose. "That is disgusting."

"It sure is," Nash said, picking up steam. "He told Rory he wanted to fuck you."

"Oh, my God," Maggie said with a horrified look on her face.

"So, tell me, little Miss Harvard Law, how do you feel now about jumping all over your son? How do you feel about not letting him tell his side of the story?"

She was speechless for a moment and then said, "Obviously, I let my emotions get the best of me. But there was a better way to handle this," she added with a bit of an indignant tone creeping back into her voice. "Rory can't go around punching his friends every time they say something that upsets him."

"Can you ever just admit you're wrong?"

"I'm not wrong, Michael."

"Oh . . ." Nash sighed. "The kid did the right thing."

"No, he didn't. Sidwell has a zero tolerance policy."

"Fuck Sidwell, and stop acting like a lawyer. This is our son we're talking about."

"Don't talk to me like that."

"Do you know how many times I've heard you tell your clients to shut up?" he shot back. "That when they get blindsided by something, to shut their mouths until they get all the facts? That's your motto, and you chose not to live by it tonight. Rory came home, you jumped to a bunch of conclusions, and you hammered him, like a petty third-world dictator."

"That is debatable, but the one thing that isn't is that violence is not the answer. It is not the way to solve problems."

"Shut up, Maggie," Nash said hotly. "I love you and I'll always love you, so I'm going to tell you to just shut that pretty little mouth of yours. Stop being a lawyer and start being a mother. Rory gave that little shit plenty of warnings and he chose to ignore them. He pushed and then Rory gave him exactly what he deserved."

Maggie tried to speak, but Nash put out his hand. "Don't! Don't say another word. It was your idea to send him to that damn elite school. I was fine with Shannon going there. They have a great theater program, but it's not the right place for Rory. It's a damn dilettante factory."

Maggie crossed her arms across her chest and looked defiantly at her husband. "Is that all?"

Out of sheer frustration, Nash started to walk away and then turned back and said, "You have a son up there who loves you. Loves you enough to defend your honor, and in this day and age that's something you should be proud of. He's in a lot of pain right now. He's confused because he thinks he did the right thing."

"I feel bad about not giving him a chance to tell his side of the story, but Michael . . ."

"Don't but me. I don't want to hear any buts. Would you rather have him walking around telling his friends how big of a bitch you are . . . because I'll tell you right now, there's plenty of kids his age doing exactly that."

Maggie nodded slowly and seemed to be thinking about what she would do.

"If you love him as much as he loves you," Nash said, "you'll go up there right now and apologize, and you won't bring up any of this zero tolerance bullshit."

"Fine," she relented. "Just give me a minute."

CHAPTER 52

WASHINGTON, D.C.

RALPH Wassen sat at the bar and took a sip of his Manhattan. It was his second in a little less than an hour. At a quarter to twelve on a Tuesday evening the place had plenty of open seats. The person he was supposed to meet was late, and it didn't surprise him one bit, even though he didn't know the man. He knew enough about him, though, to understand that he would make him wait. He had no hard evidence that told him so, it was more intuition. Wassen had canceled a date for this little rendezvous, and he was hoping he wouldn't regret the decision, since his love life had all but dried up in the last year. He kept telling himself it was the demands of work, but he knew it was more than that. He was growing tired of all the jetting around to New York and Miami. Turning fifty had sobered him to the fact that there were fewer years ahead than behind.

Wassen didn't even notice that the man had arrived until the bartender came over and asked if he could get him something to drink. The man answered in his deep, steady voice. Wassen looked up and saw the man's reflection in the mirror behind the bar. The sight of him standing behind him and the sound of his voice sent a stab of fear through Wassen's veins. Wassen swiveled his chair to the left and realized the man must have come through the back door. He was wearing a black field jacket with a mandarin collar and plenty of pockets. Wassen imagined them filled with all types of gadgets, most of them lethal.

Rapp threw a twenty down on the bar and grabbed his bottle of Summit Pale Ale. "So, Ralph," he said casually, as his eyes looked at everyone except the person he was talking to, "what's on your mind?"

"Ah . . ." Wassen was caught off guard. "Thank you for coming." There was no apology for being nearly forty-five minutes late. No acknowledgment, really. Just a nod.

"Should we take that booth over there?" Rapp pointed to an empty one on the far wall.

"Sure."

Rapp left the bartender a buck and picked up the rest of the bills. Both men slid into the high-backed booth, Rapp facing the front door and Wassen the back. Wassen clutched his small drink with his long fingers and thanked Rapp again for coming.

"It's not a problem," Rapp said in an easy tone. "What can I help you with?"

"You've got a big day tomorrow."

Rapp shrugged as if to say that it was bigger for some than others.

"My boss is pretty keyed up."

"I'm sure she is. A nationally televised hearing is a lot of free advertising for them."

"Yes it is, and you seem," Wassen said with a grin, "very calm for a man who is about to be grilled on national television."

Again, Rapp shrugged his shoulders. "Let's just say I've been in worse spots."

"Oh . . . I'm sure you have, but this is different." Wassen took a sip. "This group won't play fair. They will stack the deck in their favor."

"I'm sure they'll try."

Wassen noticed a bit of cockiness. "That doesn't worry you?"

"I can take care of myself," Rapp replied with a grin.

Wassen studied him for a moment; the alert eyes, behind the handsome rugged face. Sitting here in the bar he seemed like a decent fellow. Not the immoral animal some made him out to be. Although, it was not difficult to imagine that he was capable of extreme violence. "Why do I get the feeling that you know something that no one else does?"

Rapp grinned, a lopsided dimple appearing above the scar on his left jawline. "I know a lot of things that others don't, Ralph. That's my job."

"But you're supposed to pass all of those secrets on to the Intelligence Committee, aren't you?" Wassen asked in a sarcastic tone.

"We both know that would be a mistake."

Wassen nodded and then stared into his drink for a long moment.

Rapp watched him intently and then said, "You're going to have to put your cards on the table. You're not the one in a vulnerable position. I am."

"Do you want to bet? If Babs found out I was here, she would pluck my testicles out with her pretty little French manicured fingernails."

"That might be true," Rapp laughed, "but no one is looking to indict you."

"Fair enough." Wassen took another sip and then in a slightly embarrassed tone said, "You know not all of us think you're a monster."

"Just your boss."

"She can be passionate at times."

Rapp said nothing.

"I got a call this afternoon from a friend in New York. He asked me, 'What makes your boss think that we Americans want to extend our constitutional rights to a bunch of homophobes who recruit retarded children to be suicide bombers?' "

"Did you pass along the message?"

"No."

"You should."

"I might," Wassen said without much enthusiasm. "Maybe in the morning . . . which, by the way, they are talking about closing the morning session."

"I heard." The Judiciary Committee Meeting Room was secure, and it was not uncommon for them to shut the spectators and the cameras out when they didn't know what to expect.

"Why are you doing this?" Wassen blurted out.

"Doing what?"

"Testifying. Any sane man would take the Fifth and make it hard on them."

"One could argue my sanity, but I think taking the Fifth makes it easy on them. It's the game they are used to playing. Being open and forthright is something this town is not used to."

"You're right, there. That's why they're moving to close the morning session. They're nervous you might say something that will embarrass them."

Rapp took a sip of his beer and smiled.

"I think you've got something planned."

"The only thing I have planned is to go before the committee tomorrow and answer their questions."

Wassen nodded and then finally admitted, "I have tried to convince her to drop this whole matter."

"I can't see that happening."

"No." Wassen shook his head. "As much as I'd like to see her do it, I don't think she will."

"Then she and I will be locking horns in the morning."

Wassen nodded sadly and then said, "I would like to help, if there is a way. This infighting is bad for all of us."

"Agreed," Rapp said, "but we appear to be pretty far apart on some major issues."

"Which brings me to my main question—why?"

"Why what?" Rapp asked.

"Why risk your entire career on an operation like this?"

Rapp smiled. Wassen was the first person to get it. "Ralph, that's the million-dollar question."

CHAPTER 53

KARIM finished tying the gag around the man's mouth and then removed his shoes. He held the tip of the knife a few inches from the man's eyes and said, "Toenails can grow back, but toes will not."

It was a line he had heard an Afghan use on a British paratrooper they had captured one night during a battle. He had learned much that evening watching the Afghani methodically wear the man down. He had always assumed there was a real skill to torture, but he'd had no appreciation for it until he'd seen it firsthand. There were several truisms. The first was that everyone broke. No matter how tough they were, eventually they cracked. The only time that wasn't true was if the subject was overstressed and died prematurely of a heart attack. The other truism was that you could get anyone to say anything. In this instance Karim thought that was the more important lesson to keep in mind. The subject was fit and looked to be under thirty. His heart would be able to handle a great deal of pain.

He did not want to start out asking the man if he worked for the CIA, because eventually he would admit to it only to stop the pain. He needed to get him to flatly admit who he worked for. No leading questions.

"I have found in these situations it is best to show the subject that I am serious." Karim looked up at Aabad, who was standing behind the man, and said, "Hold him tightly around the chest." Karim grabbed the man's right foot and placed the tip of the knife under the nail of the big toe. Looking into the frightened eyes of the man, he said, "I can make this one toe last for hours."

The man began to fight. Karim held the foot firmly and jammed the tip of the knife under the nail bed. The man went stiff with pain and his eyes rolled back into his head. Fifteen seconds later he stopped fighting them and his breathing became labored.

"Take off the gag," Karim ordered Aabad. After it was removed he asked the man, "Your name, please. The one you used when you were a Ranger."

"Tony . . . Tony Jones."

Karim smiled. "I don't believe you, but we will check." He stood and grabbed a mobile phone from a shelf, and he dialed a number and then gave the person on the other end the name.

"Put the gag back on," Karim ordered.

"No," the man screamed. "You haven't even found out if I'm lying to you."

"I know you are lying." Karim smiled.

"No, I'm not," the man pleaded.

"Really . . . tell me then why you were trying to get into the storage room across the hall."

"I . . ." the man stammered, "was looking around . . . that's all. I swear. It's my job to know what's going on around here."

Karim nodded for Aabad to put the gag back on. The man struggled and fought him every step of the way. When it was secure, Karim stuck the tip of the knife back under the nail and slid it back and forth. The man bucked and writhed in pain. Karim waited for it to pass and then asked him, "Who do you work for?"

With the gag off the man sputtered, "I'm a carpenter. I work for myself." He craned his head around and said, "Aabad, please tell him. You know me."

"He doesn't know you," Karim laughed. "No one here really knows you, do they?"

"That is not true."

"Yes it is." Karim held up the knife. A drop of the man's blood ran down the silver blade. "I will ask you one more time, who you work for. If you lie to me the toe comes off. Now . . . who do you work for?"

The man's eyes were filled with fear. "I told you who I work for. I work for myself. I don't know why you're doing this."

Karim gave the signal and the gag was slipped back on. It took all their combined strength to hold him down this time. Karim sat on the man's legs and when he had him reasonably still he pressed down on the big toe of the right foot. The man jerked and the cut was imperfect, the blade slicing through most of the big toe as well as the one next to it. The man's screams were muffled by the gag, but he was writhing in pain. Karim waited for him to lie still for a moment, and then he quickly cut the remaining tendons on the big toe. Things continued like this for thirty more minutes and two more toes, until the man, sobbing uncontrollably, uttered the acronym that Karim had been looking for.

"The CIA."

It was a strange victory. He had broken him, but he had also confirmed their worst fears. "Who is your handler?" Karim asked, his mouth only a few inches from the man's ear. The gag was off. The man no longer had the energy to fight. He hesitated, so Karim jammed the tip of the knife into one of the stumps on the right foot. The man started to scream, but Aabad was right there with a towel. He stuffed it in the man's face and waited for him to stop.

"Who is your handler?" Karim repeated.

"Mike . . ." the man's voice trailed off.

"Mike who?" Karim asked while grabbing him by the shoulders.

"Mike Nash."

Karim let him go. It was a name he knew. Al-Qaeda had key sources inside both Saudi Intelligence and Pakistani Intelligence. As part of his plan, Karim had asked for the flowchart of American counterterrorism operations. He wanted to know who he was up against and how they would respond to his attacks. He also wanted the ability to turn the hunter into the hunted.

"Mike Nash," Karim said to the man. "Former U.S. Marine, married, four children, lives in Arlington or Alexandria, I can't remember which one. Is that the same Mike Nash you work for?" The man did not answer. "The same Mike Nash who reports to Mitch Rapp?" he asked in a lighthearted voice.

The man looked up at him with confused eyes and said, "Who are you?"

"Ah," Karim said in a happy voice, "you don't know how pleasing it is to me that you have no idea who I am. Now let's get back to what we were talking about."

Over the next hour Karim coaxed as much information out of the man as he dared. He knew there would be protocols in place for an operative like this, but since he had no way of checking them, he wasn't sure it was worth pursuing. Instead, he focused on what the man had discovered at the mosque and what he had already passed on to his handlers. What he learned was that nothing of any value had been relayed. Indeed, the *only* thing that had been passed along was the fact Aabad had been shooting his mouth off that something big was going to be happening. That and the delivery of the supplies that had been placed under lock and key. Karim questioned him for thirty minutes on this one point alone. When he was done he felt extremely confident that the CIA had nothing more than suspicions.

Karim left the room and took a long moment to make sure he had everything figured out. Was it worth it to push it a little more? That was the question he kept asking himself. It was now nearly 1:00 in the morning. He doubted the man had a midnight check-in, but even if he did, this Mike Nash was likely asleep. Nothing would happen until morning, Karim decided, so he called Hakim using one of the disposable phones and ordered him to remove the back three benches from the van and return to the mosque with two of the men.

There were twenty-five cardboard boxes, each one weighing forty pounds. They were sealed and had USAID stenciled in blue on the sides. The contents of the boxes were courtesy of the U.S. government, but they could hardly be considered humanitarian aid. Each box was loaded with U.S. military C-4 plastic explosives. The shipment had been lost in Kuwait and ended up on the black market. Karim ordered Aabad to unlock the storage room and have his men begin placing the boxes on the delivery elevator. Hakim arrived twenty minutes later. His lack of enthusiasm for the change in plan was apparent from the moment he set foot in the door.

He came down to the basement and said, "We need to leave right now."

Karim smiled and calmly said, "We are fine. I have thoroughly interrogated him. I will explain it all to you later. Right now we need to load the boxes into the van." Karim pointed at the delivery elevator, which already had eight boxes loaded.

"But they will come looking for him," Hakim said as he nervously moved about.

"Yes, eventually, but I do not expect them before morning. Now, don't argue with me," he said in a surprisingly happy tone. "Let's get moving."

The first load of twelve cases was sent up, as more boxes were brought down the hall. It was like a fire brigade, with four men in the basement, passing the boxes from the room, down the hall, and onto the rusted metal platform of the elevator. Then up they went and into the back of the van. With seven people helping, they had the van loaded in less than fifteen minutes.

As they were preparing to leave, Aabad inserted himself between Karim and Hakim and in an extremely agitated state asked, "What should we do with him?" He pointed back down through the hole in the sidewalk where the delivery elevator was descending.

The *him*, they had found out, was a twenty-nine-year-old American named Chris Johnson. He had done two tours in Afghanistan and another in Iraq with the 101st Airborne Division. After his last tour he was recruited by Mike Nash to join a counterterrorism group within the CIA. There was actually no question what would be done with him, it was simply who would do it.

"Kill him," Karim said, as if he was ordering him to move another box.

Aabad looked at the ground and began mumbling to himself as he shifted his weight from one foot to the other. "I . . ." he started to say, and then stopped.

"You can do it," Hakim hissed as he looked at Karim.

Karim looked from one end of the block to the other and thought they were pushing their luck. Now was not the time to stand around and debate the issue. To Hakim he said, "Wait for me in the van." To Aabad, he said, "Follow me."

Karim walked back into the mosque and down to the storage room. He looked at the bloody prisoner on the floor. He had already inflicted a great deal of pain on the man, but he still didn't feel it was enough. He decided he would not simply put him out of his misery. Struck by a sudden inspiration, he said to Aabad, "Do you have a video camera?"

"Yes, in the office."

"Get it." He ordered.

Aabad went down the hall and returned ten seconds later with the camera in hand.

"Turn it on and make sure you do not get my face." Karim pulled the hood on his sweatshirt over his head and turned his back to Aabad. "Is it recording?"

"Yes."

"Move in for a close-up after I'm done." Karim reached down and pulled Johnson's head back. He looked into the agent's tired eyes and said, "You are a deceiver, and you have insulted all of Islam. There will be a special place in hell for you."

Karim placed the blade against the throat just beneath the Adam's apple and drew the knife across the thin layer of flesh. The cut opened up pink, and then white, and then crimson as the blood began pouring out in a sheet. Karim stood upright and watched Johnson begin to choke on his own blood. It took a good thirty seconds for the agent to submit to his own death, and then he lay still on the blood-soaked floor.

Karim wiped the blood off the blade with what was left of the man's torn shirt and then said to Aabad, "Wrap him up in a prayer rug, bring him to an area where no one will see you, douse him in gasoline, and burn him."

CHAPTER 54

ARLINGTON, VIRGINIA

N ASH woke up to the sound of his beeping watch at 6:30. He slid out of bed without any thought of the night before or anything else, for that matter. He knew if he did not keep his head down and his mind focused he would never get out the door. The shorts, socks, shirt, and long-sleeved pullover were sitting on the overstuffed chair in the corner of the bedroom where he had placed them before bed. He picked up the stack and quietly slid downstairs. In the mudroom he stripped off his sleep pants and put on his running gear. After a glass of cold tap water he stopped by the back door and opened the cupboard at the top of his cubby. On the top shelf sat a black biometric gun safe. He placed his right thumb over the glass eye, and a second later the safe beeped and the door popped open. There were three pistols and two extra magazines of ammunition for each.

Nash grabbed the Glock 23 off the top shelf, put it in his right hand, and with his left hand pulled back on the slide. He looked down and confirmed that the chamber was empty. He then yanked the slide all the way back and put one round in the tube. That left him nine more in the grip. He stowed the compact .40-caliber pistol in his fanny pack with his keys and one of his phones, which he didn't bother to turn on. Nash turned the alarm off and then turned it back on before leaving and locking the door again. He did all of this without putting any thought into it. "Good habits breed success," was what his high school wrestling coach had always said. In the Corps, the mantra was, "Discipline is what gives us the edge." Now in this next stage of life it was Rapp telling him flatly, "You fuck up one time and you're dead."

Nash hit the sidewalk running. There were only two cars parked on the broad tree-lined street and they were both familiar. The Jeep Wrangler belonged to the Gilsdorfs, and the Honda Accord belonged to the Krauses. He headed for Zachary Taylor Park. There and back was three miles, and if he couldn't do it in less than twenty minutes it would probably ruin his day. Right up until the explosion, he consistently did it in under eighteen minutes.

Nash ran for a lot of reasons, but more than any other, it was the clarity of thought it gave him. He'd made his toughest decisions during runs. He'd solved some of the biggest problems he'd faced, or at least figured out ways to get out of some pretty tough jams. This morning was no different. As his feet got lighter and he hit his stride it was like the beat of a drum in his head. First and foremost on his mind was Rory. The pain Nash felt over not being there for his family hurt every bit as bad as a piece of hot shrapnel slicing through his skin. Some things were going to have to change. He wasn't sure what, but he did know that Rory needed him in his corner. He knew his wife well enough to know that despite what he had told her last night, she would strut that pretty little ass of hers into school and try to smooth things over.

"Not going to let that happen," Nash said to himself as he pounded it out.

He was on call to go up to the Hill and testify. Kennedy had made it clear there was no way she would allow him to testify in an open hearing. If the Judiciary Committee closed it, they could compel him, but not if it was open. He hadn't a clue as to how that whole mess was going to turn out, but Rapp seemed extremely confident that it would be fine. For the rest of the run he put together a mental list of things he needed to get done. Some were mundane, like the call he had to make to personnel about the auto-deposit they kept fucking up on one of his overseas operatives, and others were a little more tricky. Like explaining to Rapp and Ridley that he'd allowed Chris Johnson to stay in the field. Rapp probably wouldn't give a shit but Ridley was likely to pop a bolt.

When he got back to the house, Maggie was in the kitchen feeding Charlie the gourmet baby food that made his poops smell so bad. He kissed the head of fine blond hair first and then the head of thick black hair.

"Good morning," he said as he walked to the sink for a glass of water.

"Morning," she replied, without any warmth.

"How'd you sleep?"

"Like crap. How about you?"

"Surprisingly well." Nash reached for the hand towel to wipe the sweat from his face.

As Maggie slid a spoonful of food into Charlie's mouth, she said, "You'd better not be using one of my dish towels to wipe your sweaty face."

Nash looked at the back of his wife's head and wondered how she'd known. He set the towel down and walked around the island. Charlie looked up at him with a gummy smile and a blob of something green at the corner of his mouth. Nash looked at him wildly and mouthed the word Charlie had been so fond of the day before. Charlie's little feet started dancing and he blurted it out. Maggie groaned and put her head down on the table, defeated by a one-year-old.

"Nice work, honey," Nash said as he left the room and headed upstairs for a shower.

Thirty minutes later he was back downstairs, cleanly shaven and dressed in the gray three-button Joseph Abboud suit his wife had got him for his birthday. Nash sat down at the computer in the office and logged on to his personal e-mail account. There were nine new e-mails since he'd checked it last night. He quickly scanned the From column for Johnson's name. He frowned that there were none. Nash walked over to the bookcase and grabbed his work BlackBerry. He quickly scrolled through thirty-four messages and again came up empty.

Nash felt his stress begin to build as he racked his brain to come up with a reason why Johnson would have disregarded the new protocols. He could think of no good reason and a lot of bad ones. Nash knelt down and opened the cupboard door, revealing a safe. He put his thumb on the reader and then opened the safe and retrieved a Motorola phone. Once the unit was powered up, he called Johnson's apartment. After eight rings, the answering machine came on and he hung up. He then tried his mobile number and again ended up listening to his voice-mail greeting.

The first pinprick of a headache started in his left temple. Nash put his hand up to his head and pressed down. "Not today, please. Not today."

"You all right?"

Nash looked up and saw his wife in the doorway dressed for work. "Yeah, everything is fine."

She looked as if she knew he was full of shit but also knew he more than likely couldn't talk about it. "Rosy just called. She's having car trouble, so she's jumping on the bus. Can you hang out with Charlie until she gets here? I would, but I have a really important client breakfast."

A small kernel of apprehension pushed its way into Nash's thoughts. This was one of those moments in a marriage where something relatively small could blow up into something really big. Nobody liked being wrong, and Maggie had blown it with Rory. And then in her typical stubborn way she'd dug in her heels, and now instead of apologizing for her behavior and putting it behind them, she was throwing out this test. *Show me that I'm more important than your job. Show me that you still love me.*

She was hurting in her own very real way from what had happened with Rory. She probably wasn't feeling like the best mother at the moment. Nash thought quickly about how he could make it work. He'd brought Charlie into work before; the problem would be getting him back to the house and then getting downtown for the hearing that was scheduled to start at 9:30. He realized they would never start on time because half the senators would be late, so he said, "Yeah . . . I can take him into the office with me, and then drop him back off before I go downtown for the hearing."

Maggie's tense expression melted away and a hint of a smile, not a happy one, but a relieved one, formed on her lips. "Great," she said. "I'll get him ready."

CHAPTER 55

ANACOSTIA RIVER,
WASHINGTON, D.C.

THE warehouse looked like something out of an Eastern European country before the fall of the Iron Curtain. More than half of the glass panes were missing from the skylights, and the roof itself was missing small sections. The corrugated metal walls were rusted, dented, and even peeled back in a few spots. Animal droppings dotted the oily concrete and rotted pallets; shredded tires and garbage littered a space approximately half the size of a football field. None of it, however, could cast a pall over Karim's mood.

Aabad had returned just before sunrise with the three men who had helped him, just as Karim had ordered. The body of the spy had been stuffed into the trunk of a stolen car, driven to an abandoned lot, and the entire vehicle set ablaze. Karim thanked all of them for their devotion, and then as the first rays of the morning sun began to poke through the dirty and broken windows, he asked them to stay and pray. All thirteen men faced Mecca and knelt on the dirty floor. Karim's men were not bothered by the filth. They had long ago learned to shut out such things. Aabad and his men, though, were obviously bothered.

For a full thirty minutes they prayed, and when they were done, Karim hugged each man and thanked him for his sacrifice, even the three men whom Aabad had brought along.

He asked to have a word alone with Aabad's men and led them back toward the door where they had entered. Karim spoke to them for a few minutes, and then without any consultation or warning, he drew his silenced 9mm Glock and shot each of the three helpers in the head.

Hakim was thunderstruck by the brutality of his friend. He looked around to see if the others shared his reaction, but all he saw were seven men acting as if nothing had happened. Karim had turned them into compassionless robots. Only Aabad was bothered by what had just occurred, but Hakim knew he was too feeble to protest.

Karim came to them across the open space, carrying with him the smell of gunpowder. He smiled and shook his head in a solemn fashion and said, "That was an unfortunate necessity."

Hakim had had enough. "Why?" he blurted out in a confrontational tone.

"Because," Karim said taken aback, "they had seen our faces."

"And what does that matter?"

"The CIA will come looking for their agent. We can hardly afford to leave any loose ends."

"Loose ends," Hakim said, as he pointed at the bodies. "Is that what we call believers now?"

Karim would not allow his upbeat mood to be diminished. "Come now, Hakim, we have discussed this many times. Many have martyred themselves ... millions of our brothers ... but American Muslims have given nothing. Those three men have martyred themselves and they will be rewarded by Allah. They are on their way to paradise as we speak."

They did not martyr themselves, Hakim thought. *You martyred them, or more to the point, killed them.* He did not say it, for fear of his own life. He looked at his friend's placid, almost euphoric face and finally realized just how much he had changed over the last year.

"Come now," Karim said. "We have much to do. I have decided to move our plan up by two days."

This got everyone's attention. Karim's men were too well disciplined to question their commander, but Aabad was not. "Today?" he asked in an unsteady voice.

"Yes, today," Karim said proudly.

"But I am not ready," Aabad said with his hands fluttering. "My office needs to be gone through . . . my apartment . . . there are final things I must do."

"It is out of our hands. The CIA will come looking for their man, and we cannot wait for that. Once they have discovered what has happened, they will raise alarms and our job will become extremely difficult."

"But my plane ticket . . . I am not to leave until tomorrow. What am I going to do?" Aabad was beside himself.

Karim put a fatherly hand on his friend's shoulder. "Do not worry. I will take care of you. I want you to go to your apartment right now. Get only what you need. One bag," he cautioned him, "and come right back here."

"But . . ." Aabad started to say.

Karim covered his mouth. "Do not argue. This is a direct order. You must do exactly as I tell you. Now go and be fast." Karim released him.

With great irritation, Hakim wondered why Karim didn't simply shoot the imbecile like he shot everyone else. Instead he watched Aabad anxiously hurry toward the door, looking back every few steps. When he stopped at the door, Karim urged him on by repeating his instructions one more time.

"Now," Karim said to Hakim as he put a gentle hand on his shoulder, "as you can see, my men are ready. Their martyr vests are all but done."

The men had spent much of morning breaking the C-4 into smaller blocks and pressing ball bearings into the malleable explosive and then placing the blocks in vests that they would put on, and if everything went according to plan, die in.

"Are you sure," Hakim asked with great concern, "about moving things up?"

"Yes."

"I'm afraid by rushing we will make a mistake. A mistake that will cost us."

"No," Karim shook his head. "My men are ready. This is the right decision. Waiting is risky. This . . . this is seizing an opportunity."

"What about the traffic cameras?"

"I was hoping you could call your man."

"Right now?" Hakim asked as he computed the time difference between the Netherlands and Washington.

"Yes."

"I can try," Hakim said without much confidence. This had been arranged months in advance.

"You will succeed, my friend. You have always succeeded. That is why, despite your lack of faith, I have allowed you to be part of this great battle."

"And if he can't crash the system?"

"We will proceed with or without him. Is my message ready?"

He was referring to the prerecorded message that would be launched across the World Wide Web. A message that proclaimed Karim to be the Lion of al-Qaeda. When Zawahiri saw it, he was likely to have a heart attack. "Your message is ready. He should have no problem releasing it."

"Good."

"If he cannot crash the system"—Hakim leaned in so none of the others could hear—"you and I need to leave the city this afternoon."

"Check with your man first," Karim said casually. "Allah is on our side. I am confident you will come through for me once more. I have not come all this way to complete half the mission. We will succeed, or we will all die. Am I clear?"

"So you have changed your mind?" Hakim asked quietly.

"I have given myself up to my destiny. If Allah wants me to survive, I will survive."

What about me? Hakim wanted to ask, but he could see that his friend's conversion to religious fanatic was finally complete. Hakim had seen the look in the eyes of far too many men in Afghanistan. Men that would stand up under withering American fire, convinced Allah would shroud them in protection. As Hakim looked into the wide, believing eyes of his friend he began for the first time to question why he was involved in this. His participation had been purely logistical. He would help get them into the country. He was to obtain separate financing, and to recruit the hackers that could help them crash the thousands of cameras that monitored the streets of Washington. And lastly he was to get himself and Karim back out of the country. All of this talk of Allah and destiny was suddenly beginning to sound like a suicide mission.

CHAPTER 56

ARLINGTON, VIRGINIA

NASH hit the key fob, and the side door of the minivan popped out and rolled back on its own. He sat just behind the two front seats in the middle and then dumped King Charlie into his plush car seat. After wrestling with all the different straps, buckles, and clips, he started the van and began backing out of the driveway with his little, cursing one-year-old yapping it up in the backseat. The National Counterterrorism Center was less than five miles away. Nash had time for one, maybe two phone calls at the most. He thought of calling Rapp or Ridley, but there was no sense in alarming them at this point. They had enough on their minds. There was one obvious choice, and it was Scott Coleman. Nash called him and passed along Johnson's address and the construction site where he was currently working. Coleman was read in on the program, so Nash did not have to explain to him what was going on. Coleman told him he'd have some answers within the hour.

At the security checkpoint for the NCTC the guard jokingly asked to see Charlie's badge. Nash laughed along with the middle-age guard even though he wasn't in much of a joking mood. After he was cleared and Charlie was given his visitor's badge, Nash pulled into his spot in the underground garage and freed Charlie from his restraints. With the diaper bag on one arm and Charlie in the other, Nash took the elevator up to the sixth floor and into the bullpen. This was Charlie's third trip to the National Counterterrorism Center and he'd been out to Langley at least as many times. Usually on Saturday mornings, so he could give Maggie a chance to sleep in.

By the time Nash reached his assistant's desk she was on her feet with arms out.

"Come here, Charlie."

Nash handed him over and set the diaper bag down on the side chair. He looked up at the wall of TV screens and asked, "Anything new this morning?"

Jessica had worked for Nash for three years. She also helped out with two other Langley guys assigned to the NCTC. "That Coast Guard chopper that went down yesterday . . ."

"Yeah?"

"Last night the divers recovered all four crew members. Preliminary report says they all drowned." She took her finger and rubbed the wattle under Charlie's chin. "They went back down first thing this morning and found seven bullet holes. Four of them appeared to have pierced the engine compartment. The FBI has a team headed down to verify, but the divers say they were fifty-caliber rounds. Armor-piercing."

"And they think it was a drug shipment?"

"Yep, but there's only one problem." Jessica pointed across the floor at a cluster of desks and said, "Alberto from DEA says they rarely shoot at our birds, and he's never heard of them doing it so close to shore."

Nash wondered if the cargo was more than drugs. "Let me know what the FBI finds out." He looked over at the corner office and asked, "Is Mr. Crabby Pants in?"

"Yep," Jessica replied as she gave Charlie a little tickle under the arm. "You'd better leave the kid with me."

"He's in that bad a mood?"

"No worse than usual."

"That's all right," Nash said. "I'll use him as a shield." He took Charlie back and said, "One more thing. Call the dean of students at Sidwell and find out when he's meeting with my wife."

Jessica frowned. "Shouldn't I just call Maggie?"

"No . . . in fact, tell them you're checking on her behalf."

"What's going on?" she asked suspiciously.

"Rory beat up some kid . . . it's a complicated story, but the short version is that the little spoiled shit had it coming."

Jessica was a mother of two young boys. She understood the program. "Was it on school property?"

"Yes."

"And knowing Sidwell, I'm sure they have a zero tolerance policy."

"That's right. And if I know my wife, she's going to go in there today and kiss some major ass and make this thing go away."

"And you're not invited?"

"That's my guess."

"I'm on it." She said as she sat and reached for her phone. "I'll let you know what I find out."

Nash walked over and knocked on Harris's door. A loud voice told whoever was there to go away. Nash knocked again and then grinned as he heard a slew of curses erupt from the other side.

As the door started to open, Harris could be heard growling, "What kind of dumb mother . . ." The last word got stuck in his mouth as soon as he saw the smiling little towhead in Nash's arms.

"I need to have a word with you," Nash said in a grim voice.

Harris took a step back and motioned for them to come in. As soon as he closed the door, his entire demeanor changed. He rubbed his hands together and then reached out for Charlie, who willingly lunged forward. Harris held him tight and kissed his big pudgy cheeks. "Oh . . . Sheila is going to be jealous when I tell her you stopped by the office."

Nash smiled. Sheila was Harris's wife, who leapt at the chance to watch Charlie any chance she got. The show Nash and Harris had put on for everybody in the office on Monday had been prearranged. The two worked very hard behind the scenes to share information, and Nash thought it would be best if Harris let everyone in the office believe he was furious over the story in the *Post,* when in fact he had known about the basics of the operation from the beginning.

Harris saw Charlie looking at his desk, so he sat down in his chair and said, "I don't let anyone touch my desk, but you, little buddy, you can touch anything you want. Go ahead." After a moment he looked up at Nash and said, "What's wrong? I can see by the way you're standing there like you need an enema that you're not having such a good morning."

"I've got a problem."

"How bad?"

"It depends." Nash shrugged his shoulders, and then appeared to be lost in thought.

"Buddy," Harris said, "you can trust me."

"I know I can, I just don't know if I want to lay this mess at your feet."

"We've talked about this before." There was a clang as Charlie knocked over a blue FBI mug filled with pens. "That's okay," Harris said reassuringly and then looked back up at Nash. "I'm with you on this thing. I'm not going to break any laws on my end, but I'm not going to turn your ass in either."

"You need to be really careful on this. No electronic fingerprints . . . No paper trails. I'd prefer it if there weren't any phone records."

"I know how to work the system. Tell me what you need."

Nash looked out the window for a moment and then said, "A friend of mine has gone missing."

"Good guy or bad guy?"

"Good guy."

"How long?"

"Not sure."

"When was the last time you heard from him?" Harris asked while he reached out and squeezed Charlie's thigh.

"Yesterday afternoon."

"That's not very long."

Nash sighed. This was going to be hard to express, why he was so worried. He settled on saying, "Considering the circumstances . . . it's an eternity."

Harris nodded. "You want me to check the morgue?"

Nash hoped it wasn't the case, but it had to be done. "You told me you had some buddies downtown . . . D.C. Metro."

"I know a bunch of guys down there. A few owe me some pretty big favors."

"Good. Just keep it real quiet. You don't want this traced back to you."

"I know how to handle it. Just give me the basics." Harris stuck out his big mitt, palm up, and said, "Charles, may I please use that pen?"

Charlie looked at the pen and then carefully placed it in Harris's hand. He smiled at his own accomplishment.

Harris rubbed Charlie's back and said, "You're a smart little boy. Too smart for the Marines. You'll have to go into the Navy like your uncle Artie." Harris grabbed a sheet of paper and said, "Shoot."

Nash thought of a dozen off-color remarks he could make about the men who sailed the seven seas, but kept them to himself. Thinking about Johnson, he said, "Six feet tall, African American, approximately one hundred and eighty pounds."

"How old?"

"Late twenties."

"Anything else?"

"He has an Airborne tattoo on his left bicep."

"Name?"

Nash shook his head.

"All right. I'll have a buddy of mine check the morgue for John Does."

"Thanks," said Nash while plucking Charlie off the desk. If some-thing had happened to Johnson, he would never forgive himself.

"Don't you have to get your ass downtown?"

"Yeah."

"Well, good luck. Don't take any shit from those peckers."

At the door Nash stopped and said, "I'm not the one who's going to need it. Rapp's the one they have in their sights today."

CHAPTER 57

CAPITOL HILL

R APP stood in front of the witness table, his right hand in the air. He repeated after the committee staffer who swore him in. It was possibly the first time he'd ever taken the oath in front of this or any other committee, for that fact, where he actually planned on telling the truth. He knew this was one of the reasons so many of them hated him. His lack of respect drove their overfed egos wild. Professional parsers, bullshitters, and liars, they couldn't get through a day without bending the truth in some drastic way, but God forbid someone come before their hallowed committee and do the same.

When he was done he sat down and looked up at the nineteen senators arrayed before him. They were sitting in judgment behind a heavy wood bench that curved around him and back like a horseshoe. The Judiciary Committee was without a doubt the most partisan in the Senate, due almost solely to the abortion issue and the fact that, in addition to the myriad of issues they faced, the committee was also charged with the confirmation of federal judges. Unfortunately, it affected everything that came before the committee. Of the nineteen members a dozen could be considered the most radical in the Senate.

Rapp was alone at the long witness table. He had chosen to make a statement that this problem started and ended with him. He had mixed feelings about how this was going to proceed. A very weary part of him had hoped they would be reckless enough to do this in front of the media. It would finally bring things to a head. It would force them to confront their lack of discipline and leadership. Anna would have loved that. His face being flashed all around the world would have all but assured that his days as a field operative would be done. In all the nights he'd been thinking about this, though, he knew they'd blink. These hearings were for show, and these vain men and women did not like to be embarrassed.

Their chairman was moving this thing along faster than they were used to. She wanted Rapp in her crosshairs before he changed his mind and lawyered up. But there were others who simply didn't like the idea of a hearing with so many unknowns. They were used to getting written testimony in advance—kind of like getting the answers to a test and then making up your own questions. The whole system was rigged to their advantage, and Rapp was looking forward to dropping a few surprises on them. This was the one silver lining of a closed hearing. They were far more likely to grant him some latitude. If the cameras were present, and they sensed anything embarrassing, they would rally around each other like a pack of hyenas, howling and snapping until the clamor reached such a level that it would drown out the words of the witness. In a closed-door session, he stood a far better chance of being able to finish a point, and hopefully get them to put party politics on hold.

Chairman Lonsdale removed her reading glasses and set them in front of her. Rapp looked up and noticed that her demeanor had changed drastically during the fifteen-minute recess. The first ninety minutes of the morning had been spent hearing the testimony of Captain Leland, who had been flown back from Afghanistan. Lonsdale and her colleagues had treated him with the sensitivity a prosecutor would afford a rape victim. Now they were going to get their pound of flesh from the rapist.

With a disapproving frown, Lonsdale said, "Mr. Rapp, I trust you paid close attention to Captain Leland's testimony."

Rapp had been ordered to sit in the gallery during Leland's testimony. "I did, Madam Chairman."

"I considered it to be very truthful, yet," Lonsdale said as she held up a sheaf of documents, "quite in contradiction to the written statement you have provided us."

"Are you saying that you find my statement to be false?" Rapp asked.

"I do, as a matter of fact. You look perfectly healthy, Mr. Rapp, whereas Captain Leland has obviously been physically assaulted." Lonsdale gestured to Leland, who was now sitting in the sparsely populated gallery flanked by his two recently hired attorneys.

Rapp looked over his shoulder at Leland, who was in his Air Force dress blue jacket and a matching sling. His head was tilted in a way that made his black eye impossible to miss. Rapp returned his attention to Lonsdale. "So without hearing my verbal testimony, you've already made up your mind?"

"You will be given an opportunity to plead your case, but at this point it is obvious that you have an uphill battle, Mr. Rapp."

"Well, it certainly is reassuring to have such a fair and impartial chairman presiding over this hearing," Rapp said in a voice full of sarcasm. "And you wonder why such an alarming number of people choose to exercise their Fifth Amendment right when called before this committee."

Lonsdale's eyes narrowed, and she was about to respond to Rapp's charge, when there was a commotion at the back of the room. Rapp resisted the urge to look over his shoulder, since this was the cue for the first big surprise. Lonsdale and then every other senator turned their attention to the center aisle of the committee room. Rapp heard the deep baritone voice and resisted his desire to smile. He knew what was about to happen, and understood perhaps better than most that it was going to be a historic moment. One where the legislative branch was about to be challenged on their home turf by a cabinet member of the executive branch.

"Madam Chairman," the voice boomed louder than anything that had been heard that morning. "I apologize for the intrusion, but I have something here that has a direct bearing on the matter before you."

Rapp found it safe now to turn and look at England. The secretary of defense was in his mid-fifties and had a full head of gray hair. He was widely known in Washington to be one of the more amiable cabinet members. He walked past Rapp's table without looking at him and stopped at a long wooden table that sat between the witness table and the raised dais. The senators all began sharing looks that ran the gamut from amusement to concern.

"Secretary England," Lonsdale said with trepidation into her microphone, "this is a closed-door hearing, and since you are not on the witness list, I am going to . . ."

England slammed a four-inch sheaf of documents down on the table and loudly announced, "I won't take but a minute of your time, and since you, Madam Chairman, have seen fit to involve yourself in the day-to-day affairs of the Department of Defense, I find it my duty to return the favor."

"I beg your . . ."

"That's quite all right," England shouted, refusing to yield the floor. "Esteemed members of the committee," he said as he looked from one end of the bench to the other in a casual sweeping motion, "I have in my hand a signed statement from General Garrison, the commander of the Bagram Air Base, Afghanistan. That would make him Captain Leland's commanding officer. He was present during the incident that you are now discussing."

"Secretary England," Lonsdale said in a sad, irritated voice, "this is highly irregular. If you . . ."

"No more irregular," England said in a singsong voice, "than the chairperson calling a friend at the Justice Department in the middle of the night, and having that friend initiate an investigation on one of my bases."

"Mr. Secretary," Lonsdale started in a strained, casual tone.

England was not to be denied his moment, though, and once again refused to yield. "The United States military has a long history of policing itself. On the rare, and exceptional, occasion when they have failed to do so, the Justice Department has intervened. But never," roared England, "in the history of this great country has the Justice Department moved to investigate an incident so clearly under military jurisdiction a mere forty-eight hours after it has occurred."

"Mr.—" Lonsdale tried to speak.

"Which," hollered England, "leads me to the conclusion that this entire thing is politically motivated."

"How dare you come before my committee and put forth such baseless allegations?" Lonsdale shot back.

"Baseless . . . Please explain to me, Senator Lonsdale, why your boy at Justice would only bother to get a statement from one person involved in this incident?"

"Because," Lonsdale shouted, matching England's intensity, "he was the aggrieved party."

"Did your man think of getting a statement from General Garrison? He was, after all, the only neutral party to the incident." England took a quick look at the panel and saw all heads turned to Lonsdale to hear her response. After an uncomfortable silence, England waved the document in the air and said, "Never fear, the air force did it for you. They are actually quite competent at this kind of thing." England motioned to a staffer that was sitting to his left. "Please do me a favor and hand these out to the committee members."

"Mr. Secretary," Lonsdale said, her anger barely in check, "I do not need to remind you that all documents are to be submitted to this committee in advance . . ."

"I'd like to make a motion for an exception."

Lonsdale didn't have to look. She knew Gayle Kendrick had made the motion. She reached for her gavel, but before she could get her hand around the mallet, the motion was seconded by another half dozen senators from both parties.

"The long and short of it, ladies and gentlemen," said England, "is that General Garrison corroborates Mr. Rapp's testimony, and says that Captain Leland has either misremembered the events of that evening or has made them up."

Lonsdale felt as if she were drowning and someone had just thrown a brick at her head. Her mind splintered, running off in eight different directions trying to find a way to regain control and momentum. She felt a touch on her shoulder and out of habit leaned back. Wassen was there, as he'd always been. He threw her the lifeline she needed to stay afloat by giving her a question.

With her cheeks still flushed from the embarrassment of England's revelation, she grabbed her microphone and said, "I would like to remind the committee that Mr. Rapp striking Captain Leland is but a single issue before us. Secretary England, as long as we have you here, I would like to know why you don't seem at all bothered by the fact that an employee of the CIA put on the uniform of a United States Air Force officer and snuck onto one of your bases with the express intent of circumventing the Uniform Code of Military Justice and the Geneva Conventions."

The room fell quiet, and all eyes turned to England for his response. With an incredulous shake of his head he said, "That's his job, people. This is what he's supposed to do." He made eye contact with several of the senators who were nodding agreeably. "We might not want to talk about it in civilized circles or, God forbid, in public, but his job is to go kill these bastards before they kill us." England's plain words had a sobering effect on the committee. In a softer tone he added, "We get caught up in all the crap that goes on in this town, and we forget one simple thing." England pointed at Rapp and said, "He's on our side."

CHAPTER 58

AFTER Secretary England had walked out of the committee room, several members called for a fifteen-minute recess so they could read General Garrison's statement. Lonsdale made no attempt to defeat the motion, for the simple reason that she needed to regroup and figure out how she would proceed. She went back to her office in Dirksen and huddled with Wassen and a few other senior staffers. They were all of the opinion that she needed to table the Leland issue for now and let the air force finish their investigation.

As no one had yet read General Garrison's statement, one of the committee staffers eagerly did so while the debate about what to do roared around her. When she was finished she offered her boss the hope she was looking for. Nowhere in Garrison's statement was there any mention of how Rapp had abused and mistreated the prisoners. Unlike Leland's statement, which went into specific detail about Rapp's abuses. Wassen was skeptical of this, raising the point that Leland's entire statement was now cast in doubt because his commanding officer had all but called him a liar.

Lonsdale, though, needed something. She wasn't going to call the whole thing into recess after just having been embarrassed by England. She wanted her pound of flesh from Rapp, and she was going to get it. Lonsdale announced that she would hit him hard on his abuse of the prisoners and directed the group to hastily assemble a list of questions while she went back and got things started. There would be a good five to ten minutes of motions and procedural nonsense before they got back to questioning Rapp.

On the way back to the committee room, Lonsdale asked, "What's wrong? You were awfully quiet back there."

Wassen looked down at the ground and said, "I've been with you long enough to know when I'll be wasting my breath."

"You don't agree with me?"

"There are plenty of times I don't agree with you."

"But you usually speak your mind."

"I have made myself very clear on this matter, and I think Secretary England framed the issue rather nicely."

"Secretary England is a capitalist windbag," Lonsdale said, while flashing a passing senator a fake smile.

"Have you ever stepped back far enough to really look at what's going on here?"

Lonsdale didn't answer immediately. "Of course. I do it all the time."

"Bullshit," Wassen said flatly. "All of you politicians are like parents. You adopt an issue and it's like it's your child. You lose all objectivity."

"That's not true."

"It's absolutely true, and the secretary of defense just proved it."

"How?" Lonsdale asked.

"When he reminded us that Rapp is on our side."

"I'm not so sure about that," Lonsdale said dismissively.

"God," Wassen groaned, "you are impossible sometimes. You think the terrorists are on our side?"

"Don't be silly."

"Then tell me . . . just whose side is Rapp on? Based on his record I think he's pretty firmly in the let's-kill-all-the-bastards camp."

"Then you tell me, Ralph," Lonsdale said in an irritated voice, "just who in the hell is on the side of the Constitution and the Bill of Rights?"

"History is your Achilles' heel, Barbara. I don't think you want to go there with me."

"Just what in the hell is that supposed to mean?" Lonsdale asked as the committee room came into view down the hall on their left.

"Those two documents are bathed in blood. They did not spring forth from the pen of men like Jefferson and survive on high-minded ideals alone. They have been bathed in blood over the years."

"You are so damn dramatic sometimes."

"And you are as pig-headed as ever."

Lonsdale stopped and grabbed Wassen by the arm. "So you think this is a mistake?"

"Barbara, you just got your pretty little ass kicked by the secretary of defense in your own backyard. That's not supposed to happen."

"What would you have had me do?" she hissed at him.

"Maybe nothing." He shrugged, "I warned you from the outset not to rush into this."

"Well, I disagree. We are a nation of laws. We can't have animals like Rapp running around doing whatever the hell they want."

"That's a lovely platitude. Would you prefer the terrorists run around and do whatever they like?"

"You are so damn infuriating sometimes."

Wassen looked over the top of her head and said, "This is why I kept my mouth shut. You don't want to hear what I have to say."

"Not on this issue. That's for sure." Lonsdale turned and entered the committee room. A few of her colleagues wanted a word with her, but she brushed them off and took her seat. After a quick look up and down the bench she gaveled them back into session.

CHAPTER 59

RAPP sat at the witness table and tried to follow what was going on. The various esteemed members of the committee seemed to be in great disagreement over how they should proceed. Even a few members of Lonsdale's own party were upset by the fact that she had rushed them headlong into this. Rapp wondered how they would react when he dropped the next bomb on them.

Finally, after a good ten minutes of wrangling, Lonsdale looked down and said, "Mr. Rapp, I would like to remind you that you are still under oath."

Rapp nodded.

"Speak into the microphone," she snapped, her patience used up by the bickering of colleagues.

"I am aware that I am still under oath."

Looking like she was afraid that someone might try to make another motion, Lonsdale quickly asked, "Do you deny striking Abu Haggani while he was bound and in U.S. custody?"

The room went completely silent and all eyes turned to Rapp, who was again alone at the witness table. *It all comes down to this,* Rapp thought. *Give them something and let them know you're serious.* "Madam Chairman, I will gladly answer all of your questions truthfully and to the best of my ability if you will clear the chamber of everyone except you and your fellow committee members."

Before anyone could react, Lonsdale snorted and said, "That is not going to happen."

Rapp nodded as if to say fine and then said, "Then you will leave me with no choice but to exercise my Fifth Amendment right."

Lonsdale sensed the stirring on both the left and the right. Ignoring the chatter, she said, "Mr. Rapp, you are not in control of this committee." She gestured to the nearly fifty staffers sitting behind the nineteen members. "These people have all passed stringent background checks, and I am deeply offended that you would call into question their integrity."

Rapp could spend the rest of the morning arguing with her about the leaks that came out of this committee and every other one on the Hill, but that wasn't what he was here for. He looked back at Lonsdale with a face that said, *You have to be kidding me,* and said, "Madam Chairman, in light of the fact that I am offering to answer all of your questions truthfully and honestly, I think it is a reasonable request."

The vice chair reached over and pulled Lonsdale in for a quiet conference. Rapp watched as both members covered their microphones with their hands and eagerly chatted in each other's ear. After nearly a minute of back and forth, Lonsdale returned to her microphone and cleared her throat.

"Mr. Rapp, we would be willing to entertain a motion to clear the room of everyone except committee members and yourself, including your delegation from the CIA, but I want to be crystal clear on your offer. You will make no attempt to evade our questions or invoke your Fifth Amendment right . . . is that correct?"

"That is correct. On issues pertaining to the matter before us, I will answer all of your questions truthfully and to the best of my ability."

Lonsdale and the vice chair covered their microphones again and began whispering. Rapp was betting on two things. The first was that Lonsdale had already been smacked by England, and she would not want her day to end in a defeat the town would be talking about for weeks. The second, he was betting on the collective hubris of the committee. Any of them would be sure of their ability to rip him to shreds in a proceeding like this. Together, all nineteen members would be fearless in the face of one man.

As Rapp had hoped, Lonsdale emerged from her conference and ordered that the room be cleared of everyone with the exception of the witness and the committee members. Rapp did not bother to turn around and look at his departing colleagues. Kennedy knew what was going on, and for now, the others did not need to be involved to this extent. Rapp was about to go way out on a limb and there was no sense in sending more than one person into the dangerous situation.

Lonsdale looked around to make sure everyone was gone. The large room seemed massive now that it was just the twenty of them. She wondered briefly if this had ever been done before. It happened on the Intelligence Committee from time to time, but she was not aware of the Judiciary Committee ever having met in such a manner. She looked down at Rapp and was surprised to see that he too appeared nervous for the first time all morning.

"Mr. Rapp, I would like to warn you . . . if I get the slightest sense that you are lying to me or any other member of this committee, I will . . ."

"I hit the prisoner," Rapp said clearly into the microphone. He knew he needed to give them something; show them that he had not made an empty promise. He also had no desire to sit there and listen to another round of threats form Lonsdale.

"So you are admitting to striking a bound prisoner?"

"He was not bound at the time, but I did strike him."

"I'm not sure that makes any difference. He was in our custody."

"Yes, he was."

Lonsdale felt suddenly vindicated, but she wanted to make sure her opponents on the committee were clear on this point. "So you admit to striking him?"

"Yes."

Lonsdale glanced at her notes. "And choking him?"

"Yes."

"Was he restrained while you were choking him?"

"Yes," Rapp said.

Lonsdale paused for a second to let the gravity of the admission sink in. "I see in one of the reports here that there was an electronic stun gun found in the interrogation room. Did you use that stun gun on the prisoner?"

"Yes," Rapp answered without hesitation.

Senators began mumbling to themselves.

"Madam Chairman," said Bob Safford, the chairman of the Intelligence Committee, "I would like to remind the witness that at any point he may still invoke his Fifth Amendment right."

Lonsdale shot Safford a look that said, *Shut the hell up*, and said, "Maybe the senator didn't hear, but the witness has already said he does not wish to invoke his Fifth Amendment right."

"Senator Lonsdale is right. I have no intention of invoking the Fifth."

Lonsdale turned back to the witness table and was surprised to find Rapp walking in front of it.

"Have any of you," Rapp said, "bothered to ask yourself why I would risk running an operation like this?" Not a single one of the nineteen answered, so Rapp continued. "Several weeks ago I was contacted by a source who works for a foreign intelligence agency. He informed me that two terrorist cells had been intercepted en route to the United States. One was headed to Los Angeles and the other to New York City."

"Why are we only hearing about this now?" asked Senator Safford, the chairman of the Intelligence Committee.

"That's a complicated answer, but the short version is that this ally no longer trusts us on this particular issue."

"What particular issue would that be?" Lonsdale asked.

"Enhanced interrogation methods."

"You mean torture," Lonsdale said.

"Call it whatever you'd like, ma'am, but please do not delude yourself into thinking it doesn't work."

"Mr. Rapp, I . . ."

"Please let me finish, ma'am. This is very important. This intelligence asset has reason to believe that a third cell may exist and might already be in the United States." Rapp slowly looked from one end of the long bench to the other. Not a single senator made an effort to speak.

Lonsdale exhaled a heavy sigh and said, "I find the timing of this phantom intelligence to be entirely self-serving."

"I thought you would say that, Senator, so I am prepared to make a deal. I would like to repeat what I just said in an open session. Hopefully, this afternoon. If you want to investigate and prosecute me for striking Abu Haggani, a man who is responsible for murdering over one hundred U.S. service personnel . . . a man who specializes in attacking grade schools filled with children . . . a man whose contribution to terrorism is that he was the first to recruit mentally retarded people to become suicide bombers . . . If that is the case you would like to put before the American people, then I welcome it. I am more than willing to publicly stand behind my position."

"And what exactly would that position be, Mr. Rapp?" Lonsdale said with derision. "That you think it should be the official policy of the United States of America to torture prisoners of war?"

The conversation had been brought to the crossroads that Rapp had been hoping for. Rapp watched as a good third of the panel snickered at their chairman's quick retort. He took the hatred he felt for them and doused it with pity just as Kennedy had told him to do. "My position, Madam Chairman, and members of the committee, is that it should be the *unofficial* policy of this government to reserve the right to use extreme measures in instances where we are threatened from terrorist attacks."

"Extreme measures," Lonsdale said with a disappointed look. "No doubt a euphemism for torture."

"Ma'am, about ten years ago I spent a week in the custody of the Syrian Intelligence Service." Rapp spoke without malice or dramatic effect. "I can tell you from firsthand experience that there's a big difference between torture and extreme measures." Rapp looked to the most liberal members of the committee as Kennedy had advised and said, "Ladies and gentlemen, I respect your position on this issue. No one who I work with likes torture. None of us enjoy inflicting pain on a prisoner, and it is not something that we do because we are bored and have decided to satisfy our sadomasochistic streaks. We do it in the rarest of instances, and we do it to save American lives."

"Mr. Rapp, what if this person is innocent?" asked the chairman of the Foreign Relations Committee.

"I only know of one instance where that has happened, and I was not involved in it. The person was never tortured in the sense that most people would define torture; however, I will freely admit that this person was subjected to environmental stress that is designed to get people to break. It is not something that is remotely pleasant, but this person was released without any physical harm."

"What about mental harm?" Lonsdale asked.

Rapp nodded. "That is a very good point. I have no doubt that the person suffered mental trauma. We have done our best to try and compensate this person and offer him medical assistance. Again, I am not proud of it, I was not involved in it, but I admit to you that a mistake was made. One mistake among hundreds of interrogations."

"I don't find your words reassuring, Mr. Rapp."

He turned to face the senior senator from Vermont. "This is an ugly business, Madam Senator. These religious fanatics want to do us great harm, and it is my job to try and stop them. That is why I launched this risky operation. We have two men in our possession, both senior Taliban members with heavy ties to al-Qaeda. Men who have the blood of thousands of innocent people on their hands, and I am not allowed to talk to them. One of those men, Mohammad al-Haq, acknowledged the existence of the third cell without us even laying a hand on him."

"That," said Lonsdale, "was because you were threatening to hand him over to the butcher of Mazar-i-Sharif . . . General whatever his name is."

"That's right," Rapp said without shame. "That's how you get these guys to talk. Mohammad al-Haq is not an American citizen. He is a terrorist."

Lonsdale said, in a surprisingly even tone, "Mr. Rapp, you would be well advised to remember that this committee, as well as several federal judges, have already weighed in on this issue. This country is bound by the Geneva Conventions. We must afford all prisoners of war the protection mandated by law."

"And the terrorists who intentionally target civilians?" Rapp asked. "Who holds their feet to the fire and makes sure they follow the Geneva Conventions?" Rapp looked at the right side of the bench and added, "We all know the answer to that. They did not sign the Geneva Conventions and never will. They in fact go out of their way to break almost every rule the Geneva Conventions set forth, yet in our infinite wisdom we have decided to afford them the protections of a document that they spit on."

"Mr. Rapp," Lonsdale said, in an almost tired voice, "we are a nation of laws."

"Yes, we are," Rapp said respectfully. "An open democracy. A government of the people, by the people." He took a step closer to the bench and lowered his voice. "Ladies and gentlemen, I don't want to do this," he said in almost pleading tone, "but you are leaving me with no other choice. I've been doing this for close to twenty years, and tension between the CIA and Capitol Hill has never been this bad. We have forgotten who our true enemy is. It is not us." Rapp pointed back and forth among the various members. "Secretary of State England said it earlier. We are on the same team. I remember after nine-eleven, when the pain of that day was still fresh, many of you came to me and asked if we were doing enough to make these terrorists talk after they were captured. You didn't think we were being aggressive enough, and then Abu Ghraib hit and we went right back to fighting each other."

Rapp paused for a brief moment and then directed his words directly at Lonsdale. "Madam Chairman, it is my sincere belief that we are going to be attacked in the near future. I know for a fact that at least one of the two men I tried to question last week has information that could help us to stop this attack." He looked from one end of the table to the other and said, "I am begging each and every one of you, think of the ramifications. Think of how the American people will react when they find out that this committee and its members were more concerned with protecting the debatable rights of a couple of bigoted, sadistic terrorists than they were in protecting their own citizens, who each and every one of you has sworn to protect and defend."

"If this country is attacked," said Lonsdale, "then you and the CIA will be to blame. Not this committee."

Rapp's anger was barely in check. He'd set aside all of his disdain for these men and women, and their ever-shifting set of principles, in hopes that they could find a middle road. He was giving them an opportunity to save themselves, and Lonsdale could not see fit to get off her pedestal and take the necessary course, the course that would protect the country. His every fiber wanted to let loose on the self-serving chairman, but Kennedy's voice kept him in check. Her words admonishing him that they would need these people, especially after the bombs went off. The president had assured them that the CIA would not be blamed should an attack take place. He had guaranteed them that he would place the blame firmly at the feet of a group of elitist senators and rabid congressmen who had for years harassed and hamstrung the CIA.

Knowing that the president would be there as a backstop, Rapp allowed the slightest hint of a grin to form on his lips, and then he said, "If you really believe that, Madam Chairman, I propose we convene for lunch, and when we come back for the afternoon session, we open it to the public. Let's get the press in here." Rapp turned around and motioned toward the gallery. "Fill the place up. I'll admit everything in front of the cameras. You can tear me apart," Rapp said triumphantly. "Your constituents will love it. I'll state my case for the use of extreme measures, you can all call me a barbarian if you'd like, and if this terrorist cell that you believe doesn't exist never materializes, you will be able to make great political hay out of the entire matter. If you push hard enough, you will surely get me removed from service and probably prosecuted."

Rapp paused and let a moment pass before he put forth the uncomfortable alternative. "But, if I'm right and this cell does manage to reach D.C. . . . and the bombs start going off . . . every last one of you is going to have to face the wrath of your constituents." Rapp looked up and down the long bench. Most of the senators were as solemn as they'd been all morning. Rapp was reminded again of Kennedy's words. How she had cautioned him to resist his instinct to tell them off. This was supposed to be about bringing them into the fold. Not deepening the divide. In a slightly conspiratorial tone he said, "There is another route we can take, however."

No one spoke at first and then Senator Valdez asked, "What would that be?"

"You can quietly refer this entire matter back to the Intelligence Committee, where things can be handled in a more discreet manner." Rapp gave them a moment to weigh their options and then said, "So, what is it going to be? An open session this afternoon, or back to the Intelligence Committee?"

Lonsdale looked as if she might take her gavel and throw it at Rapp's head. She started moving her perfectly lined lips toward the microphone and was just about to let loose when both the vice chair and Kent Lamb, the esteemed chairman of the Appropriations Committee, reached out and grabbed her. After a tense fifteen-second conference, Lonsdale made it to her microphone and said, "Mr. Rapp, you are excused. The committee will now meet in private to discuss the issues before us and then break for lunch. We will reconvene at two this afternoon."

"I will stay in the building, and make myself available should any of you want to discuss this matter in private." Rapp gave a grimacing Lonsdale a nod and then left.

CHAPTER 60

NASH waited as long as he could for Rapp to emerge from the committee room, but he'd run out of time. His administrative assistant had come through as she almost always did and informed him that his wife was scheduled to meet with the dean at 11:45. Nash left word with Kennedy to have Rapp call him as soon as he got out and then he left to race across town. Sidwell was only five miles from Capitol Hill, but Nash knew it would take at least fifteen minutes to get there, and that was if he hit all the lights and traffic wasn't too bad. As he pulled out of the Dirksen parking lot, he was relieved to find the street empty. Nash's hopes that he would make it to the meeting on time were dashed a few blocks later as he reached a jam-packed Columbus Circle. With his options extremely limited, he nosed his way onto Massachusetts Avenue and headed northwest.

A cab cut him off a block later and he laid on his horn with everything he had. The cabby flipped him off. Nash looked through his windshield and for a split second imagined how satisfying it would be to run the guy off the road and whip him with his own antenna. He quickly banished the idea and turned his mind to his son. He could spend the next fifteen minutes getting angry about it and carefully plotting out the confrontation, but in the end this was about Rory. He and his wife would have to sort their problems out later.

The traffic was a mess at Thomas Circle, and for a minute Nash was tempted to take to the side streets, but he'd made this trip enough to know that could be a risky move. As he was nearing Dupont Circle his phone rang. The readout told him it was a private call.

"Hello."

"Irene said you wanted to talk to me." It was Rapp.

"Yeah," Nash said, "How'd the rest of the hearing go?"

"Well enough. I'll fill you in later. What's up?"

"I've got a bit of a problem." He paused and carefully chose his words, keenly aware that the call could be recorded. "That dinner we were planning . . . the one we canceled. I talked to everybody and they were fine with shutting it down, except Chris."

"What was his problem?"

"He said he'd put too much effort into it to just call it off, and he felt like he was nearing a breakthrough."

"So he's still on the job?" Rapp said casually.

"Yeah, except there's a slight problem. We had coffee yesterday, and he said he would check in with me last night and this morning."

"And?"

"Nothing so far."

"That's not good. What are you doing about it?"

"I called Scott. He's trying to track him down."

Rapp didn't answer right away and then said, "Irene said you had a family thing to attend to."

"Yep."

"When will you be done?"

"If all goes well, I'll be back up there by one."

"All right. If you hear anything, call me."

"Will do."

"And when you get back here, we might have to make a trip over there."

"Over there?" Nash asked a bit anxiously. He wondered if Rapp meant the mosque.

"Yeah, I don't like this. Chris is no flake. If he hasn't called you back, we've got a problem."

"I agree, but who in the hell are we going to bring it to?"

"We're not. That's why you and I are going over there. Get back here as soon as you can."

"Will do." Nash hit the end button and set the phone down.

Traffic eased up as soon as he crossed Rock Creek. A few minutes later he was turning on to Wisconsin Avenue and passing the National Cathedral. He checked the clock on the dashboard and swore. It was 11:51. Sidwell was the type of place where things ran on time, so there was no telling what kind of damage his wife had already done. Nash parked the van in the small lot in front of the school and raced in. He knew where the administration office was located, but not the dean's office. A student pointed him in the right direction and a moment later Nash found himself standing in front of the dean's door. He could hear people talking on the other side, but they weren't clear enough for him to know what they were saying.

Nash tapped on the door lightly and then opened the door. He stepped into the room and said, "Sorry I'm late." Nash gave his wife a fake smile and then approached the neat, organized desk of the dean. Sticking his hand across the desk he said, "I'm Mike Nash, Rory's father."

A serious woman with short salt-and-pepper hair offered Nash her hand and said, "I'm Peggy Barnum Smith, dean of students here at Sidwell. Please have a seat."

Nash noted that there was no warmth in the woman's voice. He grabbed a chair that was sitting near a bookcase and set it down next to his wife, who made no attempt to look at him. He glanced over at Todd and Kristy De Graff, whom he barely knew, and noted the tissue in Mrs. De Graff's hand, as well as her red eyes and nose. "What have I missed?"

Dean Barnum Smith leaned forward and folded her hands, placing them atop her leather desk blotter. She tilted her head toward Nash and in a solemn voice said, "Kristy had just finished explaining to us the extent of Derek's injuries. Your wife," the dean said while gesturing to Maggie, "is hoping that we can find a middle ground short of expulsion. She has offered to pull your son off the lacrosse team and thinks that one hundred hours of community service, either here at Sidwell, or an organization of the De Graffs' choosing would be fair."

Nash took the anger that he felt toward his wife at that moment and set it aside. He looked back at the dean and said, "That's not going to happen."

"You would prefer he be expelled?" The dean asked sincerely.

"No."

"I'll be honest," Barnum Smith said, "my hands are tied. We have a zero tolerance policy against fighting."

"What is your policy for foul-mouthed kids?"

"Pardon me?" Barnum Smith said, looking very caught off guard.

"Have any of you bothered to ask themselves why a kid like Rory, who has never been in trouble before, would suddenly decide to beat up a classmate?"

"What are you trying to insinuate?" Kristy De Graff asked, obviously offended.

"There are two sides to every story, Kristy. Have you asked your son if he provoked Rory?"

"Provoked!" she said in shock. "My son's face looks like something out of a horror movie. I can't believe we are even having this conversation." She turned to her husband. "I told you we should call the police."

"I think that's a great idea," Nash said as he sat back and crossed his legs. "I'm sure the administration here at Sidwell would love the P.R. they would get out of having D.C.'s finest on campus. The police can take statements from each of the boys and any witnesses, and then it will all go away because the D.C. juvenile courts have a hell of a lot more important things to worry about than a couple of wealthy kids getting in a fistfight, because one kid said he wanted to fuck the other kid's sister."

The word hit like a mortar shell. Barnum Smith sat back like she'd been slapped in the face, and both De Graffs sat in their chairs slack-jawed, not believing what they had heard. Maggie simply lowered her face into her hands and Nash said, "Yeah, your little angel was telling Rory about all the things he wanted to do to my daughter Shannon . . . who, by the way, is fourteen. Derek said she was really hot and that he wanted to *fuck* her."

An appalled Kristy De Graff said, "My son would never say such a thing."

"Oh . . . he did," Nash said as lightheartedly as he could. "In fact, he said it several times. Rory told him if he said it again he was going to beat him up. Apparently, Derek didn't take him very seriously, because he thought it would be funny to then insult my wife by telling Rory that Maggie here is a MILF. Which stands for Mom I'd Like to . . ." Nash didn't want to push it, so he mouthed the word.

Dean Barnum Smith was seriously offended. She turned to the De Graffs and asked, "Have you talked to Derek about this?"

"I don't need to talk to my Derek about this," Kristy said. "He would never talk like that."

The dean gave her a look that said, *Don't be so sure about it.* She pressed the intercom button on her desk and said, "Please send word that I want Derek De Graff and Rory Nash sent to my office."

As the dean took her finger off the intercom button, Kristy De Graff turned to her husband and said, "I told you we should have brought our attorney with us."

Nash felt his BlackBerry vibrate. He reached into his suit coat breast pocket and grabbed it. It was an e-mail from Art Harris. Nash opened it and read the small letters: *I think I found your guy. Not good. Call me ASAP!*

The room suddenly got very hot. Nash pulled at his tie and stood. "I'm very sorry," he said to the group. "I have to leave."

Maggie looked up at him and saw what she took to be genuine fear on her husband's face. "What's wrong?"

"Something at work. I'll call you the first chance I get." Nash squeezed her shoulder and left. By the time he hit the front steps of the school, he had Harris on the line. "Art, what's up?"

There was a heavy sigh on the other end and then, "The D.C. fire department responded to a call last night just before four in the morning. There was a burning car in an abandoned lot. When they got the thing put out, they popped the trunk and found a body. Based on the coroner's report, everything matched your description except one thing."

"What's that?" Nash asked, holding out a sliver of hope.

"He was missing three toes on his right foot. The doc said they looked like they'd been cut off one at a time, and not by a surgeon. He also said it looked like it had been done recently. Probably around the time of murder, but he wouldn't know until he was finished with the full autopsy."

"Shit," Nash said as he lost all hope.

"What do you want me to do?"

"Forget we ever had this conversation." Nash hung up and looked back at the school and then at his phone. He knew what he had to do and he hoped Rory would understand. Nash jumped in his car and dialed Rapp's number. After six rings he got his voice mail. Nash hesitated for a second and then decided to call Kennedy's office. When her assistant answered, he said, "This is Mike Nash. I need you to get Rapp on the phone ASAP. I have an emergency."

CHAPTER 61

CAPITOL HILL

L ONSDALE did the walk of shame back to her office from the committee room. Only those who really knew her could have guessed that she was on the verge of cracking. She was a professional politician, after all—a woman who could look happy after three straight months on the campaign trail. What was a little two-minute walk from the Judiciary Committee room to her office? She'd almost snapped three times, though, twice at a couple of her incompetent staffers who couldn't read her emotions for shit, and once at a fellow senator who had rushed up to her to find out what happened behind the closed-door session. Each time Lonsdale looked like a petite version of the Heisman Trophy with her hand extended palm-out to keep would-be tacklers at bay.

When she finally made it to her office suite, she slid through her private door and walked right past a half dozen senior staffers who knew her well enough to keep their mouths shut. She breezed through the small reception area with a plastic smile on her face and entered her office. A split second later the heavy wooden door slammed shut.

All eyes turned to Wassen. He looked with a heavy dose of trepida-

tion at the door his boss had just gone through and knew she was waiting for him and only him. If anyone else dared go through that door,
they would get their head bitten off. Ralph Wassen motioned for everyone to get back to work, and then he very carefully opened the door
and slid in, closing it behind him. Lonsdale was on the long couch—
her shoes off, her feet up, and a cigarette in her hand. Wassen noticed
that she hadn't bothered to turn on the smoke eater, which he took as
another bad sign.

He crossed the room, turned on the machine, and then went and
joined his boss in the seating area. He took one of the ultramodern
armchairs with the big chrome base and said, "What in the hell happened?"

Lonsdale didn't bother to look at him. With her head tilted back,
she looked up through a cloud of smoke and said, "Probably the worst
day of my life."

Wassen thought of her dead husband. "Worse than the day John
died?"

"No," she answered frankly. "No . . . not worse than that. It was the
most embarrassing failure of my political career," she corrected herself.

"What in the hell happened?" he asked again.

"They all turned on me. They pissed right down their pants legs."

"Why? What did Rapp say?"

Lonsdale rocked her head forward and looked at Wassen for the
first time. "He did basically what you told me he would do. Not exactly
the same, but the same general theme. He scared the piss out of all of
them. Made them think we're in danger of being attacked, and if they
don't let him loose so he can break as many laws as he wants, he's going
to blame us when we get hit."

Wassen swallowed. "So where does it go from here? We've been
flooded with calls. Are you going to open it up to the press at two?"

Lonsdale took a long drag and then, after she'd exhaled, began
laughing hysterically.

"What's so funny?"

"There isn't going to be any hearing this afternoon. At least not in front of my committee."

Wassen was stunned. "How is that possible?"

"That little shit," she said, "put the fear of God into all those little pussies I serve with. He wanted to have a public hearing this afternoon. He was willing to admit to hitting and choking and electrocuting that damn terrorist in front of a roomful of cameras, and he was going to say he did it all to protect us against an imminent attack by some phantom terrorist cell. And then he gave them a second option, which was to refer the entire matter back to the Intelligence Committee, where things could be handled in a more secret manner."

"And?"

"My own damn party ran out on me. There was a heated thirty-minute debate on the matter, a vote to refer it back to the Intelligence Committee, and it was over."

"How did the vote break?"

She waved her hand dismissively. "It wasn't even close. It was seven to one before it even got to me, and that was on my side of the aisle."

Wassen winced and asked, "Anything else?"

She had her head all the way back again. She groaned and said, "Ted Darby whispered in my ear, at one point, that if I didn't calm down and begin acting reasonably, he would make sure my chairman-ship was taken away from me."

"Oh my God," Wassen mumbled. Ted Darby was perhaps the most powerful man in the entire Senate and not someone who was prone to making empty threats. "So where do you go from here?"

"I don't know. I suppose I can go after him when he comes before the Intel Committee, but I don't think I'm going to get much support."

Wassen looked at his watch. It was a few minutes past noon. She was already late for her lunch appointment. "I hate to do this to you, but you have a lunch date with Joe Barreiro."

Lonsdale grabbed her forehead with her free hand and said, "I can't do it. No way. I don't think I could hold it together. I'll end up saying something that could land me in hot water with the Ethics Committee. Hell . . . probably even the Justice Department." She paused for a moment and then started laughing. "Wouldn't that be something? After all this, I'm the one who ends up getting indicted."

"You're not going to get indicted. Do you want me to go in your place?"

"No." She waved her hand. "Just cancel it."

"Bad idea."

"Why?"

"Barreiro doesn't like getting stood up. He's likely to write something really nasty about you, and from what it sounds like, the last thing you need right now is some bad press."

"You're right."

"What should I tell him?"

"Tell him my party has abandoned me. That they no longer care about government employees following the law."

"How about I tell him that Rapp brought some disturbing information before your committee, and you have decided that, for the sake of national security, you would refer the entire matter to the Intelligence Committee, where it can be handled with sensitivity."

"Take credit for it?" she asked in near total exasperation.

"That's the general idea."

"No way in hell. This thing will turn someday, and I'll be standing there looking at all these gutless bastards . . . and we'll all know whose fault this was."

"Fine." Wassen stood. "Would you like me to tell him the vote was eighteen to two? Let me guess: the only other person to join you was our stalwart communist, Chuck Levine?"

"Do you really think I need this right now?"

"What you don't need is more bad press than you're already going to get."

"Fine . . . I don't care," she said without looking at him.

Wassen looked down at her and hesitated to bring to her attention that he had warned her about this. He wanted to say to her, *And what happens if Rapp is right? How will you handle it when all of your col-leagues look at you with derision?* But he couldn't. Not now, while she was so thoroughly beaten. It would be cruel. He would wait for a few days to pass and then try to talk some sense into her. And in the meantime, he would give Barreiro a version of the events that would make his boss look more moderate.

CHAPTER 62

RAPP, Kennedy, O'Brien, and Ridley went up to Hart 216 and ensconced themselves in one of the secure conference rooms, so they could have some privacy and take advantage of the phones. Rapp's club sandwich and fries lay half eaten in a Styrofoam container. He was up and moving. His jacket was hung over one of the empty chairs and he had his arms crossed while he slowly walked from one end of the conference room to the other. O'Brien and Ridley paid him no attention. They were used to the fact that the man seemed to be in perpetual motion, and they were too interested in finishing their own lunch. Kennedy, however, was watching him with her sad, thoughtful eyes. She'd already closed the lid on her salad and pushed it aside.

She took a sip of Diet Coke and asked, "What's wrong?"

Rapp scratched his hand with his left hand. "I've got a bad feeling."

"You said things went well," Kennedy said reassuringly.

"They did. I'm not talking about that stuff . . . I'm worried about what's going on out there." Rapp waved his hand toward the walls.

Kennedy smiled. He had never been comfortable in this role of bureaucrat. Not that he wasn't good at it—he was. He was just infinitely better in the field, left to his own devices and judgment. His true talent was wasted in these meeting rooms, but she'd needed him to make a statement. She could have said everything he'd said, and the majority of the senators would have dismissed it out of hand. But Rapp was something different. A dirty, muddy, and bloody soldier returning from the front lines to report to the generals that the situation was quite different than it appeared from the safety of the rear. Rapp was a man of action who had bled for, and done great things for, his country. Few, if any, knew the specifics of what he'd done, but the rumors were enough for them to give great weight to his words. There would be a few like Lonsdale, however, who so despised what he stood for that they would never listen. But the majority would be sensible, for in the end, they were politicians, and the one thing they could be counted on doing was to act in their own self-interest.

"Just a few more hours this afternoon and then hopefully we can move forward with their support."

"I'm not worried about that," said Rapp in a grave voice. "I'm worried about this damn third cell. According to the Brits, D-day was set for next week."

O'Brien and Ridley stopped talking and looked at Rapp. They knew if he was concerned, they should be concerned. "Mitch, we don't even know if this third cell is for real, and if they do exist, there was a good chance they were scared off after the other two failed to report in."

Kennedy watched Rapp and could tell there was something else on his mind that he wasn't saying. "What's wrong?"

Rapp looked at the two men and then Kennedy. "I talked to Nash right before lunch. He says one of his guys has missed his last two check-ins."

"Which guy?"

"It sounds like Chris Johnson."

"What check-in? We pulled the damn plug on the whole thing." O'Brien said with anger. "It was supposed to be shut down."

"Don't go all HQ on me, Chuck," Rapp shot back with every bit as much anger. "We've all been in the field before. We all know what it's like to bust your ass on something for months and then have HQ hit you over the head with some asinine order."

"This is different, Mitch," a red-faced O'Brien said. "There was way too much heat coming down on us."

"And none of us were there." Rapp said, pointing at the table. "I don't know what in the hell Johnson told him that convinced him to leave him on the job, but I'm not going to get all pissed off about one of our guys putting his nuts on the line. I trained Nash. I taught him to be aggressive, just like you two were when you were running around in Europe, Charlie, and when you were working your magic in the Middle East, Rob. So if you want to be pissed at someone . . . take it out on me."

Ridley held up his hands and said, "I think it's safe to say Nash had a good reason for leaving Johnson in place."

"It's not his call," O'Brien said. "If he has something, he comes to us, and we make the decision."

"Bullshit!" Rapp said while frowning at O'Brien. "You gonna tell me when you were slinking around East Berlin you never made a couple frickin' on-the-fly decisions and never told your boss?"

"Gentlemen," Kennedy said without looking at any of them, "do any of you know Mike Nash to be a reckless man?"

One by one they all shook their heads.

"Good," she said, "then we should all calm down and think about what this might mean."

The secure phone in the middle of the table started ringing. Ridley reached out and grabbed it. "Hello." He listened for a second and then gave Rapp the handset. "It's Nash."

Rapp grabbed the phone. "What's up?"

"It's not good." Nash's voice sounded heavy.

"Let's hear it."

"I'm almost certain Johnson is in the morgue. I gave a friend his profile and he just called me to report that a body fitting his description was found at four this morning, in the trunk of a burning car."

"Shit."

"And there's one other thing, Mitch. I think he was tortured. The body was missing three toes from the right foot. The coroner said they were not removed by a surgeon."

Rapp felt his guts turn and he told himself, *not now.* "You have all of his reports, right?"

"Yeah."

"He had six good suspects, right?"

"Yeah."

"Get out to NCTC as fast as you can and you get those six dumped into the system and kicked to the top of the watch list. You get any heat from anyone, you tell them the order comes directly from Irene. If they still piss and moan about the protocols, you tell them to put them on the list first and then call me.

"What about a source? They're going to want a source."

"Tell them I got it from my counterpart at Mossad and call me with confirmation as soon as it happens. I gotta run." Rapp hung up the phone and looked at Kennedy. "Johnson's in the morgue, missing three toes. We have to open this thing up. You have to tell the president and you have to get the National Security Council together."

"And tell them what?" O'Brien asked. "That contrary to everything we've been saying, we actually did send an undercover operative into a mosque and now he's dead? We'll all be thrown in jail."

Rapp grabbed his suit coat and started for the door. "I don't give a shit what you tell him. Blame it all on me, tell him the Israelis tipped us off. Think something up. The bottom line is, if Johnson is in the morgue, those fuckers are in this city."

As Rapp reached the door, Kennedy asked, "Where are you going?"

"I'm sure they're long gone, but I'm going to over to that mosque to see what I can find out."

"Not by yourself, you're not."

"Irene, trust me. They have more to fear than I do."

Kennedy watched him leave and looked at Ridley. "Go with him,"

she ordered. "And make sure he doesn't kill anyone . . . unless he absolutely has to."

Ridley jumped up and chased after Rapp. Kennedy picked up the
phone and punched in the secure number for the White House Situation Room. When the watch officer answered on the other end, she
identified herself and said, "We have a situation. I need to speak to the
president."

CHAPTER 63

KARIM was dressed in a dark blue suit, white shirt, and blue and gray striped tie. His well-oiled pistol was holstered on his right hip and a radio was clipped to his left hip. A small flesh-colored cord coiled its way past his shirt collar and around and into his ear. An American flag pin was proudly displayed on his lapel. He stood ram-rod straight and inspected his men from left to right as if they were on a parade ground. In a manner of speaking, they were. On his far left, Farid stood in front of a blue Ford Fusion. He was dressed almost exactly the same as Karim, minus the earpiece. The car had forged U.S. government plates. No one had an easy job today, but Farid would be the first to move into position. If he failed, it could have a cascading effect on the operation. Next in line were three identical white Chevy vans. Each vehicle had FedEx emblazoned in purple and orange on the side. In front of the vehicles stood three men, each wearing the uniform of a FedEx driver. The cargo pockets on the right side of their pants had been modified to holster their pistols with the silencers attached.

On the far right, two men stood at parade rest in full SWAT gear. Parked behind them was a big black Suburban, also with forged government plates. The windows were heavily tinted and there were LED emergency lights mounted on the grille as well as the back window. Karim was filled with pride over the well-disciplined, transformed men before him. He stepped forward and approached Fazul, one of the Moroccans who was in a FedEx uniform.

Karim extended his hand palm-up and said, "Your sidearm."

The man did exactly as he had been taught. Using only one hand, he reached into the cargo pocket, retrieved his gun, and held it out with the silencer pointing down for inspection.

Taking the weapon, Karim turned it over in his hands and admired the well-oiled slide. After a few more seconds, he handed the weapon back and continued down the line. He did the same thing with each man, and then returned to the center of the formation, where Hakim was waiting. He smiled at his old friend and turned to address the men.

"We are poised to strike a mighty blow. You have trained hard for many months, and we are at the end of a great and glorious journey." He gazed from one man to the next, and slowly a sly grin spread across his face. "But before we rush off to paradise, we will have some fun."

The men laughed and shared looks of confident agreement.

"Does anyone have any questions?" Karim asked, secretly hoping there were none. They had been over each part of the plan in such detail that there should be no room left for interpretation or doubt. The assignments had been choreographed down to the minute. Maps had been studied over and over. Metro schedules had been checked and rechecked. The routes were all programmed into GPS devices, so that no one would get lost and they would all arrive at their targets within minutes, if not seconds.

Farid took one large step forward and came to attention with his eyes front and center. "Sir," he said in a crisp voice. "I would like to say, on behalf of the men, that it has been an honor serving under your command."

Karim looked over at perfect Farid. His fellow Saudi. He was the only one of the group who showed signs of possible greatness. It was a shame that he would have to die with the others. "It has been my privilege," Karim announced, "to lead you men. Allah looks down on each of you with favor. They will talk about this day for centuries. They will revere our courage, admire our skill, and celebrate our victory. Now is the time. We have been on the defensive for many years. Today is the day that we strike at the heart of our enemy for all of Islam."

Karim looked at his watch and then turned back to Farid. With a curt nod he said, "It is time." Looking over his shoulder at Hakim, he said, "Open the door." Ten seconds later Karim watched the blue sedan roll past a black Lincoln Town Car and out into the sunlight. He marked the time on his watch. They were exactly on schedule. Now the important part was pacing. He wanted everyone to arrive as close to 12:30 as possible. Sending the vehicles all out at once would mean that the ones with the closest targets would have to park and wait, and that would only create an opportunity for something to go wrong.

Two minutes later he ordered the first of the FedEx vans to depart, and then he ordered the rest of the men into their vehicles. Karim climbed into the front seat of the Lincoln, and Hakim got behind the wheel.

"Your man has assured you?" Karim asked skeptically.

"Yes. He said it is not a problem." Hakim pointed at the dashboard clock and said, "At precisely twelve twenty-three Eastern Standard Time, the entire traffic surveillance system will crash."

"Did you make sure that it will only be the cameras? If the signals go down as well, we will never get out of the city."

"He assured me," Hakim said, tired of having to repeat himself. "Besides, that is why the Suburban will wait for us, just in case."

"And everything is fine with Ahmed?" Karim asked anxiously.

Hakim sighed. Early in the morning, right before the sun came up, he had dropped the sniper off near their second target so he could observe things and provide intelligence for the assault. "Yes, he is fine. I spoke with him not more than thirty minutes ago."

"Good." Karim studied his watch and then pointed toward the open door. "It is time to go."

Hakim started the car and put it in drive. The other three vehicles followed closely as they wound their way through the run-down industrial park. After crossing the Anacostia River, three of the vehicles turned onto Kentucky Avenue, while one of the FedEx vans stayed on Pennsylvania Avenue. Karim ticked off the landmarks. He'd seen photos of each of them but this was the first time in person. As they reached Stanton Park, Karim felt his heart begin to pound.

Farid's voice crackled over Karim's earpiece. "This is Bill. I am clear. Do you copy?"

Karim pulled back his suit coat and turned his radio to the transmit mode. "I copy you, Bill. Good luck."

The Lincoln turned onto C Street off of Stanton Park. The FedEx van followed, but the Suburban continued on to Massachusetts Avenue, where it turned north. Karim could see the U.S. Capitol looming just a few blocks away, and then it disappeared as the road dropped down and their view was blocked by the immense Senate Office buildings. At 1st Avenue, Karim felt as if his heart would leap out of his chest at any moment. Hakim whistled some song he did not recognize. It bothered him that his friend could be so calm at a time like this. They turned right and were headed north, their target only a block away. Karim glanced to the right and smiled at the sight of the blue sedan that Farid had parked in the lot only minutes earlier.

At 1st and D Street Hakim took a right and pulled over, leaving enough room for the FedEx van to nose in behind them. Karim looked up just as the clock changed from 12:27 to 12:28. He looked at his own watch and confirmed that they were now only seconds away.

"This is Joe. I am clear."

Karim sighed and said, "I copy you, Joe. Good luck."

Hakim drummed his fingers on the wheel and said, "Two down
. . . one to go."

It came just seconds later. "This is Thomas. I am clear."

"I copy you, Thomas. Good luck." Karim wiped his sweaty palms
on his pants and tried to take a deep breath. He was not used to feeling
such nerves and wrote it off to the importance of the situation.

"Are you ready?" Hakim asked.

"Yes," Karim said.

The Lincoln began rolling once again with the FedEx van right on
its bumper. A half a block later the Lincoln stopped in front of a green
awning. Printed in white letters were two words: *The Monocle.* Almost
directly behind the Lincoln, the FedEx van took a right turn into the
parking lot. Forty feet later, the van stopped almost at the midpoint of
the building. Karim could not see the parking lot, but he knew what
was going on. He exited the car and opened the back door. As he was
reaching in to grab a briefcase, he received confirmation from the van's
driver that he too was clear. Karim gripped the briefcase and, without
saying a word to Hakim, closed the door.

He entered the restaurant and took a quick glance at the packed
dining room on the right. The maitre d' greeted him. Karim gave him
a forced smile and turned into the bar area, which ran along the left
side of the building. He couldn't have been more pleased that he had
to thread his way through a packed crowd. As he worked his way down
the bar, it became less crowded. Near the end, he set his briefcase down
on the floor and continued toward the bathrooms. He passed a waiter
in the narrow hallway and flattened his back to the wall and then continued right out the back door. He held his hands over his eyes as if he
was screening them from the sun.

Steadily he picked up the pace, heading straight south. He threaded
his way through a couple of parked cars on his left and turned east.
Only fifty more feet, he told himself. Karim was sweating now. He
reached into his pocket and grabbed the remote detonator. He flipped
off the safety. A few seconds after that, he faintly heard his watch beep-

ing. It was 12:30. He wanted to break into a sprint, but he fought the instinct to panic.

"Just a few more steps," he said out loud this time. When he reached the rear of the next building, which dwarfed the relatively small restaurant he'd just left, he gave Allah a quick thanks and flipped the switch on the detonator.

CHAPTER 64

RAPP tore down Constitution Avenue at speeds approaching 70 MPH, right down the centerline, sending oncoming cars lurching to get out of his way. All Rapp could do to warn them was flash his brights and hit the horn. Ridley nervously clutched the door. At Tennessee a red light was waiting for them. Rapp slowed down to 30 MPH, looked both ways, and gunned it. The big Hemi V8 in the Dodge Charger set Ridley back into his seat. A few blocks later the black Charger shot through the intersection at 15th Street going 74 mph.

"You might want to slow down," Ridley said nervously. "I don't think we want the cops with us."

"I really don't give a shit." Rapp slipped his foot over to the brake and yanked the wheel almost a half turn to the right. The tires squealed as the rubber tried to grip the pavement. They came out of the turn racing south on sixteenth Street.

"Mitch, I think you need to calm down," Ridley said nervously, with one hand on the dash and the other on the door.

"Rob, when we get there, I'll stay as cool as the situation dictates, but this isn't some covert sneak-and-peek. We're going in hard and I'm planning on rattling some cages."

Ridley winced. "Maybe we should call Irene?"

Rapp looked over and said, "I can pull over right now and let you out."

Ridley shook his head and grumbled, "I'm in. I just wish we'd slow down. I don't see why we need to rush over there and announce ourselves."

"We're going to do what someone should have done months ago." Rapp gripped the wheel and let loose a string of obscenities.

"Just don't hit anybody."

Rapp shot him a look that told him not to bring it up again.

"Unless they have it coming, of course," Ridley offered.

"Check your BlackBerry. See if Nash sent those photos."

A couple seconds later Ridley said, "I got them. There's six."

"Are they the same six we've been looking at?"

"Yeah."

"Take a good look at the photos." Rapp glanced at the clock on the dashboard. "The place is going to be crawling. They're going to be in the middle of noon prayer."

"Well," said Ridley lightheartedly, "at least they'll all be there."

Two blocks away Rapp laid off the gas. Keeping his eyes on the street he asked. "You ever been here before?"

"Not exactly my part of town. Plus it wouldn't look too good if the deputy director of the National Clandestine Service got picked up hanging around a D.C. mosque. Which reminds me . . . why are we doing this?"

"We're not going to bug the place, we're just going to walk around and take a tour."

"Two guys from the CIA?" Ridley said, thinking of the article that had appeared in the *Post*. "This isn't going to look good."

"Relax . . . this isn't the first time I've been here."

"What?" Ridley asked, shocked.

"I've been down here a couple times."

At first Ridley thought he was kidding, and then realized he wasn't. "You're serious?"

"Hell yeah. I came down on a Friday about six months ago. Couldn't believe the sermon the imam delivered. You would have thought you were in Mecca listening to one of those crazy Wahhabis."

Rapp slowed way down as they reached the front of the mosque. He turned the corner and pulled over, stopping the car directly in front of a fire hydrant. Rapp popped the trunk and got out. Ridley met him around back, where Rapp popped open a hard case. Inside, resting in foam cutouts, were an M-4 rifle, two extra pistols, and a half dozen spare magazines.

"You carrying your Sig?" Rapp asked.

"Yep."

"How many extra mags?"

"Two."

"Good." Rapp already had a 9mm Glock 19 in a paddle holster on his left hip with two spare seventeen-round magazines. He grabbed the silencer for the 9mm, threw it in his right front pocket, and then grabbed the .45-caliber Glock 21, in case he needed a little more punch.

"Jesus Christ, Mitch. I thought we were just going to take a look around."

Rapp grabbed a right-draw paddle holster out of his shooting bag for the .45. An extra thirteen-round magazine was already in the holster. "Chris Johnson was no pussy." He pulled back the slide on the .45 a half inch to make sure a round was in the chamber, then slid the paddle between his shirt and dress pants. "I'm not going to end up in a trunk, burnt to a crisp." Rapp opened another case and grabbed two radios and a couple of wireless earbuds. He handed one set to Ridley and said, "I go in, you stay outside and keep an eye on things."

"Well . . . I'll be damned," Ridley said in near shock.

Rapp followed Ridley's gaze down the street and saw four men moving from the side door of the mosque to a waiting sedan. The first man had to be six foot five and the last man had to be almost a foot shorter. The trunk of the car was open.

"Let's go." Rapp gently shut the trunk of his car and started walking with Ridley.

"What's the name of the short guy Johnson was worried about?" Ridley asked.

"Aabad bin Baaz."

"That's right. I think that's him . . . the last guy."

"I think you're right."

"And one of them was tall," Ridley said. "I think that's him . . . the first guy."

"Yeah," Rapp said, "I wonder why they're not inside praying like everyone else?"

Rapp got out a half a step ahead of Ridley. His eyes were moving efficiently from one man to the next, assessing their potential threat. Two of them were wearing sport coats with an open collar and dress pants. The other two were wearing dress slacks and dress shirts. From what he could tell, none of them seemed to be armed. The big guy was the first to notice them. He'd already reached the car and had placed a bag in the trunk. He made eye contact with Rapp, and then, without a word, he moved to intercept them.

Rapp did not like what he saw in the guy's eyes. He was no stranger to violence. With the hopes that he could distract the big guy, he glanced over at the last of the four and said, "Aabad, how have you been?" His casual tone caused the big guy to hesitate for a half step. They were now only thirty feet away. "I need to talk to you." Rapp knew he was entering that gray area where a gun would be all but useless unless it was drawn. The big guy moved to put himself between Rapp and Aabad, so Rapp stopped and put out his hand to keep Ridley back as well.

Aabad looked at the big man and said, "I do not know them."

"Get in the car," the large man ordered, and then started walking toward Rapp.

His left hand came up and was waving them away like a couple unwelcome dogs. Suddenly, the guy had a small wooden truncheon in his right hand.

"Easy there, big guy, "Rapp said.

"You must leave," he ordered. "You do not belong here."

"Is that right?" Rapp said in an easy voice. "You ever heard of a public sidewalk?"

"This is the property of the mosque." He pointed at the three-story brick building. "You must leave."

"I don't think so."

"You must leave now!" the man yelled. He took another step closer and brought the club up, brandishing it in an attempt to scare Rapp and Ridley.

It occurred to Rapp that the big goon had probably used the same club on Johnson. Rapp glared at the man and said, "Get that thing out of my face, or I'll shove it up your ass and turn you into a popsicle."

The guy kept coming. The club was now raised above his head.

Without turning, Rapp said to Ridley, "If you have to shoot him, don't kill him." He rocked back on his heels like he might move away, knowing it would cause the man to continue rushing carelessly forward with all of his vulnerable areas exposed. Suddenly, like a pole-vaulter's, all of Rapp's energy came forward and he charged. His gamble paid off. The big man was used to people backing down. The sight of someone charging him caused him to freeze for a second, and that was all Rapp needed. He made a head fake to the right and then charged straight in. His left hand shot up to grab the wrist with the club while his right hand went for the big guy's throat. Rapp kept all of his weight moving forward. He clamped his right hand under the big guy's chin and drove it up, accelerating through the target. The goon toppled straight back. On his way down he managed to grab ahold of Rapp's right shoulder but it wasn't enough to break his fall. Rapp didn't resist. He went down with the man, driving his head into the concrete sidewalk.

Rapp came to a stop with his right knee in the guy's stomach. He watched as the guy's eyes fluttered and then rolled back into his head. After that, he went completely limp. The wooden truncheon fell from his hand and rolled across the sidewalk. Rapp's eyes were drawn to the underside of the man's wrists, where he saw three distinct scratch marks. There were more marks on the guy's neck. Rapp was suddenly aware of a familiar smell. He lowered himself down and took a whiff of the man's shirt. It smelled like a fire. Like burnt food.

"Mitch," Ridley called out, just as the car started. "What do you want me to do?"

Rapp stood. His right hand grabbed his silencer while his left hand drew his 9mm Glock. He watched as the car backed up to get out of the space. Rapp spun the silencer onto the end and leveled the gun just as the car was beginning to pull away. Two rounds spat from the end of the silencer and both passenger side tires went flat. Rapp walked between two parked cars out into the street, leveled his gun, and shot out the driver's-side tires. The car limped along for another twenty feet, the engine straining to transfer its power into any real momentum. Rapp shot the driver's-side mirror clean off the car. The engine roared louder. He took careful aim at the driver's window and sent a round through the forward-most portion, instantly shattering the safety glass into thousands of pieces.

"Put your hands where I can see them," he yelled, "or I'll blow your fucking brains out!" He approached the car from the oblique, saying, "You two in the backseat, get out this side, hands in the air. Let's go!" he yelled. "Right now!"

The two men spilled out of the car and dove to the pavement. Rapp moved to his left so he had a clear view of Aabad, who was behind the wheel. "Aabad, get out of that car right now."

The door opened slowly and Aabad got out with his hands up in the air. Rapp waved his gun toward the back of the car. "Hands on the trunk! Let's go!" Rapp followed him and kicked his feet apart, and then shoved his gun into the back of his neck. While he searched his pockets with his free hand he asked, "Where in the hell you going in such a rush, Aabad?"

"Nowhere," Aabad answered nervously.

"Why aren't you inside, praying?"

"I . . ."

"That's right, you don't have a fucking answer, do you?" Rapp smelled Aabad's suit coat and discovered the same burnt smell he'd gotten from the big guy's shirt. Rapp practically stuck the silencer through Aabad's skull. "You been barbecuing lately?"

"What?" Aabad asked, his voice cracking.

"Barbecue! Cooking pork on a grill!"

"I don't know what you are talking about."

Rapp grabbed the man's right wrist and wrenched it up behind his back. Aabad howled in pain. Rapp moved his face within inches and spat, "I know what you've been up to, you crazy motherfucker. You tortured my guy last night, didn't you? You cut off three of his toes, stuffed him in a trunk, and burned him." Rapp saw the recognition in Aabad's eyes—the shock that he had been discovered. He twisted the arm further.

"I want to talk to my lawyer!" Aabad screamed. He now had tears in his eyes and was grimacing from the pain.

Rapp laughed, "That ain't gonna happen. You know why? Because I'm not a cop." He stuck his gun into Aabad's face. "You know many cops who carry silencers, you idiot? I'm going to give you two choices, Aabad." Rapp wrenched the arm a little further and over Aabad's howls, he said, "You either talk to me, or I cut your toes off, just like you did to my guy. Except I doubt you'll make it to three. In fact, I bet you start blabbering before I make the first slice."

"I want my lawyer!" he cried.

Rapp turned to Ridley and was about to tell him to get the car, when the sounds of the city were dwarfed by a booming clap and then a rumble that carried over their heads and rolled toward Maryland. To the uninitiated, it could have been confused with thunder, but not to Rapp and Ridley. They both knew exactly what it was, and before they could verbalize it, two more explosions ripped through the air.

CHAPTER 65

McLEAN, VIRGINIA

NASH stood at the back of the Operations Center on the sixth floor of the National Counterterrorism Center and stared up at the wall at the far end of the room. The big fifteen-by-twenty-foot screen was divided in four. One section showed the estimated casualty numbers from the attack, and the other three showed images of each blast site. The smaller screens along each side were providing live feeds from FOX, BBC, CNN, Al Jazeera, Al Arabia, and the local NBC affiliate.

They had hit three restaurants at almost precisely 12:30. Right in the middle of the lunch rush. The estimated numbers of casualties were staggering. The number on the board right now was at three hundred. Nash was so shocked by it that he had to ask Art Harris if it was a typo. The FBI's deputy assistant director for the CTC Division said his guy actually thought it might be low.

Nash stood there and stared in semi-disbelief. He'd seen carnage up close over in Afghanistan and Baghdad, but he was just a visitor over there. It was different when it was the city you lived and worked in. On top of all of that was the agonizing fear that the terrorists had gotten their hands on one of the NCTC's own threat assessments. This attack was right out of a scenario they'd been warning about for several years. All three targets—the Monocle, Hawk 'n' Dove, and Bobby Van's—were actually named in the report as locations of extreme concern.

Nash's assistant, Jessica, approached and said, "The director is on the line for you, and so is your wife."

"Tell Maggie I love her and I'll call her later." Nash stepped forward and put his hand on the shoulder of the man who ran the floor, Senior Operations Officer Dave Paulson. "Dave, you mind if I use one of your phones?" Paulson had four computer screens and three phones on his desk.

He pointed to the one on the far right.

Looking to Jessica, Nash said, "I'll take it here."

Five seconds later, the phone began beeping. Nash picked it up and said, "Hello."

"Mike," said Kennedy, "I'm in the Situation Room at the White House. When are we going to get those traffic cameras up and running?"

"Any minute, I'm told."

"Do we know what happened?"

"The system was hacked. They thought they could handle it, but that's obviously not the case, so I put Marcus on it. I talked to him five minutes ago and he says he's close."

"There's a bit of an incident here. The CBS correspondent just asked the press secretary to confirm a report that these were radiological devices. She claims to have a source in Homeland. Do you have any information that would support that claim?"

Nash could tell by the tension in her voice that she was pissed. "I have heard nothing of the sort. We're barely an hour into this thing, but our sensors would have picked up a dirty bomb immediately."

"That's what I told the president," she said with frustration, and then asked, "Have you heard any rumors?"

"No, and I'm standing in the Ops Center right now. DOE has their teams at each site, and they've given us the all-clear."

"You're positive, because the president wants to address the nation in ten minutes. He wants to step on this thing before it creates a panic and people try to flee the city."

"Hold on a second." Nash leaned over and asked Paulson, "Dave, have you heard anything about a radiological device?"

"Nothing." He shook his head vigorously. "Fire and rescue reported nothing, Metro said nothing, and DOE gave it the once over and came up all clear."

"Thanks." Nash took the phone off his chest and said, "We've got nothing here. She's either fishing or the rumor mill is working over-drive."

"I agree. Hold on a second."

Nash could hear Kennedy passing his assurances onto someone else. After about twenty seconds she came back on the line. "Before I let you go, could you clarify these casualty numbers for me? Why is the Hawk 'n' Dove so low and Bobby Van's so high?"

"Apparently a city bus full of people was stopped in traffic when the bomb went off at Bobby Van's. Also, Bobby Van's seats more peo-ple. The Hawk 'n' Dove is smaller, and they're saying the meters were full in front so the guy had to double-park next to a pickup truck, which, fortunately, absorbed most of the blast."

"Do you have any names for me?"

Nash was afraid this was coming. The Hawk 'n' Dove was located on the House side of the Capitol and was a favorite haunt for congress-men. The Monocle was on the Senate side, and on any given day you could easily find a half dozen senators having lunch. Bobby Van's was a block away from the White House, and right across the street from the Treasury Department. Nash had heard nothing concrete at this point, and he wasn't going to be the one to start any rumors. In a non-committal voice he said, "I don't have anything yet."

"Well," Kennedy said, her voice hinting of bad news. "This is not for distribution, but Secretary Holtz and Secretary Hamel were having lunch at Bobby Van's."

"Shit," Nash said softly as he looked at his bird's-eye view of the rescue effort on 15th Street. The secretary of the treasury and the secretary of commerce in one fell swoop. Two cabinet members.

"We're not getting much information from the Monocle. Do you have any updates?"

Nash glanced up at the big screen and looked at the image that was being provided by an air force Predator drone circling over the city. He had just spoke to Art Harris, who had spoken directly to one of his agents on the scene. "It's not good."

"Elaborate," she said.

"Complete structural failure. The initial blast tore away half of the building, and then the upper floors came down on whatever was left. Harris told me a few minutes ago that one of his guys on the scene says the only way anyone survived was if they were in the basement, and even then it's iffy."

"So these estimated casualties at the Monocle are likely to be fatalities."

"I'm afraid so. We're calling every senators' office to see if we can get an idea of who might have been in there." Again, he listened while Kennedy relayed the news to someone else. He thought he heard the president's voice, and then Kennedy came back on.

"What about these suspects that Mitch picked up?"

"They should be here any minute. Last I heard they were stuck in traffic. He wanted me to make sure you talked to Senator Lonsdale, though."

"I did. The president dispatched a car and two agents to pick her up. I'll have someone follow up with an update."

Nash looked nervously over each shoulder and saw that no one other than Paulson was close enough to hear what he was about to say. He turned away from Paulson and asked, "What are we going to do about these guys that Mitch is bringing in?"

"I'll leave that up to Mitch."

"Irene," Nash said anxiously, "a third of the people in this building are Feds. I'm talking real Johnny Law types. This isn't the Hindu Kush. We can't drag these guys out in back of some mud hut. The Feds aren't gonna to like any rough stuff."

Kennedy sighed, "Just let Mitch be Mitch. We'll sort it all out later."

Nash was not reassured. "That's the damn problem, boss. All these gutless pricks will look the other way today, when it's convenient, but a year from now, when the panels and committees are doing their after-action reports, they're all gonna act shocked that the suspects were manhandled."

"I don't know what to tell you, Mike. You're probably right, but the priority right now is to get answers and make sure we find these guys."

"Why is he bringing them here?"

"It doesn't matter at this point. The cat's out of the bag. The FBI has agents crawling all over the mosque. Bringing them to Langley is out of the question. NCTC is a shared facility. You guys are the lead agency on counterterrorism, so you're the logical choice."

"Why can't we just lose them for a couple of hours? Let him do the rough stuff off-site."

"Trust me . . . I've wondered the same thing, but if I've learned anything over the years it's to let him do what he wants to do in these situations. He has it all figured out. He wants a rapid-fire interrogation. Set them all up in separate rooms, and go right down the line. Plus, he needs a secure video feed to Bagram. He's convinced the best way to get al-Haq to talk is to have Lonsdale tell him their deal is off. He either talks or we hand him over to General Dostum."

"Did Lonsdale say she'd cooperate?" Nash asked in near shock.

"I think this attack has crystallized the issue for a lot of people."

"I suppose."

"I have to run. Call me in thirty with an update."

"You got it." Nash placed the phone back in its cradle and looked up at the casualty tally on the big board. There were 327 injured and

31 confirmed fatalities, and that wasn't counting anyone at the Monocle. Nash thought of Johnson. His was a name that would never be added to the list, even though it should. Nash felt a pang of recrimination for not raising the alarm earlier. Maybe the entire disaster could have been averted.

CHAPTER 66

Two of the men started their escape on the Orange Line, and were out of the downtown area five minutes after the first blast. The other two had to take the Red Line and then transfer to the Orange Line, so it took a bit longer for them to clear the area, but even so, by 1:00 they had all emerged from the West Falls Church Metro Station and were boarding buses for their next destination. They traveled in pairs as they had been taught. The FedEx shirts and ball caps had been discarded and stuffed into garbage cans. The men were not concerned about leaving any DNA, just getting clear of the city. They had long-sleeved T-shirts under the FedEx uniforms to make the change easy. Karim had hammered the point over and over. The bombs would cause traffic mayhem and it was possible that out of fear of future attacks they might shut the Metro down until they got a handle on what was going on.

All four men rode the same bus to the Tysons Corner Shopping Center. One pretended to listen to an iPod while the others pretended to read newspapers. When they got off the bus, they walked in pairs away from the mall. Karim had schooled them to look casual. To laugh and smile, so as to not attract any unwanted attention. Their next destination lay a little over a mile to the northwest. Unlike the previous warehouse, this one was relatively new and in near perfect shape. It sat in an upscale mixed-use industrial office park. Farid had the keys and he entered the space from the front, where the offices were. The other three men, with their baggy pants and long-sleeved T-shirts, went around to the back, as if they were day laborers coming in to unload a truck.

Less than five minutes after their arrival, the black Lincoln Town Car and the Suburban rolled into the all-but-empty warehouse space and the big door was closed. Karim had been so thorough in his planning that he had even anticipated this moment. He had told them the reunion would be sweet, but their celebration would be silent. Karim stepped from the front seat of the sedan with a massive smile and his fist in the air. He walked steadily over to the four men. He approached Hakim first, shook his fists in the air, and then wrapped his arms tightly around the man's shoulders.

"We did it," Karim whispered in his ear. "We did it. I am so proud of you." Karim moved onto the next man and hugged him as well. He moved down the line telling each man, in a hushed emotional voice, how well he had done. When he was finished, there were tears in his eyes.

He stood in front of them and said, "I have never been so proud in all my life. This truly is a great day for us, but we are not done," he was quick to add. "You must hurry and change clothes." He clapped his hands together. "Hurry now. All of your stuff is in the back of the truck. I want guards posted on twenty-minute rotations. Eat, poop, and drink some water. You all know what to do. We've covered this a thousand times. I want to be ready to move in thirty minutes, if we need to."

Karim turned to Hakim and put a hand on his shoulder. "You have done an amazing job, my friend." He looked around the fifty-by-thirty-foot space. "This is perfect. Do you have the TVs I requested?"

"Yes." Hakim motioned toward the front. "They're in the office up front. Three of them."

"Good. Let's go." He began walking. "I want to see."

The office was good-sized with a desk, a couch, and a credenza with three 27-inch flat screens. Karim stood in front of the desk while Hakim turned on each TV. He then grabbed the remotes and turned them to the channels he thought would provide the best coverage.

Karim's eyes floated from one screen to the next. He was not surprised to see that there was no aerial footage, since the airspace over the Capitol and the White House was restricted. Most of the shots were of reporters standing behind barricades while emergency vehicles raced past. You had to look very hard to assess any damage. Karim was actually disappointed for a second and then he heard the female newsperson on one of the American channels say that early estimates of casualties were as high as five hundred. Karim was ecstatic. He had been hoping for numbers as high as three hundred. The TV on the far right switched to a new reporter and then the screen changed to what Karim at first assumed was a shot from a helicopter until he realized it was being taken from a building.

Pointing, Karim said, "Turn the volume up on that one."

"What you are seeing," said a male voice, "is what is left of one of Washington's most storied restaurants . . . the Monocle. It appears that the blast completely leveled the restaurant."

Karim moved closer to the screen while the reporter talked with an anchor up in New York. There was nothing left of the building except a half wall on the southwest corner. "It's gone." Karim practically giggled. "Look!" He pointed at the screen. "There is nothing left. There is no way anyone survived that."

Hakim looked at all the emergency vehicles. Men with axes and shovels were climbing over the rubble, and two dogs could be seen sniffing the pile. "I think you're right."

A new image came up on the screen of hundreds of people standing at the south end of the parking lot. A reporter was sticking a microphone in the face of a young girl who was crying. Hakim thought she couldn't have been more than twenty.

"Look where they are standing!" Karim said with great enthusiasm. He checked his watch. "This is perfect. We will have front-row seats this time."

Hakim wasn't so sure he wanted a front-row seat.

"Oh," Karim said, clapping his hands together, "I almost forgot. I must check in with Ahmed." He grabbed his mobile phone and pressed down on the number seven. The phone automatically dialed Ahmed's phone. After three quick rings, the Moroccan answered. "How are you?" Karim asked.

"Good," the man answered in a quiet voice. "Things are very busy here. I assume everything worked on your end."

"Yes . . . to perfection." Karim imagined the Moroccan lying in the woods, burrowed into a pile of leaves and pine straw.

"Congratulations. As you predicted, this place is busier than a bee-hive."

"Wonderful. We will stick to our original timetable. If anything changes, I will inform you."

"I'll see you in a little bit."

CHAPTER 67

RAPP stepped off the elevator with his ragtag crew. In addition to Ridley and the four men he'd picked up, he had two of D.C.'s finest with him. Both cops were roughly the same size as the man Rapp had knocked out. After Rapp had cuffed all four men and duct-taped their mouths, he stuffed two of them in the back of the squad car and brought Aabad and one other with him.

Ridley moved ahead and entered his number into the cipher lock on the door to the Operations Center. Rapp entered first with Aabad, and then the cops brought up the rear, one on each arm of the big man. Apparently, he had given them some trouble while in transit. After the man had tried to break one of the side windows with his feet, the cop riding shotgun was forced to hit him in the face with a blast of pepper spray. With his wrists cuffed behind his back, the man was left to writhe in anguish as the spray burned his eyes. If it was up to Rapp they'd all have canvas bags over their heads right now, but he didn't have any.

Nash and two other agents met the group as they came through the door. Behind him the big screen went blue. "Where do you want them?"

"Upstairs," Rapp said, looking up at the balcony. They didn't have four separate conference rooms, so Rapp had to come up with a solution. "Take these three," Rapp pointed to the big guy and the two others, "and put them in one room, facedown on the floor. If they so much as look at each other, you guys have my permission to kick the shit out of them."

Nash looked nervously at the two cops. He was surprised to see that they were nodding with approval.

One of them actually offered to help, and Rapp took him up on it saying, "That'd be great. Follow these two agents." As the men moved off, Rapp said to Ridley, "Why don't you take dumb-ass here upstairs and get started. I'll be along in a minute."

"Gladly," Ridley said, "Come on, dumb ass." Ridley grabbed him by the elbow and Aabad howled in pain.

"My shoulder!" he screamed in pain. "I think it's dislocated!"

Rapp got right in his face and said, "It's not dislocated. If it was, you'd probably pass out from the pain. It's only separated, but when I get upstairs, if you don't tell me everything I want to know, I'm going to rip that fucking shoulder clear out of its socket, and then I'm going to stick your hand up your own ass."

"Come on," Ridley said to the prisoner, this time pulling him by the collar of his jacket.

Nash looked around the big room and noticed the majority of the analysts had been watching Rapp's tirade. He put himself between Rapp and the rest of the room and said, "I need to talk to you about a couple things."

"Make it quick."

Nash put his hands on his hips and was about to start talking, when Art Harris came walking up.

"Guys, you didn't hear this from me," Harris said in conspiratorial whisper. "I just got a call from HQ. They're sending a team."

"What kind of team?" Rapp asked.

"Prosecutors and Investigators. They found heavy trace amounts of explosives at the mosque as well as blood."

"So," Rapp said, still not getting it.

"It's the FBI, Mitch. Someone realized after the fact that we didn't have a search warrant. They're all freaked out. They think a judge will kick all this evidence."

"So they're going to come out here and take over the interrogation?"

"I think so."

"Fuck that. Let 'em try."

"If I were you," Harris said, leaning in closer, "I'd do whatever you need to do in the next thirty minutes." Backing away, he added, "If you know what I mean."

Rapp grabbed his forehead and moaned, "Does it ever end? This is the same type of bullshit that got us into this mess in the first place."

"Let me handle the interrogations. I'm the one who fucked this thing up."

"What in the hell are you talking about?"

"If I'd brought Johnson to your attention sooner, maybe this whole disaster could have been avoided."

Rapp grabbed him by the arm and led him into the corner. "Shut the hell up."

"But . . ."

"But, nothing. A disaster is when a hurricane hits. You can't stop God or Mother Nature. This," he pointed at the big board, "was going to happen sooner or later. There was no way we were going to be able to hold these guys off forever. Especially when we're playing by all these Mickey Mouse rules. If you had pulled Johnson on Monday like Chuck and Rob had told you to, we wouldn't have these four right here. We haven't arrived at this spot by being too careless. We're in the middle of this shit storm right now because we haven't taken enough risks. This Johnson thing sucks, and when the time is right we'll honor him, but that's not now. We can't let up for a second. The Feds are going to come in here and throw their weight around, and Mirandize these pieces of shit. They're going to get lawyers, and a couple of years from now they might actually go to trial.

"I don't give a shit about any of it. It's all a fucking sideshow. You know what two of those guys smell like?"

"No."

"Barbecue, Mike. They smell like burnt meat. How much do you want to bet they're the ones who fucking torched Johnson?"

Nash looked up at the balcony where the four men had been taken and said, "Let's get this done before the suits show up."

CHAPTER 68

AN ashen-faced analyst stood outside the conference room door and tried her best to ignore the loud but muffled noises that were coming from inside the room. She'd been asked by Mike Nash to stand there and wait. She'd asked him, "For what?" and his reply had been a simple one-word answer: "Information."

It had been five minutes, and while she had no sympathy for the man who was being interrogated, it was very uncomfortable to know that it was her boss in there who was doing a good deal of the shouting and God only knew what else.

Suddenly the door opened and Nash appeared with a piece of paper. "Run those names through TIDE and call me on the conference room phone as soon as you get a hit."

TIDE was the database they operated. It stood for Terrorist Information Datamart Environment.

"Hurry up," Nash ordered, before closing the door. At the far end of the conference table Aabad bin Baaz was sitting in a chair with his hands still bound behind his back, tears streaming down his cheeks, his thick black hair sticking out in different directions.

Rapp put both hands on the table and said, "Aabad, I swear to you, the biggest computer in the world is chewing up those names right now, and if it comes up empty . . . the arm is coming out of the socket."

"I have not lied. Those are their names. You can go ask them."

"Of course I could go ask them," Rapp said in a reasonable tone, "but how do I know they're not going to give me some bullshit name that you guys have agreed on?"

"I am telling you the truth. It was just the four of us."

Without any warning, Rapp wound up and cracked him across the back of the head with an open hand. Aabad let out a yelp like a scared dog.

"I told you," Rapp warned him, "every time a lie comes out of your mouth, I'm going to smack you. Let's go back to last night. During evening prayer you said you found my guy poking around in the basement of the mosque. Rashid, the big, stupid idiot, offered to torture my guy and you took him up on it."

"Yes."

"You then found out he was CIA, so Rashid killed him, rolled him up in a prayer rug, stuffed him in a trunk, drove him to an abandoned lot, and lit the thing on fire, but you weren't there for that part."

"Yes!" Aabad nodded enthusiastically.

"So between then and the time we ran into you, you and your little four-man terrorist cell managed to place three separate car bombs around the city, get back to the mosque, and make your break for . . ." It occurred to Rapp that he hadn't bothered to ask one obvious question. "Where in the hell were you headed, Aabad?"

"The airport."

"Which one?"

"Baltimore."

"Ticket already purchased?"

"Yes."

Nash snapped his fingers and jerked his head toward the far corner.

The two walked over and Nash whispered to Rapp, "He's full of shit. Twenty minutes ago Treasury called. They took a look at their 15th Street cameras. They have the whole thing on tape. A FedEx van pulled up in front of Bobby Van's at 12:29. The driver jumped out and started running north with a package in his hand. Twenty-six seconds later the van exploded. You had eyes on all four of these guys. They were a mile away at the mosque. Can't be in two places at once. How much do you want to bet the other two blasts went down the same way, which means there were at least three more guys involved . . . probably more than that."

Rapp looked back over his shoulder at Aabad, who was nervously watching them. "All right," Rapp said, "I'm done fucking around." He walked back over to the prisoner and said, "Aabad, you know what I think . . . that gerbil in your underdeveloped brain? I don't think he can run fast enough on that wheel to keep up with all your lies."

It was obvious by the confused look on Aabad's face that he hadn't followed a word that Rapp had said.

"What he's saying," Nash said, moving in to translate, "is that you're too fucking stupid to run an operation like this, and on top of all of that, you definitely aren't smart enough to keep all your lies straight."

"I am not lying!" Aabad screamed.

"Give me the other names," Rapp said in a no-nonsense tone.

"I have given you all the names."

"All right," Rapp said without missing a beat, "here is how this is going to go down. I'm going to dislocate your right shoulder. I already told you," Rapp said as he registered the look of horror on Aabad's face, "it was not dislocated. Just a minor separation, which is proof, that in addition to being stupid, you're also a puss."

"I have not lied," he whimpered.

"Shut up and listen to me."

Before Rapp could finish, there was a knock on the door. Nash walked over and opened it a crack. Harris was looking back at him, and without wasting a second, he said, "They're downstairs in the lobby," and then walked away.

Nash walked and whispered the news in Rapp's ear. Rapp turned his attention back to Aabad. "I've dislocated my shoulder before, and I can honestly say it's one of the most painful things I've ever gone through. There's a good chance you will vomit or pass out or both, in which case I'd gladly watch you choke on it and die right here. So!" Rapp yelled as he clapped his hands together. "Last chance!"

"I have told you everything," Aabad pleaded.

"Wrong answer." Rapp shoved Aabad's face down onto the table and grabbed his cuffed wrists. With both elbows locked, Rapp torqued the wrists up and toward Aabad's head until there was a loud pop.

Aabad howled in pain. So loud in fact, that Nash walked over to the door and leaned against it in case someone tried to come in.

Rapp bent to within inches of Aabad's face and said, "I can put it back into the socket in two seconds. All you have to do is tell who the real brains was behind this operation."

Aabad was now crying in agony.

"I can make it go away. Tell me right now." Rapp waited a second then lifted the arms again."

Aabad somehow managed to scream even louder this time.

"I know about the FedEx vans. You lied to me!" Rapp screamed.

Aabad had snot flowing out of his nose and tears streaming down his face. He mumbled something, but it came out completely unintelligible.

"Say the name and I can make all the pain go away."

"Karim," Aabad cried.

"Karim who?" Rapp grabbed his wrists just in case Aabad was thinking of not following through.

"Karim Nour-al-Din."

Rapp took a knife from his belt, flipped the blade out, and cut the plastic flex cuffs. After stowing the knife, he sat Aabad up and leaned him back in the chair. "Don't move," he ordered. "This will only take a second." Rapp grabbed Aabad's right wrist and pulled it up and across his body. Placing his other hand on Aabad's good shoulder, he gave the bad arm a yank, and the ball slid back into the socket.

"Keep an eye on him," he said to Nash. To Aabad he said, "Give him the rest of the names. I'll be back in five minutes. If the name you just gave me is bullshit, or you haven't come up with the rest of the names, I'll go to work on the other shoulder."

Rapp left the conference room, closed the door behind him, and rushed down the spiral staircase to meet the delegation from the Justice Department and the FBI.

CHAPTER 69

ALL six men stood at parade rest, their hands clasped behind their backs. Each one was dressed in black SWAT gear replete with Kevlar helmets and goggles. Their tactical vests were loaded with extra ammunition, grenades, and ribbon charges. Underneath those vests each man wore his martyr vest; thirty pounds of C-4 with hundreds of imbedded ball bearings. It was a physical feat just to be able to stand with so much gear, let alone maneuver and attack an enemy stronghold.

Karim was about to give them his final address, when Hakim tapped his shoulder. Karim turned and said, "Yes?"

Hakim was hesitant and then said, "Are you sure you want to do this?"

"Do what?" he asked, surprised.

"Send them to their deaths."

"Of course," Karim responded in an almost lighthearted way.

"Haven't we had enough success for one day?"

Karim began to laugh. "You can never have enough success in one day. You can never deliver too big a blow to your enemy."

"The other bomb is set to go off in minutes. You have already achieved so much." Lowering his voice, he said, "Why not let them live to fight another day?"

Karim searched his friend's eyes for a moment and then said, "You do not understand . . ."

"Oh, I understand," Hakim answered hotly. "This is about you and your glory. It is about you making a name for yourself."

"Really?" Karim gestured toward his men. "Go ahead and ask them. Ask them if they would like to leave with you right now?"

Hakim looked at the young faces again. He doubted any one of them would abandon the group.

"You doubt me," Karim said, and then turned to address his men. "Hakim thinks that some of you would prefer to live today." There was a grumbling among the men. "I think his faith is not as strong as ours. Would any of you men like to skip this mission and leave the country with Hakim?"

In unison, they barked, "No, sir!"

"Would any of you men like me to accompany you on this mission?"

"No, sir!" Their response rang out as one, even louder than the previous response.

Karim turned to his friend and shrugged his shoulders as if to say, "Oh well." Turning back to his men, he said, "You all know how strongly I feel about this next part of the operation. It is one thing to attack unprotected civilian targets. Many less talented could have done the same, although probably not with the precision that we achieved today. This next part of the plan is different, though. This is where we strike at the heart of the enemy. This is where we turn the hunters into the hunted. Are you men ready?"

"Yes, sir!" they barked enthusiastically.

"Good. It has been a great honor leading all of you. I will make sure that all of Islam learns your names and gives thanks every time you are mentioned." Karim looked from one end of the line to the other and did not allow himself to think of their deaths. He instead chose to think of their arrival in paradise. He glanced at his watch and said, "It is time to leave. Let's go."

The six men all hustled over to the black Suburban and climbed in.

Karim stood next to the black Town Car and asked Hakim, "Are you ready?"

"Yes," said Hakim.

"Then let us leave this place." He took a final look around and said, "We have done such a good job of hiding our tracks, it is possible the Americans will never know that we have used this place."

Hakim looked at his friend and with a bit of regret in his voice said, "After today, I am afraid the Americans will hunt us to the ends of the earth."

"Let them try. You have arranged our departure?"

Hakim nodded. "Everything is taken care of."

CHAPTER 70

RAPP saw them when he was halfway down the spiral staircase. They were hard to miss. There must have been fifteen of them, at least half of whom were carrying briefcases. They looked like a team of litigators who'd been sent over from a rival law firm for an afternoon of depositions. Rapp saw Art Harris talking to the two men at the front of the pack. It appeared, by the way he was pointing and gesturing, that he was trying to buy Rapp some time.

Rapp let loose a heavy sigh and rolled his sleeves up one more turn. He didn't have much of a strategy, but one thing was for sure: if these guys wanted to, they had every right to simply push him out of the way and walk out the door with his four prisoners. He had only a couple of cards to play, and neither was likely to intimidate these stone-faced bastards. His only real hope was that these guys would be every bit as pissed-off as he was that three bombs had just gone off in downtown Washington, D.C., killing and injuring hundreds.

Harris turned as Rapp came walking up, and said, "Speak of the devil. Here he is." Harris gestured to the two men at the head of the group. "Mitch, this is Abe Ciresi, Deputy AG, National Security Division, and Malcolm Smith, Deputy Assistant AG, Criminal Division."

Rapp stuck out his hand. Ciresi was a little shorter than Rapp and had light red hair. He looked as though he'd probably played football as a kid. Smith was Rapp's height and whip-thin. Rapp figured him to be one of those guys who got up and ran five miles every morning at 5:00 a.m. "Sorry we're not meeting under better circumstances."

Ciresi agreed with the sentiment, but Smith had only one thing on his mind. Looking over Rapp's shoulder, he asked, "Where are the prisoners?"

Rapp ignored him and returned the slight by looking over Smith's shoulder. "Boy, you sure did bring a lot of people. I would have thought you guys would be out trying to catch your own bad guys."

Harris let loose an uncomfortable laugh and took a step back.

Smith, with a troubled frown on his face, looked Rapp over from head to toe and then said, "Let's step over here, where we can talk in private."

Ciresi followed and the three of them moved about twenty feet away. Smith unbuttoned his suit coat and set down his briefcase. "I was warned about you, Rapp."

"Really . . . by who?" Rapp couldn't have cared less, but he figured the longer he could keep this guy talking the more time he would give Nash with Aabad.

"Let's just say that in certain circles your reputation is well known. I don't want this to escalate into some big pissing match between the DOJ and the CIA."

"We know you've done all the heavy lifting," Ciresi quickly added, "and we're not here to steal any of the credit for breaking this thing."

"Although, you might want us to, before this is all said and done," Smith added.

"And why would I want you to do that?" Rapp asked.

"For the life of me," Smith said as he shook his head and looked around the room, "I'm still trying to figure out what a couple of spooks from Langley were doing poking around a mosque right about the time these bombs started going off."

"I . . ."

"No . . ." Smith said, cutting him off, "I don't want to hear it. I want you and Ridley to get your stories straight before you talk to any of us."

"I know Rob," Ciresi offered. "He's a good man."

Rapp was starting to get the idea that maybe these weren't pricks after all.

"So our problem," Smith continued, "is that we have a body in the morgue. It appears that the guys you picked up had something to do with that."

"Yeah . . . one of them has already admitted to the whole thing."

"Without being Mirandized?" Ciresi asked.

"Of course not," Rapp said. "I don't Mirandize people."

"And that's why we're here," Smith said. "I think a lot of people in this town are going to jump to the conclusion that the guy in the morgue was working for you. I seem to remember something in the paper about this the other day."

Rapp played dumb and offered, "Maybe he was working for Mossad. Maybe one of my contacts over there called me and asked me to check in on him."

Ciresi nodded. "I like the way you think."

"You see," Smith said, "we're not here to bust your balls or take away your thunder. But we have a problem. At least two of the guys you have are American citizens, and while I personally couldn't give a shit if you dangled them off the roof by their ankles and threatened to drop them on their heads, as an officer of the court I cannot condone such behavior."

"If we were to witness such behavior," Ciresi added, "we would be duty-bound to report it."

Rapp was liking these guys more and more. "So how would you guys like to proceed?"

"Where are you in your interview phase?"

"One of them is starting to talk. It took a little prodding."

Both men shook their heads, and Smith said, "Too much informa-tion, Mr. Rapp."

"I could use a little more time with him. To make sure he isn't lying to me."

"Which one is it?" Ciresi asked.

"Aabad bin Baaz."

"He has dual citizenship." Ciresi frowned

"How much more time?" Smith asked.

"An hour would be nice."

The two men shot each other an uncomfortable look. Smith said, "We can't give you an hour."

Rapp was about to find out how much time they would give him when one of the female analysts in the bullpen let loose a scream. A rumble of shock spread across the big gymnasium-sized space, and analysts began to stand and point at the big screen. Rapp looked up at the big board but couldn't figure out what was going on. All he saw were the three TV feeds and casualty tally.

He raced over to the Operations Officer's perch and said, "Dave, what the hell just happened?"

Paulson was feverishly working one of his keyboards. The big screen went from four separate shots to one complete picture. As Paul-son reached for his mouse, he said to Rapp, "I think we just had a latent explosion."

"Which location?"

"The Monocle. Hold on a second, I'm rewinding it."

The cloud of dust on the big screen began to retreat as if a giant vacuum cleaner was sucking it out of the air, except when the tape was rewound far enough, there was a blue sedan at the epicenter. The tape now began to play forward in super-slow motion, frame by painful frame.

Rapp looked at all the emergency workers in the immediate vicin-ity of the explosion. There were dozens, plus he knew the original bombs had used ball bearings to increase kill ratio. Any civilian within a half mile stood the risk of getting hit. The ones that were lined up at the barricades would drop like Confederate soldiers making the final charge at Gettysburg. Rapp could taste the bile in his throat. He'd seen the same thing done in Beirut, Tel Aviv, Baghdad, and Kandahar. Of all the tricks of the terrorist trade, he considered this to be lowest. To set up a bomb designed to intentionally target those who rush to the aid of others showed just how little these people cared for innocent life.

"What just happened?" Smith asked.

With barely contained rage, Rapp said, "Another bomb just went off."

"Where?"

Rapp told them and then put his hand on Paulson's shoulder and said, "Pull everybody out at the other two scenes, ASAP! Get on the horn and alert all levels, and get the bomb units in there to make sure these areas are cleared! That was supposed to have been taken care of right away." Rapp stared up at the chaos on the big board. They had practiced all this before. He had warned the people at Homeland that the terrorists would try something like this.

"There might be more?" Smith asked.

"We don't know. That's the problem." Almost as an afterthought, Rapp looked up toward the conference room and said, "But I think I know where I could find out."

Smith and Ciresi looked at each other and came to an agreement without exchanging words.

Ciresi looked at his watch and said, "We should go downstairs and get a cup of coffee," Ciresi said.

"Good idea." Smith handed Rapp his business card and said, "My mobile number is on there. Traffic is really bad out there. When the prisoners arrive, please give me a call."

Rapp nodded slowly and then said, "Will do."

CHAPTER 71

KARIM sat in the backseat of the Town Car, directly behind Hakim. It seemed to him that his friend was in a rather glum mood, considering how successful the day had been. He was used to being the one who brooded in an angry-faced silence, and found it rather uncomfortable when the shoe was on the other foot. He did not like his normally upbeat friend casting a pall over their victory. Karim wanted to clear the air, but there were only a few minutes before they got to the facility. There would be plenty of time after the attack, but they would not be alone. Ahmed would be with them.

Ahmed was the only one Karim would let live. They were close enough now to use radios, so Karim toggled the button and said, "Thomas, how does everything look?"

Four seconds later the radio crackled and a voice said, "Good. More people are arriving every minute."

Karim frowned and wondered if security was being increased. He would normally never ask such a question on an open channel, but at this point there wasn't much the Americans could do to stop them. "Has security increased?"

"A few more people are out patrolling the grounds, but nothing I can't handle."

"Good. We will see you shortly." Karim set the radio on the seat next to him and looked at Hakim's reflection in the rearview mirror. "The RV is ready?"

"Yes."

Karim thought of the plan. With any luck they would be in Canada by tomorrow afternoon. An RV loaded with provisions was waiting for them at a pole barn in Ashburn not more than twenty minutes up the road. "And how far can we make it before we have to stop for gas?"

"Iowa." Hakim offered him nothing more.

Karim was sick of his friend's pouting. "What is wrong with you?"

"Nothing."

"Don't lie to me. You are like my brother. I know when something is bothering you. Tell me. I want to hear it."

"You have changed." Hakim hit the turn signal and took a left onto Dolley Madison Boulevard.

"We all change as we grow older."

"Not always for the better."

"I am not sure I like your implication," Karim said.

"And I know for a fact that I do not like how you have brainwashed these young men."

"I have brainwashed no one. These men are great warriors who are about to give their lives in the greatest struggle of our time," Karim said with absolute sincerity. "Do not demean them."

"I am not demeaning them. I am demeaning you. You have embraced this cult of death where you gleefully offer up the lives of others. And for what? To satisfy your own . . ." Hakim shook his head and stopped short of finishing his thought.

"Say it!" Karim demanded.

"I don't want to."

"Say it. I order you to tell me."

Hakim looked back in the mirror at his childhood friend. "We have always been equals. I see that is no longer the case."

"We are equals, but not in the middle of an operation. There can be only one commander."

"There are only two of us in this car. Just two friends who grew up together. One of us seems to have forgotten that."

"And one of us," Karim shot back, "has grown soft with all his travels."

"Soft," Hakim repeated the accusation. "I would rather grow soft than carelessly waste the lives of others."

Karim's jaw tightened. "I care about these men more than you will ever know."

"And you show it by sending them to their deaths."

"You are a fool." Karim grabbed the front passenger headrest and pulled himself forward. "We do not have billion-dollar planes and laser-guided bombs to fight with. This is how we must wage war. This is how we will defeat them. Six brave men are about to give their lives today, and you are too self-absorbed in your own emotions to admire their sacrifice."

"And you are too self-absorbed in your own greatness. If this is such a wonderful idea, then why aren't you going in with them?"

Karim threw himself back into his seat. Under his breath he was cursing his friend, and then himself for being so stupid to bother bringing this up. As they passed over the freeway that went to the airport, Karim saw the woods off to their left and the roofs of several buildings. "Don't miss the turn," he barked.

"I know where it is," Hakim shot back bitterly.

Karim thought about really giving it to him, but they didn't have the time. They were less than a minute from the facility. He grabbed the radio, pressed the transmit button, and said, "Thomas, we will be with you in less than sixty seconds. Do you copy?"

"Copy."

Karim looked behind them and saw the Suburban close on their tail as they took the left turn. They were only five hundred feet from the big looping service road that would take them up the hill. Karim said a quick prayer, and was relieved he had put Ahmed in the woods so he would have some eyes on the target. He imagined, for a second, how unnerving it would be to make this drive with no knowledge of what waited at the security point.

Hakim made the turn and accelerated. The Suburban followed close behind.

"Men," Karim said into the radio, "remember your training. Stay together, do not use the elevator, and go straight to your primary target."

The road swung around to the right, and then there it was. The six-story building looked no different from any of the other office buildings in the area. Even the guard shack up ahead seemed practical. Hakim turned left and stopped at the guard shack. As planned, he rolled down his window and pointed to the backseat. Karim began rolling his window down, and as the guard approached; he looked at him through his sunglasses, smiled, and shot him three times in the face. Before the guard had hit the ground, one of the men was out of the Suburban. He marched straight up to the bulletproof guard shack and stuck a block of C-4 on the door. Two guards sat on the other side of the thick glass, trying to make sense of what was happening.

Hakim gunned the engine, and the car raced forward. He pulled into a parking spur on the left just as they heard the explosion. A moment later, four shots rang out, and then a few seconds after that, the Suburban sped past with four of the men standing on the running boards and holding on to the luggage rack.

"Thomas, you may engage targets at will." Karim smiled with pride and made a last-minute decision. "Follow them."

Hakim turned around and looked at him with complete surprise. "But that is not part of the plan."

"I know, but I want to see them enter the building."

"This is not wise."

"We are fine. As you can see, they have been caught completely off guard. It is yet another sign of their arrogance."

"I'll drive up and we'll come right back out. You are not going to change your mind and go in with them."

"No," Karim said, patting him on the shoulder. "Go! I want to savor this great moment. I want to watch them enter the building."

Hakim took his foot off the brake and hit the gas. They drove to the corner of the building and took a hard left. Along this side of the building, two wings angled back to form a shallow V. The Suburban had jumped a curb, ran over a flagpole, and come to a halt approximately fifty feet from the front door. The men were in a straight line, weapons up, and heading toward the front door. A man and a woman came out and moved to the side to make room. The lead man in the conga line ignored them, but the second man swung his M-4 over and fired two quick shots, striking each person in the head.

"Look at them," Karim said, full of pride. He watched as the men disappeared into the building, and then he heard a steady stream of shots. His eyes traveled up the façade of the building to the sixth floor. That was where his men were headed. To the heart of America's war against Islam. This wouldn't get the media attention that the blasts would receive, but it would hurt the Americans far more. Karim could barely take the thrill of knowing that America's best and brightest were gathered at this very moment on the top floor of this building—their National Counterterrorism Center. They were gathered to manage this crisis, trying to find the very people who were now on their doorstep. The psychological blow would be devastating. If only he could be there to see the looks on the faces of the smug Americans as his men mowed them down.

"I'm leaving," Hakim announced.

"Wait," Karim said as he looked wild-eyed out the window. He heard the first explosion and felt the pull, the desire to join his men. The car began to move. "Just a little longer."

Hakim jammed his foot onto the break and turned around. "You either get out or we leave."

"Fine," Karim answered in a sad voice. "Go."

CHAPTER 72

RAPP was about to head back upstairs when Lonsdale came walking through the door with two Secret Service agents. The normally put-together and well-styled Lonsdale looked absolutely disheveled. As Rapp approached, he realized that she'd been crying. It dawned on him that she quite likely knew more about who was under that pile of rubble that used to be a favorite haunt of senators than anyone else in the building. A few of those people were also undoubtedly her friends.

Earlier in his career, Rapp would have never felt an ounce of compassion for this woman, but with age he had begun to realize that most of the players in this drama did not intend to do harm. They simply downplayed or ignored the threat. Some were naïve and merely thought the terrorists would go away if we understood them better. Others, like Lonsdale, thought the letter of the law was the most important thing. That we as a nation must never lower ourselves to their level. In Rapp's world, where he saw up close the mayhem that these groups caused, the first sentiment was simply naïve and the second, while honorable, was not very practical.

Rapp looked at her cheerless, bloodshot eyes and wondered if the murder of her fellow senators would cause her to see things differently now. "Senator Lonsdale," Rapp said in a polite voice, "thank you for coming."

Lonsdale looked nervously around the room, and said, "Where are they?"

"Excuse me?" Rapp said not understanding what she was talking about.

"The men you captured," she said, looking him in the eye for the first time. "I spoke with the president. He told me you have four men in custody."

Rapp wondered if any of these politicians knew how to keep their mouths shut. "Senator, maybe after we handle the video conference with al-Haq, I can . . ."

"I want to see them now!" Lonsdale said forcefully.

The force of her demand took Rapp aback. "I can assure you, they are being taken care of, ma'am."

Lonsdale clenched her fists and stepped to within a foot of Rapp. Looking up with her bloodshot eyes, she said, "I do not care about their welfare, Mr. Rapp. I want to see them right now."

Rapp was suddenly very curious to see how this would play out. "Fine . . . follow me."

After a couple steps he turned and told the Secret Service agents that they could stay put. It was bad enough he was bringing Lonsdale up. The last thing they needed was more men with badges. Lonsdale followed him up the spiral staircase in silence. When they reached the door to the conference room, Rapp knocked and said to Lonsdale, "Give me a second."

Rapp opened the door a crack and saw Aabad sitting at the far end of the heavy wooden table, cradling his right hand across his chest.

Nash was sitting on the edge of the table, looming over Aabad. When Nash saw Rapp, he got up and walked over to the door. Rapp stepped in and shut the door.

"I'd told him he'd better give me something good before you get back up here or that other arm would get torn out of its socket. Now he's going on and on about these SWAT uniforms. He's admitted that there's nine other guys still out there."

"Nine," Rapp said, surprised by the number.

"Yeah, he says they are going to use these SWAT uniforms to get into and attack a federal facility."

There was a loud knock on the door. "That's Lonsdale. She wants to see him. Let's make this quick, and then we'll get this new info out." Rapp opened the door.

Lonsdale entered the room and looked down the length of the table at the small man who appeared to be grimacing in pain. "Who is he?" she asked in a cold voice.

"Aabad bin Baaz. Saudi national," Rapp said as he closed the door. He decided to leave out the part about the dual citizenship.

"I demand to see my attorney," Aabad said in a pleading voice.

"Is he responsible for the explosions?" Lonsdale asked.

"He's part of the cell."

Lonsdale approached the prisoner and asked, "Do you know who I am?"

"No," Aabad said with wide hopeful eyes.

"I'm Senator Barbara Lonsdale."

"I am an American citizen," he said earnestly.

Lonsdale ignored him. "Do you know where I was supposed to have lunch today?"

"No," he said with a confused face.

"The Monocle. I sent my chief of staff there instead."

Aabad looked nervously back and forth between Lonsdale and Rapp and Nash. "I know my rights. I demand to see my attorney."

Lonsdale suddenly reached out and slapped him across the face. "He was my best friend."

Aabad looked up in shock and in a more pleading voice said, "I am an American citizen. I have a right to see my attorney."

"If you are an American citizen, then you are a traitor," Lonsdale hissed, "and I will do everything in my power to see that you are executed."

Rapp, who was still standing by the door, thought he heard a noise. He looked to Nash and they exchanged a quick glance. The noise came again. It was distant. Muffled.

"Are those gunshots?" Nash asked.

Rapp was about to open the door, when there was a much louder noise. The room shook just slightly. The one thing about combat was, you only had to go through it once and you were left with the sound, feel, and smell of battle for the rest of your life. Rapp had been in more than his fair share of dustups. He looked over at Nash, his face showing a deep concern. "I think that was a hand grenade."

"I think you're right," Nash agreed.

Rapp reached for the door and asked Nash, "Do you have any flex cuffs on you?"

"No."

Rapp opened the door, his primal instincts screaming that something bad was on the way. He glanced at the big screen and wondered briefly if the rumble of noises had come from some audio that they had just obtained. Without warning, the main door to the Operations Center was blown open. A split second later, a man dressed in full SWAT gear stepped through the cloud of dust and debris, his weapon raised. He pointed it straight ahead where the two Secret Service agents who had delivered Lonsdale happened to be standing with their arms tentatively raised in the air. Without provocation the man in the SWAT gear shot both agents in the head.

Rapp flinched as his brain tried to reconcile the irreconcilable. A second and third man in SWAT gear followed the first man through the door and began shooting analysts who were diving to get out of the way. Rapp's left hand was already wrapped around the hilt of his gun.

With the rifle shots ringing out from below, Rapp turned to Nash and screamed, "Knock him out!"

At the sound of rifle shots, Nash was already reaching for his gun. He'd been in combat with Rapp before and trusted him completely. He drew the heavy .40-cal from his holster and cracked Aabad across the temple with the weapon. The man fell out of his chair and tumbled to the floor.

"Senator," Rapp yelled, "get in that far corner and stay there!"

Nash joined Rapp at the door. Both men had their guns drawn, and as they looked down at the floor, they watched the lead man in the line stop and look over his shoulder. He raised his right fist up in the air and paused for a moment. A final shooter joined the line, making it six total. The lead man motioned forward with his hand and the group began to move as one, shuffling forward into the room, unleashing a torrent of bullets. They were in a textbook raid line. Rapp and Nash had watched the drill hundreds of times. The first man is responsible for the first slice of pie immediately in front of the group. The second man takes the next slice on the left, and the third man takes the first slice on the right. They alternate their way back to the sixth man, who is responsible for all six.

The entire group opened fire, but it wasn't the undisciplined fire of poorly trained insurgents shooting from the hip. These guys were firing only one or two rounds at a time.

"It's got to be them," Rapp yelled.

"Let's take them out!" Nash shouted back, and began to move.

Rapp held him back. "They've got body armor on." He surveyed the situation. The men were moving roughly from right to left in front of their position. If they started taking shots at them from up here, they'd be lucky to get two or three before the others returned fire. With almost no cover, the rifles would shred them.

"I want you to crawl up to the edge of the balcony and sight in the first guy. That's their weak point. You drop him, and I can run right down their throat."

"You're going to charge them." Nash was shaking his head. "That's fucking crazy."

Rapp ignored him. He could see it all in his mind's eye. Lifting his right elbow up, he tapped his own side and said, "Put the first one into his helmet and then aim for the weak spot in his body armor. Right here on his side." Rapp pushed Nash toward the floor and then got into a crouch and ran along the wall.

Nash crawled to the edge of the balcony, mumbling to himself. In the middle of something like this, there wasn't enough time to question and dissect a plan. You simply had to go with it and hope it worked. He wedged himself up against one of the vertical supports and leveled his sight on the first man.

Off to his left he heard Rapp scream, "Now." Nash placed his sight square on the man's helmet and squeezed off his first round. The muzzle jumped an inch and came right back down. Nash lowered his aim a touch and squeezed off another round. He was going to zipper this guy right down his left side. After his fourth shot the sight came down and the guy was crumbling to the floor. Nash went to sight in the second guy and found himself staring straight down the hot muzzle of an M-4 rifle.

Rapp bounded down the steps two at time. There was only one way to do this, and it wasn't complicated. It was a full-on blitz, and it was the last thing these guys would expect. Rapp hit the floor and charged forward at a near full sprint, his left hand extended with his Glock leveled right down the axis of the shooters. He knew Nash was doing his job, because the lead guy was looking to his left instead of straight ahead. Rapp closed in with lightning speed. At fifteen feet he squeezed off his first round, hitting the lead man in his goggles.

The second man was turned to the side and looking up. From ten feet away Rapp sent a round into his exposed throat. The third guy sensed the motion and was beginning to turn on him, but while he could swivel his head to face the threat almost immediately, he had a harder time bringing his muzzle to bear. Rapp shot him from six feet away, right in the bridge of his nose. He stepped over the first guy as he shot the fourth guy twice in the neck and then the fifth guy in face.

The sixth and last guy had his back to him. Rapp saw him reaching into his vest with his right hand for a fresh magazine, oblivious to the fact that the rest of his line had fallen. Stepping over the next two bodies, Rapp grabbed the back of the guy's vest, stuffed the muzzle of the 9mm Glock into the man's lower back, and shot him twice through the spine.

CHAPTER 73

THE only thing Farid noticed before it happened was that, for a split second, it seemed as if everything had gone strangely quiet. The initial push into the building had gone perfectly. He'd taken out the three security guards at the turnstiles and led the team straight to the staircase, where he flipped positions and provided rear security. He fell slightly behind on their climb to the sixth floor when he had to stop and kill two women and a man who had stumbled upon them. By the time he reached the lobby on the sixth floor, the ribbon charges had already been placed on the cipher lock. Hauling seventy-eight pounds of gear plus yourself up six flights of stairs was no easy thing, but they could rest in paradise. In a few minutes it would all be over.

They knew their prize lay in the big room on the other side of the door. Karim had estimated that somewhere between two hundred and three hundred men and women would be in the Operations Center managing the crisis, trying to find out who was behind the attacks and coordinated the collection of evidence. Karim said they would represent the heart and soul of America's satanic war on Islam. It may have seemed as if it was the American military who doggedly pursued them with unmanned aerial drones through the mountains of Afghanistan and Pakistan, but they were merely the instruments. These people were the thinkers, the trackers, the investigators. Their collective wealth of knowledge was America's greatest asset in their war. They had more planes and tanks than they could ever throw into a hundred battles. If they lost one, they simply put another into service. That would not be the case with these people. It would take America years to replace them, and it would give al-Qaeda the time they needed to rebuild.

This is what Karim had preached to them for months, and Farid believed every word of it, but he couldn't help think that his capable commander was withholding one aspect of the operation from them. Zachariah, Zawahiri's nephew, had sensed it as well, and he had been the first to openly complain. He told the other men, and they had taken to grumbling about it when Karim was not around. Farid went to Karim with the problem. Zachariah was telling the men that while the martyrdom mission was honorable and would strike at the heart of the enemy, it would undoubtedly also make it far easier for Karim to escape. Two days later Zachariah was dead.

Even before the confrontation with Zachariah, Farid could see Karim was beginning to worry about certain people's devotion. They had practiced the assault for months on end, and Farid was always at the vanguard. He was to lead them into the building, up the staircase, and into the Operations Center. They were to stop for nothing. If targets presented themselves, that was fine, but they were not to pause to engage a threat. The prize lay on the sixth floor. So, Karim ordered that once they reached the stairwell, Farid would cover their entry, and then take up the position at the rear of the attack.

Farid sensed there was a deeper purpose to the move, but he hadn't been a hundred percent sure until just today. After all the men had their vests on, Karim pulled him aside and handed him a master detonator. Each vest had a digital timer that was to be started when they rolled through the gate. Those timers could be shut off or restarted, should they need more time to get to their target. They had five min-

utes to kill as many people as possible; moving through the room laying down a 360-degree cone of fire. Thirty seconds before detonation,
the men were to spread out so as to maximize the blasts that would
hopefully tear the roof off the building, kill any remaining survivors,
and render the entire space useless. If any of the men had second
thoughts about completing their mission, or they were somehow met
with stronger force than they had anticipated, Farid was to hit the
master detonator.

As he lay on his back trying to piece together what had just happened, this thought was floating on the periphery of his mind. He did
not understand what had gone wrong. The SWAT uniforms had
worked perfectly. Every security guard and agent they had encountered froze. Just as Karim had said they would. Everyone except this
man standing above him. Farid remembered the bolt on his rifle locking in the back position. His thumb hit the magazine release, expelling
the empty box, while he reached for a fresh one. It occurred to him
that the rifle fire had suddenly gone silent. He sensed movement behind him, and then there was the stabbing hot pain in his back. He had
dropped his rifle and fallen to his left, hitting the ground and then rolling onto his back.

Now lying there, Farid realized he couldn't feel his legs. He tried to
move them, but it was as if some great unseen weight had smothered
them. Farid raised his head and looked at his lower body. Everything
appeared to be fine. He tried desperately to move his legs again and
then the harsh reality struck him that he was paralyzed. That hot pain
that he had felt earlier was no doubt bullets slicing through his spinal
column. Low enough, however that his arms still worked. Farid imagined himself in a wheelchair for a second, and then realized it was an
extremely foolish thought. They were all wearing their vests.

Farid turned his head to the right to see what had happened to the
others. All he saw was a jumble of black boots, vests, gloves, and helmets. They were all dead. The man standing above him started yelling
at others, and that was when Farid remembered Karim's order. He had
told him if it appeared that they would be overwhelmed, he should not

take any chances. He should hit the master switch and blow all the vests. He wondered how much time had passed since they'd come through the gate. Farid tried to remember where he had placed the detonator. Everything else had been rehearsed, but this had been a last-minute addition to the plan. He reached for his vest and then realized he'd put it in the cargo pocket on his left thigh. His hand began groping for the device, when there was a loud noise and a flash followed by searing hot pain in his elbow.

CHAPTER 74

RAPP stood over the last man and surveyed the damage, his weapon trained on the blown-out main door, fearing that more men would come through at any moment. Moans and cries of pain were coming from every direction. To his right, Art Harris emerged from his office with a bloodstained shirt. He was stepping unsteadily over broken glass, but otherwise appeared fine. Rapp had one round in the breach and eight more in the grip. He popped out the half spent magazine, put it in his pocket, and grabbed a full one.

More people were up and moving now. Rapp could see a few of them had guns in their hands. "Art!" Rapp screamed. "Get some people over on that door and secure it!"

Harris started yelling orders to his fellow agents.

Rapp caught some movement beneath him. He looked down and saw the man on the floor reaching for something in his pocket. The image of a grenade popped into Rapp's mind. His 9mm swung down and he sent a round into the man's elbow socket. The arm jumped a few inches in the air and then lay flat at a slightly odd angle. The fingers twitched as the man strained to make his hand respond.

After stepping on his other arm, Rapp bent down and patted the pocket that the man had been reaching for. There was something square inside. Rapp reached in the pocket and pulled out an electronic detonator roughly the size of a pack of cards. He studied the device for a second and then looked down at the man. "Too bad you're not going to be able to use this."

"It doesn't matter," the man said in near perfect English. With a smile he added, "It would have only sped up the inevitable."

Rapp moved his gun to the man's face and tore off his goggles. "What's that supposed to mean?"

"I am not afraid to die. I have already martyred myself. I have killed many Americans today. Allah will be very pleased with me."

Rapp hated that word—martyr. He'd learned long ago that guys who liked to throw it around had a particularly crazy religious bent. The fact that this guy had just had his spinal column blown out and his left elbow shattered, and was looking up at him as if he was experiencing some kind of religious nirvana, was extremely unsettling. Rapp began looking him over from head to toe. His tactical vest was packed with extra magazines for his rifle, but not much else. At the neckline, though, he saw the seam of what appeared to be a second vest under the first. Rapp stuffed the detonator in his shirt pocket and yanked at the Velcro and zipper on the man's tactical vest. The vest fell open to reveal a sight that caused Rapp's entire body to tense for a second. There was a second vest under the first, and the pockets that were designed to hold ammunition were instead filled with blocks of pasty gray C-4 plastic explosives. Like the bombs that had been set off earlier in the day, these too had ball bearings pressed into the C-4.

In the pocket just above the man's heart, near the neck of the vest, he found the detonator. Rapp carefully slid it out and looked down at the small digital readout as it ticked from forty-three to forty-two seconds. He resisted the urge to pull the wires from the device, knowing that it could very well trigger the explosion. Rapp looked around the room that was now swimming with the walking wounded and people crying for help. There was no way in hell he could get all of these people out of here in just over half a minute. His eyes fell on the windows that looked to the northeast. At the base of it, six floors down, was the ramp that went down into the underground parking garage.

Rapp couldn't be certain that the glass was blastproof, but it was a pretty good possibility. Then again, blastproof glass was designed to keep the blast wave of an explosion out. It wasn't designed to keep things in. Rapp quickly looked over the other five bodies. He had to assume they were all wearing vests.

Just as Nash came up, Rapp swung his pistol around, aimed it at the window, and squeezed off four quick rounds that punctured and spidered the glass but did not shatter it. Rapp started shooting again, the rounds popping off in rapid succession. In less than four seconds he emptied the rest of the seventeen-round magazine into a two-by-two-foot section of the window that was starting to give way.

The entire room had stopped to watch this one man shooting at an inanimate object as if he'd lost his mind.

As Rapp reached for his last full magazine, he screamed, "They have suicide vests! Art," Rapp yelled as he hit the slide release on his gun. "I need help with these bodies! We have less than thirty seconds before these vests start . . ." Rapp's words were muffled by his and Nash's gunshots as they emptied their magazines into the window.

A jagged hole had now appeared; roughly big enough to fit a garbage can through. Rapp holstered his gun and yelled to Nash, "Grab the other side."

They bent down and grabbed the paralyzed man by the legs and the side of his vest. They lifted him and started running across the room toward the partially punched-out window. Rapp began yelling at others who were standing by, watching. "Grab a body! Hurry up!"

As they neared the window, Rapp shouted, "Don't slow down."

He and Nash continued at near full speed and chucked the man headfirst into the uneven opening. The glass bent and then gave way as the body sailed past and down to the concrete ramp below. Rapp and

Nash did not wait to see the impact. They turned and ran back to the floor. More men and women were jumping in to help now, some of them wounded. Rapp and Nash grabbed the last of the six men and started back across the room. Up ahead, they could see others throwing the terrorists out in the same fashion they had.

Three more bodies quickly went out the window. Rapp was beginning to think it was going to work when the people in front of him and Nash lost their grip and dropped the body. Nash started to slow and Rapp yelled, "My side," and kept moving.

They ran around the two agents, one of whom was now collapsed on the floor with blood dripping from his right arm. The hole was now much larger, so Rapp and Nash tossed their body out the window from a couple of steps away and then raced back to help the agents who had stumbled. Others were stepping in to help at the same time. Four of them ended up each grabbing a limb as they hoisted the body toward the opening, and then threw it clear into the open blue sky.

Rapp was about to stick his head through the opening to verify that the men had in fact ended up in the concrete-walled drive that led down into the parking garage, when he realized how stupid that would be. Nash grabbed him by the shoulder and began pulling him away from the window. They pushed everybody back as they went, and then the blast echoed from below, rolling up toward the shredded window.

Rapp turned to Nash, elated that they had pulled it off. He saw his friend looking down at the ground in semi-shock and followed his gaze. There on the ground with a bullet hole in her forehead was their assistant, Jessica.

CHAPTER 75

I T was almost midnight when Nash pulled into his driveway. He wedged the minivan into the garage, put it in park, and just sat there for a minute, both hands on the top of the steering wheel, his forehead resting on his knuckles. He hadn't wanted to leave the office. It had nothing to do with not wanting to see his wife and children; he just didn't want to leave while there was still work to be done. The death toll at NCTC had reached thirty-eight, with another seventeen injured, three of them critically. The only consolation was that it could have been so much worse.

That was the mantra that had been picked up by virtually everyone as a way to offer comfort to those who had gone through it. Men like Rapp and Nash, who had seen death up close were more equipped to deal with the situation, but for quite a few of the analysts who had witnessed close colleagues and friends blown away in the place they worked every day, it was too much. A few got back to work, because subconsciously they knew it was the only way they could take their mind off what had happened, but a surprising number either became hysterical with grief or went into shock.

As Nash helped move the mentally wounded to the cafeteria, the realization hit home that these people were civilians. They were not trained for combat like his marines. Langley sent over people to help, as did the FBI and other agencies. There had been a hell of an argument early on between Art Harris and another bigwig from the bureau who wanted to quarantine the entire Operations Center and treat it as a crime scene. Harris was adamant that they get the Ops Center up and running again as soon as possible. The other agent wouldn't budge, however, and ordered everyone to stop the cleanup. He wanted the bodies left exactly where they were until forensic teams showed up. The two men began screaming at each other, and then Rapp decided to settle the issue. He walked over, coldcocked the agent, and ordered everyone back to work.

Nash had talked to his wife just once. He'd called her to let her know that she might start to hear some things from the press. He couldn't talk about it, but he was fine and he would call as soon as he had a chance. Nash couldn't even remember how long ago he'd made the call. He guessed it was probably around dinnertime. Maggie would be worried sick.

He pulled the keys out of the ignition and got out. After shutting the garage door, he walked up to the house. The light over the kitchen sink was on, as was a lamp in the study. Otherwise, the house was completely black. Nash slid his key into the back door and entered the mudroom. He turned off the alarm, closed and locked the door, and turned the alarm back on. He put his gun and holster in the gun safe and made a mental note to fill the magazines for the .40-cal in the morning.

Nash took off his suit coat and set it on the back of a chair in the kitchen. He quietly walked down the hallway and looked in the study. Maggie was sitting in the big chair next to the fireplace with a blanket and a book on her lap. She must have sensed his presence, as her eyes fluttered open, and she looked up at him with a warm smile that vanished almost as quickly as it had appeared. Her eyes traveled from her husband's face to his shirt.

Nash had forgotten that his shirt was stained with blood.

"What happened?" Maggie asked with concern.

Nash didn't know how much he could say, and he really didn't want to relive what had happened. "I'm fine, honey. This isn't mine."

"When you called, you said you were fine," she said as she tossed the book and blanket off her lap. "You never said you'd been in danger."

"I wasn't, honey. This is from helping with the wounded."

"That building in McLean ... the one that they showed on TV with all the emergency vehicles racing in and out—is that where you were?"

Nash was hit suddenly by the bizarre requirements of his job. His own wife didn't even know exactly where he worked. She knew only that he had an office at CIA headquarters. She knew nothing about his role at the National Counterterrorism Center. She probably didn't even know the organization existed.

"I was there," he admitted, "but I can't tell you much more than that."

She wrapped her arms around him and gave him a tight squeeze. "The kids were really worried."

"I know. I wish I could have gotten home sooner but ..." Nash's voice trailed off.

"You can't talk about it," she finished for him.

It was the company line. It represented the strange nonbalance of their marriage. She talked about her job whenever she wanted and as often as she wanted. He didn't speak of his even at times like this, when it would have made his life a lot easier. "How did things go with the dean and the De Graffs after I left?"

Maggie took a half step back and looked up at her husband with a proud smile. "Let's just say Dean Barnum Smith and I got the De Graffs to drop the entire matter."

"Really?"

"Yes, and Rory and I sat down and had a good talk this afternoon. I asked him if he was happy at Sidwell."

"And?"

"His answer was less than enthusiastic. So, I told him, if he stayed out of trouble for the rest of the semester, I'd let him go to Georgetown Prep next year."

"What about lacrosse camp this summer?"

"I told him that was between you and him."

Nash drew her in close and kissed the top of her head. Knowing how stubborn she was, Nash knew it couldn't have been easy for her. "Thank you, honey." He squeezed her tight and rubbed her back.

She tilted her head back and offered him her lips. "You were right. I allowed myself to get too caught up in all of it."

"I'm not exactly the easiest person to deal with," Nash said as he stepped away and looked down at his dirty shirt. "You put up with a lot of shit, honey."

"Yes, I do."

"I'm sorry," Nash said in a tired but sincere voice.

"Don't be," she said as she pushed him toward the stairs. "Go upstairs and take a shower. I'll be up in a minute."

Nash started walking up the stairs.

"Michael," his wife said softly, "I know you can't talk about it, but I'm sorry about what happened today." Maggie placed her hand on the railing. "I'm sure you knew some of those people who were killed."

With a blank stare Nash looked past his wife into the near dead embers in the study's fireplace. He didn't have it in him right now to tell her that Jessica was dead. For some reason he couldn't picture any of the faces of those who had died. In a detached voice, Nash said, "It wasn't a good day for us."

She rubbed his hand. "I'm sorry, honey."

Nash looked down at her beautiful, perfect face and gave her a reassuring smile. "I'm fine."

He climbed the stairs and was about to check on each of the kids, when he decided he'd better shower first. They did not need to see their father in the dead of night in a bloody shirt. Nash peeled off his clothes and stepped into the shower. As the hot water cascaded down his shoulders, he took a deep breath, and as the tension began to release, the faces came to him. Chris Johnson was first. He imagined what his final hours must have been like, and shuddered to think of the pain they'd put him through. Then the images of the people he worked with at the NCTC. He thought of Jessica lying there with a bullet hole in her head. He thought of her little boys. They were only nine and six. Their mother gone forever.

A lump welled up in Nash's throat. He tried to fight it, but there was no stemming the tide. The tears began to fall. Nash slowly sank to the floor of the shower. As the water poured down on him his chest heaved and he began to sob uncontrollably. He was not all right.

CHAPTER 76

LONSDALE stood on the terrace of her Capitol office. As she looked to the north she could see the glow of the emergency lights coming from the other side of the Dirksen Senate Office building. The recovery operation there had ended only a few hours ago, roughly thirty hours after the attack. One survivor, an employee of the restaurant, had been found in the basement. Everyone else was dead. Seven United States senators and another nine high-level staffers, including her own chief of staff, Ralph Wassen. Seventy-three had perished in the Monocle attack alone. The death toll for the day stood at 185 killed and another 211 wounded.

Lonsdale took a drag off her cigarette and thought how quickly her entire life had been turned upside down. A little less than a day and a half ago she'd been sitting in her other office too embarrassed to make a lunch date with a reporter. She was devastated over the loss of Wassen. He was her oldest friend and closest confidant. The fact that she had asked him to go in her place only added guilt to the grief. *How had she ever been so blind to the threat?* She had asked herself the question a hundred times in just a day.

At the moment the press did not concern her, although she knew they would come after her soon enough. With five years left in her term, she wasn't so sure she'd seek reelection. She knew what she must do, though. It had come to her during her sleepless night while she tossed and turned with self-recrimination. Words kept coming at her like big, bold headlines at the top of a newspaper: Naïve, Self-Righteous, Foolish, Idiotic, Irrational, Sanctimonious. The list went on and on. She had been so convinced that she was right that she had fallen prey to one of Washington's oldest games. Rather than taking a hard, serious look at the issue, she gravitated toward a position that would give her the most political clout. And then in an effort to further delude herself, she had assigned ignoble characteristics to her enemies —Kennedy, Rapp, Nash, and many others. She had convinced herself that they were the real threat.

Now, with the echo of the blasts still reverberating around the world, the charade was over. Two choices lay before her, and although Wassen was not here to consult, she knew what his advice would be. She looked at the Supreme Court, and felt a stab of regret. Of all the buildings on Capitol Hill, the court perhaps meant the most to her. Her decision would not be without some discomfort.

"Senator Lonsdale," the voice of a staffer called from the doorway. "Your visitors are here."

Lonsdale stabbed her cigarette out and turned. She waved for the staffer to bring them out. "You can leave now, Stephanie. I'll lock up." Lonsdale watched her aide leave and the two men step onto the terrace. She did not expect this to be easy, but it was something that had to be done.

The two stone-faced men approached and stopped eight feet short of Lonsdale. Rapp looked at her and said, "You wanted to see us, Senator?"

"Yes," Lonsdale said a bit anxiously. "I hear you have some leads."

Rapp and Nash nodded but neither verbally confirmed the comment.

"The president told me you think three of the terrorists are still at large."

"That's right," Rapp said.

"And you think you'll catch them?"

Rapp shrugged. "That all depends, ma'am?"

"On what?"

"Our rules of engagement," Nash said, cutting straight to the heart of the matter.

Lonsdale nodded and reached for another cigarette. "This isn't easy for me, gentlemen," she said as she flicked her lighter and took in a draw, "but I have to say this. I'm sorry. I'm sorry for the way I've acted, I'm sorry for the way I have called your characters into question, and I'm sorry that my interference in your investigation may have hindered your ability to prevent this attack."

Rapp and Nash exchanged a surprised look. They thought Lonsdale wanted to see them so she could explain her momentary lapse of composure when she'd slapped Aabad yesterday afternoon. Rapp nodded his acceptance and said, "Thank you, and I'm sorry about your chief of staff, Ralph Wassen. I didn't know him, but he seemed like a very nice man."

"He was the best." Lonsdale folded her arms across her chest and her eyes became unfocused in thought. After a moment she said, "He thought very highly of you two."

"Us?" Nash said with surprise.

"Yes," Lonsdale said. "He thought you two were on the right side of the issue."

"I wasn't aware there was a *wrong* side," Nash asked with a tinge of anger in his voice.

Ignoring Nash, Rapp asked, "And he thought you were on the wrong side?"

Lonsdale nodded and then was quiet for a long moment. She

looked at the two of them and asked, "Would either of you like a cigarette?"

"No, thanks," Rapp replied.

Nash shook his head.

"In addition to apologizing to you, I wanted you to come here tonight so I could offer you certain assurances. I already spoke with the president and Director Kennedy about this. As I'm sure you're aware, Senator Whaley was killed yesterday. That means the Intelligence Committee needs a new chairman. I want it."

"Excuse me?" Rapp said, not certain he had heard her right.

"I'm going to give up the Judiciary Committee in exchange for the Intel Committee, if they'll have me."

Rapp and Nash were shocked. There wasn't a senator they could think of that wouldn't kill to join the Judiciary Committee. "Why would you do that?" Nash asked.

"Call it penance." Lonsdale half smiled. She saw the look of concern on their faces, so she quickly added, "Don't worry. I've seen the light. As I already said, I was wrong."

Rapp shifted his weight from one foot to the other as he stared at Lonsdale. "You've seen the light?"

"Yes."

"May I ask about the extent of your conversion?" Rapp inquired.

Lonsdale took a few seconds to consider and then said, "I want you to hunt this Karim and these other two men down, and anyone else who helped him, for that matter, and I want you to kill them."

"Kill them?" Nash said, not quite believing his ears.

"That's right. I don't want to know how you do it . . . just do it."

"Kill them." Nash said again.

"Yes."

"You don't mean bring them to trial?"

Lonsdale looked directly at Nash and said, "I mean, kill them. I think we would all be better off if you saved us from a circus trial."

"And your colleagues?" Rapp asked.

"I have spoken to a handful of the ones who matter. The really important ones are on the Intel Committee. I will make sure you have all the money you need. Anything you ask for, I'll get it."

"Senator, you'll have to excuse me," Rapp said in his wry tone. "I've been doing this for a number of years. If I've learned anything, it's that as the political winds shift in this town, people tend to lose their appetite for stuff like this."

Lonsdale gave him a curt nod. "Director Kennedy told me to expect this from you. So . . . as much as I might someday regret this, I have prepared a letter." Lonsdale slipped her hand into her jacket and retrieved an off-white envelope. She handed it to Rapp and said, "Please put that in a safe place and show it to no one other than Mr. Nash and Director Kennedy."

Rapp held it in his hands and asked, "What does it say?"

"In short . . . it says that I offer you and Mr. Nash my full support to use whatever means you deem necessary to hunt down and kill this Karim fellow and his associates. Legally speaking, it offers you no protection."

Rapp held it up and said, "But it assures your support."

"And demise, should I fail to protect you from my more politically motivated colleagues. I am offering you cover, gentlemen. I am promising that I will do everything in my power to aid you in bringing these men to justice. And should you fail . . . I will still protect you."

Rapp looked at Nash and the two men shared a confident nod. Turning back to Senator Lonsdale, Rapp said, "Senator, we will not fail."